Also by Jennie Marts

COWBOYS OF CREEDENCE
Caught Up in a Cowboy
You Had Me at Cowboy
It Started with a Cowboy
Wish Upon a Cowboy

CREEDENCE HORSE RESCUE
A Cowboy State of Mind

WHEN A *Cowboy* LOVES A WOMAN

JENNIE MARTS

sourcebooks
casablanca

Published by Sourcebooks Casablanca, an imprint of Sourcebooks
P.O. Box 4410, Naperville, Illinois 60567–4410
(630) 961-3900
sourcebooks.com

Printed and bound in the United States of America.
KPC 10 9 8 7 6 5 4 3 2

This book is dedicated to
Mandy Morfitt Watson.
Your sunny spirit lit up so many lives.
I miss you, Friend.

CHAPTER 1

EVERYTHING HURTS, THOUGHT ELLE BROOKS AS SHE SANK lower in the bathtub. Her back and shoulders ached from carrying bales of hay and brushing the horses that morning at the Heaven Can Wait Horse Rescue, where she volunteered. Although she preferred the physical labor over the headache she got from spending the afternoon with her financial advisor, going over the trust and through her finances. Between his company and his considerable life insurance policy, her beloved Ryan had left her with a substantial amount of money. But she'd give it all away for one more day with him.

She pushed a bubbly pile of suds across the spacious garden bathtub as the final strains of one of her favorite Pink songs faded in her ears. Usually the pop star's music could energize her, but tonight she felt more like a sinking stone than any kind of rock star. With a sigh, she pushed the drain release with her toe and pulled the earbuds from her ears.

That's when she heard the sirens.

Hair raised on the nape of her neck, and a chill that had nothing to do with the cooling bathwater raced up her spine. She slammed her eyes shut against the onslaught of memories. It had been over a year since Ryan died, but the images of the ambulance's throbbing lights and the mournful sounds of the sirens were as vivid as if it had happened the day before.

She caught the first whiff of smoke as she heard the fire trucks pull up in front of her house. Water sloshed over the side as she stumbled to get out of the tub. Grabbing a towel, she scarcely had time to run it over her body before she heard the slam of her front door and raised voices.

Reaching for her pajamas, she pulled on the cotton shorts and wrenched the tank top over her head.

Move, her brain screamed. *Get out.*

The fabric clung to her damp skin as she snatched up her short robe and raced out of the bathroom. From the landing, she could see a flurry of men in yellow coats dragging a gray hose across the Italian marble of her foyer toward her kitchen.

She choked on the acrid smoke filling the air. There were no blazing flames, but the smoke scorched her throat, and she blinked against the sting of it to her eyes.

An older fireman caught sight of her. "You need to get out of the house, ma'am."

Panic gripped her as she wildly looked around at the chaos invading her home. Then her gaze caught and held on the familiar eyes of the tall cowboy who'd just stepped into view. He was dressed in jeans and boots and a black Stetson hat, and the sight of his broad shoulders filling the doorway somehow grounded her.

She didn't really know him—she'd briefly met him a few weeks ago. But that one time had shown his ability to stay calm and steady in a crisis situation. His name was Brody—*Doctor* Brody Tate. He was her best friend Bryn's veterinarian. But why was a veterinarian at a house fire?

A plume of dark smoke billowed out of the kitchen, and Elle caught the distinct sound of the crackle of flames. She coughed, then turned around and ran back down the hallway.

She heard the older fireman's voice yelling, "Get her out of here, Tate," followed by the sound of cowboy boots sprinting up the stairs as she raced to the closed door at the end of the hall.

She pushed through, ignoring the rush of emotions that normally flooded her when she opened the door to the room decorated in pink-and-white stripes. A hand-knit pink blanket lay in the seat of the rocking chair. Elle grabbed it and clutched it to her chest. If she could only save one thing, it had to be this.

She turned back to see Brody in the doorway. He didn't say anything, just reached for her hand and led her quickly back down the hallway.

They reached the top of the stairs, and she froze again at the commotion below—the rush of the firefighters' feet, the commanding tone of their voices as they shouted orders, the pulsing flash of red lights against the white walls of her entryway.

Brody pulled at her hand, but she couldn't move. He turned back and must have seen the panic in her eyes. His tone was soft as he swept her up, cradling her to him as if she weighed nothing at all. "It's all right, darlin'. I've got you."

She buried her face in his chest, clinging to him, as he carried her down the stairs and out the front door. Elle lifted her head and gulped at the fresh air.

"Is there anyone else in the house? Any pets?"

She shook her head. "No. Only me."

"You remember me? We met a couple of weeks ago at Bryn's?"

"Yes, I remember. But what are you doing here?" And why was she clutching his neck like he was a life preserver? A handsome, tall cowboy life preserver.

A scattering of neighbors stood on their front lawns, but the older woman from across the street hurried toward them. "Oh my word. Are you all right, honey?" she asked, her head tilting up to search Elle's face. She stood barely over five feet, and a mass of silvery-blue curls covered her head. She had on pink-and-white-checked capri pants, a hot-pink T-shirt, and a white coat with a pink fur collar. The T-shirt matched the hot-pink shade of her toenails, poking out of her orthopedic tan sandals. As Elle looked closer, she also noticed pink streaks interspersed throughout the woman's curly hair.

"She's okay, Aunt Sassy," Brody told her. "Just a little shaken up." He gazed down at Elle. "Ms. James is the one who called the fire department."

"Thank you so much," Elle said to the older woman.

"You can put her down now, Brody," Ms. James told the tall cowboy.

He set her gently on the ground and eased her robe from her hands. Shaking out the thin apparel, he held it as she slid her arms into the sleeves. Still clutching the blanket, she awkwardly maneuvered into the robe. The back of his fingers brushed the bare skin of her neck as she pulled the belt around her, and she froze at the sensation. Goose bumps rose on her arms as a heated thrill raced over her shoulders and down her back.

Stunned, she swallowed at the dryness in her mouth. It had been a long time since she had experienced any kind of thrill, heated or otherwise. Her shoulder warmed where Brody rested his hand.

This was the absolute worst and most awkward time to be feeling any kind of warm, other than from the fire. There was smoke billowing out her kitchen window, and she was feeling hot for the cowboy who had just carried her down the stairs in nothing but shorty shorts and a thin tank top.

"What happened? How did the fire start?" she asked him, already dreading the answer.

"I'm not sure. I think I heard someone say something about a skillet on the stove. Were you cooking something?"

Elle pressed her palm to her forehead. How could she be so stupid? "No, but I was going to. I put some oil in a skillet to make some fried rice, but I got distracted, then decided to take a bath, and I can't remember if I turned off the burner under the pan."

"That'd do it. Hot oil can easily catch fire."

At least the house was paid for, her banker had reminded her that afternoon. And Ryan had been meticulous about having more than enough insurance. Still…how did she make such a dumb mistake?

"Don't be too hard on yourself," he told her, almost as if he could read her mind. Which she hoped wasn't the case, since she'd just been thinking about how hot he was. "It could have been much worse, and thanks to Aunt Sassy here, the fire department got here quickly."

"I can't thank you enough," Elle told her. A shiver coursed down her back as she thought of what could have happened.

Brody gave Elle's shoulder a squeeze. "I'll be right back. And I'll see if I can learn anything more about the fire."

Elle stared after him, not knowing quite what to do and missing the comfort of his hand on her shoulder.

The older woman put her arm around Elle's waist. "Everything's going to be all right."

Shame heated Elle's cheeks. This woman was being so nice to her. And of course she knew Elle's name. Why hadn't Elle ever accepted her invitation to tea? It's not like people were knocking down her door to get to know her.

They had at first. After Ryan's funeral, they'd shown up in droves, filling her counters and freezer with casseroles and meals. But she wasn't used to the crush of small-town hospitality, the constant questions and offers to help. She didn't know what to say. There was nothing anyone could do. They couldn't bring Ryan back. And Elle hadn't had the energy for small talk or *any* talk. She'd just wanted to curl under the covers and sleep.

"Thank you, Ms. James," she said, putting her hand on top of the other woman's. "I didn't realize you were Brody's aunt."

"Oh, I'm not. But he's friends with my nephews, so I've known him since he was a boy. My real name is Cassie." She offered Elle an impish grin. "But hardly anyone calls me that anymore. My nephews started calling me Aunt Sassy when they were little, and it seems half the town picked up on it, and now they all call me Sassy. I kind of like it. It suits me."

It did. The older woman definitely carried a sassy vibe.

A light breeze picked up, carrying the scent of smoke through the air, and another shiver ran through Elle.

"You must be freezing," Sassy said, reaching to take off her coat. "Here, honey, take my jacket."

"No, I couldn't."

"Oh, don't worry. It's not real fur."

Elle laughed—a real laugh that surprised even her as it burst from her lips. She didn't do spontaneous laughter much anymore. She shook her head, trying to imagine what kind of animal would have a hot-pink coat. "Okay." She agreed and let the woman drape the jacket over her shoulders. The fake pink fur tickled her neck, but it *was* warm and cut the chill of the Colorado night air.

"There's not much we can do now but wait," Sassy told her. "Would you like to come over to my house? I could make you a cup of tea. Or a lasagna if you're hungry."

Elle laughed again but tears pricked her eyes at the woman's generosity. "Thank you. You're very sweet. I'm ashamed I haven't accepted your offer to stop by sooner."

"It's okay, honey. Everyone grieves in their own way. And until someone has gone through a loss like that, they won't understand."

Elle peered at the woman's face. Sassy's eyes, soft and kind as she nodded, displayed a kind of compassion that only another survivor of deep loss could convey.

Sassy cut off any further discussion of the topic by pointing toward the house. "Here comes Brody."

The tall cowboy crossed the lawn, Elle's purse and a pair of her sandals clutched in his hands.

"I'm not sure that purse matches your outfit," she teased.

He grinned and held her charcoal-colored designer bag up to his soot-covered shirt. "Shoot. I thought these grays went together." He passed her the items. "I saw these by the front door and figured you could use them. I found your phone and put it in there too."

"Yes. Thank you." Her feet had been getting cold standing in the damp grass. She balanced on one foot to put the first sandal on. Brody held out his hand, and she grabbed his forearm to steady herself. Dang, this man had muscles. Even his forearms were hard as rocks.

Stop thinking about the man's muscles and put the shoe on, she scolded herself. But they were hard to ignore.

"I got the scoop from the fire chief. I went to school with his son and have known their family for years," Brody told them. "He said he'd let you know when it's safe, then you can go in the house and get anything else you might need for now. They've got the fire out. Most of it's contained in the kitchen, but it's a mess of smoke and water damage in there. You're not gonna be able to stay there tonight."

"It's fine. I can stay at the motel," she said, waving his concern away. In a town the size of Creedence, there was only one.

A grin tugged at the corners of his lips. "Good try. I was at the diner when two of the volunteer firemen got the call. Bryn recognized your address and told me to get my butt over here ASAP. She wanted to come get you herself but still had thirty minutes left of her shift and they were pretty busy. So she sent me. Under threat of bodily harm if I don't obey, I'm to bring you to her house." He offered her a coy grin. "I've grown quite accustomed to this body and would like to spare it the wrath of Bryn Callahan. So I'd appreciate it if you let me give you a ride out to her place as soon as they release you."

"I'd better go with you then. I don't want to be responsible for anything happening to your body." Elle laughed, despite the surge of heat talking about his body—and thinking of the things that could happen to it—sent through her. Dang. Where had that come from? She hadn't felt that kind of warmth in a long time. The fire must have melted her brain. Or thawed her frozen libido.

"She said the guest room is already made up and to tell you there's no discussion. I've known that girl since we were kids, and there's no use arguing with her."

Although it was fairly new, she was thankful for the bond of friendship she'd already developed with Bryn. "I'm learning that myself."

Brody grinned. "It doesn't take long." His expression sobered as he peered down at her. "All kidding aside, I think it's a good idea. Then you won't be alone. This is a lot to deal with."

Watching my husband die in front of me, that's a lot to deal with. Her kitchen catching on fire, that was nothing.

CHAPTER 2

STAYING WITH BRYN WOULD BE NICE. ELLE HAD BEEN volunteering at her friend's horse rescue ranch for the past month, so at least she'd be close to work when she woke up. And the tipping point was the five puppies they'd recently rescued who were tumbling around Bryn's living room. There wasn't a lot that a lapful of puppies couldn't make better.

"Thanks again," she said, not knowing what else to say. She felt like a dork standing there clutching her purse while wearing just her pj's, a pair of sandals, and a hot-pink faux-fur jacket.

Brody nodded. "I'll check back with you in a bit. I'm gonna go see if there's anything I can do to help. I'll keep you posted if I find out anything else."

It took another hour and a half for the fire to be ruled completely out and for Elle to talk to the fire chief.

"There's nothing else to be done right now," the fire chief said. "We caught it before it moved to the rest of the house, but there's always smoke and water damage in a situation like this. You'll want to contact your insurance agency, and we can put you in touch with some companies who do cleanup after this sort of thing. You'll need someplace else to stay for a bit." He gave her his card and a few more instructions.

Brody stood next to the chief, looking down at her with concern. Elle had seen him helping one of the volunteer fireman haul a hose back to the truck, and his clothes were smudged with dirt and debris. He'd taken off his Stetson, and his light brown hair stood up in damp tufts. He had a little soot on his cheek and a light scruff of whiskers lay across his chiseled jaw, but he still looked hotter than the flames in her kitchen.

"Thank you," Elle said softly, her body suddenly too weary to move. But oddly enough, not too wiped out to notice the beard of the hunky cowboy. She *must* be exhausted.

Sassy had stuck by her side, offering her water and more food and dragging out a couple of dented lawn chairs to use while they waited. She wrapped an arm around Elle's shoulders. "You look ready to drop on your feet, honey. I think it's time to get you out of here. You can come back tomorrow to get your things." She nodded to Brody, who cupped his hand lightly under Elle's elbow and led her toward his truck.

He opened the door, then swore at the collection of items filling the seat. He pulled open the back door of the club cab, pushed a kid's scooter to the side, then moved a bag of horse feed, a roll of baling wire, and his toolbox into the back. "Sorry, about that. I've been meaning to get this thing cleaned out." He shoved a pink sweatshirt and a stack of books to the center, then tossed a crumpled fast-food bag over the seat. "Should be good enough now, but I can't guarantee you won't still find a Cheeto in the seat."

She shrugged. "I love Cheetos."

"Then if you find one, it's all yours." He grinned, then wiped his hand down the front of his shirt in an effort to brush away the soot and grime.

"Sorry you got so messed up."

He peered down at his front. "This is nothing. In my job, I'm always getting dirty. I've learned to carry a stack of spares." He jerked a thumb toward the vet box on the back of the truck. "Give me a second to clean up, and we'll head out."

Sassy had followed them over, and she tucked a plastic sack onto the floor of the pickup. "I put a spare toothbrush and some other toiletries in there. I'm sure Bryn can loan you whatever else you might need. Now I don't want you to worry about a thing. I'll keep an eye on the house and let you know if there's any trouble."

Elle rubbed a hand over the woman's shoulder. "Thank you

so much. And thank you again for calling the fire department. I feel like such a fool, but this would have been so much worse if it weren't for you."

Sassy waved a dismissive hand. "Don't give it a thought. You just get some rest. And take a little time to appreciate the view of your cowboy taxi." She wiggled her eyebrows and nodded to the other side of the truck, where Brody had stripped off his soiled shirt and was wiping his bare chest down with a towel.

Elle swallowed as he leaned forward to dump a bottle of water on his hair, then stood back up to shake his head like a dog getting out of a lake. The muscles of his hard abs flexed as he took another towel and rubbed it vigorously over his hair.

"Whew boy," Sassy said, her breath coming out in a whoosh. "I think another fire just started..." She lowered her voice to a conspiratorial whisper and gave Elle a wink. "I might be old, but I'm not dead yet."

"Apparently not." *And neither am I.*

It was the worst time to be laughing and ogling a handsome cowboy, but Elle couldn't hold back her giggles as she snuck another glance at the heat-inducing hottie.

She pressed her hand to her chest. Her heart was getting quite a workout tonight, between the fright of the fire and the crazy palpitations the hot cowboy was causing. A niggle of guilt slipped in, as if admiring Brody's abs was being disloyal to the memory of Ryan.

She shook it off as she gave Sassy a quick hug, then returned her pink jacket before climbing into the truck. Brody got in the other side and passed her a light-blue T-shirt similar to the one he'd just yanked on. "Here. You can have this one if you want. It'll be a little big, but it's clean."

"It's great. Thank you." She tugged the shirt over her head, then pulled her hair free. It *was* too big for her but worked out fine, since she'd pulled it on over the top of her robe. The fabric was warm and smelled of laundry detergent. The words *Tate Family*

Veterinary Clinic were stamped across the breast pocket. Sinking back into the seat, she let out a shaky breath as Brody started the truck and maneuvered out onto the road.

"You okay?" he asked. "What do you need?"

Elle shook her head. "I honestly don't know."

"How about some food?" he asked, pointing to the golden arches ahead of them. "My daughter seems to think that fries and chocolate shakes are the cure for just about everything that ails you."

Elle swallowed. "Fries and a shake sound perfect." They turned a corner, and she grabbed at the stack of chapter books sliding into her lap. She held up a couple of Baby-Sitters Club books and a title by Judy Blume. "Doing a little light reading?"

He chuckled, the sound of his laugh as warm as the T-shirt she was wearing. "Yeah, *Kristy's Great Idea* is my favorite. That girl's a real thinker." He pointed to the thick copy of *Harry Potter and the Goblet of Fire*. "I am actually reading that one. My daughter loves the series so much, I promised I'd check it out."

"I love them too. I've read them all three times now."

"I wasn't expecting to like them so much, but they're really good. And I never imagined I could spend thirty minutes in a conversation with a ten-year-old discussing which house at a wizarding school a magical sorting hat would put us into, but that's what happened over breakfast this morning."

"And?"

He offered her a sheepish grin. "Gryffindor."

She laughed. "Me too."

He pulled into the McDonald's drive-through and rolled down his window to place the order.

They inched forward, and Elle rubbed at a spot of soot covering the back of her hand. "Thank you, Brody. This is so nice of you. Do you often take perfect strangers to McDonald's after their houses catch on fire?"

"Occasionally," he said with a shrug and an impish grin. "Nah. I'm just kidding. And you don't feel like a stranger to me. That might sound weird, since we only met the one time when you rescued those puppies, but after the girls' night sleepover my daughter had at the farm with you and Bryn, she hasn't stopped talking about you. She holds you in pretty high regard, and for a girl of only ten, Mandy is a pretty good judge of character."

Elle smiled. "I hold her in pretty high regard as well. She's pretty special. And smart as a whip."

"Yeah, sometimes she's too smart for her old dad."

I doubt that. "I've been helping Bryn with the marketing and business end of the horse rescue, and even taking care of the animals a little. Whenever Mandy is over, she's a great help. She's seems older than ten."

He chuckled. "That's what happens to an only child who spends the majority of her time with adults—she starts to think she is one." He moved forward in the line. "She was pretty young when her mom died, barely five, so it's just been the two of us for quite a while now, and sometimes she acts like she's the parent of me."

"Do you need an extra parent?"

He laughed again. "Probably."

"I'm sorry about your wife," she said, softening her tone. "That must have been so hard."

He shrugged. "It was. Sometimes still is." He rested his hand gently on her knee and gave it a light squeeze. "But it does get easier."

Elle swallowed again. "Thank you" was about the most she could whisper.

"I knew Ryan. He was a couple years younger than me in school. But he was a good guy. I was awful sorry to hear about his passing."

She whispered, "Me too."

He narrowed his eyes and gave her a hard nod. "From everything Mandy tells me, you're stronger than you probably think you are. She was pretty dang impressed at the way you saved those puppies."

"For the record, Zane's the one who crawled down in that storm cellar and brought out the puppies and the mama dog. That poor girl was close to death." She shivered at the memory of that day and remembered how thankful she'd been that Brody had been at the ranch when they'd pulled in. The cowboy-slash-veterinarian was the person they'd needed the most. That was the only time she'd met him, and she'd been so emotionally wrought up in saving the half-starved mother dog, she hadn't paid much attention to him. But she was certainly paying attention to him now.

"How about we call it a joint effort and just be thankful it all worked out," Brody said. "Except I'm not sure it worked out so great for me."

"Oh?"

"Mandy's been working on me all summer trying to convince me we need to adopt one of those pups."

Elle grinned. "They are pretty hard to resist."

"Not if you're a veterinarian who sees cute puppies on a regular basis."

"True. But adding a cute, tenacious ten-year-old to the mix probably takes the pressure up a notch."

"Excellent point. And speaking of that tenacious ten-year-old, no pressure, but she seems to think you all are going to the swimming pool together sometime this summer."

Elle laughed. "She's right. I did tell her we'd do that. Thanks for reminding me."

"You don't have to."

"I want to. I love to swim. And she's good company." A grin tugged at her lips. "She offered to be my best friend."

Brody shook his head, but Elle noted the way his Adam's apple moved as he forced a swallow. "Dang, that girl does wrench at my heart sometimes."

"She got me too. I almost started bawling when she said it." Elle noticed an older model minivan pull in behind them, a tired-looking woman at the wheel. A bored preteen sat in the passenger seat staring at her phone, and two younger girls were having a heated argument in the back. A stuffed animal came flying over the seat and hit the woman on the side of the head.

As she watched the mother turn and scold the girls in the back, Elle's gut twisted in a jumble of jealousy and grief. She didn't often let herself imagine the life, and family, she and Ryan would have had—it hurt too much to go there—but sometimes the extreme unfairness of it all hit her like a sucker punch to the kidney.

"That's Kimmie Cox," Brody told her after turning to see what had captured Elle's attention. "I went to school with her, and her middle girl is in Mandy's class."

"She looks like she has her hands full."

"Yeah, she married her high school sweetheart, a big douche nugget who left her and the girls last year to run off with the rodeo queen from the Colorado State Fair. Poor girl had no idea what she was getting herself into."

"That'll be nine seventy-five," the teenage cashier told them as she passed two shakes out the drive-through window. Brody handed her a ten-dollar bill. Elle took a shake and passed Brody her debit card. She raised her voice to the cashier as Brody passed over the card. "Please use that to pay for the meals of the car behind us."

The teenager raised her eyebrows as she took the card and passed out the bag of fries. "You sure? They ordered a *lot* of food."

Elle nodded. "Yes, I'm quite sure."

Brody handed the fries to Elle, then poked straws into their shakes. "That's nice of you. I didn't realize you knew Kimmie."

"I don't. But it looks like she could use a kind gesture."

Brody took the debit card and receipt, and passed them to Elle before pulling out of the drive-through and onto the road. "Do you do that often?"

Elle was shaking a packet of salt onto her fries. "What? Use too much salt?"

He laughed. "No, pay for other people's meals?"

Elle shrugged. "I don't know. I help when I can, I guess. I got a bunch of money from Ryan's life insurance, which feels weird, because I'd rather eat ramen noodles every day and live in my car if it meant I could have him back. But it somehow feels better if I can spend some of it to help other people."

"Hmm," he said, narrowing his eyes again. "Bryn told me someone paid off her entire account at the grocery store last week. She asked if I knew anything about it, hinting around that she'd really like to thank the person who did it, but I told her it wasn't me. Was it you?"

Elle kept her gaze trained on her freshly salted fries. "I'm sure I wouldn't know anything about that."

"Yeah, I bet not," he said with a laugh, then nodded to the bag of food. "Toss some of that salt on my fries, would ya?"

She sprinkled salt on his fries, then passed him the carton, thankful for the distraction and that he was willing to let the awkward conversation go. The whole point of helping someone anonymously was to stay anonymous. And she knew Bryn used her account to buy pet food and groceries to feed the friends who stopped in to help volunteer with the horses. The few hundred dollars she'd paid off on the account wasn't a big deal to her, but she knew it would help Bryn, who survived on her waitress salary and would still give the shirt off her back if someone were in need of it.

Elle settled into her seat, and they passed the ten-minute drive in comfortable silence, munching on fries and sipping their shakes.

"Is that a deer?" Brody asked, squinting into the headlights as he turned into Bryn's driveway and slowed the truck.

"No, that's Shamus," Elle responded, recognizing the mini-horse Bryn had recently rescued. "But what the heck is he doing out of the corral?"

"And why is he hanging around with that ornery goat? Otis is bound to get them into trouble."

The horse stood in the middle of the driveway, grazing on a small patch of grass and eyeing the truck. As they got closer, Elle spotted the black-and-white goat, a dandelion hanging from his lip, standing behind Shamus. She laughed as she watched the unlikely pair trot off together toward the barn. "They probably heard we stopped at McDonald's and were hoping to steal a fry."

"I'll go put them back in the corral after we get you inside." Brody cautiously drove down the final part of the driveway and stopped in front of the two-story farmhouse. "I just realized we probably should have waited to eat. Bryn's most likely set out enough food to feed an army. And you know she won't be happy until she convinces you to eat something."

"You're right," Elle said, gazing at the yellow house with the big wraparound porch. Something in her settled as she took in the soft glow of light shining through the windows, and she could almost smell the scents of cinnamon and vanilla that hung in the air of the farmhouse kitchen. "Knowing Bryn, she probably whipped up a Three-Alarm Kitchen-Fire Casserole while she waited for us to get out here."

He chuckled. "I'm laughing, but only because it's true."

Elle gathered her things as Brody walked around the front of the truck and opened the passenger door. He held out his hand to help her from the truck. She slid her palm into his—an innocent enough gesture, yet the touch of his hand sent a dart of heat down her spine. He held on just a fraction of a second too long, making her wonder how it would feel to hold his hand and walk up to the porch, to have him pull her into the circle of his arms and lean down to kiss her goodnight as if they just arrived home from a date.

The screen door flew open, and Elle dropped Brody's hand as Bryn and her fiancé, Zane stepped onto the porch. Bryn came flying down the steps, saving Elle from delving any deeper into her date-night fantasies with the dashing cowboy.

"Oh my gosh, I'm so glad you're here. I've been worried half to death," her friend cried, throwing her arms around Elle. "Are you all right?"

"I'm fine. There's no need to make a fuss."

"Oh, this little fuss is only the beginning. I've got the kettle boiling water for tea, and I can make you anything you want to eat. I've already been setting out food."

A grin tugged at her lips as Elle snuck a glance at Brody. He was grinning back, causing a battalion of butterflies to take flight in Elle's stomach. She tried to focus on Bryn as she told her, "That's so nice of you, but we just stopped at McDonald's, and I couldn't eat another bite."

Bryn's shoulders sagged. "Okay, but I have to pamper you somehow. How about a nice hot shower? Or a bath? Or are you sure I can't make you something to eat? It would only take me a few minutes to put together a casserole."

"I promise I'm fine. I don't need a bath or a casserole," she said, sneaking another grin at Brody. What was happening? She barely knew this man, had only been around him a few hours, and yet, they were already sharing secret smiles and private jokes?

"All right, give the girl a little space," Zane said, sauntering off the porch and leaning down to pull Elle into a hug. "You okay, darlin'?"

"Really, I'm fine," she said, her words muffled against Zane's broad chest.

"Good," Bryn said, muscling her way between them and wrapping her arm around Elle's waist. "Because space is the last thing I'm giving you. First, you're getting at least six more squishy hugs, then I'm wrapping you in a cozy blanket on the sofa, and I may sneak into your room to snuggle you in your bed tonight. I was so scared for you. It took everything I had not to race out of the diner and drive to your house. If we hadn't been so busy, I would have done it. Thankfully, Brody had stopped in for some pie and was willing to come in my place. Then it killed me to come home and just wait after my shift ended." She held a hand up to Brody. "Yeah, I know having half the town show up to a fire only makes it harder for the firemen to do their job. Blah. Blah. Blah. I've heard it before. But it's never been *my* friend whose house was on fire."

"My *house* wasn't on fire," Elle explained. "It was just the kitchen."

"Only you would bring up that distinction. Now come inside and tell me everything." She waved to Brody as she led Elle up the steps. "You too, Brody. I've got coffee on and enough food to feed half of Creedence. Unless you need to get home to Mandy."

He stopped at the bottom of the stairs. "I'm good. She's staying at her grandparents' tonight." He jerked a thumb toward the barn. "We saw Shamus and Otis standing in the driveway when we pulled in. I was gonna try to round them up before I came inside."

"I think they already beat you to it," Bryn said, pointing toward the corral where Shamus, Otis, and the new colt, Mack, stood peering at them through the fence.

Mack, short for MacGyver, so named for his skill at stealthily escaping the stable and corral, was the usual culprit in a breakout.

Beauty and Prince were standing at the trough, more interested in eating the fresh pile of hay than spying on the newcomers. Beauty, the gorgeous, brown quarter horse, had been Bryn's first rescue, bought off a couple of dirtbags who'd stopped for lunch at the diner.

But the waitress had gotten more than she'd bargained for because the quarter horse had been pregnant. Mack must have realized no treats of apples or sugar cubes were coming, and he left the fence and pranced over to nibble on some hay next to his mom.

Brody shook his head as he followed the others inside. "Crazy animals."

Lucky, Bryn's dog, was waiting inside the door to slather the newcomer's with affectionate puppy kisses and licks. Elle bent down to pet the dog, and he tried to scramble into her arms, which was a pretty impressive feat, considering that, thanks to a hit-and-run car accident, the dog only had three legs. Grace—the dog that she, Bryn, and Zane had rescued from the storm cellar—raised her head and let out a whine. Now that the puppies were mobile, Zane had constructed a pen to keep them corralled in one corner of the kitchen. Grace lay inside it on a dog bed, her five pups snuggled into her belly as they nursed.

Elle crossed to the corner and sank down next to the dog pen, reaching through the bars so she could scratch Grace's neck and not disturb the puppies' nightly feeding. Lucky, who had happily hopped along at her heels, climbed into her lap and rested his head on her thigh.

Within minutes, Bryn stuck a warm mug in her hands, and the scent of chamomile rose in the steam around her, providing a sense of comfort. Elle sipped at the hot chamomile tea as she watched the puppies fall asleep, then moved to join the others at the kitchen table.

Bryn added another box of crackers and a plate of sliced cheese to the impressive array of snacks already assembled in the middle of the table, then dropped into the chair next to Elle. "Okay, now tell me everything."

CHAPTER 3

BRODY LEANED BACK IN HIS CHAIR, TRYING TO HIDE HIS SMILE behind his cup as he listened to Elle tell Bryn and Zane about the fire.

She seemed like a different woman from when he'd first met her. Granted, saving the puppies had been his highest priority, but he had recognized the sadness in the young widow. It was nice to see her laughing and joking and ribbing Zane.

He still couldn't believe Zane and Bryn were engaged. He'd known them both a long time and remembered the night Zane's father had used a beer bottle to create the scar running from Zane's eyebrow down his cheek. But Zane, aka the horse whisperer, seemed to have found his place here at the Heaven Can Wait Horse Rescue.

Although more than just horses had found their way to the ranch, and Bryn now had a slew of abandoned and unwanted animals, ranging from the deserted puppies to a style-conscious swine. Which meant there was always something to do for them, from feeding and bathing to cleaning out stalls. And Zane worked on training the horses as well, in hopes they would eventually get adopted.

Bryn had a way of finding strays and offering them a home, and it looked like Elle had found a place here. "Got any more coffee?" he asked after she finished recounting the events of the night.

"I got ya," Zane said, holding up the carafe and pouring more coffee into Brody's outstretched mug.

"Thanks," Brody said, then turned the conversation to Bryn. "Tell us what's happening with the horse rescue. How's it going?"

"It's going great," she answered. "I got a call from the Western

Slope a few days ago with a request to take on a new horse. And thanks to Elle's stellar marketing skills, I've got the money in the bank to be able to say yes."

"That's great."

"Yeah, I'm excited but nervous. It's an abandoned quarter horse that the sheriff's department found. They're bringing her out next week."

The discussion turned to the horses and their antics and to the latest gossip Bryn had heard at the diner where she waitressed. Brody was content to listen and smile with amusement as he watched Elle's hopeless attempts to try to refuse Bryn's endless efforts to pamper her.

"Really Bryn, I'm not cold anymore," Elle was saying as Bryn wrapped a throw around her shoulders and pressed a fresh cup of steaming peppermint tea into her hands. "You don't have to fuss over me."

"Yes, I do," Bryn replied, nodding to the cup. "Drink."

Elle obediently took a sip. "Fine, I'll drink the tea, but I'm not taking your bed. I've slept in the guest room before, and the mattress is fine. It's wonderful, I mean."

"Fine. You can sleep in the guest room, but I'm giving you my good pillows."

Elle glanced at Brody, her expression pleading for his support.

He shrugged and offered her a grin. "I don't think you're gonna win this one. Best just to take the good pillows."

"A lot of help you are." She playfully tossed a cookie at him.

He caught the cookie and took a bite, trying to keep his thoughts from roaming to the image of Elle's long, chestnut hair spread out over his own pillow.

Whoa. Where did that come from? He didn't often let his mind wander to images of women in bed, especially not *his* bed. And this hadn't been the first crazy thought he'd had about Elle tonight.

It had been a long time since his brain had been taken over with notions of a woman. Not that he didn't still think about Mary—he did. But it had been five years now since she'd lost her battle to breast cancer. And these days, his focus was solely on the pint-sized woman in his life.

He shook his head to clear the vision and grinned at Elle. "I've known Bryn way too long. You won't win this argument."

"Fine. I'll use the dang pillows. But if you try to force another nice thing on me, I'm going out to sleep with the horses in the barn." Elle razzed Bryn, but Brody could see the easy affection the two women had for each other.

He was glad, especially since Bryn had told him how long it had taken for Elle to feel comfortable around her and to accept her attempts at friendship. They seemed on great terms now, and he was genuinely happy for both of them. A yawn snuck up on him, and he covered it with his hand. "I'd better call it a night. I've still got to stop by the clinic and check on a dog I did a surgery on this afternoon."

"I'll walk you out," Elle said, as Brody stood.

"Thanks for everything," he told Bryn as he gave her a quick hug, then held the door open for Elle to walk through.

The night air was cool and felt good on his heated cheeks. He breathed in the scent of hay and horses, and caught the subtle scent of whatever soap and shampoo Elle wore. It was something flowery and light, and had him wanting to bury his face in her neck and inhale her.

A shiver ran through her as she walked beside him.

"Here. Take my jacket." He unzipped his sweatshirt and put it around her shoulders before she had time to protest.

"Thanks," she told him as she pushed her hands through the sleeves. They were too long, but she didn't seem to care as she wrapped her arms around her middle. "What a crazy night. I don't even know what to do or how to feel."

"If they've come up with a handbook for how to have the

correct emotions at the proper time, I sure haven't heard of it." He offered her a kind smile, then nudged her arm with his elbow. "You can act however you want with me. No judgment here."

"Thanks." She offered him a pained smile. "Everyone's acting like this is such a big deal, so maybe I should be freaking out more. But I'm just not that worried about some damage to my kitchen. It's just stuff, no one got hurt, and all of it can either be repaired or replaced. It's inconvenient, sure, and I'm humiliated that it was my own fault, and I feel bad for putting all of you out, but as far as tragedies go, it's not much of one."

"I hear ya." He nodded. The kind of loss they had both experienced couldn't be repaired or replaced. The ones they lost were gone forever. He swallowed back the sudden ache in his throat.

She stopped at the door to his truck and looked up at him, her eyes narrowing as if she were studying his face. "You're pretty easy to talk to."

You're pretty easy to look at. She *was* beautiful, even in the half-dark shadows of the night, her beauty shone through. Even with her hair pulled into a messy ponytail and wearing his too-big jacket and a guarded half smile. "I'm happy to listen. Anytime you want to talk." He pulled out his phone. "I wanted to give you my number anyway. In case you had any questions about the fire. Or whatever."

"Thank you."

"I mean it. Anytime. I'm used to getting calls at all hours because of the vet clinic, so you don't have to worry about the time. Half the time I'm up in the middle of the night anyway. Not that you'd call me in the middle of the night. But I'm just saying you could." Why was he rambling?

She smiled as she raised her hand as if to touch his arm, then hesitated and let it drop instead. "I hear you. And I know what you're talking about. People like us—we get it. It's usually late when the ghosts decide to visit."

He nodded, somehow knowing she understood, sure that she had spent the same lonely hours lying awake in the middle of the night missing the warmth that was supposed to be on the other side of the bed.

He wrinkled his brow as he looked down at his hand. "I'm not sure why I just got *my* phone out to give you my number." Maybe because he couldn't remember the last time he'd exchanged numbers with a beautiful woman. *I'm not asking her out. I'm just offering a friendly ear if she needs someone to listen.*

Mmmhmmm….keep telling yourself that, Tate.

Nodding at his phone, she said, "Why don't I give you *my* number, and you can send me a text? Then I'll have yours."

"Smart."

She recited her number, and he punched it in, then held his fingers over the message line. What should he text her? Something flirty? *Flirty?* Or all business? Or something in between?

He typed, Hey, it's Brody. *Wow. That'll impress her.* He added a smiley face emoji, then deleted it. He held his thumb over the keyboard, debating what else to type. Why was this so hard? It was just a simple text.

The longer he stood there staring at his phone, the more awkward he felt. *Just type something.* He tapped the letters on the screen, I'm here if you need me. Then he pressed Send before he could change his mind.

"It seems like a lot of thought went into that text. I'm excited to read it," she said, teasing him.

He offered her a sheepish grin. "I know. That was dumb. I don't know why that was so tough."

She chuckled. "I'll check it when you leave and try to think of something superawkward to text you back."

He laughed. "Please do."

One of the horses whinnied, and she looked out toward the corral. "I love this place."

He watched her gaze toward the barn. Her expression was wistful, her eyes slightly sad. The breeze blew a strand of her hair across her cheek, and he was tempted to reach out and brush it away. A pensive smile pulled at the corners of her lips, as if she were reflecting on a happier time.

Dammit, why couldn't he stop looking at her mouth?

"I should probably go," he told her. "Let you get back inside."

"Thank you for everything," she said, taking a step toward him. She opened her arms as if to hug him, then started to close them, then opened them again and committed to the hug.

He grinned as he wrapped his arms around her, pulling her close and inhaling the scent of her hair. He probably smelled like smoke, but she didn't seem to care. Now that she'd committed, she really hugged him, pressing herself to him and resting her cheek against his shoulder. She fit perfectly into the circle of his arms, and he closed his eyes for a second, something in him settling for just that moment, then taking off in a flight of winged nerves.

As he pulled back, a sudden urge had him pressing a quick kiss to her cheek. But she turned just as he did, and he caught the corner of her lips with his.

He paused for just one tenth of a beat, one millisecond of indecision, of want and need and a bone-deep desire to slant his lips over hers and take that gorgeous mouth he'd been staring at all night. He could smell a mix of Oreos and peppermint from the tea on her breath and could almost taste the chocolate of the cookies. He tried to swallow, then tried to make a joke, but his words stuck in his throat.

"I'll check in on you tomorrow," he finally managed to say as he pulled away and let her go.

Her eyes were round, and she blinked, her breathing a little shaky as she nodded and said, "Yeah, okay, that would be great."

He turned and opened the door, climbing into the truck before he said anything more. Or did anything more—like pull her back into his arms and issue her a proper kiss. One that would take both of their breath away. He offered her a quick wave, then pulled the door shut.

She waved as she took a few steps back. It took everything he had to keep his eyes on the road and not check the rearview mirror. *Dang.* His hands were shaking on the steering wheel. This woman had really unnerved him. He'd done a femoral head ostectomy the day before to remove a dog's fractured hip and his hands had been steady as church on Sunday. But a few minutes in the company of Elle Brooks, and he was shaking like his grandma's Jell-O salad.

Turning onto the highway, he shook his head as he tried to settle himself. He jumped as his phone buzzed in his pocket. Pulling it out, he looked down at the screen and couldn't help the smile that spread across his face as he saw he'd received a text from Elle.

He laughed out loud as he read the promised "awkward" message:

I like your pants.

Brody shook his head at his dashboard clock the next morning as he pulled up in front of his parents' house. He'd told Mandy, his ten-year-old daughter, he'd be there to pick her up at eight, and it was already five after. Not that she would care—she loved being with his folks and usually spent a few nights a week with them, especially when he was on call. But he didn't usually run late.

He also didn't usually spill coffee on his shirt or misplace his phone or forget to start the dishwasher. But this morning, his mind had been all over the place and mostly consumed with thoughts of the woman he'd been hanging out with the night before. He'd lost five minutes that morning just ruminating over the way her face had looked as she stared out over the farm and the snug fit of her pajama top, which had hugged her curves just enough to send his mind to sinful places.

He was still shocked that he'd kissed her. Well, not *exactly* kissed. More of a *missed* than a kissed. Had he meant to catch the corner of her lip? Or had his body betrayed his brain and actually *tried* to kiss her? He shook his head, the idea of wanting to kiss another woman so foreign.

His mom had been dropping not-so-subtle hints about him getting back on the dating horse, and he'd even asked a woman out last month. He'd asked out a friend, Bryn actually, thinking it would be a safe way to ease into the dating pool. It was before he knew she had a thing for Zane, although it became apparent when he showed up at the same restaurant where they were having dinner. The whole thing had been awkward and had ended with a disastrous attempt at another good-night kiss that hadn't quite landed on its mark. Like his lips didn't want to betray Mary, although it had been five years since they'd kissed hers.

And the experimental kiss with Bryn had been nothing like the tantalizing one with Elle. It had been more like a peck he'd give his cousin—none of the heat that swirled through him when his lips had brushed Elle's. All that from a simple touch of the corner of her mouth.

He shook his head, trying to clear the image of her face after the missed kiss—her eyes wide, her lips barely parted, as she stared up at him, the same kind of wonder and confusion that was surging through him evident in her expression.

He swallowed as he pushed the thoughts away. That part of him was closed, shut down. It had died in that hospital room the night Mary had taken her last breath.

Now there was only one woman in his life, the one who was waving as she pushed through the front door. A smile lit her face as she strode down the sidewalk.

His heart swelled with love at the sight of her, her long, blond hair already escaping the braids he was sure his mother had meticulously plaited that morning. She wore a teal T-shirt, cut-off jean shorts—he swore that girl had grown an inch in the last week—and her favorite purple cowboy boots. She clambered into the passenger side of the truck, tossing her purple, glittery backpack onto the floor before throwing her arms around her dad's neck for a quick hug. "Hi, Dad."

"Good morning, beautiful girl," he said, hugging her to him and inhaling the sweet scent of her shampoo mixed with a hint of maple syrup. "Did you have fun with Gramps and Grandma last night?" He glanced at the house and offered a wave to his mom, who stood in the doorway. She waved back, then her eyebrows lowered as she raised her outstretched thumb and pinkie to the side of her face and mouthed *Call me later*.

Uh-oh. Brody didn't like the sound of that. She hadn't given any indication what she wanted to talk to him about, but she was his mom. He could read her expressions from a mile away, and the tight set of her jaw told him he wasn't going to like the conversation.

"Yeah, it was fine. Grandma and I finished working on our costumes for the Hay Day Celebration. Shamus is going to look so cute."

"I'm sure you both will. I'll bet you'll be the cutest girl-and-mini-horse team in the costume competition."

"I hope so." She held up her crossed fingers. "Grandma did a really good job on the sewing."

"I know the costume competition is important to you, but there's other things to do at Hay Day. I want you to have fun at the whole celebration."

"Don't worry, Dad. I will. It's one of my favorite parts of summer." She dropped into her seat and buckled her seat belt. "Oh, and guess what. I beat Gramps at Uno for like four games in a row." She wrinkled her forehead. "I still can't tell if he's letting me win or if he's just not trying hard enough."

Brody chuckled and pulled onto the road. "Who cares? I can't believe you got him to play *four* games in a row. *Especially* if he was losing."

"Good point." She turned in her seat, her eyes drawn with concern. "Hey, I heard Gramps say there was a fire in town last night."

"Yeah, there was. I was there."

"You? Why?"

"I was at the diner when we heard about it, and I went over to help."

"What happened? Was it a bad one?"

"Not too bad. It could have been worse, but no one got hurt at least." He put a hand on his daughter's shoulder. "It was Elle Brooks's house."

Mandy gasped. "Oh no. Is she okay?"

Mandy had spent more time with Elle than he had. She'd done a girls' night sleepover with her and Bryn the month before, when he'd had an out-of-town conference. His daughter thought highly of her, talking nonstop of the mother dog and the puppies Elle had helped to rescue, and even at her young age, Mandy proved to be quite a good judge of character. Although how could his daughter not love a woman who saved puppies, treated for pizza, and taught her how to apply a beauty mask?

Beauty masks? Another weird woman thing he had no clue about. And only one of many. He was beyond thankful for his mom and the help she offered as his daughter was quickly transforming into a preteen. His gut clenched at the hope that his mom's phone call didn't have to do with any of that.

Oh no. What if Mandy had started her period? No—she was still a little girl.

He was a doctor, for Pete's sake. He could explain menses and knew the reproductive system details of numerous species, but he fumbled like a nervous quarterback when it came to the notion of all that and *his* little girl.

"Yeah, she's okay," he said, pushing away the thoughts. "A bit shaken up, but she seemed all right. She stayed at Bryn's last night."

"We should stop over there and check on her before we go home."

He raised an eyebrow as he snuck a glance at her. "Check on Elle or check on the puppies?" He may not be great at conversations about periods, but he knew his daughter and knew she'd been eyeing one of the rescued puppies. Hardly an hour went by that she didn't find a way to drop the little black-and-gray puppy into their conversation.

"Both," she said, then giggled as he reached over to tickle her side.

The sound of her laughter filled the truck as he turned down the highway toward Bryn's farm. And despite his moments' earlier declaration to push Elle from his mind, his stomach had just done a funny, little jump at the thought of seeing her again. He'd had the idea of checking on her today but was glad his daughter had been the one to bring it up.

"Hey, I almost forgot, how was the birthday party yesterday? Did you have fun?" The idea of spending even one hour with a bunch of ten-year-olds was enough to make him cringe, and he wondered if his daughter had felt the same way. She hadn't seemed very excited about the party for Jasmine Riley, one of the girls in her class, even though it was being held at the Bounce House Trampoline Park, a place she normally loved. He'd all but had to convince her to go.

Her smile fell. She gave a slight shrug as she turned to stare out the window. "It was fine."

"Fine?" *Hmm.* "I thought you loved jumping on those trampolines. We had so much fun that time we went."

"I do love jumping on them. With you."

His brow furrowed at her quiet response. "But not with your friends?"

She shrugged and mumbled something that sounded like "What friends?" But he didn't quite catch what she'd said.

"I think it would be fun to eat pizza and get to play around with a bunch of kids."

"That's because nobody cares that you smell like a horse."

Brody jerked his head back as anguish tore through him. His fingers gripped the steering wheel as anguish quickly changed to anger. He wanted to pummel whatever stupid kid said something mean to his precious girl. Slowly exhaling, he fought to control his reaction, somehow knowing he needed to tread carefully with his next choice of words. He was sure that offhand comment wasn't as casual as his daughter made it sound. "Did someone say you smell like a horse?"

Her gaze stayed trained at a spot on the truck seat where she picked at a loose seam. "Some girls do."

Damn. Much harder to think about pummeling ten-year-old girls. Calling them names probably wouldn't help either. Another stab of grief pierced through him as he missed Mary. She would know how to handle this, what to say. He tried to imagine how she would deal with it, what kind of mature, thoughtful response Mary would have. "Maybe they're just jealous. Being around horses doesn't seem like a bad thing. Doesn't every little girl wish she had a pony?"

"Not really. At least not anymore. Now they all just want iPhones and boyfriends."

Oh.

Wait, boyfriends? She was only ten.

"And it's not like I even *have* a pony," she complained. "Not one of my own anyway."

"Mandy, we board four horses on our property. It's practically the same thing. You can see them and ride them whenever you want."

"I know. But it's not the same as having my *own* horse."

How did this conversation go from mean girls to him buying his daughter a pony? He was so in over his head. "If you ask me, those girls sound awful. I'd rather have horses than an iPhone any day. And who wants a boyfriend? Talk about someone that smells." He gave her shoulder a playful nudge.

"Da-add." Her expression didn't change to her normal smile at his jokes and teasing. Her mouth stayed set in a tight line.

Oh-kay. This was really upsetting her. "Do you want me to talk to their moms?"

"NO! No way. That will only make things worse. I can handle this myself. It's not that big a deal."

It seemed to him like a fairly big deal. Otherwise, she wouldn't have brought it up. Mandy was pretty even-keeled and didn't let much get her down. He wanted to say more, but they were pulling into Bryn's driveway, and Mandy was already leaning forward in her seat, her lips pulling into a grin as she caught sight of Shamus, the miniature horse that trotted toward the fence to greet them. He was another of Bryn's rescues, and the transformation in the little horse over the last month had been remarkable. He'd come in with a lackluster coat, hooves long and curling from neglect, and an overall sad demeanor. But after a few weeks in Bryn's and Zane's care, he was a different horse, his coat shiny and his foot pain gone as he pranced along the fence.

At least he was still behind the fence and not standing in the middle of the driveway like the night before. The sneaky, little escape artist.

Brody's shoulders dropped as he noticed Bryn's car was gone. He may have gotten himself worked up for nothing. Elle might not even be here. Bryn could have already taken her back to her house.

It was probably for the best. He had no business getting all worked up over Elle. He'd probably blown those feelings out of proportion anyway. He had more than enough of a woman to take care of in his life right now. Even if she was only four feet tall and missing her right canine. He grinned over at his daughter.

Sometimes it took his breath away to try to grasp the depth at which he loved her. *And* at how much she looked like her mother. Even though she'd been gone for years, Mary was always with him, in the expressions and nuances of his daughter. He'd had his shot, had felt the all-consuming breadth of perfect love and the bone-deep grief of losing it. He'd sworn he'd never let himself get that close to another person ever.

He caught sight of Elle as he got out of the truck. She stood on the other side of the screen door, the light from inside radiating around her, giving her an almost angelic appearance. Her hair was down, and she wore black leggings and the T-shirt he'd given her the night before. She smiled and gave him a little wave, and his stomach tumbled to his boots.

Dang, Tate. Get a grip. She's just a woman.

He'd noticed she was pretty the first time he'd met her. He wasn't blind. But they'd been preoccupied with trying to save the dogs' lives and hadn't had a chance to talk. Now that he'd spent time with her, talked to her, heard the soft cadence of her voice and the warm lilt of her laughter, he realized she was even more beautiful on the inside.

"Thank goodness you're here," she called to them through the screen door as they got out of the truck. "I've been trapped in the house for the last thirty minutes." She pointed to the front porch.

Mandy stopped in her tracks. "Oh wow" was all she could whisper.

Brody's eyes widened as he caught sight of the source of Elle's entrapment. *Oh wow* was an understatement.

CHAPTER 4

BRODY CAUTIOUSLY WALKED UP THE PORCH STEPS AS HE stared down at the creature blocking the front door.

Elle offered them a thankful grin. "Boy, am I glad to see you guys. I've been stuck in here for half an hour. I didn't see her out there and hit her shell with the screen when I tried to open the door. Between that and the way I shrieked, I think I must have scared her because she pulled into her shell and hasn't come out for the last thirty minutes."

"Why didn't you just use the back door?" he asked.

"I would have, but there's a giant hog sprawled out in front of that one."

Mandy placed a hand on her hip. "You know Tiny doesn't like to be called a hog."

Elle raised her hand. "You're right. My mistake. There was a petite, two-hundred-pound pig sunning herself and blocking the back stoop."

Satisfied that the proper terminology had been applied to the pig, Mandy turned her attention back to the turtle. "Where the heck did she come from?"

"I have no idea. She was just there when I opened the door."

"She's huuuggge," Mandy said, her voice carrying a tone of awe. "I've never seen a turtle that size."

"Hmmm, not a turtle," Brody remarked. "It's a tortoise. And by the looks of it, I'd say it's a sulcata. Third-largest species in the world. This one's got to weigh sixty pounds. No wonder you couldn't move the door."

Elle's tone softened as she looked down at the giant tortoise. "You don't think I hurt her, do you?"

"*She's* actually a *he*," Mandy said.

Brody leaned his head to check the turtle, noting how the back end of the shell went straight down to protect the tail versus leveling off. "Between the shape of the carapace and the roundness of the shell, I'd say you're right. I could tell for sure if I turned him over, but he seems to be in enough stress right now without me messing with him." He raised an eyebrow at his daughter. "How did you know he was a male?"

Mandy pointed into the large cardboard box that sat next to the wall of the house. "Because it says so on the note. His name is Spartacus, and you're right: he's a sulcata tortoise."

"Well thanks, honey," he answered wryly. "Glad to know those years of vet school weren't a waste of money." He held out his hand. "Pass me the note."

"It looks like someone left him here for Bryn," she said, peering into the box as she handed him the note. "There's all sorts of stuff in here, like food bowls, and some lights, and some blankets."

Brody scanned the note. "It says here that Spartacus's owner is apparently a ski bum named Chad who had to leave the state in an emergency and couldn't bring the tortoise with him. He met Bryn at the diner, and she told him about the rescue ranch, so he knew she'd be the perfect person to leave the tortoise with. He said he's going to try to come back for him. And he left her some cash for food. He said the tortoise is friendly, digs having his neck scratched, and loves anything red, especially berries or cherry tomatoes."

"Does Bryn have any berries or tomatoes?" Mandy asked Elle. "Maybe we can use them to lure him away from the door."

"Good idea. I'll check. Be right back." Elle disappeared into the house and returned a minute later with a small plastic bowl with three large strawberries in it. "Found some." She pushed the door open a few inches, careful not to hit the tortoise's shell, and passed the bowl through.

Mandy took it and picked up the largest berry. Holding it by the leaves, she waved it in front of the opening in the tortoise's shell. The animal's legs were drawn together just inside the shell, as if its tortoise knees were touching, providing a cover in front of its head. "Here, Spartacus. Here's a beautiful strawberry, just for you." She laughed as the tortoise's legs slowly parted, and he carefully poked his head halfway out of the shell and sniffed at the berry. "It's working." She took a small step back and the tortoise's head pushed further out, its neck pulsing like a bullfrog's. "Come on, buddy." She let the tortoise take a small nibble of the strawberry, then pulled it slowly back, trying to lure him away from the door.

Thrusting his legs fully out, his toenails clicked on the wooden slats of the front porch as he pushed himself up and took a slow, tentative step forward.

"He's moving." Mandy cheered as she let him take another bite. The red pulp of the fruit clung to his lips, making the girl giggle. "He looks like he's wearing lipstick."

Elle lifted her shoulder and pushed out her lips, effecting a pursed, kissy face. "It's the latest rage, don't you know? They're calling it Very Strawberry, and *everyone* is wearing it."

Mandy laughed again and pursed her lips. "Ooh la la. It's the latest in turtle fashion." She made kissing noises at the tortoise. "Come on, Spartacus, you're making fashion history here."

Brody shook his head. Not a chance in heck was he getting in on this game. But the tortoise was moving. He could easily pick it up and set it in the grass, but his daughter was having so much fun solving the dilemma with the fruit, he hated to take the victory from her.

Two strawberries and ten slow minutes later, the tortoise had finally moved from in front of the door. "Yay," Elle said, clapping her hands, then pushing the door wide. "I'm free."

"Were you going somewhere?"

Elle laughed, and the sound played over his ears and sent a wave of warmth through him. "I was going outside to look at the horses while I drank my coffee, but I've drained my cup while standing here checking out the turtle...er, tortoise, I mean. I had been thinking of making some breakfast. You two want to join me?"

"What are you makin'?" Mandy asked before Brody had a chance to reply.

Elle shrugged. "I don't know. What are you hungry for? Eggs? Bacon? Pancakes? French toast?"

"Yes."

"Yes to which ones?"

"Yes to all of them," Mandy said resolutely. "And we can help. My dad makes the *best* pancakes."

Elle cocked an eyebrow at Brody. "Here I thought your talents lay in running bravely into burning buildings and saving the lives of animals. Who knew you were also a skilled pancake chef?"

He lifted a shoulder. "What can I say? I'm a man of many talents. I'm also pretty proficient at grilled cheese sandwiches, chocolate shakes, and getting tough stains out."

"I'm impressed."

"*And* he can french braid hair," Mandy added, beaming in pride at her father.

Brody cringed. "Now we didn't have to tell her that one. Just when I was starting to impress her."

"What? French braiding hair *is* impressive. It's hard. You watched like twenty YouTube videos to figure it out."

"Wow. Now I really am impressed," Elle said.

"Don't be. You haven't seen my french braids. But I *can* make fairly decent pancakes."

Elle stood back from the door. "Your griddle awaits."

The kitchen that normally seemed so large suddenly felt tiny as Elle maneuvered around Brody's tall body and Mandy's short one. Although Mandy wasn't making her pulse race the way Brody was every time his arm brushed hers or their hips bumped into each other.

Brody started the bacon frying while Elle and Mandy cracked eggs into a bowl. They had already spent ten minutes cooing over and cuddling the puppies before washing their hands and getting down to the business of breakfast.

They worked well together, each doing separate tasks that contributed to the whole meal process. Mandy found the griddle and plugged it in. Elle pulled the pancake ingredients from the cupboards as Brody called them out and mixed them together. Familiar with being at Bryn's house, Mandy found plates and silverware to set the table while the griddle heated.

"We need some music," Mandy said. "Dad, you should play your pancake party playlist."

"Your *what* playlist?" Elle asked, barely holding back a laugh.

He raised an eyebrow at her. "What? You don't have a pancake party playlist?"

She pressed her lips together, the giggles building in her throat. "No, but I should. I can't wait to hear yours."

He pulled out his phone and connected to the Bluetooth speaker sitting on Bryn's counter. The cheerful strains of a popular pop song blared from the speaker. He offered her a slow head bob and a flirty grin. "This is my pancake-making jam."

The laugh finally burst free. "Nice. Are those your pancake-mixing moves too?"

"You know it. I call this one the hotcake." He moved his arms in a wave. "It's all groove, baby."

Mandy jumped in front of him, getting in on the game with a wild wiggle of her hips followed by a straight-armed clap. "And I call this one the flapjack."

Elle twirled her arm in the air. "This is my spatula-spin step."

Brody chuckled as he shook his head. "That's weak. You're going to have to try harder if you want to make it into this elite dance club."

"Spin me, Dad," Mandy said, grabbing Brody's hand and twirling under his arm. "We can call this move the mixer." She giggled as he spun her around, then dropped his hand and pointed to Elle. "Now spin, Elle."

He held out his hand and Elle hesitated for just a second, then—*Oh, what the heck?*—slid her hand into his outstretched palm. Her heart felt dizzy as he spun her under his arm, her body brushing against his, the scent of his aftershave surrounding her with each turn.

She'd noted the scent the night before, something woodsy and masculine. He'd also smelled like smoke, but the hint of his aftershave was still there as she'd stepped into the circle of his arms and pressed into him. It had been an impulse move, she hadn't planned to hug him. But once she'd gone in, she had to commit. And it had been worth it.

She'd found herself wrapping her arms around his waist and holding him tighter than she'd anticipated, shutting her eyes as she sank into the warmth and comfort of his arms. It had been so long since she'd taken comfort from a man's arms. But with Brody, it had felt easy. Just like talking to him had been. And how spending time with him and Mandy felt this morning.

The *kiss*. Now that was something else entirely. Had he meant to brush her lips? Or was it an innocent buss on the cheek, and she'd blown it by turning her head? Had her body betrayed her, veering in at the last second in hopes of connecting to his mouth? Had she wanted him to kiss her? She couldn't imagine that. He was cute and a great listener, and he had big, solid shoulders and great hands, *and* he was funny. But she wasn't looking for any of that. She'd had her shot. And it had been taken away. And she didn't think she could withstand even another ounce of grief. So why was she letting Brody spin her around the kitchen and inhaling his aftershave like it was the scent of a fresh summer day?

Mandy cheered and clapped her hands, twirling around as her body wiggled and shook to the music. "Woo-hoo! Dance party mayhem!" She scooped a handful of flour off the counter and tossed it into the air.

Brody stopped, his arm falling around Elle's shoulders as the bits of white dust fell on them like floury snow. He stared down at Mandy, who peered up at him, her arms pressed against her sides, doing her best to look remorseful as an unabashed smile took over her face.

"Sorry, Dad," she said, trying not to laugh as she brushed flour from the side of his and Elle's arms. "Sorry, Elle."

Elle shrugged, sliding out from under Brody's arm. "No worries, kiddo. We're having fun. You just got a little carried away." Was that what she was doing now? Swirling and dancing with Brody? Getting carried away in the moment and acting silly? She brushed flour from her hair as she stepped toward the stove and picked up a fork. "I'd better take this bacon out before it burns."

"You can grab a broom, little miss, and sweep up the flour," Brody told his daughter. He kept his tone stern, but Elle saw the smile on his lips as he turned back to the mixing bowl. "Sorry about that," he said softly as he brushed the white dust from Elle's arm.

"It's no big deal," she answered, trying to control the shiver that ran down her back at the soft touch of his hand on her arm. "I love her enthusiasm."

He chuckled. "Me too. I would be lost without that kid."

"She's great."

"Thankfully, she didn't inherit her dad's skill on the dance floor." His grin was back as he scooped batter onto the griddle.

"I'm thankful for that too," Mandy said, teasing her dad as she came out of the pantry with a broom and dustpan.

Elle lifted the crispy bacon onto a paper towel and drained away the majority of the grease from the pan before pouring in the bowl of cracked eggs. She sprinkled salt and pepper over the egg mixture as she stirred, then added a handful of grated sharp-cheddar cheese into the fluffy yellow pile.

Mandy finished sweeping the floor and disappeared into the pantry to put the broom away.

"The eggs are done," Elle said, sliding them from the pan into a cheery red bowl. She stepped up to the counter, bumping her hip against Brody's as she squished in next to him. "Anything I can do to help you?" She surveyed the perfect circles of batter bubbling on the griddle. "Wow, Mandy was right. You *are* an excellent pancake maker."

"Just wait until you taste them," he said. "Melt-in-your-mouth delicious. Add a little butter and some warm syrup, and you'll think your mouth has died and gone to heaven."

Speaking of melting, she was softening like heated butter just listening to him describe the meal. Between the rumble of his deep voice and the sinful-sounding description, her stomach was doing little flips that had to do with more than just excitement about the food. Since when did a stack of pancakes turn into an orgasmic experience? Apparently since Brody Tate was the six-foot-plus chef flipping them.

"I can't wait to take a taste." *Of the pancakes and of you*, her inner vixen spoke up. Whoa, Elle hadn't heard from her in a long time. But suddenly, with the arrival of Brody in her life, the saucy minx part of her mind was back and ready for action.

No. No action, Elle told herself. She was definitely *not* ready for action.

You were ready for that kiss last night, her vixen argued. *And you're standing close enough to Brody to feel more than heat from the griddle.*

Her hip was pressed against his, and she could feel the warmth of him, even through the fabric of her leggings. She took a tiny step to the side.

"They're almost done," he said, flipping the final one. The undersides were golden brown, the edges crisp, and the scent of warm vanilla wafted up from the griddle. "And they'll be worth the wait." He peered down at her, then laughed as he lifted his hand. "You've still got flour on your face."

He brushed her cheek, pausing for just a second to let the ends of his fingertips linger on her skin. Her eyelids fluttered closed and she leaned in, just the slightest bit, to his touch.

Instead of lowering his hand, he raised it tenderly to cup her cheek. The feel of his hand on her face had her breathless—such a small gesture, the lightest touch. It had been so long since a man had touched her so intimately.

She dared to risk a glance at him as she tipped her face up to his. He was staring directly into her eyes, and she was stunned at the raw hunger she saw in his gaze. And even more astonished at the same kind of wanton passion spiraling through her.

His gaze dropped to her lips, and her knees went weak. She gripped the edge of the counter, the hard surface offering something solid to cling to, to keep her from falling into the depths of this man's gaze.

Was he going to kiss her again? A real kiss this time? Not an accidental brush of connection, but a deliberate crush of his mouth on hers? Her lips parted in anticipation as he leaned in. There was no questioning his intention—he was going to kiss her, and every part of her yearned for the connection.

CHAPTER 5

ELLE'S BODY ACHED WITH A BURN SHE'D ALMOST FORGOTTEN she could feel. Brody's lips were so close, the air felt sparked with an energy of need and hunger.

"Hey, anybody want chocolate chips in their pancakes?" Mandy asked, stepping out of the pantry, a yellow bag in her hand. "I found some in here. Remember that's how Mom used to like them?"

Brody's hand dropped from Elle's face, his expression stricken, and the speed with which he stepped away from her was like her skin had just caught fire and was too hot to touch. His gaze dropped to the pancakes, his attention suddenly razor focused on lifting them from the griddle to the plate. "It's too late..." he started to say, but his voice faltered and he paused to clear his throat. "Sorry, honey, it's too late to add them. They're already done."

Mandy shrugged and tossed the bag back onto the shelf. "Oh well. No biggie."

Elle stood frozen in place, still gripping the counter, seeming unable to transition from the moment of pure desire reflected in Brody's eyes to his sudden unwillingness even to stand close to her.

The mention of Mandy's mom had shut him down tighter than a seaside cottage during a Maine squall. She understood. Of course she did. The ghost of Ryan's memory pushed against her as well, blanketing the new emotions of need with a thin layer of guilt. Was she really ready to make out over the pancake griddle with a man she'd barely met before the previous night?

That thought urged her into action, and she busied herself with setting the eggs on the table and filling the glasses with water as

Brody flipped the rest of the pancakes onto a platter. She'd heated the syrup in the microwave, and she retrieved it now as they all sat down to the table.

Mandy reached for Brody's hand, then Elle's, as she bowed her head for grace. Brody's hand was on the table, and he turned it over, offering his palm and a wisp of a smile. She slipped her hand into his and bowed her head.

"Thank you, God, for this yummy food," Mandy said. "And for keeping my very good friend Elle safe and not letting her whole house burn down. Please help Dad to save every animal and to reconsider letting me have a puppy of my own. Amen."

Brody squeezed her hand and grinned. He shook his head, chuckling as he turned his smile to Elle. "See what I have to deal with? This girl has even got God in on her pursuit of a puppy."

Elle nodded at the girl. "I'm on your side too."

Mandy fist pumped the air. "Yes. Girl power."

"Don't encourage her," Brody said, slapping a hand to his forehead. "She's already got her grandma working on me too." He lifted his fork and pointed to the pancakes. "Eat first. Talk about puppies later." He scooped eggs onto his plate, then passed the bowl to Elle. "Have you had a chance to make any calls about the fire?"

"Yes, several," she said, taking the eggs. It seemed their easy camaraderie was back. "I called my insurance company last night, and they're sending out an adjuster, but he can't make it over until tonight. I'm meeting him at the house around five. I also got ahold of the fire restoration company you and the chief recommended. They are finishing up a job today so won't be able to start on my house until tomorrow. I'm going to meet them over there in the morning, so they can give me an estimate."

"Then you get to stay here another night," Mandy said, gazing wistfully at the dog bed full of puppies in the corner. "Lucky."

Brody nudged her leg. "It's not lucky that Elle had a fire in her house."

"Oh, gosh." The girl put her hand on Elle's arm. "I'm very sorry, Elle. I didn't mean it like that."

Elle put her hand over the young girl's, ignoring her slightly sticky fingers. "I know you didn't. It's okay. And I am lucky. But if the restoration takes more than a few days, I'll probably get a hotel room."

"Good luck with that," Brody said. "No way Bryn is going to let you stay in a hotel. She'll want you to stay here, no matter how long it takes. And in my experience, with a fire like that, you're looking at the cleanup taking a few weeks, not a few days."

Elle groaned.

"It's like a long slumber party," Mandy said.

"That I invited myself to."

"I'm sure Bryn doesn't see it that way." He aimed his fork at his plate. "These eggs are delicious, by the way. You'd better eat yours before they get cold."

She picked up her fork, thankful for the distraction.

Twenty minutes later, she was less thankful as she leaned back from the table. "Oh my gosh. I'm so full." Elle narrowed her eyes at Mandy. "I never should have let you talk me into that pancake-eating contest."

"I tried to warn you," Brody said. "My girl can put away flap-jacks like nobody's business."

"I never met a pancake I didn't like…" Mandy said, grinning, "…to eat."

"Well, I am duly impressed with your pancake consumption skills. Now if you two will roll me over to the sofa and pass me a remote control, I'll commence with my plans of spending the day binge-watching bad television."

"Binge-watching bad television?" Mandy cried, waking up the puppy sleeping in her lap. "You can't spend a perfect summer day inside watching TV."

"I can't?"

"No way. Dad and I are spending the whole day outside today. We're packing a picnic lunch and spending the day at the lake. You should come with us. You told me you love to swim." She jerked her head toward Brody. "She can come with us, can't she, Dad? You're always trying to get me to invite a friend over. And Elle and Bryn are just about the best friends I have. I mean, besides you."

A lump formed in Elle's throat, not just at the adorable girl telling her dad that he was her best friend, but also by the inclusion of herself in the girl's friend circle. It had been a long time since she'd been considered someone's best friend.

Brody shook his head as he looked from Mandy to Elle. "Are you sure Elle even *wants* to come with us? Maybe she has other plans."

"She doesn't," Mandy insisted, stroking her hand over the puppy's back to soothe it back to sleep. "She just said she was going to spend the whole day watching a bunch of awful television shows. Which sounds terrible. You're always telling me television is bad for my brain, and you also say we should do our best to try to help other people when we can. And Elle definitely needs our help. We have to save her from frying her brain."

Brody raised an eyebrow at Elle.

She lifted one shoulder. "A day at the lake does sound better than a fried brain."

"I guess you're coming to the lake with us. Hope you like bologna sandwiches."

"Ugh," she said, laughing and holding her stomach. "How can you even think about food?"

It was his turn to shrug. "I'm a man. We're always thinking about our next meal." He pushed back from the table. "But before we go to the lake, we need to clean up this mess." He pointed to the sticky plates pooled with syrup. "Why don't you clear the table, Mandy, while I start some dishwater running?"

The puppy had fallen back asleep, and Mandy gently put him

back in the enclosure next to his siblings, then raced back to the table to stack the plates. "The faster we clean up, the faster we can go swimming."

"Oh, shoot," Elle said. "I just realized I don't have a bathing suit."

Brody stood behind his daughter so she couldn't see his face, but Elle caught the salacious grin that tugged at his lips. A grin that had heat darting up her spine and swirls of nerves taking off in her pancake-stuffed belly. She smiled back, unable to help the impish grin that took over her face.

Brody raised his shoulders in an innocent shrug.

She tossed her napkin at him.

"Don't worry about it," Mandy said, oblivious to her father's flirty antics. He *was* flirting with her, wasn't he? "We don't have our stuff either. We still have to go home and pack the lunch and get our suits. We can wait for you if you want to run home and get your things." Mandy's face fell. "Or did your things all get burned up last night?"

Elle shook her head, touched by the girl's emotion. "No. Just my kitchen caught fire. But I don't have my car. I have to wait for Bryn to get home from her shift at the diner to give me a ride back to my house to get it."

"We can give you a ride," Brody said. "I was planning to offer anyway."

"Are you sure?"

"Of course."

"All right, then I guess we better get these dishes cleaned up so we can go to the lake."

Mandy threw her hands in the air. "Yay."

———————

Twenty minutes and one clean kitchen later, they piled into Brody's truck, Elle in the front and Mandy scrambling into the back seat of the king cab. Elle peered into the back with concern. "Don't you need some type of car seat? Or at least a booster?" she asked Mandy.

"Nah. I outgrew those last year. Once you're a certain age or weight, you don't need them anymore. And I weigh plenty."

"You weigh just the right amount," Elle said, trying to push down her fears about the car seat.

She rolled her eyes. "Not according to the girls in my class."

"The girls in your class sound like idiots," Brody said. "You only weigh more because you're tall."

"I'm the tallest girl in my class," Mandy confirmed.

Elle nodded. "That's tough. I grew tall fast too. Then I stopped. But I still remember what it was like to be one of the tallest girls. No fun."

"Being tall is awesome," Brody corrected. "You can see over other people's heads, and you get in to all the rides at the county fair. I think you're perfect just the way you are. Both of you are beautiful."

Elle raised an eyebrow at him.

"I'm working on her positive body image," he said quietly, then backpedaled as he shook his head. "Not that I don't think you're beautiful too. I do. I mean, oh, just put on your seat belt."

She grinned as she buckled in.

Ten minutes later, they pulled up in front of her house. Elle pulled her keys from her bag and peered at the two-story home as they walked up the front sidewalk. "From the outside, you can barely tell anything happened."

"The inside is a different story," Brody said.

"It can't be that bad," she said, turning the key in the lock and pushing open the door. She reeled back at the stench of smoke still heavy in the air.

"Pee-yew," Mandy said, pinching her nostrils together. "It stinks in there."

"Yeah, that's why I want you to stand right here in the doorway while Elle runs up and grabs her stuff. It's a mess in here, and I don't want you getting into it or breathing in too much of this smoke residue."

Standing inside the large foyer, Elle gazed around at the destruction. Directly in front of her, a large staircase led to the second floor. The oak bannister looked almost gray, its normal wood sheen covered in a fine layer of soot. The formal living room to the left looked fine and the door to the right, to Ryan's study, usually remained closed, so Elle didn't anticipate much damage in there. The majority of the mess was along the hallway that led to the kitchen and the living room at the back of the house. Muddy boot tracks and small pools of gray water lined the tile, and broken glass littered the floor.

"It's not pretty," Brody said as he started down the hallway. His cowboy boot sent up a small splash as he stepped through a shallow puddle of water. He pointed at his daughter. "Stay there," he instructed. "There's a lot of broken glass back here. Leave the door cracked to let some fresh air in. We'll be right back." He turned his hand over, holding it out to Elle. "You ready?"

"Not really," she said, but she slipped her hand into his and tentatively edged down the hall behind him. She gasped as she stepped into the kitchen, then choked on the smoke-filled air. She covered her mouth with her free hand and stared at the mess and debris littering the once-white kitchen. The glossy cabinets above and around the stove were now inky black, their surfaces bubbled and warped. The glass door of the oven had shattered, spraying broken glass all over the floor. Gray and black soot was everywhere, covering the ceiling, the cabinets, the fixtures, and obscuring the window above the sink. Ash dusted the countertops and smudged across the floor.

She swallowed, the taste of ash even in her mouth. "Gosh" was all she could utter.

"Sorry," he said. "I know it's rough." He let go of her hand and wrapped an arm around her shoulder.

She turned to him, burying her face in his chest and inhaling the fresh scent of the laundry detergent in his shirt. Sliding her arms around his waist, she held on to him, clutching the fabric of his shirt in her fingers and letting herself sag against him.

It's just stuff, she reminded herself, taking in a deep, shuddering breath and pulling her shoulders back. "I'm okay," she told Brody, stepping away from him and already missing the comfort of his arms.

"It's a lot. I know," he said, wincing as he surveyed the damage. "Why don't you go grab your swimsuit and whatever you need, and I'll sweep up some of this glass?"

She nodded, uttering a whispered, "Okay, thanks," as she backed out of the kitchen.

In a daze of shock, she walked down the hallway and up the stairs on shaky legs. The open door of the nursery caught her eye.

She was sure she hadn't left it open. She never did, unable to bear to walk by it and spy the cheery, pink-striped walls. But she hadn't exactly been thinking in the turmoil of the fire the night before, and she could have failed to get the door shut.

The air was clearer upstairs, still smoky but not as acrid. She swallowed at the burn in her throat as she took a cautious step toward the door. She reached for the jamb of the door to support herself as she spied Mandy standing in the middle of the room, holding a stuffed rabbit in her hands.

CHAPTER 6

"WHAT ARE YOU DOING IN HERE?" ELLE ASKED, TRYING TO keep her voice from shaking.

Mandy turned, her eyes wide. "I'm sorry," she said, dropping the bunny back into the rocking chair. "I wasn't trying to snoop. I promise. I was trying to help. I thought if I could find your swimsuit, we could get out of here sooner and get to the lake. But I didn't know which room was yours, and I opened this door by mistake." Her words tumbled out quickly, and she took a step away from the rocker.

"It's okay," Elle whispered, taking a small step into the room but still keeping one hand on the doorjamb. "I'm just not used to other people being in here."

"I'm really sorry," Mandy said again, tears in her eyes. "I didn't mean to…" She looked around the room, unsure of what she'd done wrong but knowing she'd somehow crossed a line.

Elle let go of the doorway and took another few steps into the room, then sank to her knees in front of the rocker. "It's all right. Really." The girl hadn't meant any harm. There wasn't a malicious bone in Mandy Tate's body.

Mandy reached out a hand and rested it on Elle's shoulder. "Are you okay?"

Elle rested her hand on top of the girl's and gave it a reassuring pat. "I will be. I just need a minute."

Mandy sat down on the floor next to her and leaned her small body into Elle's. She put her hand on Elle's leg, offering her support in the only way a ten-year-old knew how. They sat that way for a few moments. The young girl's eyes were filled with concern as she peered up at her, occasionally rubbing her hand gently on Elle's thigh.

"I'm okay," Elle reassured her.

"Did you have a baby, Elle?" Mandy whispered.

A lone tear escaped her eye as Elle nodded. She let out a shaky breath, then tried to find her voice to answer. "I did. But she died before I ever got to hold her."

The girl inhaled a sharp gasp, then tears again filled her eyes. "She died?"

Elle nodded, unable to say anything more.

"What was her name?"

"Ava." Elle breathed the name, her heart shattering again at the memories of the night she'd lost not just her husband, but her daughter as well.

Mandy threw her arms around Elle and pressed her face into her shoulder. "Why do the people we love have to die? It's not fair."

Grief ripped through Elle as she folded the girl into her arms and whispered, "No, it's not fair, sweet girl. It's not fair at all." She buried her face in Mandy's hair, holding the girl and rocking her gently, ignoring the tears that fell from her eyes as she focused on the sobs pouring from the girl.

She didn't hear him come in, but she didn't flinch when a pair of solid arms wrapped around her from behind and folded them both into his embrace.

"I got you," Brody said softly as he held them close.

———————

Brody wasn't sure how long they sat that way, Elle pulled tightly against him and Mandy practically in his lap as his arms wrapped protectively around them. He wanted to protect them with a yearning deep in his soul. Especially his baby girl. He would do anything to keep the harm and pain of the world from touching her. But he was surprised at the gut-deep wrench of defense he felt for Elle. Something about this woman had him pulling out his armor and preparing to slay dragons for her.

He'd always been protective of his family, especially his daughter. From the second he'd held her in his arms and she'd gazed up at him with those tiny, innocent, blue eyes and wrapped her small fingers around his, he knew he would do anything for her. When it came to Mandy, he had the ferocity of a grizzly bear, ready to claw and attack anything that hurt her. He'd felt the same about Mary, but cancer was an enemy he hadn't been able to defeat, no matter how hard they fought it.

Something about Elle Brooks had him picking up his sword, even as he fought the memories and heartache of the battle he'd lost.

Sitting on the floor in the nursery so lovingly decorated, all he could do was wrap them up, buffer the storm, and hope his shoulders proved broad enough to protect them. There was nothing to say that would bring their loved ones back or ease the ache of loss; all he could do was hold on and hope that the strength of his embrace could offer some comfort.

Elle held the back of his shirt in a tight grip, the fabric pulling as she clutched it firmly in her fist. Her shoulders trembled.

"I know," he whispered into her hair. He did know. He recognized the feelings she was fighting—had fought the same emotions from the very depths of his soul. "I'm so damn sorry." A shudder ran through him, and he let out a sigh. "Man, I hate that word."

Elle nodded. "Me too."

Sorry.

"I heard it a thousand times. Everyone was *sorry*. *Sorry* this happened. *Sorry* for your loss. I know they didn't know what else to say. And I know they were just trying to help. But it got to the point where I started to resent the word, like if one more person told me they were sorry I would rip their head off."

Mandy looked up at him. "Me too. I know I was little, and I

don't remember much, but I do remember being mad and wanting to kick that old lady at church who told me it was better that Mom died "cause now she wasn't suffering anymore."'"

Another crack split through Brody's brittle heart. "I didn't know that. I remember you being mad a lot, but the counselor said you were just angry about losing your mom." He pushed back the loose strands of hair that stuck to his daughter's tear-soaked cheeks.

"I was. I still get mad sometimes. And really, really sad."

He bent his head so his forehead touched hers. "So do I."

"So do I," Elle whispered, leaning her head into theirs. She heaved a heavy sigh. "What are we supposed to do with all this anger and sadness? I don't know if kicking old ladies is the answer."

Mandy pulled her head back, a grin tugging at the corners of her lips. "What about biting them? I was a biter till I turned six."

Brody let out a chuckle. Then the chuckle turned to a laugh as he glanced at Elle, whose eyes crinkled on the sides as she lost the battle not to laugh, and suddenly they were all laughing, cracking up as they held on to each other's arms.

Elle was laughing so hard that she let slip a snort, and that did them in. They dissolved into hysterical laughter.

"You *were* a biter," Brody said and ruffled Mandy's hair. He pushed his hand to his gut. "Oh my gosh, my stomach hurts."

"Who cares about your stomach?" Elle asked. "I think I peed a little." Her remarks sent them into another gale of laughter.

"Seriously now," Elle said, putting her hand on Brody's leg. "I think we should ban the word *sorry* from our vocabulary. At least with each other. What else could we say to show regret, so we don't have to ever say *I'm sorry*?"

Brody nodded, trying to focus on Elle's idea instead of the warm pressure of her hand on his leg. "I like this. A moratorium on *sorry*. Instead, we could say *I apologize*."

"Or *I regret what I said*," Elle suggested.

Mandy tilted her head to the side as if thinking. "Or *I wish I hadn't said that.*"

"That's a good one, honey," Brody told his daughter. He softened his voice, his tone growing more serious. "Or how about *forgive me?*"

Elle raised her gaze, her eyes welling with tears. "That's a good one too," she whispered.

Dang. The last thing he wanted was to make her cry again. Her laughter had filled something in him, and he wanted to hear it again, to see her smile light her face. He grinned and relaxed his shoulders. "How about *my bad?*"

It worked. Both Elle and Mandy grinned, and his daughter nudged him in the arm. "Oh, Dad. You're such a dork."

"Yoo-hoo. Anybody home?" a singsongy voice called from the floor below.

"That's Aunt Sassy," Brody told them, recognizing the voice. He looked from Elle to Mandy. "You guys okay?"

They both nodded. He pushed to his feet and helped them up as he hollered, "We're upstairs, Aunt Sassy. We'll be down in a minute."

"Okay, honey," she hollered back.

Before they left the room, Brody turned and pointed his finger at Mandy and Elle, pinning them with a stern glare. "Now, Aunt Sassy is a sweet old lady. I don't want either of you kicking her."

"Or biting her," Mandy said with a giggle.

"Or biting her," he agreed, smiling. He loved that his girl always got his jokes.

They headed down the stairs, but Elle stopped at her bedroom door. "I'll be right down. I'm just going to grab my suit."

He nodded, then followed Mandy down the stairs to where Sassy stood in the foyer. They both gave her a hug.

"I saw your rig out front and thought I'd stop in to check on Elle." She held up a Ziploc bag of cookies. "And I brought over some cookies. Not that they're enough to help in a case like this, but…" She trailed off as she stared into the burned-out kitchen.

"Cookies always help," Elle said from the top of the stairs. She had a laundry basket of what had been clean clothes in her arms and a large tote bag over her shoulder, clothes spilling over the top. She made it to the bottom of the stairs and set the basket down to give Sassy a hug. "Thanks for checking on me. And for the cookies. That was so thoughtful."

"I've been thinking about you," Sassy said. "I'm making lasagna and bringing it out to Bryn's tonight. I already called her at the diner to tell her to expect it." She patted Brody's arm. "You and Mandy are welcome to eat with us. I've made enough to feed a family of elephants."

"That's kind of you to offer," Brody said. "We accept. What time should we be there?"

"We'll eat around six."

"Yay," Mandy said, bouncing on the balls of her feet. "I love lasagna. We're going to the lake this afternoon," she told Sassy. "We're going swimming and having a picnic. Wanna come with us?"

A grin pulled at the corners of Sassy's thin lips. "Mercy, no. I haven't been in a bathing suit in twenty years. Back in my younger days, I had this light-blue bikini, and when I wore it, I'd practically have to beat the boys off with a stick. Now if I tried to wear a bikini, I'd have to use a stick just to hold it up." She pressed her hand to her chest. "Not much left in the old ta-ta department."

"Oh" was all Brody could manage to say. But Elle cracked up next to him, another snort escaping her. Dang, but she did have a cute laugh. Even with the snort. Hearing it somehow made him feel lighter.

"But you kids have fun," Sassy told them. "You need a little fun after being in here. It's downright depressing." She touched Elle's arm. "I'm sorry, honey."

Elle shrugged and tried to hold back her smile as she glanced at Mandy and Brody. "It's just stuff."

"I like your attitude. Now take these cookies and get out of here. Go have a good time, and don't worry about this place. I'm keeping my eye on it."

Elle gave the older woman's shoulder another squeeze. "Thanks again. For everything. I've already called a restoration company, and I'm meeting the insurance adjuster here later tonight."

"Good."

Elle turned to Brody. "I'll get my car now and follow you to your house."

"Sounds good." He and Mandy gave Aunt Sassy another round of hugs, then locked the front door and headed for the truck.

An hour later, they had changed into their swimsuits, put together a picnic lunch, and packed the truck with lawn chairs, towels, a cooler, and some inflatable rafts. The lake was actually on Bryn's property, so they dropped Elle's SUV at the farmhouse, then she piled into the pickup with Brody and Mandy.

"I didn't know Bryn had a lake," she told Brody as she buckled her seat belt.

"She's got quite a lot of acreage. Her grandfather used to raise cattle. The lake is in the mountains up behind the farm," Brody explained. "There's a hot springs on the property too, and some of it feeds into the lake, so the water isn't exactly warm but it's real nice. Especially in the summer. And it's downright balmy compared to mountain-lake standards."

"We love it. It's perfect," Mandy said. "And Bryn lets us go up there whenever we want in the summer."

"Which is not as often as I like," Brody said. "But we try to get up there for a few hours every other week or so."

"It sounds great. I can't wait to see it," Elle said. She was excited, and not just about seeing the lake, but about having a free day to swim and soak up the sun and enjoy summer with good food and good friends. Which, oddly enough, she already considered Brody and Mandy.

Well, her inner vixen had been considering Brody in a lot of ways that were well beyond the friend zone, but despite the zings of heat he sent racing up her spine whenever his hand brushed any part of her body, she still felt comfortable with him. Which was a strange feeling for her. She didn't often warm up so easily to people she'd just met. Although Bryn often watched Mandy, so Elle had been hanging out with the girl on several occasions over the past few weeks and had already formed a connection with her. She was tall and a little awkward, but crazy-smart and so funny. She often had Bryn and Elle in stitches. And Elle was touched by the girl's compassion for the animals, whether it was the adorable puppies or Otis, the ornery cuss of a goat. There was something special about Mandy Tate, and Elle simply enjoyed being around her.

It felt easy and normal, talking and laughing with Brody and Mandy as they bounced over the ruts of the pasture, then headed up the rocky mountain road through the trees. Then she couldn't speak at all as they drove out of the trees and into a clearing so beautiful it took her breath away.

Nestled against the backdrop of the tree-covered slope, a waterfall poured gently over a grouping of rocks into an idyllic lake, the water so blue and still that it perfectly mirrored the reflection of the mountain above it. Shades of navy, turquoise, and green blended together to turn the water's surface into a magnificent blue tapestry.

Brody pulled to a stop close to the shore, and Mandy and Elle scrambled from the truck. They were met with the scents of pine and lake and the sounds of the gently lapping water as it broke against the rocky shore. An area had been cleared to form a sort of a beach, although the ground was covered with hard-packed dirt and pebbles instead of sand.

"It's so beautiful, it makes me want to cry," Elle said softly.

"I know," Brody agreed, his voice low and reverent as he peered at the lake over her shoulder. "It gets me every time."

Shaking her head, she swallowed back the emotion and turned to Brody. "What can I do to help?"

He nodded to the bed of the truck. "Grab a couple of those chairs. I'll get the cooler, and Mandy can set out the blankets in our favorite spot."

Mandy pulled a stack of blankets from the back seat and raced toward a giant elm tree, hollering over her shoulder as she ran. "We love it by this tree. It's shady and by the best spot to get in the water."

"Looks great," Elle said, hoisting the fold-up chairs and following Brody.

It only took five minutes to set up their space. Brody and Mandy obviously were used to their routine. They spread out blankets and set up the chairs between the tree roots and around the cooler, using it as a table between them. The roots of the tree rose out of the dirt like gnarled fingers reaching for the water's edge.

They'd filled a tote bag with chips, dried fruit, snack crackers, and Aunt Sassy's cookies, and the cooler was stocked with drinks, sandwiches, and a giant tub of sliced watermelon.

Mandy spread a blanket between the roots, dropped a glittery, purple backpack onto it, then beamed up at Elle. "This is my spot. It's a perfect reading nook because I can sit between the roots and lean against the tree."

"It all looks perfect to me." Elle took a deep breath, inhaling the fresh mountain air. "I didn't realize how much I needed this."

"Nothin' like a day in the mountains to cure what ails ya," Brody said, toeing off his sneakers. Until that afternoon, Elle had only seen him in jeans and cowboy boots, but he looked dang good in swim trunks. His legs were long and muscled, and something about seeing his bare feet felt intimate and familiar. "A good swim, a little sunshine, and one of my famous bologna sandwiches adds up to a perfect day in my book."

She cocked an eyebrow. "*Famous* bologna sandwiches? I think I was there when you made them and they looked like Wonder bread, bologna, and mayo to me."

"It's all in the ratio of mayo to bread, and it takes a keen hand to spread it all the way to the edges." A grin tugged at his lips. "And I'm a doctor, so we're known for our skilled hands."

Elle chuckled as she glanced down at his hands. "Is that so?"

He held them up and offered her a flirty grin. "These hands are known to perform magic."

She swallowed as she imagined his large hands roaming over her skin, his long fingers sliding along her curves.

He nudged her arm, a knowing smile splitting his face. "Get your mind out of the gutter," he said, teasing her. "I meant like magic tricks, like pulling a quarter from your ear, or…" He glanced to where Mandy was already wading into the water. "Or rocking a baby girl to sleep."

A tight fist clutched Elle's heart as she inhaled a quick breath.

His face fell as he realized what he'd said, and he laid a hand gently on her shoulder. "Oh shit. Elle, I'm sorry. I wasn't thinking."

She tried to shake it off, knowing he hadn't meant any harm.

He scrubbed his free hand across the back of his neck. "Idiot," he mumbled.

"It's okay," she said, putting her hand over the one of his still holding her shoulder. "Remember we don't have to say that to each other."

He peered down at her, his expression apologetic as he nodded. "You're right. What I meant to say was *forgive me*."

She gripped his fingers. "Always."

He smiled and reached out to touch her cheek, then closed his hand at the last moment and dropped it to his side. "I have this insane urge to hug you right now. And I don't think I can control it, so if you don't want to be hugged, you'd better take a step back."

A grin spread across her face, and instead of taking a step back, she took one forward and let herself be pulled into his embrace. It felt so good to be pressed to his solid chest, his arms wrapped securely around her.

She let herself sink into him. How could it feel so natural to be in his embrace? She didn't know, but she did know that if she didn't put a little distance between them, she wouldn't ever want to let go. And that would be awkward for him as he tried to resume his vet duties with a woman clinging to him like a baby monkey.

She let go and took a step back, exhaling as she tried to figure out where to put her arms.

He cleared his throat and looked around their picnic site as if grasping for something to do. He nodded toward the water. "You ready for a swim?"

"Sure." She pulled at the back of her tank top where it had gone damp against the truck's seat. Or maybe it was sweaty from the heat she'd felt during their hug. Whatever it was, she hesitated to pull the top off.

In her haste, she'd grabbed the first swimsuit in her drawer, a red bikini she'd worn on her and Ryan's honeymoon, not realizing it probably wasn't the best choice for a family swim day. It covered all her bits, but just barely, and she was suddenly shy about taking off her shorts and tank in front of Brody. Especially since he kept sneaking glances at her as he set out their lunch.

Here goes nothing. She pulled the tank top over her head and tossed it to the blanket, then adjusted her top before unzipping and shimmying out of her shorts. Out of the corner of her eye, she saw Brody fumble the small bags of chips he'd been pulling from the tote. He reached to grab one that was falling but missed and only made it worse as the other bags slipped from his hands and fell to the blanket in a crash of crinkly plastic. He left them scattered on the blanket. "I think I'll join you. Apparently I need to cool off."

She glanced at his sheepish grin before he pulled his shirt over his head, then all she could do was stare at his tan, muscular chest. He was different from Ryan—her husband had been muscular, but he'd had a swimmer's body, lean and wiry, whereas Brody was tall and broad with big shoulders and long legs. His swim trunks hung from his hips, his stomach flat and ripped with muscles. Not the kind one got in a gym or from working out, but the kind earned from working outside and with large animals. He had to be strong to deal with two-thousand-pound bulls and solid horses and cattle that weighed eight times what he did. She already knew he was strong; he'd swept her off her feet the night of the fire and carried her down the stairs of her house as if she weighed no more than a bag of flour.

She was glad he'd stepped forward and was wading into the water in front of her, not just so she could admire his delicious physique, but because she was still self-conscious of the tiny bathing suit bottoms she wore. Which was interesting, since she hadn't really cared what she, or her body, had looked like the past few years.

After Ryan had died, she hadn't cared much about eating; nothing had tasted the same and the effort of cooking or even picking up food hadn't seemed worth the bother. She didn't know how much weight she'd lost, but she knew her clothes had started to hang on her, and she couldn't get by without wearing a belt.

But the last few months, she'd ventured out to the diner a few times a week, and that's where she'd met Bryn. For some reason, probably due to her natural inclination to take wounded strays under her wing, Bryn had decided to befriend her and seemed to make it her constant mission to feed Elle, often stopping at her table to chat bearing a bowl of ice cream or a piece of homemade pie or cobbler. As they'd become friends, Bryn found ways to sneak gooey grilled cheese sandwiches and plates of mashed potatoes and gravy in front of her. Elle had put some weight back on, and she was glad.

Bryn's friendship had done more than feed her body; it had also fed her soul, and she couldn't be thankful enough for the other woman's devotion.

"Are you coming in or what?" Mandy hollered from the water, breaking her out of her reverie.

Forget the stupid swimsuit, and just let yourself have fun, she scolded herself. "Yes, yes, I'm coming," she answered, laughing even as she tensed for the cold water to lap over her feet. But the water wasn't the icy cold she was expecting. It was cool, but the top layer was almost warm from the sun, and she laughed again as she waded in up to her waist. "I thought it would be freezing, but it's not even cold."

"I know. We told you. It's from the hot springs. Isn't it awesome?" Brody had turned, and his gaze raked over her body. Obviously *he* hadn't forgotten about the swimsuit.

A thrill ran through her at the look of desire on his face at the same time a quiver of caution skittered over her skin. *Careful, Elle.*

She waded in farther, then dipped down to her neck, tipping her head back to wet her hair. The cool water lapped luxuriously over her skin. She closed her eyes and went under, loving the different temperatures of the water, layered levels of cool and warm, like the tiers of a chocolate torte, dark and rich cake on one layer, then cool and light mousse on the next.

She broke the surface with a laugh and another feeling she hadn't had in so long, she almost didn't recognize it. It was joy—a pure, genuine feeling of happiness. Brody was right: sun and water and a perfect summer day were the ingredients to a soul-healing tonic.

Brody dove into the water and came up next to her, grinning and shaking the water from his hair like a giddy golden retriever. "It's great, isn't it?"

She smiled back. "Yes, it's wonderful. It's been a long time since I've been swimming and years since I've swam in a lake. Last time I can remember, I was a little girl. My mom surprised me and took me to one for the day. I don't know how she knew about it, and we never went there again, but that day was hot and the lake was practically deserted. It felt like we had the whole thing to ourselves."

"Sounds like fun. And seems like a good memory."

"It was. One of a very few." She tilted her head, lost in the recollection. "I haven't thought about it in a long time. I don't even know where it was. But we played in the water and ate warm peanut butter and jelly sandwiches and sunned ourselves on these giant slabs of rocks that jutted into the lake."

"It sounds cool. Are you pretty close to your mom, then?"

She shrugged. "When it suits her." Which hadn't been during Elle's most crucial time of need. No, her mom didn't *do* sad and grieving. She'd given Elle a few months to grieve, then taken her for a week at a good spa and explained that Ryan had left her plenty of money, and she needed to get over it now. Elle hadn't told her about the baby.

She let out a sigh. This day was perfect, she felt good, and she didn't want the issues she had with her mother to spoil it. "My relationship with my mom is complicated. Let's just say I'm not usually her first priority."

"Who is?"

"Herself."

"Ah. That sucks." He turned to watch Mandy playing in the shallow water next to a rock. "I work really hard to put that little girl first in my life. I didn't always. For a lot of years, I put my work and myself in front of my family. I went from spending all my time studying in vet school to spending all my time working and trying to rebuild our family's veterinary clinic. I took it for granted that my wife and baby would always be there."

He paused, and his gaze left Mandy as he seemed to stare into the past. "But then my wife died. And somehow my *baby* was already five years old. I'd missed so much. So I made a promise then and there to always put my child first."

She hurt for him, knowing all too well the pain of loss and regret. "And have you kept that promise?"

"For the most part. The few times I've blown it and acted self-ishly or put myself or my needs above hers have backfired in the most glorious ways."

Elle narrowed her eyes as she studied him. "I admire you. And I'm impressed with your commitment." Not like *her* absent father. "Mandy's a great kid. You must be doing something right."

He held her gaze, his expression solemn as he stared into her eyes. "Thanks. That means a lot."

She got lost in his eyes, their blue the same shade as the water, and she had to tear her gaze away for fear of doing something crazy, like throwing her arms around his neck and kissing his perfect mouth.

Behind him, Mandy was climbing up the rocky bank. A set of makeshift stairs had been formed in the dirt that led up to a flat ledge. Panic gripped Elle as she pointed to the girl. "Is she supposed to be doing that?"

Brody turned, and his eyes widened in alarm. "Mandy. Get down from there," he hollered.

The girl turned at her dad's voice, and her foot missed the next step. Dirt rained down the side of the path as she scrambled to regain her balance. She let out a cry as her arms pinwheeled and she fell backward off the bank.

CHAPTER 7

MANDY'S BODY HIT THE WATER WITH A SPLASH AS ELLE frantically dove into the lake. But she was no match for Brody, whose strong arms cut easily through the water. He made it to Mandy in what seemed like barely ten strokes.

The girl's head popped up just as Brody reached her and pulled the girl to him. "Are you okay?" He held her out, checking for injuries. "Are you hurt?"

"No, Dad. I'm fine," Mandy said as Elle finally made it to the pair.

"Are you all right?" Elle asked, her hand fluttering out of the water as she fought the urge to check Mandy's hair for a head wound. "Did you hit your head? Are you bleeding?"

"No, I just fell." She furrowed her brow at Elle and her father. "Stop looking at me like I almost died. I just slipped and hit the water. I'm not even hurt." Her expression changed from exasperation to alarm as she looked into the water. "But you are, Dad. You're bleeding."

"Shit," he said, lifting his foot out of the water to reveal a gash on his lower leg. "I must have cut myself on something."

Elle reached for Brody's arm. "It's okay. I'm trained in first aid. Do you need help getting back to shore?"

Brody turned to her, an amused expression on his face. "That's good to know. But you do realize that I'm a doctor."

"And a dad," Mandy said, obviously sensing Elle's panic. "So he's good at cuts," she said, her tone full of reassurance.

Elle tried to quell the alarm building in her at the sight of the blood. "Do you have a first aid kit? Some bandages? We should have brought my car. I always carry a full emergency kit. Do you think you need stitches?" She was rambling, her sentences running together in a rapid stream of words, as her legs vigorously scissors kicked under the water.

Brody put a hand on her shoulder and peered directly into her eyes as he spoke in a calm voice. "It's okay, Elle. I'm okay. It's just a cut. It doesn't need stitches. We're going to swim back to shore, throw a Band-Aid on it, and everything will be fine. Okay?"

She nodded, holding his gaze and trying to keep her lip from trembling. "Oh-oh-kay." *Pull it together, girl.* He was the one bleeding, and she was the one losing it.

Mandy swam over and put a hand on her other shoulder. "I'm sorry, Elle. I didn't mean to scare you. I just wanted to show you and Dad how I could jump off the ledge into the water."

Elle ran a shaky hand over the girl's hair and cupped her cheek. "It's okay. I'm sorry. I didn't mean to freak out. Wait," she said, remembering their early vow. "We're not saying we're sorry to each other." She glanced from Brody to Mandy, an impish grin teasing her lips. "I meant to say *my bad.*"

The three of them looked at each other, then broke into laughter. Elle's panic eased as they grinned at each other and their own private joke.

"You okay to swim back?" Brody asked as their laughter died. "We can get out here and walk around the lake if you'd rather."

She shook her head. "No, I'm good now. I can swim."

He smiled reassuringly. "Good. Let's go back and chow down on those bologna sandwiches." He turned his gaze to Mandy and narrowed his eyes. "And don't worry. I haven't forgotten about you. We'll still be having a talk about you trying to go up to that ledge by yourself."

Mandy lowered her eyes and ducked her chin to the water. "I know, Dad." She offered him a shrug and a sheepish grin. "My bad?"

He narrowed his eyes further.

"Too soon?" she said in a tiny hopeful voice.

He tried to hold the glare but couldn't do it and grinned back. "You goofball. Let's go eat."

They swam back across the lake to their picnic spot. Elle was surprised how shaky her legs were as she stepped out of the water and was glad to sink down onto the blanket.

Brody handed her a towel, then pressed a couple of napkins to the cut on his leg. "It's fine. Barely a scratch."

Mandy had wrapped a towel around herself and crammed her feet into a pair of pink flip-flops. The soles flapped against her heels as she headed to the truck then brought back a small blue plastic box. She passed it to Elle. "See? We do have a first aid kit."

Elle popped open the box and stared dismally into the contents. "This isn't a first aid kit. All that's in here is some Band-Aids and a tube of Neosporin."

Brody shrugged. "There's a couple of packets of ibuprofen in there too." He chuckled at her obvious look of dismay. "That's farm first aid. You get hurt, you slap a Band-Aid on it. That kit combined with some duct tape and a little baling wire, and you can fix just about anything."

Elle shook her head, resolving to buy a full emergency kit and sneak it into his truck later. For now, she'd use what she had. She held out her hand. "Just show me your leg."

He raised an eyebrow. "I can do it."

She wiggled her fingers. "Your leg."

He chuckled again as he swung his leg toward her and rested it on the blanket in front of her knees.

She peeled off the soggy napkins, now soaked with lake water and tinged pink with Brody's blood. She peered at the cut. "You're right. It's not too bad. More of a scratch than a cut." She took the Neosporin from the case and squeezed a thin line of the ointment along the cut, then covered it with a Band-Aid, trying to ignore the intimacy of the gesture, the brush of her fingers over his shin. She patted his leg next to the Band-Aid, resisting the urge to skim her hand along his skin. "I think you'll live."

He grinned. "Thanks, Doc."

She nudged his leg good-naturedly. "At least tell me you have some antibacterial gel in that tote bag to clean our hands before we eat."

———————

"Four to six *weeks*?" Elle stared at the insurance adjuster later that night. They'd been through the rest of the house already and were just finishing up in the kitchen. The acrid scent of smoke still hung in the air.

The adjuster, a guy by the name of Stan Weber, told her he was a Creedence local, and that he'd lived in the town since he was a boy. He was in his midfifties now with a balding head and a rounded belly that revealed a fondness for jelly donuts—that and the dusting of powdered sugar still evident on the front of his shirt. He wore black slacks, a blue polo shirt with the insurance company's logo embroidered on the breast pocket, and scuffed hiking boots, though his soft body didn't show signs that he'd done much actual hiking. He also had a bad habit of clicking and unclicking his pen between scribbling notes on a red clipboard stuffed with papers. He seemed nice enough, but he wasn't giving her much in the way of good news.

Click. Click. She blinked twice, almost in time with the clicks, as if hoping he might be a mirage. As if this whole mess of a kitchen fire would just disappear. "It's going to take a *month* to repair this damage?"

"Ayup. At *least* four to six weeks. Could be more," Stan answered absently as he made another note on his clipboard.

"But it's only one room." Elle sagged against the counter, then pulled away as she remembered it was covered with soot—just like everything else in the house, apparently. *Oh well. I'm going to have to wash these shorts anyway*, she thought, and leaned back against the counter again.

Her afternoon had gone so great, she'd almost forgotten about her troubles with the fire. She, Brody, and Mandy had spent hours eating, swimming, and lying in the sun at the lake. She'd even snuck in a short nap while Mandy and Brody read their books.

Next time, she'd have to remember to bring a book. Not that there would be a next time. Today might've been a one-off. But if it was, it was a great one. They'd talked and laughed and teased each other. She'd had fun. And being with Brody and his daughter had felt so easy.

Brody had a late-afternoon meeting scheduled with his ranch foreman and had cattle to feed, so after the lake, they'd dropped her at the farm, where she had taken a shower, then driven into town to meet the insurance guy. Nothing had been easy since then.

"I know it doesn't seem like much, and I'm awful sorry to be the one to have to tell you, but even small fires can amount to big damage. It's not just the destruction caused by the fire, but also the act of putting the fire out—the water from the hoses, the smoke damage, and that dang soot gets into everything. You'll need to call a restoration crew. They'll come in and clean all this up, get rid of the ruined stuff, and then they'll have to repaint all the walls. And you're definitely going to need new carpet. In here, you're gonna need new cabinets, countertops, and appliances. Basically a whole new kitchen. You've got good coverage, so we'll take care of most of this, but you need to plan to be out of the house for a good month at least."

Bryn was a gracious host and had assured Elle she could stay at the farm as long as she needed, but a *month*? Six weeks? That was pushing it for any friendship. She'd make some calls tomorrow to see about finding a hotel or a short-term rental. Unfortunately, in a town as small as Creedence, her choices were limited. The

Lamplighter Motel was the only option in town, and she imagined the list of VRBOs would be slim as well.

Her shoulders, and her spirits, sagged as she listened to Stan detail the staggering amount of damage from the one small fire. The fact that she'd done this to herself just made it worse. She raked her fingers through her hair. The soot in the air was burning her eyes; panic and anxiety pressed in.

She needed to get out of here.

She took a step back, and her shoulders collided with a broad masculine chest. She knew it was Brody even before she turned around. She recognized the sound of his boots and the scent of his aftershave and the feel of his arms as they wrapped around her.

"Hey." His deep voice rumbled in her ear. "I thought maybe you could use a friend."

Closing her eyes, she leaned back into him, just for a moment, allowing herself to draw strength from his solid embrace. She *could* use a friend right now, but how did he know? How did this man keep showing up exactly when she needed him?

She opened her eyes and turned around, still in the circle of his arms as she laid a hand on his right pec. "You thought right. This is disheartening, to say the least."

"I know. But I've seen a lot worse."

"True." She took a step back, breaking their contact, and peered around his shoulder. "Did you bring Mandy with you?"

"Nah. I dropped her off at Bryn's, then thought I'd come over to see if you needed any help or if the adjuster had any questions about the fire that I could answer." He held out his hand to the insurance guy. "How you doin', Stan?"

"Not bad. Good to see you, Doc. Although not in the best of circumstances."

"No. This kind of thing never is."

"Say, I took your advice and sprinkled some pepper in my cat's litter box, and my dog hasn't eaten her poop since."

Elle covered her mouth with her hand to keep from laughing.

Brody offered her a shrug as if saying *What are you gonna do?* then nodded at Stan. "Glad to hear it." He gestured to the stove. "Anything I can answer about the fire? I was here the night it happened. I mean, not here *when* it caught fire, but I showed up right after to check on Elle."

"Ayup. It was a dandy, all right. But it seems pretty cut and dried. I'm just finishing up. I've already taken pictures and jotted down the notes I need. I'll write up a report and get in touch with you soon, Ms. Brooks. In the meantime, there's some good information in here on what steps to take now." He handed Elle a folder of paperwork.

Elle stared down at the folder in dismay.

"I'll walk you out, then," Brody said. He put a hand on her shoulder. "I'll be right back, and help you get anything else you might need out of the house."

Stan followed Brody to the door, and Elle half heard the continued conversation of the insurance adjuster's issues with his cat-poop-eating canine. She set the folder on the counter and peered around the kitchen, shaking her head at the destruction.

She heard Brody come back in but didn't turn around as she felt him slip her hand into his and entwine their fingers.

"Did you know the three wise men were actually firemen?"

She turned her head and cocked an eyebrow at him.

He lowered his voice to an exaggerated drawl. "Right in the Bible, it says they came from *a fire*." He elbowed her rib. "Get it? Afar? A fire?"

The corners of her lips tugged up in a grin. "Yes, I get it. That was a terrible joke."

"But it made you smile."

"Um, it *almost* made me smile. There's a difference."

"How about this one? What award do you give a firefighter?"

She shrugged.

"Most extinguished."

She groaned. "Your material is getting worse. But thanks." She nudged his shoulder with hers. "I mean it. Thank you for coming over. How do you always seem to know exactly when I need you?"

He shrugged, then offered her a wink. "It's what I do. I'm a doctor *and* a dad—I drink juice boxes and I know things."

She groaned again.

"And I'm good at fixing stuff."

"Like offering helpful advice for dogs with questionable appetites?"

He chuckled. "Exactly. And that's just one of my many talents." His lips curved into that flirty grin that made Elle's stomach do funny flips. But maybe that was just his grin. And *she* was the one whose mind was going to the dark places of imagining his *other* talents.

This was all new territory to her. Not that she hadn't been flirted with before. But it had been a long time since she'd felt like someone was actually interested in her. And an even longer time since she'd felt that interest in return.

It somehow felt both exciting and as dangerous as the fire in her kitchen. She didn't know how to act, how to respond, or what to say. But she did know that he was still holding her hand, and for right now, that was okay. She searched her brain for something, anything, even semi-witty to say. "Wow," she finally choked out. "A veterinarian, a cowboy, *and* a comedian. You *are* talented." Ugh. That would have to do. Put the focus back on his daytime occupations instead of imagining what his nighttime talents might be.

He chuckled and pulled her hand. "Come on, let's grab the rest of your stuff and get out of here. There's a lasagna with your name on it waiting for you at the farm."

"Good idea." Her phone buzzed, and she pulled it from her pocket, then let out a groan. "It's my mom. I've got to take it. I left her a message that I had a fire in my house."

"Sure. Go ahead. I'm sure she's worried about you." He leaned his hip casually against the side of the counter, oblivious to the soot dusting his jeans.

"I'm sure you don't know my mom."

She tapped the screen and put the phone to her ear. "Hi, Mom."

"Oh, honey, I got your message, and I've been so worried. Is your house okay?"

Wow. Her mother was so worried it only took her an entire day to call her back. And even then, her first question was about the condition of the house. "Gee, thanks for your concern, Mom. No really, I'm fine, didn't get hurt at all. By the way, you should check your mail—I'm sure your Mother of the Year Award will be arriving anytime now."

"Don't be ugly," her mother scolded. "I just think that house is so beautiful, and I would hate to see it ruined by a fire."

"Then you'll be glad to know it wasn't ruined. But it did have considerable damage, so I'm staying with a friend while they clean it up and replace the appliances and the flooring."

"Oh, well, then it sounds like you'll at least get new carpet out of the deal."

"Yeah, it was practically a blessing." It was hard for her to keep the sarcasm out of her voice.

"Make sure you fill out all the forms. And you can pad those lists of damaged items. They'll never know if you add in an extra television or some more clothes. You could end up with a whole new wardrobe. Oh, I just bought a gorgeous pair of Jimmy Choos. I could give you the receipt to use."

"Yep, that's just what I'd been thinking, Mom. Six weeks of inconvenience, expense, and ruined items, but hey, at least I can score some new outfits. And if I use your receipt, maybe an insurance fraud allegation too."

"You know, snide comments are really unattractive, dear. I was only trying to help." Her voice took on a pouty tone. "All I've ever done was try to be a good mother to you. And all I seem to get in return is sass."

"Sorry, Mom." How did their conversations always wind up with *her* apologizing?

Her mother let out a long-suffering sigh. "Don't worry about me. I'll be fine."

Wait—wasn't Elle the one whose house had caught on fire? She rolled her eyes and tried to hold back her own sigh. "I'm fine too."

"All right then. I'd better go. I've got a spa appointment in twenty. Talk to you soon."

"Bye, Mom," Elle said, but her mother had already hung up. She shoved her phone back in her pocket, then shrugged as she met Brody's eye. "She's not really what you'd call a giver."

"No, I guess not." He nodded to her phone. "I wasn't trying to listen. She was just talking kind of loud."

"She's always been like this. Even after the accident. She was more concerned about the life insurance than my husband's actual life. Which probably accounts for why she's now on her fourth marriage."

"Fourth?"

"Yep, and her main consideration when looking for a husband is the size of his...you know."

Brody raised an amused eyebrow.

She nudged his arm. "The size of his bank account, of course. What were you thinking?"

He offered her a look of wide-eyed innocence. "What? That was exactly what I was thinking." He laughed, and the sound of his laughter swirled through her as if something was blooming inside her. "What about your dad?" he asked, and the bloom withered and died on the vine.

"Which one? There have been several who have tried to fill the role. My real dad has never been in the picture, but I got close to one of my stepdads. He was the one who was around the most when I was growing up, and he actually made an effort to be a father to me. He's the closest thing I have to a dad, but even so, we haven't done very well at keeping in touch. When I left home for college, I never went back. Then I met Ryan, and he and I became the family I never had. He was everything. Then in the space of four and a half minutes, he was gone."

Brody nodded, his expression somber. "I get it. Although with my wife, we had months filled with false hope and trying to prepare for her death. Not that it mattered. It was still the hardest thing I've ever had to do. But at least we had a chance to say goodbye."

Elle swallowed, the memories crushing in around her. "The night of the accident, we were going out to dinner with some people from Ryan's work, and I didn't want to go. I'd been grumpy and pissy all night, and the last thing I said to him before the accident was 'I don't think that tie goes with your shirt.' What a stupid thing to say."

"That's rough."

"I guess that wasn't the *very* last thing I said to him. I had a few minutes before he died when I told him I loved him and begged him to hold on."

He picked up her hand and held it gently in his.

They stood in silence for a moment, a comfortable moment of not having to say anything more.

Finally he gave a light press to her hand and offered her an encouraging nod. "You ready to go get that lasagna?"

She nodded back and offered him a brave smile. "I'm always ready for lasagna."

Elle and Brody walked into the farmhouse twenty minutes later to hearty laughter and the heavenly scent of tomato sauce and garlic.

Bryn wiped her hands on a towel as she stepped out of the kitchen and pulled Elle into a hug. "Are you really okay?" she whispered into her ear.

Elle nodded as she hugged her friend back. "I really am. But I'm not sure you will be. It looks like I'm going to have to be out of my house a lot longer than I thought."

"Don't worry about that," Bryn assured her. "You'll just stay here. No arguments."

"Hope you're hungry," Zane called from the kitchen where he was slicing a loaf of garlic bread.

Aunt Sassy was scooping up the slices and putting them in a bread basket. She wore a lime-green apron covered in hot-pink strawberries over her outfit of turquoise Bermuda walking shorts and a blue-and-pink floral T-shirt. When Sassy turned, Elle could see the front of the apron read *Sassy, Classy, and a little Smart-assy*. The older woman grinned as she wiped her hands on a paper towel and came across the room to give Elle a hug. "It's all gonna be okay."

Elle hadn't had this many hugs in a year, and frankly, she wasn't supercomfortable with all the attention being focused on her and her problems. "I'm fine, really."

"Speaking of fine." Sassy tilted her head toward Brody and gave Elle's middle a nudge. "I notice the cute cowboy has been hanging out with you quite a bit today. Is this the start of another kind of fire?"

Warmth flooded Elle's cheeks. She had never met an older lady with Sassy's spunk. Elle lowered her voice and tried not to smile. "Has anyone ever told you that you have a dirty mind?"

Sassy shrugged and waved away her admonishment with an exaggerated wink. "You say dirty, I say flirty."

Brody looked up at her then, as if he knew she was thinking about him, and flashed her a grin. The butterflies took off in her stomach, swooping and swirling.

Mandy kissed the heads of the two puppies she'd been cuddling, then put them down and ran toward her. Jeez, did that girl ever just walk anywhere? Elle wished she could embrace life with the zeal of the spirited ten-year-old. Mandy grabbed her hand and pulled her toward the table. "You're sitting next to me, Elle."

The group converged on the table, the sound of chairs scraping the floor and silverware clattering as napkins were drawn out and placed in laps.

As soon as grace was finished, everyone held out their plates to Zane who slid heaping mounds of lasagna onto each one. Then they passed around a green salad, freshly grated parmesan, and a bowl of green beans from Bryn's garden that had bacon and tiny slivers of onion mixed in.

Elle wiped her mouth with a napkin and tried again to thank her friends. "This is so nice of you all to let me stay."

"Don't thank us too much," Zane said. "It's a bit of a zoo around here. And we won't be your only roommates. That goat of Bryn's is always sneaking into the house. He was standing by the bed staring at me when I woke up the other day—about scared me to death. And last week he snuck into the pantry and ate an entire box of Cheez-Its."

"Bah-ah-ah." As if on cue, Otis bleated from the front door.

Elle turned around and burst out laughing at the sight of the goat and his wingman, Tiny the pig, standing on the porch and staring in through the screen door.

"See?" Zane said, pointing his fork at them. "Your new roomies are a bunch of animals."

Bryn chuckled. "They must have smelled the garlic bread."

Elle peered under the table at the new wet noses on either side of her knees. "They aren't the only ones. Hope and Lucky are standing by my legs hoping I'll drop something," she said, referring to the tripod dog and Zane's border collie.

"Seriously, Elle, if you can handle this wacky bunch of beasts, you'd actually be doing us a favor if you stayed," Bryn told her.

"A favor? How do you figure that?"

Bryn glanced to Zane, then back to Elle. She gnawed at her bottom lip. "We were going to tell you. We've got sort of a crisis on our hands."

CHAPTER 8

UH-OH. THIS DIDN'T SOUND GOOD.

"Oh, are you preggers?" Sassy asked with glee. "Got a bun in the oven? Good job, Zane."

"Aunt Sassy!" Bryn admonished.

Zane just rolled his eyes.

The older woman shrugged. "Sorry, would you rather I say *eating for two*?"

"No, I'm not pregnant. It's nothing like that," Bryn said. "It's not even *our* crisis. It's my cousin Cade's crisis."

"I didn't know you had a cousin," Elle said.

"Yeah, we were pretty close to him and his brother when we were kids. They stayed here with our grandparents for a few weeks each summer. Cade still sees my brother, Buck, quite often. They're both big in the rodeo scene. But Cade's fallen on hard times lately, and he needs some help."

"And we all know how Bryn loves taking in a wounded stray," Zane said, rubbing an affectionate hand across Bryn's shoulder.

"Taking in?" Brody asked.

"Yeah." Bryn nodded. "He's up in Montana. Buck ran into him last week and found out he's getting evicted from his apartment. I think they're tearing the place down. I called him and offered him a place to stay. He wasn't too excited about the idea at first, but I convinced him."

"You know how she gets," Zane said.

Elle, the woman who was currently camped out in her guest room, nodded.

"Anyway," Bryn said, ignoring Zane's comment. "We thought we'd drive up to Montana and spend a couple days in Glacier

National Park, then help Cade pack up and move him down here."
She turned her gaze to Elle. "Which is where you come in."

Elle shook her head in confusion. "I don't get it. It sounds like
you need me to move out so your cousin can stay here."

"No, not at all," Bryn assured her. "We've got plenty of room,
and he's going to refurbish the old bunkhouse out east of the barn.
Gramps's ranch hand used to live out there, but now it's just full of
junk. Cade's agreed to fix it up and help out around the ranch until
he finds a job."

"What we need from you is to help out with the animals while
we're gone," Zane said. "We were hoping we could talk you into
feeding all of them and keeping an eye on the puppies while we're
away."

"Of course I can."

"We'll take Lucky and Hope with us, but that still leaves Grace
and the puppies, plus all the horses, the pig, the goat, and a slew
of barn cats."

"And don't forget Spartacus, the tortoise," Mandy piped up.

Bryn chuckled. "And Spartacus. Who, by the way, now, thanks to
Zane, has a new enclosure in the barn and isn't just wandering around
the front yard." She peered at Elle. "I know it's a lot to take on."

Elle shook her head. "No, I'd be happy to do it."

"And I can help too," Mandy offered. "I've helped Bryn feed the
animals tons of times. I know just what to do."

Bryn smiled at the girl. "It's true. She does."

"I can help too," Brody said. "I can stop by and help with the
horses after I finish my morning chores and feeding my cattle."

"That would be great," Bryn said.

Brody shrugged. "It's no big deal. You help me take care of my
little animal all the time." He grinned at his daughter.

"Da-ad," Mandy said, narrowing her eyes, then smiled back at
her father.

"It's settled then," Bryn said. "We're leaving day after tomorrow."

"Wait, if you're doing all that stuff, does that mean you won't be back in time for the Hay Day Celebration?" Mandy cried. "You can't miss it. We already entered Shamus in the costume contest. And we've been working on our costumes for weeks."

"Shoot. I forgot about the Hay Day Celebration," Bryn said. "We'll try, but I'm not sure how long it's going to take us once we get to Montana. But if we're not back, you can still show Shamus. You don't need me."

Mandy sagged in her chair. "I guess I could. But it won't be the same."

"Maybe Elle could help."

Elle nodded. "Sure, I'd be glad to."

"Sorry, kiddo," Bryn said. "Make sure you take lots of pictures for me though."

"Okay."

"Good. That's settled then. And I'll be in the audience cheering for you," Sassy said, slapping her hands on her thighs. "Now, who's ready for dessert?"

Elle couldn't turn down a slice of chocolate cake, especially since Zane was already pulling a tub of vanilla ice cream out of the freezer to go on top of it.

Minutes later, Mandy set a plate in front of her. Dark chocolate ganache frosting gleamed on the cake as the ice cream melted along its side. Elle groaned as she took a bite. "This is delicious," she told Sassy.

"Thank you. It's my signature recipe. It's got three kinds of chocolate in it. I call it the Dang Devil Cake, because that's who I blame when I've stuffed myself on it." She laughed as she raised her hands in surrender. "Don't blame me for eating three pieces, the dang devil made me do it."

Elle understood. She was contemplating licking the remaining frosting off her plate when an ancient pickup rumbled down Bryn's driveway.

"That's Doc Hunter's truck," Bryn said. "Wonder what he's up to." The former pediatrician was an old friend of her grandparents and a frequent customer at the diner. He was one of Bryn's favorites, and he had an equally soft spot for the waitress. The two of them made their way through the daily crossword puzzle most mornings while Doc had breakfast and coffee and greeted the majority of the diner patrons by name.

The elderly widower strode up the porch steps with surprising agility for a man pushing eighty and one who frequently complained about his bad hip to anyone who would listen. He knocked on the screen door, then let himself in at Bryn's wave.

"Come on in, Doc. You're just in time for dessert," Bryn said.

"Well then, I couldn't have timed it better." His gaze traveled over the room, and Elle was surprised to see the shy smile that curved his lips when his eyes lit on Sassy. He took off his hat and smoothed his silver-white hair, which he still had quite a bit of. "Didn't mean to interrupt, but I just stopped by the grocery store for some milk, and danged if a couple of bags of dog food didn't jump into my cart." His expression turned impish as he gave an exaggerated shrug. "So I figured as long as I was at it, I'd stop by the feed store—and sure enough, a couple of bags of sweet feed for the horses jumped in my truck bed too." He shook his head. "Just can't trust feed bags these days. And seeing as I have neither a dog nor a horse, I figured I might as well bring those pesky bags out here to you."

Bryn laughed. "You'd better bring your pesky self over here and see how fast a piece of Sassy's chocolate cake falls onto a plate in front of you."

"I'd be much obliged if a little scoop of that ice cream fell on my plate as well," he said with a wink as he crossed to the table.

"Here, take my seat, Doc," Brody said as he stood up and gestured toward his chair. "I'll go out and see if I can't convince that horse feed to toss itself into the barn."

Doc Hunter clapped him on the shoulder. "You're a good man, Brody Tate."

"I'll come help you," Elle said, pushing away from the table. "I need to stretch my legs and walk off some of this cake."

He raised his arm to allow her to lead the way. "We'll be back in a few."

They put the feed bags away, then he showed her where the different feed and grain was stored and went over how much to give the horses, goats, and pig each day.

"I've been helping Bryn feed all these animals for weeks now, but suddenly I feel like I should be writing this all down."

He chuckled. "You don't have to get exact measurements. Usually if you just dump in a scoop or two, you're good. And don't worry about the horses. I'll stop over and help with them. I mean, if you want me to."

"I'd like that." They were in the main area of the barn. At the front of the building, a tack room was on one side and a long workbench on the other. An alleyway ran down the center, with stalls on either side. The back end of the barn was open to a large corral, where Bryn's four rescued horses roamed. They must have known Brody would have treats for them, because they all made their way to the barn to check him out.

Elle leaned against the counter of the workbench and checked him out as well as she watched him greet the horses by name.

"Hey, Beauty. How you doing, girl?" he asked the brown quarter horse as she nudged her head into his shoulder while Shamus tried to sneak his nose through the bars of the fence and into the cowboy's pocket. Beauty had been Bryn's first rescue, and Elle never tired of hearing how Bryn had bought her with the hundred-dollar tip Zane had left for his breakfast.

Not wanting to miss out on a treat, Prince trotted up to Brody, who patted his neck and gave his ears a scratch. The gray was so light, he was practically white. He'd been their second rescue—abandoned, half-starved, and trapped in a section of barbed wire when they'd found him at the same derelict farmhouse where Elle had rescued Grace and her puppies. Shamus had been anonymously and unceremoniously dumped on Bryn's doorstep. Now, thanks to Brody's veterinary care and Zane's horse-whispering skills, all three horses, plus Beauty's colt, Mack, were healthy and thriving.

Shamus and the colt vied for Brody's attention as he passed out sugar cubes and more pets.

"You are really good with animals, you know," Elle told him as she watched him chat with the horses and pat their necks. "You should consider becoming a vet."

He cocked an eyebrow as he sauntered back to where she stood. "Now who's the comedian?"

She chuckled softly. "Certainly not me. I couldn't sell a joke to a man on fire, or is it sell a glass of ice to a burning man? See? I always flub the punch line. But seriously, you *are* good with animals. *And* with kids. *And* with sassy old ladies." She grinned as she tilted her head. "What *aren't* you good at, Dr. Tate?"

"Apparently staying away from you." He was facing her, only a half a step away, and his arm brushed her hip as he reached for something on the counter behind her.

She placed a hand on his forearm, holding it in place and keeping him close to her. Not close enough that they were touching anywhere other than her hand on his arm and his arm against her hip, but the tension between their bodies fairly crackled in the air.

She stared at his arm, noting the fine dusting of hair over the corded muscles. "Do you *want* to stay away from me?" she asked, her voice soft and husky.

He raised his free hand to her face and gently guided her chin, tilting her face up so she looked into his eyes.

Her mouth went dry at the hunger she saw reflected there, and she couldn't speak. He brushed a strand of hair from her cheek, his fingertips skimming lightly over her skin. Heat shot up her spine.

Brody huffed, the sound a cross between a laugh and a sigh. "I don't think I could stay away from you if I tried." He shook his head. "And I *have* been trying. I told myself *not* to go to your house tonight. I ordered my hand *not* to hold yours. But apparently I can't control myself when it comes to you, Elle Brooks."

His eyes conveyed pain mixed with passion, like he wanted her but that want was somehow hurting him. She understood the complexity of that feeling. Her body was awake, alive, like it hadn't been in years, but her mind was screaming at her to protect her fragile heart and to shut down where this was headed. But her hand rose to his cheek as if it too had a mind of its own.

Her fingers softly grazed his cheek, then he closed his eyes as she skimmed her fingertips over his bottom lip. Her nerve endings tingled with anticipation as she leaned closer to him. "What about your lips?" she whispered. "What have you been commanding them *not* to do?"

A low growl emanated from his throat. He raised his hands, placing one on each side of her face as his gaze shifted to her mouth. His thumb grazed her bottom lip, and a shiver of heat raced along her spine.

His voice was deep, gravelly, as if his throat were full of rocks. "I'm begging them *not* to kiss you." He leaned closer still.

She could smell the woodsy scent of his aftershave, and it was making her crazy. She traced the line of his jaw, skimmed the pads of her fingers over the light scruff of whiskers, as she imagined the feel of their scrape against her delicate skin. She ran her fingernails down the side of his throat and had the impulsive urge to press her lips to the same spot and lick his neck.

"Are your lips listening?" she whispered.

"Not even a little bit." He leaned the rest of the way in, pressing his lips softly to hers. One gentle, sweet kiss, so achingly tender, she wanted to weep. Then another. And another still.

Each press of his lips a little firmer, a little more pressure, a little more insistent. Until his mouth slanted over hers, greedy with want, as he kissed her hungrily. He tasted like chocolate cake, with a hint of vanilla ice cream, and summer and danger. And he felt so enticingly good as she slid her arms around his neck and dragged him closer, taking what he offered and demanding more.

He slid his hand from her face, down her neck, over her shoulders. They skimmed the sides of her breasts, making her nipples pebble with need. Over her waist, then down her hips, where he paused, his fingers tightening their grip over her hip bones.

Then his broad hands slid around to cup her butt before lifting her onto the workbench. Throughout his whole exploration, he never stopped kissing her. Now she wrapped her legs around his waist, pulling him closer, feeling his desire pressing hard into her most tender spot. A spot that hadn't been pressed into in years—that she wasn't even sure still worked. But it was working now.

She melted against him, her bones going soft as her limbs dissolved into a pool of desperate yearning. Her body came alive, as if waking up from a long sleep, stretching and begging for Brody's attention. She gripped his shoulders, arching her back to press closer to him, her breasts tight and aching.

Elle wasn't sure how long they kissed, if she could even call it that. *Kissing* seemed too simple a word to describe their connection but *a melding of their two souls* might be a shade too dramatic.

Whatever they were doing, kissing or melding or just making out like two turned-on teenagers, it could've lasted for two minutes or two hours. All Elle knew was that she didn't want it to end.

When he pulled away, leaving her panting and trembling, she missed his heat against her like cold feet miss warm socks.

"What's wrong?" she asked.

He looked dazed, his expression bewildered, and he shook his head as if to clear it. "Nothing's wrong. It just felt so damn good, I was afraid I was going to drown in you." He pressed his hands flat against the workbench on either side of her hips. "I needed to stop for a second and convince myself I still knew how to breathe."

She pressed her fingers to her kiss-swollen lips. "I can't figure out what you're saying. I mean I know what you're saying. I feel the exact same way—like I was losing myself in the moment. But I can't tell what you think. Is this a good thing or a bad thing?"

He sighed, a sound so desolate it ripped at the already-shredded pieces of her heart. "I don't know. So help me, I do not know." He touched her cheek again, and she leaned into his hand, wanting to close her eyes but afraid to miss the expressions playing over his face—afraid to miss her chance to understand what he was thinking. "All I do know is that I am drawn to you like a moth to a flame. I can't stop thinking about you, and every single one of my Neanderthal caveman instincts wants to throw you over my shoulder and carry you off to my cave, where I can protect you from anything else bad happening."

Her lips curved into a coy smile, and she lowered her voice. "Is that all you want to do to me in your cave? Just protect me?" Geez. Listen to her being all flirty and seductive. Where had this brazen hussy come from?

"No," he growled, sliding his hand from her cheek into her hair, to cradle her head. He dipped in to take another kiss, this one deep and full of heat as he pressed his mouth to hers. A thrill of excitement shot through her, making her feel reckless and wild as she kissed him back, parting her lips and exploring his mouth with her tongue.

His lips slid to the side as he pressed a soft kiss to the corner of her lips, then one on her cheek and another to the line of her jaw. He spoke as he trailed hot kisses along her throat and below her ear. His breath was warm on her neck, his voice deep and husky with need, as it rumbled in her ear. "No, that's not *all* I want to do. I also want to rip off your clothes and take you naked on top of the bearskin rug."

He pulled back, his eyes wide as he raked a hand through his hair. "Holy shit. We have got to stop. I can't believe I just said that." His face flushed with color. "That's not me. I do *not* say stuff like that."

"Maybe you should, because it was crazy hot. And I love that your man cave has a bearskin rug in it. Did you shoot the bear yourself?"

He raised an eyebrow at her.

"Sorry." She laughed as she held up her hands. "I couldn't help it." She rested her hands on his chest. "I hear you though. And it's the same for me. With you. I don't usually go crazy making out with hot men I barely know."

He grinned. "So you think I'm hot?"

She laughed again. "Extremely hot."

"Maybe you should try selling me a glass of ice," he teased.

She swatted at his arm. "I told you I'm terrible at jokes."

He grinned. "You still make me laugh. I like that about you. I can't believe how comfortable I feel around you already."

"Me too. It's like I already know you so well," she said as she reached up to touch his cheek.

"I feel the same way. But this is all happening really fast."

She nodded. "Okay. So let's slow it down."

His grin turned roguish. "I can take it slow." He leaned down again and kissed her gently as he slid his hands around her waist. Then he shook his head as he pulled away again. "See what I mean? I can't keep my hands off you."

"I don't want you to keep your hands off me." She looked up at him, trying to focus but getting distracted by the gorgeous blue of his eyes. She understood what he was saying. This was moving awfully fast, and her mind warred with the sensible notion that they should slow it down and the reckless idea of stripping off their clothes and doing it in the hay. *No, the hay would be too scratchy*, the rational part of her brain asserted while the long-silent adventurous party of her body cried, *but it would feel so damn good.* She ignored both parts as she peered up at Brody. "So, Dr. Tate, what do you suggest we do about this predicament we're in?"

He let out another sigh. "I don't know. Sleep on it, I guess. That's what I usually do when I can't decide what to do."

"That sounds sensible."

He took a step back, breaking the connection between them. "We should probably get back inside."

"Yep," she said, sliding off the workbench and straightening her shirt.

She smoothed her hair as she followed him toward the barn door. But right before they exited, he turned back and swept her into his arms again, turning her so her back was against the wall and they were out of sight of the house. He dipped his head and took her mouth, kissing her fiercely as his hands slid over her butt again and pulled her hard against him.

Then just as quickly as he'd seized her, he let her go and stepped away. "Sorry," he said. "I was just trying to convince myself those kisses hadn't been that big a deal."

Oh, great. He'd been walking back to the house trying to assure himself that the last half hour or so had meant nothing. "Did it work?"

His lips turned up in one of those roguish grins of his—the kind that sent her pulse racing. "Not even a little bit."

Oh boy.

CHAPTER 9

Brody couldn't believe he'd just made out with Elle in the barn. And there was no question, they *had* made out. That wasn't a simple kiss. No, that was *lots* of kisses, and touching, and caressing, and rubbing. Oh man, the rubbing.

Stop. Think about hockey stats, the latest weather report, the current price of beef—anything to stop thinking about the rubbing. He did *not* want to walk into Bryn's house with the evidence of their time in the barn proclaiming itself loud and proud through his jeans.

Thankfully, the group had left the dining room table. Bryn and Zane were at the sink doing the dishes—she still had her hands in the dishwater, but the knowing grin on her face had heat warming his neck. How could she know? He snuck a glance at Elle. Her cheeks were a little pink with color, and her hair was a bit disheveled.

She must have seen Bryn's grin too because Elle reached up to smooth her hair. But there was nothing she could do about her kiss-swollen lips. *Damn, those lips.* He'd been thinking about her mouth all day and tasting it had been worth the wait.

Crud. He was doing it again. *Stop thinking about her lips. Night crawlers, maggots, rotten fish.*

His daughter was in the corner of the kitchen showing the puppies to Aunt Sassy and Doc Hunter. Sassy had the gray-and-white one curled against her, and she was laughing as it licked her chin. Mandy turned their way, but she was more interested in the puppy in her arms than why Elle's hair was tangled. "Geez, you guys were gone forever. Was my dad showing you stuff in the barn this whole time?" Mandy asked Elle.

Elle turned to look up at him, her lips pressed together to keep from laughing. She shook her head, then softly cleared her throat before answering. "Yes, your dad was showing me lots of stuff."

Mandy rolled her eyes. "Yeah, he loves animals. Once he gets to gabbing, there's no stopping him."

There was no stopping him tonight either. But he and Elle weren't gabbing. "Thanks for the supper," he told Bryn, then gestured to Mandy. "Come on, kiddo, say good night to the puppies. We need to get to going."

"Do we have to?"

"Yep, I've got an early appointment, so we've got to get our animals fed and be at the vet clinic by eight tomorrow."

"We?" Elle asked. "Does Mandy go with you to work?"

"Sometimes. Especially in the summer when she's not in school. But she does great. The staff loves her, and she's good at entertaining herself. She helps out too, stocking shelves and feeding the animals."

"Well, I don't want to take away your free child labor, but I'm available tomorrow, and I've been promising to take her to the pool. Would it be all right if I kept her for the day?"

"Yes," Mandy cried, hugging one of the puppies to her and practically jumping up and down. "Can I go, Dad? Please. Please. Please."

His forehead furrowed. Why would Elle offer to spend the day with his daughter? He peered down at Elle. "You don't have to babysit for me."

She drew her head back. "*Babysit?* I'm not offering to babysit. I want to spend the day with my best ten-year-old friend."

Dang. He really liked this woman. And he could see from the expression on his daughter's face that she did too. Somebody was going to get hurt here. But it wouldn't be tonight. Mandy had just had a crappy time at the stupid birthday party the day before. It would be good for her to hang out with someone who *wanted* to spend time with her.

He gave Elle one more chance to back out. "You don't have to do this," he said quietly.

"I know." She placed a hand on his arm and kept her voice as low as his. "But I want to. I really do. This is for Mandy and me. It doesn't have to do with you." She dropped her voice even quieter. "I can see your wheels spinning. Don't read too much into it. It's just a girls' day at the pool."

Maybe that's all it was to Elle. But he knew *his* girl, and this would mean the world to her. He raised his hands in surrender. "Okay, sounds like I'm outnumbered." He grinned at his daughter. "You can go, squirt."

"Yay," Mandy exclaimed as she raced across the room to give her dad a hug. "The pool opens at eleven. Can we spend all day there?"

Elle smiled. "I'll pick you up at eleven at the vet clinic. So bring your pool stuff in the morning and pack a lunch. We can eat at the pool. And I'll bring a book this time."

Mandy's face broke into a grin, and she let go of her father to throw her arms around Elle. "I'm so excited. I can't wait. We're going to have so much fun. I'll bring a book too. And my Uno deck if you want to play cards. And Dad just gave me five dollars for doing some chores, so I'll bring that and buy us some ice cream."

Elle hugged the girl to her. "You don't have to do that. I'm all in for reading and playing Uno, but the ice cream and the pool admission is on me."

"No way," Brody told them. "I'll send some cash and the ice cream is on me."

The two females grinned at each other, and Elle gave a shrug. "Okay. Ice cream is on you."

"I'm so excited," Mandy said. "I'll pack everything tonight so I'm ready."

Elle laughed. "Don't forget your sunscreen."

Brody sighed as he gazed at the happy smile on his daughter's face. Yeah, they were in trouble here. He wasn't the only one falling under Elle's spell.

———————

Later that night, Elle walked into her bedroom and was surprised to see the clothes she'd brought from her house in neatly folded stacks at the end of her bed. She'd put them all in the washing machine earlier, but with everything going on, she'd forgotten about them. Bryn must have put them in the dryer, then folded them while she was in town with the insurance adjuster. How did she get so blessed to have found such a great friend?

She had just finished moving the clothes to the dresser drawers Bryn had cleared out for her when she heard a soft knock on her door and looked up to see that same friend standing there, grinning as she held two sleeping puppies in her arms. "They're asleep," Bryn told her. "But this is when they're extra cuddly. And you look like you could use a little puppy therapy."

"I can always use puppy therapy." She climbed onto the bed and leaned her back against the headboard, then reached for a puppy. "Give me one of those cuties."

Bryn handed her the plump brown-and-white male, then pushed one of the throw pillows against the headboard and sat down on Elle's other side. "Mandy calls this one Peanut Butter because he's so chunky."

"Perfect." Elle giggled as the puppy stirred, then let out a tiny yawn. She pressed a kiss to its adorably, fluffy head. The pups were five or six weeks old now, so they were starting to get a little more playful and were twice as adorable but still fell asleep at the drop of a hat. "These guys are almost old enough to start thinking about finding homes for them. I can take some pictures of them and put a post up on the ranch's Facebook page when you're ready."

"I'm not ready. Not even close. I'm trying not to think about it all," Bryn said with a pout. "But I know I can't keep them all. I've already had some requests for a couple of them. And Mandy has had her eye on one from the first day we got them. Actually, I think it's this one." She nodded to the black-and-white female in her lap.

Elle melted as she gazed down at the sweet pup. "She is a cutie. Do you think Brody will relent and let her have one?"

"I can't tell yet. But I think there isn't much he wouldn't do for that little girl."

"I think you're right."

"Speaking of Brody…" Bryn raised an eyebrow.

The pattern on the pillowcase suddenly seemed superinteresting as Elle peered intently at it and tried to keep her tone casual. "Yes?"

"Would you *like* to speak about Brody?"

Her stupid traitorous lips curved into a sheepish grin. "What about him?"

Bryn shrugged innocently. "It was pretty nice of him to show up at your house tonight, yeah?"

"Yes, it was." It had been just what she'd needed.

"You were sure out in the barn for a long time tonight. Did anything *interesting* happen while you were outside?"

"Interesting like he might have kissed me?"

Bryn's mouth dropped open. "Oh my gosh. He *kissed* you? Like for real?"

Elle nodded. "For so real. And it was amazing."

Bryn slapped the mattress, startling the puppy in her lap. She laughed as she stroked a hand soothingly over its back. "Tell me everything."

Elle filled her in. "I'm not telling you every detail, but I can tell you Brody is an awesome kisser."

"Who knew?" Bryn said, then grinned as she playfully nudged Elle's leg. "Good for you. It sounds pretty great. A fun day at the lake, a make-out session in the barn—that all seems good. So why does your face looks like you just lost your puppy?" She leaned down to the pup in her lap. "No offense."

Elle let out a sigh. "That's about how I feel. Well, not exactly like that. Actually I don't know how I feel. Which is part of the problem. Don't get me wrong, Brody is a great guy."

"Yes, he is."

"And ridiculously hot."

"That too. *And* he's single. So I'm not seeing a problem."

"How can you *not* see a problem? We both have giant king-size baggage that we are dragging around behind us."

Bryn waved her hand dismissively. "Everybody's got baggage. Of all sizes."

"Not like ours. Everything is different when you've lost a spouse. It's not like a divorce. Death is different. Especially when it happens unexpectedly—like one minute your life is wonderful, then in the blink of an eye, everything changes. You can go from wonderfully happy to life-changing grief-stricken in thirty-five seconds. When Ryan and I got married, I thought it was for forever. I'd planned to spend my whole life with him, have a family and grow old together. But that didn't happen. And it's hard to think about setting myself up for that same kind of hurt again."

Bryn nodded. "I can't imagine what you've gone through. But I do know that *you* didn't die in that crash. Which means you get to keep living. And that might mean taking the risk of letting people into your life."

Elle sighed. "I'm not much of a risk-taker anymore. I'm sure it's hard to believe, but I used to be much more fun."

"You're still fun."

"Not like before when I was daring and reckless with my feelings *and* my life. I used to be adventurous and brave. I would try anything, do anything. Ryan and I went skydiving and zip-lining and rode motorcycles and horses. And now I can't get out of the driveway without checking three times that my seat belt is securely fastened. I go through buckets of antibacterial hand sanitizer, and I bought the SUV with the highest safety standards on the market. I don't take chances anymore. I don't take risks and certainly not with my heart. I've created a new life for myself here, one that is managed and controlled. And Brody is just the kind of guy who could wreck my perfectly protected, safe world."

"You say safe. I say lonely."

Elle shrugged, fighting the ache in her throat.

"Since I run a horse rescue, I tend to think in equine metaphors, so I know it feels like life bucked you off, but it seems like it's about time you got out there and got back on the horse." She nudged Elle's elbow and wiggled her eyebrows. "And Brody's a pretty fine horse. You know, save a horse, ride a cowboy."

Elle laughed and shook her head at her friend.

"Seriously though, you and Brody seem to have a connection." She rested a hand on Elle's arm. "You're allowed to enjoy that connection and let yourself have a little fun. Like I said, *you* aren't the one who died in a car crash. It's okay for you to start living again."

Elle swallowed, unable to speak. "Thank you," she finally managed to whisper.

"Anytime. That's what friends are for." She pushed up from the bed. "And now I'd better get these puppies back to their mom and let you get some sleep."

"Good night, Peanut Butter." Elle nuzzled his head, then passed the sleeping puppy to Bryn. "Thank you. For everything. But mostly for being my friend."

Bryn smiled warmly at her. "Back atcha, girl."

"Hey, I'm taking Mandy to the pool tomorrow. You want to come?"

"I wish. But I have to work tomorrow, and I need the hours since we're leaving the day after. Otherwise, I would have loved to."

"Next time." Elle grabbed her pajamas and toiletry kit from the dresser and followed Bryn into the hall. "Oh hey, I told Mandy I'd bring a book. Can I borrow one?"

"Sure. Take whatever you want. Good night."

Elle spent a few minutes in the bathroom, changing into pajamas, washing her face, brushing her teeth, then she plugged in her phone charger before crawling into the guest bed. Her body was exhausted, but an hour later, she still wasn't able to fall asleep. Her mind was still racing, her thoughts on Brody and the kiss they'd shared in the barn. Wait, the *kisses* they'd shared. But it wasn't just the time in the barn—it was the time she'd spent with him all day and most of the night before. It was the soft caresses and the hugs, but it was also the support he offered and the solid feel of his hand holding hers.

She picked up her phone, contemplating if she should text him, just to say thank you for everything he'd done for her the last couple of days. She tapped the screen of her phone and stared at his contact information, debating.

What would she say? *Hey, thanks for everything.* Or maybe just *thanks for being there today.* And she could offhandedly toss in, *it was nice making out with you tonight. Want to do it again sometime?* Yeah, sure, that sounded great. Not awkward at all.

As she contemplated what to say, the phone suddenly buzzed in her hand, startling her so much she dropped it. But not before she saw Brody's name flash on the screen. She fumbled for the phone as it hit the bedspread, bounced to the floor, and slid under the bed.

Gah. She threw off the covers and scooted off the bed, going down on her knees and poking her head under the bed skirt. Sweeping her arm under the mattress, she stretched her fingers to reach it and came out with the phone. Ignoring the dust bunnies clinging to its sides, she tapped the screen to read the message.

You okay?

Hmm. That felt like a loaded question. She texted back, You mean because of the fire or the kissing? Might as well get right in there.

Yes. 😊

Okay, then. He was going for the cute route. Which made sense, since he was so freaking cute. *Stay focused, Elle.* How did she want to play this? It had been so long since she'd even been in the game. *Just be honest.*

She scooted around to lean her back against the side of the bed. Then yes. I'm OK about both. You?

I didn't have a fire.

Smartass. She added a winky face back.

But it did get awfully hot in the barn.

Oh my. It was getting hot in her room just thinking about it again. Yes, it did.

Okay. Well just wanted you to know I was thinking about it... I mean you.

Her lips curved into a grin. I was thinking about you too. I had a fun day today. Thanks for inviting me along to the lake. And for being there when I met the insurance guy. *And for kissing me senseless in the barn.* Maybe best to leave that part out.

I was glad to do it. It was fun having you with us.

She paused, staring at the screen, not knowing what to say next.

The bubbles came on the screen indicating he was typing, and she held her breath as she waited for his next message.

I especially liked the red bikini.

Heat flamed her cheeks. What should she say back to that? *Thank you?* She went with honesty again. You can't see me, but I'm blushing.

Me too. Good night, Elle.

She grinned. She liked the way he showed her his vulnerability. Good night, Brody.

She tapped Send and pressed the phone to her. Maybe she still had a little daring in her after all.

⸻

The next day, Elle pulled up to the vet clinic a little before eleven. She'd spent the morning with the restoration company, and they'd told her basically the same thing the insurance adjustor had. All in all, it had been an exhausting morning, and she was ready for some relaxing time at the pool.

She checked her hair and her teeth in the mirror. All good. Her pulse raced at the idea of seeing Brody. But it didn't seem that she was going to get a chance, since Mandy was pushing through the doors of the vet clinic, her arms laden with a lunch bag and a giant tote. Elle jumped out of the SUV and helped the girl load the bags into the back.

"I've been watching for your car and came out as soon as I saw you pull in," Mandy told her as she ran to the passenger side and crawled into the seat.

Oh. Elle looked from the girl to the front door of the clinic.

"Shouldn't we go in and tell your dad we're leaving?" And say hi? *And check to see if there really is some kind of cosmic connection between him and me?*

"Nah. He can't talk right now anyway. He's in surgery. But I told Dorie, she's the receptionist, and Dad knew you were coming at eleven. So we're good."

"Okay, then. Well, buckle up and let's go swimming."

Mandy pumped her fist in the air. "Yes."

The swimming pool was on the edge of town next to the county fairgrounds. There were two pools, one shallow one for little kids with squirty fountains and a larger, L-shaped pool complete with two lap lanes and a diving board in the deep end. A multitiered grassy area rose up a hill on the far side of the pool scattered with lounge chairs and shade umbrellas in heavy stands.

Elle and Mandy found a spot on the first level and claimed two adjacent lounge chairs with a small plastic table between them. They spread out their towels, and Mandy's tote bag seemed to explode with pool paraphernalia as she unpacked the lunches, pool toys, sunscreen, and books. After Elle managed to cover Mandy completely in a thick coat of 50+ sunscreen, they took a quick dip in the water to get wet, then settled in with their books to read as they ate lunch.

The sun was warm on their skin, and the pool wasn't over-crowded. It seemed like a perfect day. Mandy was laughing and giving Elle a rundown of all the reasons she thought her Dad should let her have a puppy as they walked to the snack bar to get ice cream sandwiches.

The girl's hands flew animatedly through the air as if trying to keep up with the enthusiastic rate of her words. "I told him I'm old enough to take care of a dog now. I'd feed it and make sure it always had water and—" She stopped midsentence as her eye caught something behind Elle. Her forehead furrowed, a frown now replacing the happy expression that had been on her face.

Elle turned to see three girls walking into the pool area. They looked to be about Mandy's age, although the dark-haired one in the center wore a purple bikini that was far too old for her. She certainly had the confidence for it though, as she held court with the other two girls, who seemed to hang on her every word. She was thin and tan and walked with the posture of a ballerina, her back straight as the long hair in her high ponytail swung back and forth with her every step. She turned her head and caught sight of Mandy, and her eyes narrowed into a glare.

What the heck was that about? A shiver ran down Elle's back as she turned back to Mandy, whose whole body now seemed to droop, as if the mere effort of standing up was too much to bear. "Do you know those girls?" Elle asked her, even though it was obvious she did.

Mandy shrugged. "Yeah, they're from my school. They were in my class last year. That one with the ponytail is Jasmine, and the one with the shorter hair is Kara. The one in the blue suit is Molly. We used to be friends."

"*Used* to be?"

Mandy shrugged again, although this time it was a barely perceptible lift of her shoulders. "Yeah, that was before Jasmine moved here and started at our school." The girl stared at the ground, no longer meeting Elle's eye, and her small chest seemed to cave inward as her shoulders hunched forward. "I need to go to the bathroom." She hurried into the women's restroom, leaving Elle alone at the snack bar.

The sound of high-pitched giggling had Elle turning to see the three girls laughing as they followed Mandy into the restroom. Well, maybe not followed. Maybe they also had to go.

Elle shifted from one foot to the other. Should she go in after them? Every one of her mothering instincts was on high alert— something was going on. But she wasn't a mother. And she sure wasn't Mandy's mother. She brought her thumb to her mouth and chewed at the cuticle on the side of her nail.

Screw it. She wasn't Mandy's mom, but she *was* her friend. She hurried into the bathroom, then drew back as she heard the jeering tone of a young girl's voice.

"Nice swimsuit, Mandy," the girl was saying. "Where'd you get it? Babies R Us?"

A row of lockers separated the bathroom stalls from the shower area, and Elle charged around the lockers to see Mandy cowering in the corner of one of the shower stalls.

She was seated on her bottom, her back to the wall with her knees pulled up protectively in front of her. Her arms were wrapped tightly around her legs, and she had her face buried behind her knees as the three girls stood in the door of the shower, the pony-tailed girl leaning over her as she spewed her hurtful taunts.

CHAPTER 10

"What's going on here?" Elle asked, her voice laced with the steel and ferocity of a mother grizzly.

One of the two girls jumped back, one staring at her feet as the other darted a quick glance at Jasmine, who proceeded to smile at Elle with all the gall and fake sweetness of a stuck-up socialite. "We were just coming over here to see if Mandy was okay. She looked upset." The girl held out a hand to Mandy. "I was just trying to help her up."

Mandy peered up at Elle, her eyes pleading from under her fringe of still-damp bangs as she shook her head in small tight jerks.

"I've got it from here," Elle said, keeping her voice calm when she really wanted to rip the girl out of the shower stall by her perky, little ponytail.

Jasmine's eyes narrowed at Elle. "Who are you? Mandy's *baby*sitter?"

Elle's teeth clamped together, and her fingers clenched into tight fists. Who did this little miss thang think she was talking to? "No, I'm her friend. And I said I've got it." She narrowed her eyes at Jasmine. "So you can go now."

The girl didn't even blink as she flipped her ponytail over her shoulder and flounced out of the shower. "Whatever." The two girls skittered after her like mice racing after cheese.

Elle tried to keep her mouth from hanging open at the audacity of the little snob. How did a ten-year-old have so much confidence? *Little brat.* She turned her attention back to Mandy as she tentatively approached the shower and reached out her hand. "You okay?"

Mandy ignored her outstretched hand as she pushed to her feet. "I'm fine. It's not a big deal." She wouldn't look at Elle; instead, she stared at her hands as she twisted her fingers together. "But actually I think I'm done swimming for today."

Oh. "Are you sure?" Elle was going to suggest they go back to the pool and show those dumb girls what a good time they were having, but Mandy looked miserable.

Her head hung so low her chin almost touched her chest, and she pulled at the side hem of her bathing suit. Elle had thought the one-piece suit was cute the day before, with its light-pink fabric covered in watermelon slices and the frilly hem along the top of the bodice. But now she looked at it from the other girl's perspective and could see how the style could be thought to be more suited for a younger girl, especially since the one-piece had to stretch to fit Mandy's taller torso.

"Can we just go now?" Mandy asked. "I have a tummy ache."

Elle had a heartache. "Sure. Let's grab our stuff, and we can get out of here."

"Can you go grab it?" Mandy looked up, her eyes pleading. "Please?"

"Yes, of course. It will just take me a minute." Elle handed her the small drawstring bag she held that contained her car keys, lip balm, ID, and a little cash. She'd brought it with her to buy the ice cream. "Why don't you take this? It's got my keys in it, and you can just wait for me in the car."

"Thanks," Mandy mumbled as she took the keys and practically ran out of the bathroom.

Elle casually walked back to their chairs, not wanting to give the ten-year-old girls the satisfaction of thinking they had anything to do with Mandy leaving the pool. Not that she gave a crap about what a bratty fifth-grader thought of her, but she cared what they thought of Mandy. Once at their chairs, she pulled on her shorts and tank top and quickly gathered their things, stuffing everything into Mandy's oversized tote, then grabbed their towels and just as casually left the pool.

Once she got outside, she hurried to the car and threw their stuff in the back before sliding into the driver's seat next to Mandy. She passed the girl her clothes and one of the towels. "You feeling any better? How's your stomach?"

Mandy sniffed and swiped at her tear-stained cheeks with the towel as she offered Elle a slight shrug. "I'm okay."

"Let's get out of here." She fastened her seat belt, checked to make sure the girl was buckled in, then started the car and pulled out onto the road.

Mandy stared out the window as they headed back toward the clinic. They still had a couple of hours before Brody expected them back, and Elle had an idea as they approached the shopping center on the edge of town. Creedence was a small town, but it still boasted a McDonald's, a Dairy Queen, and a new Walmart Supercenter. She pulled into the parking lot of the Walmart and turned to Mandy. "I have to do a little shopping. Would you mind coming with me?"

Mandy shrugged but perked up a little. "I guess that would be okay."

"So many of my clothes smell like smoke from the fire," Elle told Mandy as they walked into the store. "I was just going to grab a couple basics, some shirts and a few pairs of shorts that I can wear the next few weeks on the farm."

"That sounds smart," Mandy said, cheering up a little as she wandered through the racks of clothes. "I can help you look." An impish grin curved her lips as she held up a T-shirt with a sequined llama and the words "No Drama, More Llama" on the front. "How about this one?"

"That is awful," Elle said, then cracked up. "But I'll get one if you get one. My treat."

"Okay," Mandy said, giggling as she dug through the shirts, then held one up in victory. "I found a small."

"Awesome. Throw them in the cart. What else should we get?"

Elle would buy anything in the store if it made the sweet girl giggle like that again. Anything to make her laugh and forget about the torment of the mean girls in her class.

Mandy shrugged. "I don't know."

"I mean it. Let's do a shopping spree. What do you need? Shorts? Shirts? Pajamas? Whatever you want. It's on me."

"Pajamas are fun. Let's check those out."

They found some fun sleeper sets of brightly colored pajama tops with matching shorts and bought three sets, pink for Elle, purple for Mandy, and a blue set for Bryn. They picked out several shirts and a couple of pairs of shorts for each of them.

Elle picked out a couple of simple bras and threw in a packet of Hanes panties, then turned to see Mandy staring wistfully at a rack of multicolored training bras. "I just grabbed two new bras," she told the girl. "Would you like to get a couple too?"

Mandy shrugged, the normally chatty girl suddenly quiet and bashfully looking at the floor.

Elle picked a couple of the choices off the rack. They came in fun colors and looked like little sports bras, much better than the drab white one she'd had for her first bra. "These are cute. Do you have any bras yet?"

Mandy shook her head. "No, but most all the girls in my class are wearing ones like these."

"Did you talk to your dad about getting some?"

Mandy shrugged again, saying more with her raised shoulders and pained expression than she was with her words. "I tried. But he doesn't really like to talk about this stuff. He still thinks I'm a little girl. So does my grandma."

"Well, I can see that you're not," Elle told her. "And if you'd like to pick out two or three of these, I'd be happy to buy them for you. And I can talk to your dad too, if you want."

Another shrug, but this one was accompanied by the ghost of a smile. "Okay."

They looked through the choices and determined the best size for her, then Mandy picked three and carefully laid them in the cart.

"I think while we're at it, we should each get a new swimsuit too." Elle pointed to the racks of swimwear. If she was hoping to take Mandy back to the pool, she really needed something a bit more suited to a public pool, not an island beach. "I was thinking about getting a tankini."

"Tankinis are cool."

Elle dug through the rack, then pulled one out in Mandy's size that had a pair of high-waisted black bottoms and a bright-blue top with black geometric designs on it. The top was still modest and would cover her belly, but the design wasn't as childish as the watermelon slices of Mandy's current suit. "What do you think about this? Do you like it?"

Mandy nodded. "It's great."

"Would you like me to get it for you?"

Mandy looked at the cart, then back at the swimsuit, her gaze wistful. "You're already getting me a lot of stuff. Maybe I could put the shorts back and just get the swimsuit."

"No way. We're getting it all. I want to do this. So come on, tell me, do you want this one? Or do you see one you like better?"

She shook her head. "I like that one a lot."

"Then it's settled. We're getting it. Now help me pick one too."

Mandy's smile was worth the price of a thousand tankinis. They combed through the racks and found a tankini in Elle's size that was also blue with black side panels and racer-back straps. The bottoms were black and offered much better coverage than her current bikini bottoms.

Elle tossed it into the cart. "Great. Now that we've got that covered, let's go buy some groceries. I want to stock Bryn's cupboards and find something I can make for supper for everyone tonight. Including you and your dad, if you would like to come. I was thinking I could make a pan of macaroni and cheese and do some baked chicken breasts."

Mandy held up her hand as if she had a question. "Stop. You had me at macaroni and cheese. I don't know about my dad, but I'll come. Although my dad loves mac and cheese too. It's one of our favorites."

Elle chuckled. "Good. Now let's go fill up the rest of this cart."

An hour later, Elle pulled out of the parking lot, the back end of her SUV stuffed with bags of groceries and clothes. On the way to the check out, she'd also spied a shelf of ridiculously glittered stainless steel tumblers and had Mandy pick out three in blue, pink, and purple for them and Bryn. It was another impulse purchase, but she was having such fun shopping, and it had been a long time since she'd splurged on frivolously fun girly gifts.

"You sure do drive slow," Mandy remarked as they crept along the highway. "I mean, my grandma is a real careful driver, but even she doesn't go this slowly. Four cars have already passed us. And one of them was a tractor."

"I know. I can't help it," Elle answered, checking her mirrors and trying to loosen the white-knuckled death grip she had on the steering wheel. "I've got precious cargo in the car, and I'm responsible for your safety. I couldn't forgive myself if anything happened to you."

Mandy shrugged. "You're in charge. I'm just saying I don't think I've ever been in a car that's been passed by a tractor before."

Elle rolled her shoulders, trying to force herself to relax. "I'll try to go a little faster. I'm just nervous." She inched the speedometer up to forty-five miles an hour.

"It's okay," Mandy assured her. "It's only a few miles out of town to Bryn's. And I don't mind going slow. It gives me a chance to look out the window."

Elle offered her a grateful smile and eased her speed back down to forty. She breathed a sigh of relief as she turned into Bryn's driveway. Turning off the car, she felt a weight lift from her shoulders, and her lighter disposition returned. "Let's take all this inside and put it away in the cupboards, then when Bryn sees it tonight, we'll act like we have no idea where it came from," she told Mandy.

"Okay, but why don't you want her to know you bought it for her?"

This time it was Elle's turn to shrug. "I don't know. I think she'll go crazy for the shirt and the pajamas and the glittery cup. But sometimes grown-ups get weird about people buying them too much stuff."

"Grown-ups get weird about a lot of stuff."

Elle chuckled. "True."

"But don't you think Bryn is going to want to say thanks for all this food?"

"I'm not worried about that. I don't do it for the thanks. I do it to make other people feel good. And that makes me feel good. Think about it like this. If someone gave you dozens and dozens of cookies, like amazingly delicious cookies, but more cookies than you could ever eat by yourself, wouldn't you want to share those cookies with your dad and your grandparents and people who you cared about?"

"Yeah, sure. But if I had that many cookies, I'd share them with the whole town."

Elle winked at the girl. "Now you're getting it."

They carried the bags into the house and stocked Bryn's pantry and refrigerator with the groceries. "So just to be clear," Mandy said as she stacked four cans of tomato sauce on the pantry shelf, "you were trying to say that those cookies are like money, right?"

"Yes, that's what I was saying," Elle answered with a laugh.

"So just how many *cookies* do you have?"

Elle cocked an eyebrow and tried not to smile. "Enough." She waited for Mandy to step out of the pantry, then closed the doors. "Now we'd better get you home so I have time to get back and take a shower before I start working on that mac and cheese."

The trip to Walmart and Bryn's farm had taken them longer than she'd planned, so Elle had texted Brody that she would bring Mandy home instead of back to the clinic. She hadn't been prepared for the scope of his property as she drove under a huge cedar arch bearing the name Three Creeks Ranch. A dirt driveway ran between long rows of fenced fields that led to a two-story farmhouse with rough timber siding that resembled a log home.

The house set against a backdrop of corn crops and wheat fields with snow-capped mountains behind them. At least a hundred head of cattle could be seen grazing in the green pastures to the west of the large red barn. Brody must have just finished feeding them, because several horses munched fresh hay from the trough in the center of the huge corral attached to the side of the barn. The sound of chickens squawking could be heard from the coop to the side of the house and several hens walked around loose in the yard.

The tall cowboy came out of the house when they pulled up, and Elle snuck a glance at herself in the rearview mirror. Her hair was in a ponytail, she smelled like chlorine, and she wore no makeup other than the quick swipe of lip gloss she'd put on as they drove over, but at this point, after swimming at the lake together and spending the majority of the last few days with her hair in a messy bun, Brody would probably be *more* surprised to see her with makeup and nice hair.

Mandy jumped out and gave her dad a hug.

"Did you have a good time, darlin'?" he asked, dropping a kiss on the top of his daughter's head.

"A great time." She raced to the back of the SUV to open the hatch.

Elle grinned coyly at Brody. "Are you gonna ask me the same question?"

His lips curved, and her body melted. Roguish grin—check. He lowered his voice as he took a step closer to her. "Did you have a good time, darlin'?"

The deep timbre of his voice sent a thrill racing down Elle's spine. She thought she could be flirty and cute, but him calling her "darlin'" in that low drawl had her mouth going dry and any thoughts of a cute comeback flew right out of her head.

"Elle invited us over for supper," Mandy called from the back as she pulled her stuff out of the SUV and set it on the porch. "She's making macaroni and cheese. I told her it was your favorite. Can we go, Dad?"

He cocked an eyebrow at Elle. "You're cooking?"

She shrugged coyly. "I can cook. Some things."

One of the several bags Mandy was trying to carry slipped from her hands and hit the porch. Without hesitation, Brody took three steps forward and grabbed the loose bag and the others sitting on the porch. "Here, honey, I got it." He turned back to Elle. "Do you want to come in for a minute? I can offer you iced tea or a variety of flavors of juice boxes. *And* we've got cookies."

"Sure," she said because she was curious about what the inside of his house looked like. And okay, yes, because she wanted to spend a little more time with him.

The outside of the house was gorgeous and well maintained. A long porch ran the length of the house, a porch swing on one end and two cushioned rocking chairs on the other. Whiskey barrel planters of colorful trumpet flowers sat on either side of the porch steps, and a hummingbird feeder hung from the porch railing. A blue-and-orange sign hung by the door claiming *Denver Broncos fans welcome here.*

A pair of muddy cowboy boots lay next to a wrought-iron mud scraper, the dirt drying and flaking along the heels. Some pliers and a round coil of baling wire sat on one of the steps, a pair of work gloves tossed on top of them as if Brody had just come back from fixing fence.

An orange tomcat was perched on the top step, its tail swishing as he guardedly watched Elle approach. She bent to pet it as she walked up the steps, but it ducked and raced off.

"That's Zeus," Mandy told her. "He's one of our barn cats. He likes to watch people but doesn't like to be petted or picked up. Dad has the scratches to prove it from the last time he had to vaccinate him. Cocoa is the black-and-white one. She's nice and will let you pet her." She lowered her voice to a whisper. "And sometimes I bring her in the house."

The inside was homey and comfortable, with cowboy boots and tennis shoes tossed in a pile by the front door below a row of hooks for coats and cowboy hats. Elle smiled at Mandy's small pink Ropers lying across Brody's larger brown leather boots.

The entryway opened into a great room with the kitchen on the left and a hallway leading to what Elle assumed were bedrooms on the right. A big screen television covered the wall above the fireplace in the living room, and stacks of books sat next to a large brown recliner. A square coffee table littered with coloring books and markers sat in front of an overstuffed tan couch. Blue throw pillows were tucked into one corner of the sofa, and a pink-and-purple blanket hung off the arm.

The kitchen had white cabinets in a farmhouse style, and one side of the counter was stacked with mail, paperwork, and several copies of the *Creedence Chronicle* newspaper and *Cultivating Colorado* magazines. The rest of the space was tidy and clean. Framed artwork of what had to be pictures Mandy had drawn were on the wall between the pantry and a door leading into the laundry room.

There were also several pictures of Brody, Mandy, and a blond woman. A beautiful woman with a gorgeous smile who looked like a grown-up version of Mandy. Elle's heart hurt to look at them, and she had to turn away. What a waste. Mary Tate was so young, and she looked so happy.

Brody dumped the bags on the sofa. "This is a lot of stuff. Did you take all this to the pool with you?"

"No. Well, some of it. But most of it is stuff Elle bought me after. We went on a shopping spree." Mandy bounced over to the other side of the sofa and pulled out the glittery purple cup. "She bought me this, and we got a pink one for her and a blue one for Bryn. Isn't it so cool?"

"Very cool," he said, peering at the other bags.

"And she bought me some clothes and some pajamas and a new swimsuit too."

Elle noticed she left out any mention of the training bras. She also noticed Brody's face darkening as his brow furrowed.

"That's a lot of stuff," he said.

"Don't worry," Mandy told him. "Elle has plenty of cookies, and she just likes to share them. Right, Elle?"

Elle had to chuckle. "Right."

"I feel like I'm missing the joke. I'm not sure what cookies have to do with anything, but this is too much." He took a step back and turned to Elle. "We can't accept all this." He lowered his voice again, but this time it wasn't in a sexy drawl; this time it was more of a heated whisper. "I can afford to buy my own daughter her clothes."

"I know," she whispered back. "Of course you can. I would never presume anything like that. We were just having fun."

"Oh, Dad," Mandy said, letting out an exaggerated sigh. "Elle told me grown-ups get weird when you buy them too much stuff, but I'm not a grown-up. And we had so much fun picking all this stuff. So don't be a weird grown-up, okay?"

He glanced from Elle to Mandy, then sighed. "I certainly don't want to be accused of being a weird grown-up."

"Plus, look at this great shirt she got me." Mandy cracked up as she pulled the llama T-shirt out and held it up with a flair.

"Wow," Brody said, trying not to laugh. "Speaking of weird…"

"It's not weird. It's hilarious. She got a matching one for her too."

Brody pointed at the shirt, then pointed at Elle. "You also got a pink shirt with a sparkly sequined llama on the front. Like that one?"

She beamed as she nodded. "Exactly the same. And it is glorious."

He let out a soft chuckle. "This I gotta see. I'll make you two a deal: we'll come to dinner tonight if you both promise to wear your new matching llama shirts."

Elle and Mandy looked at each other and grinned. "Deal," they said at the same time, then dissolved into laughter.

———

"Apparently, you all decided to have a party and forgot to invite me," Elle said thirty minutes later as she stepped through Bryn's front door. She planted a hand on her hip as she surveyed the partygoers.

Tiny was sprawled out on her back on the living room sofa, two of the puppies curled next to her considerable girth. Two throw pillows were on the floor, and Grace had her head on one and was curled against the other with two more puppies asleep next to her.

Otis stood in the kitchen, a bag of Goldfish crackers clutched in his teeth and a spray of the orange, cheesy crackers spread across the floor in front of him. The puppy Mandy called Peanut Butter sprawled on the floor at the goat's feet, licking at a cracker.

Tiny raised her head and let out an oink that could have meant *sorry, it was all the goat's idea*, or *do you have any more crackers?*

"Don't try that innocent act with me," Elle told her. "I can see the orange dust on your chin."

The pig laid her head back down and let out a remorseful sigh.

Otis let out a bleat and didn't act a bit remorseful.

"Everybody out," Elle told them as she pulled a broom from the cupboard. "We're having company for supper, and unless you plan to help clean up this mess, you'd better scoot before I take this broom to you."

Otis offered her a steely stare, then made a beeline for the back door, taking the Goldfish bag with him. Tiny took a little more convincing, and Peanut Butter was not happy to have his cracker swept up.

After cleaning the mess and righting the living room, Elle had barely enough time to get the chicken and the macaroni and cheese prepped and tossed in the oven before jumping in the shower, swiping on some mascara and doing a quick blow-dry of her hair. She was just slipping on her new khaki shorts and a pair of sneakers when she heard the front door open.

She had texted Bryn earlier in the day to tell her she'd be making supper, and she walked down the hall to find her friend, still in her pink waitress uniform, standing at the kitchen counter thumbing through a pile of mail.

Bryn looked up as Zane walked into the house followed by Brody and Mandy. "Hey, guys—" she started to say, then stopped as she caught sight of Elle's and Mandy's matching sequined tops. "Oh my gosh, those are hilarious," she told them as she cracked up.

Zane looked vaguely amused, which was practically akin to cracking up for the reserved cowboy. He nodded at Elle. "Now that's a slogan I can get behind."

"No drama, more llama." Bryn gasped between gales of laughter. "I love that so much. I am just praying you got one for me too."

Elle grinned. "As a matter fact..." At the last minute, she'd gone back and grabbed a matching shirt for Bryn, figuring her friend would either love it, or if she thought it was lame, Elle could return it later. "We did get you one. And a few other matching gifts. I put them on your bed."

Bryn raced down the hall and squealed at the gifts. "I love these pajamas. They're perfect."

Mandy and Elle stood in the doorway, laughing as Bryn held up the shirt. "This is so funny. And this cup is awesome."

"We got you the blue stuff," Mandy told her. "And Elle and I have matching pj's and cups in pink and purple."

"I love them. This means we need to have another slumber party when I get back from Montana."

Elle raised an eyebrow. "That might be a little difficult, since Zane and your cousin will be here. Unless you think they'd like to do chick flicks, junk food, and manicures."

"We could do it at my house," Mandy said. "My dad's always telling me to invite people over."

"You already tried that one on your dad," Elle said, remembering Mandy using that as her reason to invite Elle to the lake. But having a sleepover with Brody down the hall had her mind racing to all sorts of ideas that had nothing to do with slumber.

"We'll work on it," Bryn said. "For now, I'm starving. And that food smells delicious."

As if on cue, the sound of the oven timer beeped from the kitchen. "I'd better grab that," Elle said. "Supper will be on the table in five."

"Give me two minutes to get changed, and I'll be there."

Five minutes later, they were all seated around the table digging into the moist chicken and gooey macaroni and cheese.

Bryn had changed into shorts and her "more llama" T-shirt, and she tapped her chin thoughtfully as she said, "Maybe we should think about getting some rescue llamas."

Zane shook his head. "You don't just *get* rescue llamas. That kind of defeats the purpose of rescuing them."

"I think a llama would be cool," Mandy said as she stabbed a cheese-covered noodle with her fork. "Can we get a llama, Dad?"

"No."

"Couldn't hurt to ask." Mandy leaned toward Elle. "Maybe if I start asking for a llama, he'll give in to a puppy instead."

"I can hear you, you know." Brody's voice stayed flat. He'd been pensive and more quiet than usual throughout dinner, and Elle noticed he hadn't joined in on all the joking around as much as he usually did.

Listen to her. She'd only known the guy a few days. How did she think she already knew what his "usual" dinnertime joking-around level was? But she knew him well enough to know something was different.

They finished eating, and Bryn and Zane offered to clean up since Elle had cooked.

"Do you have a few minutes to take a walk with me?" Brody asked her after he'd taken his plate into the kitchen. "I have something I'd like to talk to you about."

"Sure." She sort of hoped he'd been thinking about showing her some "things" in the barn again, but his sober tone and drawn eyebrows suggested that what he wanted to talk to her about was of a more serious nature.

Her shoulders tensed as she racked her brain trying to figure out what he wanted to talk about. Mandy was on the floor playing with the puppies, and he told her they would be back in a few minutes.

As they were leaving, Elle heard Bryn gasp as she opened the pantry doors. "Where did all this food come from?"

Elle turned back to wink at Mandy, who was grinning like a fool as she innocently answered, "I'm sure I have no idea what you're talking about."

Way to play it cool, kid. She smiled as she followed Brody out the door and down the porch steps. But her smile fell as they crossed the driveway and he stomped into the barn.

Maybe he just wanted to talk more about taking care of the horses. But that conversation wouldn't have him turning on her with his brow furrowed and a tight set to his lips.

CHAPTER 11

A KNOT FORMED BETWEEN ELLE'S SHOULDERS AS SHE STARED at Brody's narrowed eyes and tense stance. "Is everything okay?"

He shook his head. "No, everything is *not* okay. We need to talk about some of the things you bought for Mandy today."

The lights finally clicked on, and she pressed a relieved hand to her neck. "Oh, you want to talk about the bras." The tension eased from her shoulders. "I thought it was something really serious."

He flinched when she'd said the word *bras*. "This is something really serious. I know you all went and had a 'girls' day' today." He made air quotes with his fingers. "But my daughter is still a little girl, and she's not ready for a bra."

"Actually, she is. She told me most of the girls in her class are already wearing them. And you may not see it, but she's starting to develop."

He winced again. "Well, still, if she needs one, that's up to me to decide and to take care of for her. You crossed a line."

"That wasn't my intention. She was looking at them in the store and told me the other girls were already wearing them. I *did* ask her if she'd talked to you about getting one, and she said she did, but both you and her grandmother seemed to think she was still too young. But as a woman, and as your friend *and* hers, I can tell you she's ready. So I offered to buy her a couple and told her I would talk to you. I was going to call you tonight."

"I don't recall her talking to me about getting a…one of those."

"Yeah, I can see how comfortable you are talking about them," she said, then softened her tone as she rested a hand on his arm. "But, Brody, you've got to get over it. You have to figure out a way to talk about bras and boys and cramps and periods and maxi-pads.

No matter how uncomfortable it feels, you need to act like it's no big deal, so she'll be open to talking to you. And she's going to need you to be cool about not just talking about it, but being okay about picking up a box of tampons or some Midol from the store for her."

He cringed and scrubbed a hand across his neck. "What the hell is Midol?"

"It's like Advil, but for cramps and PMS. Geez, didn't you talk about this stuff with your wife?"

He shrugged. "Yeah, I mean some. She was pretty private when it came to most of that stuff. And that was my wife, not my little girl. It's different."

"I get it. But she's turning into a young lady now, and that means all this stuff is right around the corner. Plenty of girls get their period around eleven or twelve."

He held his hands up in surrender. "Okay, I hear you. I'll work on it. And I'll talk to my mom too. She had something to talk to me about the other day. Maybe this was it."

"I don't know. I do know that I'm very sorry if I crossed a line. That was never my intent."

He shook his head and let out a heavy sigh. "This is just a lot to think about. And it feels like suddenly you're just *in* our lives."

She jerked back, a coil of hurt contracting her chest. "I certainly don't have to be."

He reached for her hand, but she wrapped her arms tightly around herself. "Look, I don't know what I'm doing here—this is all new territory for me. And I don't mean about the bra stuff with Mandy. I mean about the stuff with you. I haven't been interested in someone in a long time, and I haven't really dated since I lost Mary. I've had a few women who were interested in me, and some of them have tried to get to me through my daughter. And I just got to thinking about what happened with us last night and then about today when you took Mandy to the pool and bought her all that stuff. I just wondered if you did all that as a way to try to get in better with me?"

Her mouth dropped open as she stared at him. "What? No. Of course not. I told Mandy I'd take her to the pool weeks ago, before I'd really even met you." She narrowed her eyes. "And I kind of resent that you think I would use your daughter to get to you."

He shook his head and scrubbed his hand over his neck. "I know. I'm an idiot. Forgive me?"

Her anger dissolved at the solemnness of his request, and she loosened her grip around her middle and let her arms fall to her sides. "Okay."

He offered her a grateful smile. "I didn't really think you'd do that, but you've got to admit, that was a *lot* of stuff."

She shrugged, and her lips curved into a sheepish grin. "Okay, maybe I went a little overboard, but we were having fun, and she got so excited. And I wanted to do something nice for her." She looked away for a minute, debating how much to tell him about what happened that day. She didn't want to betray Mandy's confidence, but he was her father, and she thought he should know. "There *was* another reason I had for wanting to buy her all that stuff."

"Ohh-kay. Care to share?"

"I'm not sure how much to say. I think you should talk to Mandy about it, but let's just say she had kind of a rough day at the pool. There were some girls there, and they weren't very nice to her. Actually, they were being pretty mean."

His face went hard as his shoulders tensed. "What girls? Was one of them named Jasmine?"

"You know her? Snotty attitude and a high ponytail that I wanted to rip out of her head?"

"That's the one."

"Yeah, it was her. And another couple of girls, one that she said used to be her friend before Miss Snottypants moved to town."

He winced. "What did they do to her?"

"I don't know everything that happened. They followed her into the bathroom, and it took me a few minutes to get to her. But I could tell they were taunting her, and I heard them making fun of her swimsuit, saying it was too babyish. I told them to leave her alone, but after that, Mandy claimed she had a tummy ache and wanted to go home. On the way out of town, I saw the Walmart and had this idea about stopping to shop and trying to figure out how to nonchalantly offer to get her a new suit without embarrassing her."

"That was nice of you. I get it now. And I apologize again for what I said."

"It's okay. And the shopping helped perk her back up." She looked down at herself. "Especially these silly llama shirts. I would have bought her every shirt in the store to hear her laughing again."

Brody looked away, and Elle watched him fight to swallow. "Yeah, I know that feeling."

She smiled and nudged his arm. "The good news is we found a super cute tankini—it's still very modest, don't worry. It covers her tummy, but it's more in line with what the other girls were wearing."

"What the hell is a tankini?"

"It's a two-piece, but the top is more like a tank top, so it doesn't show your belly and comes in more flattering styles than a plain one-piece. And isn't as revealing as a bikini. In fact, I got one for me too."

"Wait. What?" Now it was his turn to flash a sheepish grin. "I told you I liked that red bikini." His gaze traveled down her body and back.

Her pulse picked up at the heat of desire in his eyes. "You did say that. And I didn't get rid of it, but it wasn't the most suitable for the Creedence City Municipal Pool. I would really like to take Mandy back there tomorrow. I think it's important to show those bullies that they can't run her off."

The flirty heat in his gaze changed to concern as he raked his hand through his hair. "Dang. I hate that idea. But I know you're right. It's the best thing to do. I only wish I could take the day off and come with you. But tomorrow's crazy for me. I'm meeting with my ranch foreman at eight to go over the sale of some cattle, then I've got patients at the clinic all morning and a surgery scheduled for tomorrow afternoon."

"It's okay. I've got this."

He nodded. "Thanks. I know you do. But honestly, I don't know what to do about these girls. I feel like I should contact their parents."

"I know. But you can't do that. At least not yet. It would only make things worse for Mandy. You have to give her a chance to try to figure out how to stand up to them on her own."

"I know. That's what Google said too."

Elle laughed and was glad to see the tension in his shoulders ease as he smiled back at her.

He reached for her hand again. "This is just a lot for me to process. I'm a dad first and foremost, and I always strive to put my daughter first in my life. And it feels like she's in the middle of some kind of prepubescent crisis, and all I should be thinking about is how to help her. But instead, all I can think about is you." His gaze dropped to her mouth. "And when I can kiss you again."

She offered him the tiniest lift of her shoulders and a coy smile. "I happen to be free right now."

He closed his eyes and shook his head as if he were trying to pull away. But instead he opened them again and let out a low growl as he pulled her to him, wrapping his arm around her and pressing his lips to hers.

His kiss was hungry, carnal, as if he were a starving man and she were his last meal. She felt a little starved herself as she arched into him and slid her arms around his neck. He felt so good, so solid as she melted into him. Her body responded instantly to his, heat surging through her as her nipples tightened with an achy need. She pressed into the warmth of his body, then suddenly that warmth disappeared as he pulled away, leaving her shaken and unsteady.

He swiped his hand over his mouth as he tried to catch his breath. "See what I mean? I have no control when it comes to you. And in my life, and my daughter's, I can't lose control. It's how I survive."

Elle nodded, willing her racing pulse to slow down as she tried to focus on him. "I get it. I'm the same way. And I understand that this thing with us feels out of control." She offered him a shy smile. "But I still kind of like it."

He chuckled. "Dammit, now I can't help it. I *have* to kiss you again."

Her laugh was cut short by his mouth settling on hers in a gentle kiss. His hands raised to her face and cupped her cheeks as he deepened the kiss, slipping his tongue between her lips and into her mouth. She kissed him back, surprised and a little thrilled at the immediate arousal her body experienced.

His hands still cupped her face as he drew back, his teeth playfully dragging at her lower lip in a move that had tingles of pleasures zinging through her. His breath was shallow as he whispered against her mouth, "This thing between us is *completely* out of control."

"Well, not *completely*. We haven't…you know."

He groaned against her lips, then kissed her again. "You're killin' me, darlin'. I'm enjoying the dyin', but you're killin' me nonetheless."

She grinned, a little pleased with herself and the effect she seemed to have on him. Although he was affecting her too. Her heart was racing like she'd just run a marathon—a really crazy marathon with a sexy cowboy running next to her in cowboy boots.

That cowboy pulled away and the absence of his heat had her

wanting to shiver. He shoved his hands into his front pockets and took another step back. "As much as it pains me, and, honey, it does pain me something terrible, I've got to stop this before it gets any *more* out of my control."

The shiver turned icy down her back, and she wrapped her arms around her middle again trying to fight off the sudden chill. She looked around the barn as if an appropriate answer were somehow lurking under a bale of hay.

"It's all just happening so fast," he said. "I feel like I'm caught up in a tornado and can't get my footing back under me. And that's not a feeling I'm comfortable with."

She nodded. "I get it. A lot has happened in a short time."

Maybe he was right—they should stop this now, before someone got hurt. She held up her hands. "You don't have to say anything else. I get it. And you've already done so much for me. More than I ever expected. But I know you have a life you need to get back to. I understand that."

"I'm not saying I don't want you in my life. I'm a little rattled, and things are going at supersonic speed, but I'm not crazy. And I'm not ready to let you go."

I'm not ready to let you go. His words echoed in her ears, and she let out her breath, surprised at the sting of tears at the relief that he wasn't completely walking away. She forced her lips into a smile. "I'm not ready to let you go either."

"Can we just take a beat?" he asked. "I feel like we hit the ground running from the moment we met. Could we just take a step back and maybe spend some time as friends?"

Friends. Yeah, she could do friends. Friends seemed safe.

She nodded. "Yes, I'd like that."

His tension eased and a smile creased his face. "I'd like that too. Friends seems more manageable. I can handle friendship. We can still spend time together. I don't want to stop hanging out with you."

"I don't want that either."

"I like talking to you. And being around you."

"Me too." She lifted her shoulder in an easy shrug. "So that's what we'll do. We'll keep hanging out and talking. Like friends."

"Like friends."

She wasn't sure if he was repeating the words for his benefit or hers. "We should probably get back inside."

"Yeah, good idea."

She turned to him as they walked back to the house. "Just so you know, the thing with Mandy and the training bras. That *is* the sort of thing a friend would do."

He nodded. "You're right. I know you are. I just wish she had talked to me about it."

"Maybe she did, and you missed it."

He let out a sigh. "That's what I'm afraid of."

———

The next morning, Bryn and Zane fed the animals early, then took off for Montana around nine. Elle spent the next hour cuddling various puppies on her lap as she sat on the phone with the insurance company and filled out forms about the fire.

The sound of an engine drew her to the door, and she was surprised to see a brown truck with the sheriff department's logo on its door and hauling a horse trailer pull up to the barn. By the time she'd tugged on her sneakers and made it outside, the driver was already unloading a gaunt brown quarter horse.

"Hey there. I'm Deputy Mitcham," he said, nodding his hat toward her. "You Bryn Callahan?"

"No. I'm Elle. Bryn isn't here right now."

"Then I'm gonna need you to sign for this horse in her place. Our department called Ms. Callahan and told her we'd be dropping off the mare."

Elle's eyes widened. What the heck was she going to do with this horse? "She didn't think you were coming till next week."

"Well, I'm here now. And I've got another long drive ahead of me, so I'll just relinquish this horse to your custody and get back on the road."

"Yeah, sure. Let's put her in a stable in the barn." She knew enough to keep the mare separated from the other horses until it had been checked over. Thank goodness Brody was coming out to the ranch in an hour.

The deputy led the horse into the closest stable and unhooked the lead rope. For the first time, Elle really looked at the horse, and the sight of the lean animal ripped at her heart. The mare hung her head, her eyes dull, her tail slack as she stood still in the middle of the stall. *Poor, sweet horse.* "What happened to her? Was she abused?"

The deputy shrugged. "We don't think so. She doesn't show signs of abuse, just neglect. And even that might not have been intentional. She belonged to an elderly widow who lived alone on a little farm outside of town. The widow didn't have any family to speak of, and she apparently passed away in her home, and no one found her for several weeks."

Elle covered her mouth with her hand. "Oh no."

The deputy filled a rubber tub with water from the barn's spigot and carried it over to the stall for the mare. "We found this one in the barn. Not sure how long it had been since she'd been fed or had any water. We've got some rain here lately, and the roof of that barn was full of holes, so that might have been what saved her, if she'd found some puddles or pooled water to drink from."

"How awful."

"Yeah, not as awful as finding the widow in the house." He pulled a folded square of paper and a pen from his pocket. "If I could get you to sign this release form, I'll be on my way."

"Sure." Elle took the paper and signed where he indicated, not really bothering to read it. It didn't matter what it said. She was taking in this horse. "Do you know her name?"

"Not sure. There was a placard hanging by her stall that said *Glory*, so we've been calling her that, and she seems to be okay with it." He nodded to the mare. "She actually looks a lot better than she did when we found her a few days ago. We had one of our county veterinarians come out and check on her, and he administered fluids and gave her a dewormer and a round of current vaccinations, so you won't have to bother with that. We've been feeding her and giving her fresh water, but you might want to have your vet come out and take a look at her too, now that she's in your care."

"He's coming out to the ranch today anyway. He'll be here within the hour."

"That's good." He tipped his hat toward her. "Well, I'll leave you to it, then."

"Wait. What should I do until Brody, I mean the vet gets here?"

He shrugged. "You most likely don't have to do anything. But you might want to give her some hay, and if you've got some oats or sweet feed, she'd probably like that."

She could do that. She pulled out her phone and called Bryn as the deputy pulled out of the driveway.

"Poor baby," Bryn said after Elle had told her what happened. "Are you sure you're okay taking care of her? Maybe we should come back."

"Don't do that. I can handle it." This was part of the horse rescue process, and she was a Heaven Can Wait Horse Rescue volunteer. What better way to learn to swim than getting thrown in the pool? Wait, that was a terrible analogy—there were a *million* better ways to learn. *Lessons, instructions, YouTube videos, anything.*

Stop, she scolded herself. She would figure it out. She had to. This horse needed her.

"Well, call me anytime with questions. In the meantime, give her some food and try to keep her calm."

Keep her calm? If this horse were any calmer, she'd fall asleep.

"Maybe try to brush her. Make her feel safe."

"Good idea. Call you later."

She hung up, and a few minutes later, armed with a can of sweet feed and a soft brush, she stepped into the mare's stall and cautiously approached her. "Hi, sweetheart. Hello, Glory. I'm Elle. I'm not going to hurt you." She held out the can of oats, and the horse warily lifted her head and sniffed the can. She swished her tail once, then stuck her nose into the can and took a few bites. "That's a good girl."

Elle kept her voice to a soothing tone as she carefully reached out and ran the brush gently down the horse's neck. The mare took a step away, her ears going back, and her tail swishing harder. "It's okay. I'm a friend. Nobody's gonna hurt you."

She stood still, giving the horse a chance to get used to her being in the stall. Should she even be in here? Was she putting herself in danger? This horse didn't seem dangerous. She seemed scared and sad. And Elle knew scared and sad.

She kept talking to the horse, keeping her voice soft and light until she was almost talking in a singsongy rhythm. Heck, the way she was going, she might as well be singing to her. Elle tried to think of a song she knew all the words to, but all she could come up with were Christmas carols. She hummed a little, then softly sang the first chorus of one of her favorites. "Oh come, all ye faithful…"

The horse's tail stopped twitching. "Joyful and triumphant. Oh come all ye citizens…" Elle poured some grain in the trough, then carefully tried brushing the mare's neck again as she continued to softly sing. It was working. The horse was calming down and leaned her head into the trough to eat.

Elle kept up the gentle brushing while she sang the rest of the song, then ran through every other Christmas carol she could think of. From there, she tried whatever verses she could remember from the oldies station, sometimes mashing an old Beatles song with a chorus from Elton John. The horse didn't care. In fact, she seemed to love it. Okay, maybe not love it. But she tolerated it as she let Elle gently brush her coat. And after close to an hour, the horse seemed to lean into her as if she were actually starting to enjoy the attention.

Since it seemed to calm the horse, she kept brushing and singing, even when she heard Brody's truck pull into the driveway. She'd texted him about the horse and told him to come straight into the barn when they got there.

"Wow, that horse is getting quite a concert," Brody said, as they walked in.

"She likes it when I sing," Elle sang to them.

Mandy giggled, then sang back as she carefully approached the stable gate. "What's her name?"

"Her name is Glor-y, and her owner di-ed and she was starv-ing. But now she's eat-ing and she let me brush her."

"Why don't you let me examine her?" Brody sang in a deep bass voice.

Elle widened her eyes. She couldn't believe Brody was singing for the horse. He surprised her. She stepped out of the stable and let him go in. Mandy gave her a hug, somehow instinctively knowing to be gentle in their movements and voices. "Poor horse," the girl whispered.

"Yes," Elle whispered back. "Poor, sweet horse."

Brody took about ten minutes with Glory, examining her teeth, her coat, running his hands over her back and her flanks, all the while on and off singing lyrics to old country and western songs. Elle was particularly impressed with his rendition of "Ring of Fire" by Johnny Cash. He finished his exam and gave the horse a bundle of hay before closing the stall and motioning for Elle and Mandy to follow him outside.

"That was very kind of you to sing to that horse," Elle told him as they made their way to the house, stopping for Brody to grab Mandy's bag from the truck.

"She looked like she could use a little kindness."

Elle shared what she knew about the horse and told him what the vet had done so far.

He nodded and agreed with the treatment and offered a little more insight. "I think it was really good for you to be with her when she first got here, and it obviously made her more comfortable, but don't think you have to spend every minute with her. She's safe now, and she has food and fresh water. She's okay being on her own for a bit and getting used to her new home. It was smart that you kept her apart from the other horses though. We can keep an eye on her for the next few days and see how she does before we try to integrate her into the rest of Bryn's little herd."

They had stopped on the front porch, but Mandy had gone into the house, racing into the kitchen to check on the puppies.

"Do you want to come in?" Elle asked Brody.

"Nah," he answered, setting his daughter's bag inside the door. "I'd like to, but I've got appointments scheduled for the rest of the morning and that surgery I told you about this afternoon."

"You didn't have to bring Mandy out here if you were busy. I could have come in to get her." Elle didn't like this too-polite manner in which they were talking to each other. She hadn't noticed it as much when they were singing to the horse, but now something felt off. Things had always been easy between them, which was one of the things she loved about Brody. But this felt odd, like they were both trying just a little too hard.

"It's fine," he said. "Gave me a chance to get out of the office, and I told you I'd check on the horse. And you know..." He offered her a slight shrug. "I wanted to see you too."

A grin pulled at the corners of Elle's lips. "I wanted to see you too." Until Glory had shown up, seeing him was all she'd been able to think about. The business with the insurance company and keeping track of all the puppies had kept her mind occupied for some of the morning, but when she wasn't thinking about the damage to her house or how cute one of Grace's pups was, she was thinking about how cute Brody was and how great kissing him had felt.

But that was over. They'd decided the night before to just be friends, and that's how it had to be. That decision was better for her too. She wasn't ready for the kind of intensity this thing with Brody brought up inside her. But she also wasn't ready to let him go. Friends was definitely the way to go.

"You girls have a great time at the pool," Brody told them. "I didn't have time to pack Mandy a lunch, so I stuck some cash in her bag for the two of you to grab some hot dogs or something at the snack bar."

"You didn't have to do that."

"I know. But I wanted to. It's the least I could do." He called over to Mandy. "Come give me a hug, kid. I've got to get back to the clinic."

Would it be awkward for her to get in on the hug? she thought as she watched Mandy squeeze her dad around the waist. Friends hugged each other, right? Yeah, they do, but not the kind of hugging Elle was imagining—the kind that led from hugging to kissing to touching to… *Whew…was it getting hot out here?*

"I'll drop her off this afternoon," Elle told Brody, reaching out to touch his arm, then dropping her hand. What was wrong with her? It was like the guy couldn't be within five feet of her without her trying to get her hands on him.

"Have fun showing off your new bathing suits," he told them, then offered Elle an impish grin that had her thinking his thoughts about her swimsuit weren't staying exactly in "friends" territory either.

An hour and a half later, Elle and Mandy parked in front of the pool. They'd spent some time playing with the puppies and singing another couple of songs to Glory, then Elle had thrown her new suit, a book, and some sunscreen in a tote bag and grabbed a towel before racing out the door. By the time they did all that, then drove into town and did a quick stop to check on the progress happening at Elle's house, it was already close to noon.

"You okay?" Elle asked the girl. Now that they were here, Mandy didn't seem as excited about getting out of the car. While they'd cuddled the puppies, Elle had brought up the subject of the incident the day before, and they'd talked a little about the behavior of the other girls. She had done some research on bullying the night before, and everything she'd read said talking about it was the best way to start. Several articles had also given some good tips for what kids could do to help themselves, and Elle had shared some of those ideas with Mandy.

The girl nodded, her expression solemn and defiant.

"So what are you going to do if Jasmine comes up and tries to be mean to you?"

"I'm going to tell her to cut it out, and I will try to laugh it off and make a joke about it if I can. And I'm not going to let myself get cornered alone with them again."

"Good girl." Elle reached for her hand and gave it a squeeze. "You are a strong, loving person with a good heart, and you don't deserve to be teased. And if I catch that girl teasing you again, I might accidentally push her into the pool." She covered her mouth with her hand. "Did I say that out loud? You know I'm just teasing, right? I absolutely, positively am *not* planning on pushing a ten-year-old bully into the pool."

Mandy cracked up. "Yes, I know you're teasing. It would still be funny if you did."

"Gah, we're terrible," Elle said. "Let's go dunk ourselves in the pool."

They were still laughing as they approached the line to enter the pool. There were only a few kids in front of them, including a boy who stood by himself, carrying only a towel and a ragged paperback copy of *The Lightning Thief* in his hands.

The boy seemed to be around Mandy's age, a good-looking kid, tall and lanky, who looked like he spent quite a bit of time outdoors. His skin was tanned, his dishwater-blond hair sun-streaked with highlights, and his blue board shorts and black low-topped Converse were both faded from wear. He wore a white T-shirt with a picture of Baby Yoda on the front, and Elle liked his style.

He looked back at them as they took their place in line behind him. Mandy nodded to the book in his hand. "I love that book. I'm a huge Percy Jackson fan. I've read the whole series."

A smile cracked his otherwise somber expression. "Me too. I haven't read the new one yet. My mom's a librarian, and she put a hold on it for me at the library, so I figured I'd reread the rest of the series while I waited."

"I couldn't wait. I bought it the week it came out. I can loan it to you if you get tired of waiting," Mandy told him. "I go to the library all the time. Which one's your mom?"

"Her name's Jillian. She's new. We just moved here a few weeks ago. You'd probably remember her though. She's the tallest woman there."

Mandy sighed. "I know about that. I'm the tallest girl in my class too."

"What grade are you going into?"

"Fifth."

"Me too. Maybe we'll be in the same class."

"We will. There's only one."

"Cool, then at least you know *I'll* be taller than you," he said with a timid smile. "I'm Milo, by the way."

"I'm Mandy." The girl grinned back, and Elle had to press her lips together to keep from smiling at how adorable they were. Mandy nodded her direction. "And this is my friend Elle."

"Nice to meet you, Milo," Elle told him. "Welcome to Creedence. Where did you move from?"

"California."

"Oh, wow. This must be quite a change."

He shrugged. "It is. I love the mountains though. And I was like the only kid in my neighborhood who liked to read more than surf, so I don't miss that."

"No, I can imagine not."

"I like to read too," Mandy told him.

They moved up in the line, and as the kids talked about books, Elle watched the boy crane his neck to see the prices on the admission board, then furtively pull a wad of crumpled bills from his pocket as if checking to make sure he had enough.

"I can cover you if you're short a couple bucks," Elle told him quietly.

"Nah," he said, stepping out of the line. "I'll just come back tomorrow."

"Oh please, don't do that. It's only a few dollars, and it would be my honor to cover the admission price of a Percy Jackson fan." Elle really had no idea who Percy Jackson was or why he wanted to steal lightning, but her comment earned her a small, amused grin from the boy, so she considered that a win. She wanted him to stay at the pool. It would be so great for Mandy to have someone her own age there to talk to. Especially if the mean girls club showed up again today.

Mandy nudged his arm. "Just let her do it. She does this all the time. Just on the way here, we stopped to fill up, and she paid for the gas of the family in the car next to us."

Milo glanced from Mandy to Elle, his brow furrowing. "You sure?"

"Absolutely," Elle assured him.

"And you can sit with us if you want," Mandy told him. "We can get a good spot on the hill."

He reluctantly gave in with a half-hearted shrug. "Okay, sure. And it'd be great to sit with you guys. I don't know anyone here."

The entrance to the pool was set up so the admission counter was in the center then the men's and women's locker rooms went off to either side. Patrons had to walk through the locker rooms to get to the pool area on the other side. Elle paid for the three of them, then told Milo that they had to put their suits on and then they'd meet him on the other side by the grass in a few minutes.

They quickly changed into their new tankinis, and Elle loved the way Mandy's shoulders pulled back, and she stood a little taller in the new blue-and-black suit. Elle was digging for her sunscreen in her bag as they walked out of the locker room, and she almost tripped over Mandy as the girl came to a sudden stop in front of her.

"What's wrong?" she asked as she followed the direction of Mandy's dismayed stare.

Then Elle could see for herself what had the girl shrinking back against her. On the grass next to the pool, Milo stood waiting for them, but he wasn't alone. He was surrounded by three girls who appeared to be fawning all over the kid, the leader of the group the high-ponytailed Jasmine.

"Why did she have to be here?" Mandy frowned. "And now Milo is probably going to ditch us to go sit with them instead."

"It's okay." Elle put a firm hand on the girl's shoulder. "We talked about this. You are not going to let her push you around. And there's no reason to think Milo is going to ditch us. He's standing right where we told him to meet us." Elle shot up a silent prayer that the kid wasn't planning to ditch them. Mandy needed other friends besides her and Bryn—like someone her own age. And the fact that he was a cute boy in her class didn't hurt either. *Please let Milo be the kind of stand-up kid I think he is.*

Mandy squirmed next to her. "I don't know."

"Come on. You got this. You're stronger than you think you are," Elle told her. "You are going to march right up to those kids, and you're going to act like you have every right to be here at this pool and talking to them as anyone else does. And remember to laugh it off if Jasmine says anything mean. Show her that her words don't hurt you. Even if they do, pretend they don't. Make it the best acting job of your life." She took a deep breath. "You ready?"

Mandy followed her example and inhaled deeply, then pushed her shoulders back and lifted her chin. "Thatta girl. I'm going to grab those three chairs on the hill. All you have to do is walk over there and tell Milo where we're sitting."

"Got it."

They walked together along the pool, then Elle veered off to grab the chairs while Mandy kept walking toward the kids. "Keep your chin up," she whispered, as she slowed her steps and tried not to act like she was watching as Mandy strode toward the kids. *Come on, girl. You got this.*

"Hey, guys," Mandy said, her voice a little too loud.

Jasmine turned toward Mandy, a sneer already on her face as she peered up and down Mandy's body. "What are *you* doing here?" she jeered.

Be strong. Elle sent silent encouragement her way.

"Um, I'm going swimming," Mandy said, adding a little derision to her own voice. "Duh, it is a swimming pool, you know."

Jasmine jerked back, probably not used to Mandy talking back to her. She glanced around, as if trying to think of something to say, then her eyes lit on Elle. "Oh, I see you came to the pool with your babysitter again."

Even from several yards away, Elle could see the pink flush of Mandy's cheeks and the slight drop of her chin. *Don't let her get to you.*

But before Mandy had a chance to say anything back, Milo

took a step away from Jasmine to stand next to Mandy. "Actually, Mandy is here with me. We just invited Elle to come along."

Yes. Way to go, kid. I knew you had it in you.

A grin tugged at Mandy's lips as she lifted her chin again and stood a little taller. She turned to Milo, completely ignoring Jasmine. "Elle's grabbing us chairs over there on the grass."

"Cool," he said. "See ya around," he told Jasmine and her posse, then followed Mandy to the grass.

Elle spread her towel on the chair and tried not to laugh at the triumphant grin Mandy offered her as she plopped down in the chair next to her.

"Geez, what was that girl's problem?" Milo asked, sitting in the chair on Mandy's other side.

"I don't know," Mandy told him. "She moved here in the middle of the year, and I thought she was okay. We got along until we both won for our grade's spelling bee. We got to go to Denver to compete in the state finals, and I made it through three more rounds than her, and ever since then, she's been a total jerk to me."

"Over a spelling bee?"

Mandy shrugged. "If I had known how she was going to act, I would have messed up my word and gotten eliminated. Or I would never have even gone."

"Don't say that. Why should you miss out just because someone else can't handle a little competition?"

Oh man, did Elle ever like this kid.

"You're right," Mandy said, nodding in agreement.

"In fact," Milo said, "I think we should make it our mission for me and you to be the spelling bee champions of our grade, and the two of us should be the ones to go to state this year. I'll get my mom to find us a book on the state spelling words, and we can study them this summer. What do you think?"

"I think that's an awesome idea," Mandy said, laughing. "A-W-E-S-O-M-E. Awesome."

Joy bloomed inside Elle, and she had to look away, surprised at the well of tears stinging her eyes. She dug in the tote bag for the cash Brody had stuck in the pocket. "Anyone else hungry? I'm buying hot dogs and sodas. And before you say anything, Milo, this one isn't on me. It's Mandy's dad's money, so he's treating all of us."

The three of them plowed their way through hot dogs, sodas, and four bags of chips, then the kids jumped in the pool, and Elle laid back in her chair to read her book. The sun was warm and felt good on her skin. She could hear the kids laughing, and smiled as she heard Mandy invite Milo and his mom to the Hay Day celebration. It was fun to hear her tell him stories about Shamus and Tiny and Spartacus, the giant tortoise.

She scooted her chair under the umbrella and leaned her head back, thinking she would just close her eyes for a minute. She must have dozed off because the next thing she knew, a hand was shaking her shoulder, and she groggily opened her eyes.

"Elle, wake up." It was Milo, and he had a concerned look on his face. "Can you go in the locker room to check on Mandy? She went in there a while ago, and those girls followed her in. The girls came back out, but Mandy's been in there for a pretty long time now."

Damn. I shouldn't have fallen asleep. She pushed out of the chair as she grabbed their things and threw them into their bag. For all their talk about being friends, Elle was still in charge of the girl. She pulled on her shorts, yanked her T-shirt over her head, then shoved her feet into her sandals and hurried toward the locker room. "Thanks for telling me, Milo. I'm sure she's fine, but I'll be back in a minute to let you know." That was a lie; she wasn't sure she was fine. In fact, she was quite nervous the girl wasn't fine at all, but she didn't need to worry the kid even more.

"I don't know. That Jasmine girl looked pretty smug when she came out of there a while ago." His face was pinched, his eyebrows drawn together as he leaned his head to the side as if trying to see into the locker room. "I'll wait right here."

He was genuinely concerned, which didn't do anything to ease Elle's worries either. "Mandy? Honey?" she called into the locker room as she searched the area around the showers and the restroom stalls. But the girl didn't answer.

Panic filled her as Elle searched the room one more time, but it was empty.

Mandy was gone.

CHAPTER 12

ELLE BURST OUT OF THE LOCKER ROOM. "SHE'S NOT IN THERE," she told Milo. "Are you sure she didn't come out?" She scanned the pool area, but didn't see any signs of the girl.

"I'm sure," he said. "I already looked all over for her."

"I'm going out front to see if the cashier saw anything." She ran back through the women's locker room as Milo ran through the men's. They met on the other side, and Elle checked the parking area, making sure Mandy hadn't gone back to her car. She couldn't remember if she'd locked it or not.

"I'm going to check the car," she told Milo, then ran to the SUV. Through the windows, she could see the car was empty, but she wanted to look inside anyway, just in case the girl was crouched on the floor. The doors were locked, and she dug through the bag to find the keys and click the fob. Grabbing the door handle, she yanked it open and thoroughly checked the car. Nothing.

Elle flung their things onto the back seat, shoved the keys into her pocket, then slammed the door. Turning back, she saw Milo racing toward her.

"The girl at the counter said she saw a girl running into the woods." He pointed to the small wooded area across from the pool. A series of trails led into the trees and up the rocky bluff behind them.

Why would Mandy run into those trees? Maybe she came out to the car and found it locked. What had those girls done to her to make her run off?

"Thanks, Milo," Elle told him. "I'll check the woods." She took off at a run across the park.

"I'm coming with you," he said, running alongside her. "You go left, and I'll check right."

It felt a little weird to be taking orders from a ten-year-old kid, but Elle was glad he was there. She followed his direction and took off down the left path into the trees.

Three or four steps into the woods and the air already felt different, cooler, and Elle hated to think it, but the word *ominous* came to mind. She raced down the path, calling Mandy's name, as she tried not to trip on the roots and branches littering the way.

The forested area was quiet, the only sound the rustle of leaves as a breeze wafted through the trees. Elle ran farther. The woods weren't deep; she could see the rocky trails leading up the bluff beyond the trees.

Panic ripped through her as she heard the hysterical scream of a child.

"Mandy!" She plunged forward, racing in the direction of the scream, oblivious to the branches and shrubs that grabbed at her legs and arms as she sprinted along the path.

"No! Get away!" Mandy's screams slashed through the air.

The screams were filled with terror and rage, and fear gripped Elle as she tore through the trees, thankful that at least she had a direction to run.

Bursting into a clearing, she froze, terrified at the sight in front of her.

Mandy was huddled over an animal that lay at the base of a rock, her face smeared with dirt and tears as she screamed at the tails of two coyotes who were racing away. Blood smeared across the back of one of the girl's legs, at least one cut visible. She wore only one flip-flop, and some kind of red liquid streaked down her hair and stained the blue section of her bathing suit. Red and pink stains covered her bare arms and splashed over her legs.

Her eyes were wild with panic as she turned and spied Elle. "Elle, help me!"

Elle ran to the girl but didn't know what to do first. She looked so small wearing only her stained bathing suit and one sandal, her reddish hair matted and tangled around her head. Elle might not be a mother, but every mothering instinct in her had her wanting to snatch this girl up and carry her to somewhere safe. She dropped to her knees, reaching for Mandy and pulling her close as Milo crashed through the trees from the other side of the clearing.

His expression was fierce, and his eyes were almost as wild as Mandy's. "Are you okay? I heard you screaming."

He crumpled to the ground in front of Mandy, looking a little lost, like he wanted to help but didn't know what to do. He patted Mandy's shoulder, and she reached out her arm and pulled him into her and Elle's embrace.

Elle held both kids, wrapping her arms fiercely around them as if trying to hold them together as she felt Mandy's shoulders shaking from sobs. Over the kid's shoulder, she finally saw the animal the girl had been huddled over. It was a small dog, probably some kind of a terrier mix, its cream-colored coat smeared in dirt and blood from several cuts on her legs and back. Her belly was swollen and dripping milk.

Realization hit her like a punch to the gut. *Oh no. Oh please no*. Her gaze raked over the area searching for the mother dog's puppies. But they were nowhere to be seen.

"The coyotes," Mandy said, between sobs. Her body was hot and damp with sweat. And her skin and hair were sticky from whatever the red liquid was. "They were attacking that dog. I didn't know what to do. And I'm sure I saw two puppies with her, but now they're gone."

"Oh no." Milo jerked his head around, searching for any signs of the puppies.

Elle rubbed her hand over the girl's back, a hard ache ripping through her. There was no way those puppies could have survived if the coyotes took off with them. "You tried. There is nothing else you could have done. But I'm so sorry you had to see that." She pulled back from Mandy and brushed her sticky hair from her face.

"Are you okay, honey? It looks like your leg is cut, and you've got quite a bit of blood on you. And something else. What happened to you?"

"I don't care about me. I'm fine." The girl suddenly pushed away from Elle and scrambled toward the terrier. "But we have to help this dog. They were biting her, and she's bleeding."

Elle crawled after Mandy to examine the little dog's injuries. A long gash ran across her back, and what looked like a bite had torn through the skin on her haunches. Another cut was on her shoulder. She lay on her side, trembling, her breath coming in rapid pants. She was in bad shape. Mandy was right—they had to help her.

Elle jerked her shirt over her head and gingerly wrapped the little dog in the cloth. She pushed a corner of the sleeve against the worst of the wounds to try to stop the bleeding, then carefully stood, cradling the dog against her.

"Where's your other shoe?" she asked the girl.

Mandy looked around, her eyes still a little dazed as she shrugged. "I don't know. I lost it when I ran into the woods."

Elle kicked off her sandal and pushed it to Mandy with her foot. "Here, put mine on. I think your foot is bleeding. Can you walk?"

The girl stood up and brushed at the dirt and leaves covering her legs and feet. She winced as she gingerly tried to put weight on her foot. "It's just my leg that hurts. I think that might be the dog's blood."

Milo pulled his T-shirt off and handed it to Mandy. "Here, put this on. I'll help you."

She pulled the shirt over her head, then he wrapped his arm around her waist. She hopped forward, using his body as a crutch.

"Let's get this baby to the clinic. Your dad will know what to do." Elle slid her foot back into her sandal and gave one last look around the clearing, praying she might see one of the puppies. Her heart ached with an impossible grief for the sweet mother dog who whimpered against her.

"What happened to you?" Elle asked Mandy as they made their way as quickly as they could out of the woods.

Mandy hung her head. "I know you told me not to go into the locker room by myself, but I had to go. And I didn't know Jasmine and the other girls followed me into the bathroom until it was too late. They were mad that Milo was hanging out with me and not them, so Jasmine said she'd make sure he didn't want to be seen with me and she dumped her cherry slushie on my head."

"That wasn't your fault," Milo said. "How could she be so mean? I'll *never* be her friend."

They made it out of the woods, and Elle ran to the car and unlocked the doors. She laid the dog gingerly on the back seat as Mandy and Milo climbed into the other side. Mandy slid into the center seat and clicked on her seat belt, then cradled the dog's head in her lap. Milo clicked into the seat next to her.

Elle started the car, then turned and gave Milo a questioning look.

"It's okay," he said. "My mom works. And she trusts me to let her know where I am. I'll call her from the vet clinic."

Elle nodded and put the car in gear. She drove as fast and as carefully as she could manage, knowing she had precious cargo in the back, but also knowing the urgency with which they needed to get the dog to help. Like everything in Creedence, the vet clinic was only five minutes away. Dirt flew around her tires as Elle screeched to a stop in front of the door.

She got out and yanked the back door open, then Mandy helped slide the dog into her arms. The girl scrambled out after the dog, as Milo came around from the other side. Elle turned just as the door of the clinic flew open and Brody burst out.

"What the hell happened?" He dropped to his knees in front of Mandy, running his hands over her hair and her shoulders as if looking for injuries. "Are you okay? Have you been crying? What happened?" He picked up her leg, examining the cut. "You're bleeding. And you're sticky? Why the hell are you sticky? And where's your sandal?"

Mandy pushed him away as tears welled in her eyes. "I'm fine, Dad. But you have to take care of the dog. She might be dying. Please, Dad. You have to help her."

He stood and took the dog from Elle, his eyes searching hers for answers. "We'll tell you everything," she said, "but help her first. Please."

Milo was holding the door open, and Brody hurried through with Elle and Mandy right on his heels. "Who are you?" he asked the boy as he ran through.

"I'm Milo. I'm a friend of Mandy's."

"The dog, Dad," Mandy scolded. "Focus on the dog."

"I'm focused," he said, taking the terrier into one of the exam rooms and laying her gently on the table. "How ya doing, girl?" he asked the dog as he carefully ran his hands over her body to check the extent of her injuries. He took a pad of gauze from a drawer behind him and pushed it to the worst of the cuts. "Where're her pups?" he asked.

Mandy sucked in her breath. "They're g-g-gone," she said, the tears already starting as she turned and buried her face in Elle's stomach. Her shoulders shook as she started to sob, and Milo rubbed his hand up and down her arm.

Brody's eyes almost bugged out of his head. "Will somebody please tell me what the hell is going on?"

Before Elle could open her mouth, Milo spoke up, talking fast as he conveyed the most important details. "Jasmine dumped a slushie on Mandy's head. She got upset and ran into the woods across from the pool, where she cut her leg, lost her shoe, then found this dog and her puppies, who were being attacked by coyotes. We ran after her, but we were too late to help. The coyotes took off with the puppies. But I'm gonna go back and look for them."

"I'll help you," Mandy said, her voice shaky.

"Then we wanted to save the mom dog, so we brought her to you. That's the gist of it," Milo said, concluding his narrative.

Brody shook his head, then looked beseechingly at Elle. "Okay, I have some questions, but first, I'll take care of this dog if you will please take care of my daughter. There's a big sink in the next room. Can you at least help clean her up?" His tone wasn't angry but more concerned, and Elle nodded as she wrapped her arm around Mandy's shoulder.

"Come on, honey. Let's get that awful stuff washed out of your hair." Elle led the girl into the next room and helped her pull Milo's T-shirt over her head, then held out her hand to help her step into the large sink. "I think it's easiest if I just rinse you off. Is that okay?"

"Sure. That's how they wash the dogs in here. Just use that sprayer thing," Mandy told her.

A sprayer hose was attached to the nozzle, and Elle turned on the water and held her hand under the spray until it was warm. Mandy tipped her head back, and Elle carefully rinsed the sticky, red sweetness from her hair, brushing out the tangles with her fingers as she went. Pink and brown water ran into the stainless steel sink as Elle ran the sprayer over Mandy's soiled swimsuit and muddy legs.

Mandy winced as the water hit the cut on her leg. "It's okay. We've got to wash it out to clean it up," she assured Elle, speaking like a country girl whose father was a veterinarian.

A stack of towels sat on the shelves above the sink, and Elle turned off the water and carefully wrapped one towel around Mandy's hair and another around her body. "Stay here a minute. I'm going to run out to the car and get our clothes."

Elle peered into the other exam room as she hurried to the car. Milo was standing next to Brody, helping him to wash the dog in the smaller sink. Elle yanked open the back door to grab their bag but pulled up short as she caught sight of the smear of blood on the back seat.

A flood of memories knocked her back a step, taking the air from her lungs. She bent forward, bracing her hands on her knees, trying to block out the flashbacks to the night of the accident, the blood in the car, the terrible slant of Ryan's leg under the dash. *This isn't the same*, she told herself. That dog is still alive. *But the puppies.* She couldn't let herself think about the puppies right now. *Focus on the living.*

She grabbed the tote bag, slammed the door, and hurried back to Mandy. She gave the girl her clothes and waited outside the bathroom door while she changed.

"Feel better?" she asked when Mandy came out.

The girl offered her a small nod but didn't smile. "Can we go check on the dog now?"

"Sure, honey." She put her arm around Mandy as they walked to the next door and leaned their heads inside. "How's she doing?"

Brody looked up and some of the tension eased from his shoulders as he caught sight of his daughter and smiled. "You look better."

"I told you, I'm fine. How's the mama dog?"

He kept his smile in place as he held out his hand to his daughter. "She's gonna be okay. Come see for yourself. Your friend Milo was a good assistant. I wanted to see where she was hurt, so we washed her in the sink and gave her a flea bath while we were at it. I stitched up the one cut on her haunches, and the other cuts were just superficial."

Mandy walked around the exam table to stand in front of her father. She lifted her hand and gingerly ran it over the dog's head. "I'm sorry, girl." She looked forlornly up at her father. "She looks so sad."

He pressed his lips together as he nodded. "She is."

"If you think she's okay, I'm going to go back to those woods and look for her puppies," Milo said. "I have to try at least."

"Sure," Brody said. "We can all go."

"What about the mama dog?" Mandy cried. "We can't leave her here."

"We can bring her with us," Brody said. "Her injuries aren't life-threatening. You and Elle can sit in the car with her while Milo and I search."

Elle handed Brody her keys, and she sat in the back with Mandy as he drove them back to wooded area across from the pool.

———

"All right, kid, show me where you found the dog," Brody told Milo as the boy led him into the woods. "And as we walk, tell me who the heck you are. I don't remember seeing you around before."

"We just moved here," Milo said. "From California. My aunt Carley lives here. She runs the Cut and Curl. My mom is a librarian, and she took a job in the library in town. I guess the last lady retired or something, and my aunt talked my mom into moving here to take the job."

"What about your dad? What's he do?"

"Apparently run out on his family," Milo said. He shrugged. "I don't know him. It's always just been me and my mom."

Brody nodded. He liked this kid. "And how do you know my daughter?"

"I met her and Elle in line this morning at the pool. Mandy saw I was reading *The Lightning Thief*, and we started talking."

"She loves that Percy Jackson series."

Milo gave him an approving glance but kept walking. Brody paid attention to what his daughter was reading. He couldn't keep up with everything, but he knew her favorites. And they'd read *The Lightning Thief* together.

"Anyway, we talked about books, then they asked if I wanted to sit with them, and that's about it," Milo finished his story as they stepped into the clearing. He pointed to the large rock. "That's where Mandy found the dogs. The coyotes headed up that bluff."

"Coyotes are such jerks," he muttered as he walked around the rock, then headed up the path Milo pointed to, checking the leaves on either side of the trail.

Brody didn't hold out much hope that they'd find anything. And he was right. He and the kid checked all around the area and they both came up short.

"What are we going to do about the mama dog?" Mandy asked when they got back to the car. The terrier had her head in Mandy's lap.

"We can take her back to the vet clinic," Brody said.

"No, Dad. We can't. She can't be by herself. Can't I bring her home with me? She can sleep in my bed."

"Sorry, darlin'. I'm on call tonight. You're going to be at grandma's house."

The girl turned to Elle. "Will you take her home with you then? Please, Elle."

"What? Me?" Elle's mouth went dry. "No, I can't."

"Yes. You can. I know Bryn would be okay with it. That's what Heaven Can Wait does. It's a rescue."

"It's a *horse* rescue."

"Tell that to the pig and the goat and the tortoise that just showed up." Mandy pressed her hands together in a pleading motion. "Please. You have to take her. She can't be by herself tonight. She already looks so sad. She'll die of loneliness."

A sharp twist of pain tore through Elle. She couldn't do it. She implored Brody with her eyes, lowering her voice to a whisper as she leaned into him. "I can't do it. I can't take this mother dog home, not after she just lost her babies. You saw...at my house... you know...I can't do it."

He wrapped an arm around her shoulders and put his mouth near her ear as he spoke softly to her. "I did see. And I do know. But maybe that's *why* you need to take this dog home with you. Maybe you're exactly the person she needs."

She glanced down at the dog. The terrier's large, brown eyes peered up at her—so sad and full of grief, but also trusting, almost as if she felt a kindred spirit in Elle. *Don't be ridiculous. This dog doesn't know what I've been through.* But it was said that some dogs had a sixth sense when it came to connecting with people. And Elle already felt a connection to this sweet girl.

Elle nodded hesitantly at Mandy. "Okay. I'll take her. Just for tonight. Or until we can find a suitable home for her." She felt Brody's hand on her shoulder and took comfort from the weight of his palm. She could do this. It was just a dog. And it was just for one night.

CHAPTER 13

THEY DROPPED MILO OFF AT THE LIBRARY, THEN STOPPED AT the vet clinic to get Brody's truck. Mandy stayed in the back seat with the dog while her dad followed them out to Bryn's farm.

Brody stopped his daughter before she got out of the car. "Why don't you let Elle and me go in first? We'll get Grace and her puppies fed and settled down a little before we bring this one into the chaos."

"Good idea," Elle told him. "We can make up a little bed, and she can sleep in my room with me tonight."

She looked a little calmer now that she had a plan. He swore the color had drained clean out of her face when Mandy had suggested she take the mama dog home with her. He didn't know all the details of what had happened with Elle and Ryan and the car accident, but the things he'd overheard and the presence of the empty nursery were enough to tell him everything he needed to know.

He was proud of Elle. He could tell this was hard on her, but he admired the way she pulled back her shoulders and lifted her chin once she'd made the decision to take the dog. She was braver than she gave herself credit for.

He followed her into the house and into the cacophony of five puppies yipping and barking as they crawled over each other to get to him and Elle. They quickly changed the papers in the makeshift pen and let Grace out the back door and gave her some fresh water, all while dispensing love and cuddles to five squirming, nipping puppies.

Brody caught Elle's tortured look as she cuddled two of them close to her. "It's gonna be okay. This is the circle of life, especially in a ranching community. Coyotes are assholes, and it breaks my heart that they took those pups, but the dog will get through it." *And so will you.* He didn't say it, but he wanted to.

She nodded. "I know." Her words were soft, spoken into the furry heads of the pups.

Dang. This woman was killing him. He just wanted to pull her into his arms and take away all her pain. He would give anything to erase the sadness and grief in her eyes. He wrapped an arm around her shoulder. "You good?"

She turned to him, pressing her face into his chest while still cradling the puppies between them. "No. Yes. I don't know. I will be."

He lifted her chin and peered down at her, trying to pour his reassurance into her eyes. "Yes, you will be. You're stronger than you think."

Elle offered him a fragile smile. "That's the same thing I told your daughter earlier today."

He shook his head, his fingers curling into fists as knots of fury roiled in his gut. "That's the next thing I've got to deal with. What am I supposed to do about this mean girl who is bullying my kid? I can't let this one go."

Elle wrapped one arm around his waist. "I don't know. I'm ready to strangle that girl myself. But I think you have to take your cue from Mandy. She stood up to her earlier today, and it helped that Milo stood up for her too. Although it sounds like that's what instigated the whole slushie incident."

"Who is this kid? Where did he come from?"

"California. But we can't hold that against him." She offered him the smallest smile. "He seems like a good kid. He's cute, and he's tall, and he likes to read, so he's pretty great in my book." She filled him in on how they met him in the line and the interaction with him and Jasmine and Mandy.

"I'm proud of Mandy for standing up to her, but I still think I need to call this girl's mom. I feel so freakin' helpless. I can't just stand here and do nothing."

"I'm not suggesting you do nothing. And maybe talking to her folks is the way to go. But I did some research last night, and from everything I've read, it seems like talking to Mandy and empowering her with tools to defuse the situation herself is the first step."

"You researched this? For Mandy?" Something happened inside him, like the feeling of warm butter melting over a piece of cornbread. The thought of Elle taking the time to google how to help his daughter only strengthened his feelings toward her. And these weren't the kind of feelings he normally had for a friend.

Elle nudged him in the side. "Of course I did. I care about that girl."

I care about you. The thought washed over him, the strength of it surprising him. He swallowed as he held her to him. "Thank you. That means a lot to me."

"I hate seeing this girl hurt her. I want to get in there and save her. It took everything I had to not tell her what I thought of her. But she is a ten-year-old who doesn't know me from Adam. Although I may have told Mandy that I was considering pushing Jasmine into the pool."

He chuckled. "We'll figure it out."

Elle lifted one of the puppies and gave him an impish grin. "Or maybe you should consider letting her have a puppy."

He groaned. "Come on. Not you too."

"It's just an idea." She waved the squirming pup in the air. "Think about it. He's pretty cute."

Elle was pretty cute too. And he was glad to see her eyes sparkling with mischief instead of tinged with grief. His gaze dipped to her mouth, and he considered leaning in for a kiss. He more than considered it—his body yearned to taste her, to slant his lips over hers in a hard kiss as he dragged her against him. But he had enough on his plate right now—between the bully and the injured dog and the trauma that his daughter most likely experienced today, he needed to keep it in his pants and maintain his priorities and continue to take care of his daughter first.

He took a step away from Elle. "We'd better get these pups put up so Mandy can bring the terrier in."

Elle nodded, switching back to business mode. "Yes, of course. I'll go find a blanket."

But when they got back to the SUV, the back seat was empty. And so was his truck. There weren't a lot of places Mandy could go. He scanned the farmyard and noticed the barn door was ajar. He pointed to the door. "I'll bet she's in there."

As they approached the barn, Brody could hear the sweet tenor of his daughter's voice. He and Elle quietly eased through the door and spotted his daughter sitting on the ground outside of Glory's stable. She had the terrier in her lap and was snuggled between Otis and Tiny.

Mandy had one arm around the pig's enormous belly, and the goat rested his head on her leg as he listened to her sing the strains of "You Are My Sunshine." Brody had been singing that song to her ever since she was a little.

Shamus and the other horses stood at the corral fence and peered into the barn, as if the little's girls singing had drawn them too.

"You make me happy when skies are gray," Mandy sang as she stroked the injured dog's back.

He felt Elle's fingers entwine with his as she took his hand. He blinked back the tears welling in his eyes as he kept a tight hold of her hand and led her toward the motley group of critters. Sitting on the ground next to the goat, he softly merged his voice with his daughter's. "You'll never know, dear, how much I love you."

Elle joined in, her voice tight with emotion. "Please don't take my sunshine away."

Glory lifted her head and gave a whinny, and Otis let out a low bleat, as if they were singing along.

Mandy peered over at her dad, and he knew all the sunshine he needed was right here.

———————

Later that night, Elle crawled into bed after checking on Glory first and then the mama dog. She'd made a makeshift bed for the dog on the floor next to the nightstand.

Brody and Mandy had stayed for another half an hour or so, enough time to bring the dog into the house and make sure she drank some water. She was still lethargic and a little groggy from the pain meds Brody had given her at the clinic, and she seemed to just want to sleep, ignoring the treats and the dish of soft food they sat next to her.

After the traumatic events of the day, Elle hadn't really been hungry either, but she forced herself to eat a half a sandwich and a few apple slices, then took a shower and washed the grime of the day off her skin and out of her hair. It was barely nine, but she was wiped out, so she'd retrieved her book and given the dog a quick scratch under the chin before getting into bed.

When they'd set up the Heaven Can Wait Horse Rescue website, Elle had put out a call for donations of old towels and blankets as well as cash donations. Bryn told her she often came out to her car after her shift at the diner to find stacks of old blankets on her back seat or found boxes of donated towels dropped off on her front porch. Bryn washed them all, then kept a stock of them divided between the laundry room and the tack room in the barn.

Elle had found a comfy, blue blanket, faded with age and worn soft from many washings, and swirled it into a small bed. The terrier had padded to it, pushed the folds around with her foot, then circled the blanket and settled in.

She tried to focus on her book, but Elle kept checking on the pup and had read the same page three times now. The sweet, little dog let out a whimper, and Elle couldn't stand it anymore. She carefully lifted the dog and the blanket together and placed them in the center of the bed.

"This is not going to become a habit," she told the dog as she climbed back into bed next to her. "This is just for tonight."

The dog peered at her with big trusting, brown eyes, then waited until Elle picked up her book again to scootch closer, until the dog's whole body was eventually pressed against Elle's leg. Elle gently stroked the dog's back, careful to avoid the injured areas, and the dog shifted again so her head rested on Elle's thigh.

There was no use fighting it, Elle thought as she let out a sigh. This little scraggly mutt was worming her way right into Elle's heart. It wasn't like she even had a choice in the matter. Giving up on the book, she placed it on the nightstand and laid down, letting the dog curl against her. "It's all right, sweet girl. You're going to be okay." She tenderly pet the terrier's head until the dog closed its eyes and fell asleep.

The despair for the dog and the memories of her own loss crept in on her like quicksand, pulling her down as it sought to suffocate and immobilize her. As she watched the dog sleep, the tears she'd been holding in all day slowly leaked from her eyes, soaking the pillow as they fell. She'd never held Ava, yet she still felt the ache in her arms where she'd spent months imagining she'd be. She never saw her daughter laugh or heard her cry, and she mourned the loss of those precious moments that were never to be.

After the first miscarriage, well-meaning friends either told her she could try again or didn't know what to say, so they either avoided talking about it, or avoided her altogether. Which she could understand in a way, especially because she felt like a crazy person at the time, flipping between feeling immeasurably sad to uncontrollable rage to incredible guilt. One minute, she was so angry it had happened, and the next she could scarcely bear the guilt of thinking she had done something to cause it. But at least the first time she'd had Ryan.

After the accident, she'd felt completely alone—so much like this little dog who lay hurt and bruised and confused about what had happened to her family. Elle's chest burned with an ache that threatened to consume her, and she fought to breathe through it, pushing slow breaths through her lips as she felt the vise of anguish tightening around her heart.

Her chest hitched, but she fought to control the sob, knowing once she let it out, she might not be able to stop. Her hand dropped to the bed next to the dog, her limbs so heavy she feared she might sink right through the bed.

Her phone buzzed on the nightstand, and she slowly reached for it, struggling to raise her hand and break free of anguished stupor but still cognizant enough to be careful not to dislodge the dog and wake her. Brody's name was on the screen, and she tapped the screen and lifted the phone to her ear.

She swallowed, trying to force her voice to sound normal. "Hey," she said quietly.

"Hey, you asleep?"

"No, but the dog is. What's up?"

"I've got a bit of a situation."

Fingers of dread slithered through her. A "situation" was never good. But at least it gave her something to focus on other than her own despair. "What's going on? Can I help?"

"I was hoping you'd ask that. I'm on call tonight, and Mandy usually goes to my mom's when I'm on call, but she's still upset over what happened today, and she doesn't want to go. I already had her take a long shower, we've read two chapters in her favorite book, I've sung her a song, but she's still got herself all worked up. She thinks she needs to see the dang dog for herself to make sure she's okay."

This was a "situation" Elle could fix. "Then bring her over."

"I was praying you'd say that. We're actually on our way."

"Good." Elle peered down at the dog, snoring peacefully against her side. "Just let yourselves in—the key is under the mat—and come back to my room. The dog is finally asleep and looks at peace for the first time today, so I don't want to disturb her."

"Will do."

He clicked off and within a few minutes, Elle heard the soft *whish* of the front door opening.

Mandy's blond head peeked around the corner of her bedroom door. "Hi, Elle," she whispered. "Can we come in?"

"Sure," Elle whispered back as she pointed to the sleeping bundle cuddled against her side.

Mandy tiptoed into the room, then quietly pulled her feet from her slippers. She wore the purple pajamas Elle had bought her, and she carefully eased under the covers on the other side of the bed. "How's she doing?" the girl whispered.

"Good. She's been asleep for about half an hour now."

Mandy curled around the dog's other side, careful not to wake her, but getting as close to the dog as possible.

Brody appeared in the doorway, and Elle smiled and waved him in. He wasn't decked out in purple pj's but was dressed casually in a pair of faded jeans, a T-shirt, and his normal cowboy boots. He leaned against the wall to pull off his boots, then climbed into the bed behind his daughter.

Apparently, Elle's bed was the party, and everyone was invited.

Mandy snuggled up against her dad. He offered Elle a sheepish grin. "She thinks we're sleeping over."

Heat flushed Elle's neck. Brody was in her bed and planning to sleep over? This wasn't exactly how she'd picture this moment happening in her head, but the fact that he was so close and in her bed had her body warming and her palms starting to sweat.

Elle smiled at Mandy. "It's fine. You're welcome to sleep here tonight."

"See, Dad, I told you it would be okay."

"It's really fine," Elle whispered, running a hand tenderly over the girl's head. "Mandy will sleep better knowing the dog is okay, and then I'll be here with her if you need to go out on a call."

The girl's eyes were already starting to drift closed. Elle reached over and turned off the bedside lamp, then snuggled back into her pillow facing Mandy and her dad. It was a warm night, and the light from the moon bathed the room in a silvery glow as a soft breeze fluttered the curtains of the open window. Sliding her arm over the head of the snoring dog, Elle brushed Mandy's bangs from her forehead and softly stroked her hair. Within a few minutes, the girl's breathing settled and fell into the rhythm of sleep.

Elle started to pull her hand back but Brody caught it in his, twining his fingers through hers, their joined hands forming a protective arch over the sleeping child and snoozing dog.

She let out a sigh, her body lighter and easing into contentment as he tenderly grazed his thumb over the side of her knuckle. It was hard to imagine that she could possibly fall asleep with him holding her hand and so gently caressing her skin, but exhaustion took its toll, and within a few minutes, she drifted to sleep.

Elle woke from a deep sleep hours later. The clock on the nightstand read close to midnight, and Brody's side of the bed was empty. The little girl had rolled to her back and had her arm and one leg flung out of the covers.

A noise in the kitchen had Elle easing out of the bed, careful not to disturb the dog or the child. She straightened her pajamas and ran a hand over her chin, hoping she hadn't drooled in her sleep. She padded down the hall, running a hand through her hair.

Brody stood next to the sink, a glass of water in his hand.

"Hey, sleepy."

"Hey yourself. Did you get called out from the clinic?"

"Nah, I just couldn't sleep."

"Bed too lumpy or was I snoring too loud?"

He chuckled. "You *were* snoring, but the distraction of you sleeping two feet from me and not being able to touch you was what got way too loud."

"Yeah, I get that." She held his gaze for a beat as she fought the urge to touch him now. The heat of their bodies simmered between them, the air almost palpable as it drew her toward him.

CHAPTER 14

BRODY HELD OUT THE GLASS, AND ELLE REACHED FOR IT AND took a sip, the water cool on her suddenly parched throat. He sheepishly held up the bag of cookies Sassy had sent over. "I may have had a cookie or three. You want one?"

"Might as well. It seems like everything else about the last few days has been upside down and sideways, so I might as well eat a cookie at midnight." She shook her head and laughed as she turned and lifted herself up to sit on the counter next to him. He passed her the bag, and she took a cookie, her fingers brushing his as she pulled it out. The chocolate flavor burst on her tongue as she took a bite, and she groaned at how delicious it was.

Somehow everything she did around Brody seemed to be bigger and more delicious. Or maybe it was more about the moment they were sharing, meeting in the dimly lit room in the middle of the night, the tension in the air, the scents of summer coming in through the front windows as the rest of the house slept around them.

She peered over at the pile of puppies curled around Grace's body, the whole family sound asleep in a mound of fur and cuteness. She smiled at the dogs as she chewed her cookie, then turned back to Brody. "Will Mandy wake up and be afraid if we're not there?"

"Nah. Once that girl falls asleep, she's down for the count. Nothing wakes her up. A train could roll through this house, and she'd sleep right through it."

"I envy her."

"Sorry we messed up your sleep. We kind of took over your bed tonight."

She shook her head. "Don't be sorry. I'm glad you all came over. I was having a pretty rough time. You made it easier."

He didn't say anything, didn't have to, the expression of understanding in his eyes was enough.

"Seeing that poor dog who'd lost her babies brought up so much stuff in me. Like all the old hurt and pain just welled up like it was trying to drown me." She took a shuddering breath, then blew it out between pinched lips. "I was five months along when the accident happened. We hadn't told anyone." She offered him a brave smile. "She wasn't the first baby we'd lost. The first time we got pregnant, we were so excited, we told everybody. Shoot, I think I even told the postman. Then I miscarried. And I had to tell everyone again. Which just made people uncomfortable, and nobody knew what to say or how to be around me. Even my own mother, who told me 'maybe what happened was for the best.'" She shook her head. "And frankly, I didn't want anyone around me. I just wanted to be by myself and mourn the loss of my baby and the failure of my body."

"I'm sure it wasn't your fault."

She lifted one shoulder and tried to smile again but couldn't manage it this time. Her throat was too tight, the memories too close to the surface. "It was. I'm broken." She blinked back the tears filling her eyes. "I had a lot of problems in my teens with endometriosis and fibroids. And I guess I had an 'incompetent cervix.' Isn't that just the shittiest term?" She stared down at herself, the old anger at her body surfacing again. She pushed back the feeling and tried to get through her story. "Anyway, we knew it was going to be a tough go, but we tried for another year and finally got pregnant again. This time, we didn't tell *anyone*. Not even my mom. *Especially* not my mom. She still doesn't know."

Brody's eyes widened, but he didn't say anything.

"Because we didn't tell anyone about Ava before the accident, I didn't know how to say anything after. Everyone was so torn up over Ryan, and I was too. But I was mourning two people—my whole family, my whole world."

"That must have been so hard." He squeezed her hand. She didn't even know when he'd picked it up, but it was held securely in his now.

She nodded. "It was hard. It's still hard."

"I get that. Taking care of Mandy was the only thing that got me out of bed in the morning. If I hadn't had her, I don't think I would have made it."

"I didn't have *anything* to get me out of bed. After the accident, I didn't want to feel anything. I had a few friends that tried to stay in touch, but I didn't want to talk to anyone and eventually they stopped calling. Ryan and I moved here shortly before he died, and I hadn't really met anyone. Then one night I stopped into the diner for a cup of soup, and this supersweet waitress brought me soup and a chunk of warm bread, and she stood at my table and talked my ear off. She made me laugh."

Elle's lips curved into a small grin. "It was Bryn, of course. I kept going back, maybe once a week, maybe twice, and Bryn kept reaching out, inviting me to visit her farm or stop by for coffee. And one day, I took her up on it. I met Zane, and Mandy too, and that's what started to bring me back. Until then, I wasn't sure if I could feel anything at all, but the last few months have shown me that I can. Then there's you."

She peered up at him and gripped his hand, looking for reassurance to say the next part. His eyes were kind, his expression understanding as he nodded. Once again, like he knew just what she needed.

"I met you, and suddenly I have all these feelings again. It's like my body is short-circuiting—I'm hot, then cold, like one second I've got shivers running down my back and the next I'm sweating. I know you said you wanted to be friends, and I'm good with that. Really I am. I'm terrified of all these new feelings, but I'm also glad to know that I still *can* feel. When I was lying in bed with that poor dog tonight, those old feelings of darkness and numbness came over me again. Then you and Mandy showed up and brought the light back in. I know that sounds like a lot. It's a lot for me too. When I'm around you, I start to feel things again that I haven't felt in a long time."

"Me too," he said quietly. "I haven't dated or cared about another woman in the five years Mary has been gone. Until you. I know that feeling of numbness. I've been in that same place. Then I met you. And all of a sudden those parts of me stirred, and I found myself craving you all the time. And not just your touch, but your smile, your laugh. And that stirring scares the hell out of me."

"It scares me too."

He stepped into the V between her legs, fitting perfectly against her as his hands flattened on the countertop on either side of her. He leaned toward her until his forehead touched hers. "I can't seem to breathe when I'm around you."

She nodded, fighting her own battle to breathe. "I know," she whispered.

"I know I said I wanted to just be friends, but whenever I'm around you, I can't keep my hands to myself. I want to touch you. All of you."

She swallowed. "For the first time in so long, I'm feeling something. And yes, it's terrifying, but it's also good. So damn good."

He growled against her throat. "You feel so damn good."

"I want to feel something again. Even if it's just for tonight. We can go back to being friends tomorrow, but for tonight, Brody, I want to live." She peered up at him, trying to convey the depth of what she was feeling. "I need to know I'm still alive—still a woman."

He raised his hand to cup her cheek. "You *are* a woman," he whispered. "You are smart and beautiful and funny. And sexy as hell." His gaze dropped to her mouth as his thumb grazed across her bottom lip. "You are everything."

He dipped his head and slanted a kiss over her lips, taking her breath away, then giving it back as his lips parted and the kiss deepened. Raising his other hand, he held her face, his touch commanding yet still tender.

Every part of her came alive. She wrapped her arms around him, clutching his back as she pressed into him, trying to get closer.

His hands slid up her cheeks and dove into her hair, clutching handfuls of it as he claimed her mouth. She moaned against his lips, and he pulled her closer.

It was as if he inhaled her, stealing her breath with his hunger, but it was the most delicious torment as she drowned in his desire.

Her hands went under his shirt, her fingers skimming over the taut muscles of his back. She tugged the fabric up, and he pulled away and dragged the shirt over his head and tossed it behind him.

He hooked his fingers under the strap of her pajama top, and she gave a soft gasp as he slid it carefully down her shoulder. He bent his head to press a tender kiss to her neck, then moved lower, his lips trailing over her skin as he placed another kiss to the spot just below her collarbone. His fingers were still looped in her strap as he slowly—so achingly slowly—pulled the fabric lower. The edge of her top caught on the hardened tip of her nipple, the graze of the fabric over the sensitive nub sending hot darts of desire to her core.

The shirt dropped, exposing one bare breast, and she heard Brody's quick inhale as the fabric fell free. He shifted his hand, filling his palm with her breast as his fingers brushed over its sensitive tip.

She dropped her head back, a silent invitation for him to continue his exploration.

He gazed down at her as he rubbed his thumb over the edge of her nipple. His head dipped to press a kiss to the crest of her breast, then moved lower to circle the hardened nub with his tongue before sucking it between his lips.

Hot surges of electricity shot from her breasts to between her legs, and she squirmed on the counter, the feeling both familiar and so foreign. It had been so long since she'd felt the tingle of anticipation, the pulse of need.

Her breasts tightened, aching for Brody's attention, and she let out a soft moan as he lavished attention on them. Her pajama shirt still covered one, but the tight tip poked through the thin fabric and Brody moved his head, closing his mouth over the tip and sucking it through the fabric.

He raised back up, dragging her to him as he kissed her lips, then her cheek, then her throat. "I want to kiss you and hold you and touch you. Lord help me, I want you so damn bad."

"Yes. Touch me. Please," she pleaded, her voice a hoarse whisper in his ear.

His hand slid inside her pajama shorts, his open palm moving over her legs and between her thighs. She opened her legs, just enough to issue the invitation, and his fingers slid between them and found their target.

She moaned again, the heat coiling in her belly as he moved his hand in firm, steady strokes. Her breath came faster as the pace of his movements quickened, and she clutched his back, holding on as the sensations curled and built, pushing her higher.

Everything else fell away—everything except the relentless ache between her legs. She was utterly at his mercy, swallowed in the heat of desire, lost in the passion that coursed through her, until the intensity crested and the sensations rushed up and seized her muscles. She cried out, digging her fingers into Brody's shoulders as the heat arced and flushed through her.

She dropped her head to his shoulder, pressing her lips to his neck as the sensations pulsed and throbbed. Her arms and legs trembled, and she was helpless to do anything but hold on.

Brody let out a ragged breath, his arms wrapping around her and pulling her tightly against him. It felt like he might be shaking too.

He pulled back, just the slightest bit, just enough to press a hard kiss to her mouth. Her lips tingled from the pressure.

Then something tingled against her leg. Tingled and buzzed.

It was Brody's phone. He winced as he pulled it from his pocket and pressed his lips together as he shook his head. "Damn it. It's the clinic. I gotta take it."

She pulled the strap of her pajamas up, covering herself as she tried to catch her breath. "Yeah, of course, take it."

He put the phone to his ear, listened carefully, inserted a couple of "okay's" and an "I'm on my way," then hung up. His expression was miserable as his eyes pleaded her forgiveness. "I've got to go. We got a call from Logan over at Rivers Gulch. He's got a cow in labor, and it looks like the calf is coming in breach. He needs my help."

I need you. So damn bad.

The thoughts hit her with the force of a gale wind, and she was thankful she hadn't said them out loud. She hadn't needed someone in a long time. And she wasn't sure she liked the feeling. Maybe it was good that the clinic had called. Who knew how far things would have gone if the phone hadn't buzzed. Like they hadn't gone far enough. He'd just taken her to O-town on the kitchen counter.

"I need to wake up Mandy," Brody said, all business as he searched for his shirt. "I'll take her over to my mom's." He dragged the T-shirt back on and scrubbed his hand through his hair as if he couldn't think straight.

"Oh no you don't. She's perfectly fine where she is. You said she sleeps soundly, and when I left the room, she was sawing logs like a lumberjack. There's no reason to wake her up. She can stay here with me."

He straightened his shoulders as if he was trying to collect himself, then furrowed his gorgeous brow. "You sure?"

"Absolutely."

"I don't want her, or me, to be a bother."

"You aren't. I adore Mandy. She's great company. And I genuinely enjoy spending time with her. The jury's still out on you, though." She grinned as she teased him, trying to lighten the moment.

"Oh yeah? You seemed to like me a minute ago when I was kissing your neck."

"That was just your lips. I definitely like your lips." She gave him a nudge. "Now go deliver a cow. And don't worry about us. We'll be fine." *That's a lie.* She wasn't sure if she'd ever be fine again. Her thighs were still trembling, and her easy teasing was just her way of hiding the emotions racing through her. She couldn't quite believe what had just happened.

"I gotta grab my boots," he whispered, already hurrying down the hall. He came back a few seconds later, carrying the boots in one hand. He crossed to the kitchen and swept his arm around her back, pulling her to him and planting a firm kiss on her lips.

She gripped his shirt, holding on as she kissed him back. "Will you come back when you're done?" she whispered.

His lips formed a teasing grin. "Try and stop me."

No way.

———

Three hours later, Brody quietly let himself back into the house. His back ached as he pulled off his boots and left them by the front door.

The delivery had been a rough one. The calf had been breach, which always came with its own set of challenges. He and Logan had worked on the cow for close to an hour getting the calf turned. They'd finally done it, but it still took both of them and the help of a calf puller to get the baby cow born. Hearing the healthy bawl of the calf as it lay in the hay next to its mother made it all worth it.

The glow of the moon coming in the window at the end of the hallway gave him enough light to see as he padded in his socked feet down the hallway and leaned his head into Elle's bedroom. He peered at his daughter curled in bed with a dog and a woman who were both grieving. He wasn't sure if it had been the right move to push Elle to take the dog, but it had felt right at the time. Something told him that her helping another anguished mother would somehow help her to heal. Even if that anguished mother was a dog.

He hoped Elle *was* healing. He knew it was slow and painful. Hell, he hadn't made it all the way through the process himself.

He shook his head. *Like I'm any kind of expert on the grieving process.* He'd fumbled his way through almost every day for the last five years. But the last few days with Elle had been different. *He* was different. Almost like being around her had lessened some of the weight of his burdens. He wasn't sure if she'd taken them or if he'd finally laid them down, but he felt their absence just the same.

But it's not about me. Mandy's happiness was what counted the most. What he needed to put above everything else.

He and Elle had committed to starting again as friends, and they'd managed to keep that commitment for a whole day. But one moment in the dark had wrecked all that. And now all he could think about was touching her again.

She was so damn beautiful. With her eyes closed and her long hair spread out on the pillow around her head, she looked like an angel. Her arm was draped over the dog and rested protectively on his daughter's shoulder. He knew he was falling for this woman. Hard. He could claim he wanted to be friends all day long, but his feelings had already gone way beyond the friend zone.

He wanted to climb into bed with her and his daughter and fall asleep, the three of them, together. But it was too much like a family. And he wasn't ready for that.

Hell, he'd only known the woman a few weeks. He had no

business even imagining her in that role. But he didn't have to imagine it, because she was already there, curled in bed with his daughter and curved snugly around his heart. She fit so easily into their lives, like she already belonged. Being around her felt so easy, even as she did hard stuff like helping his daughter deal with a bully and taking her shopping for a dang training bra.

He took a step back. He had to. This felt too fast. And not just for him. Although it appeared to be too late for Mandy too. He was pretty sure his daughter had already fallen in love with Elle.

But not every woman wanted to step into a ready-made family, especially one who had so tragically lost her own. She could just as easily put the brakes on this thing and pull away from them.

He could take that kind of heartbreak—he'd been through it before. But he wasn't sure his daughter could. Maybe he needed to back up—again. He couldn't let Mandy lose anyone else.

Calling on all his strength, he turned away and forced his feet to take him back to the living room, where he sank onto the couch. He pulled the blanket from the back of the sofa and laid down, resting his head on the lumpy throw pillow. Closing his eyes, he tried to put thoughts of Elle out of his mind, tried to focus on what he had to do at the clinic the next day and not think about how soft her skin was or how her body fit so perfectly against his.

He fought the urge to go back to her room and finally fell into a fitful sleep.

———————

Elle tried to push back the hurt she felt the next morning when she found Brody asleep on the living room couch. She'd hoped he'd come back to bed with her and Mandy. But maybe it was really late and he hadn't wanted to wake them. Or maybe he'd regretted his earlier actions and was trying to go back to being friends.

She left him on the sofa as she quietly slipped into the bathroom to take a shower and get ready for the day. As she washed her hair, she imagined ways to phrase her questions and figure out what was going on in that handsome head of his. But her rehearsing was for nothing, because by the time she came back out to the kitchen, he was gone.

CHAPTER 15

GONE? WHY WOULD BRODY LEAVE WITHOUT EVEN SAYING goodbye? Elle rubbed her fingers across her forehead. Was he already regretting their midnight make-out session? He had said he only wanted to be friends. She tried to think back to the moment they kissed—had she instigated it? Had she thrown herself at a guy who wasn't interested? No way. Brody had been plenty interested. And he'd said she couldn't keep him from coming back.

So what had happened between the time he left last night and this morning?

Quit overanalyzing everything. The man did have a ranch to run and animals to take care of. He probably needed to feed his cows and get his chores done before he went to work. That made sense.

But why didn't he say goodbye?

Mandy sat at the table hastily eating her way through a bowl of cereal.

"Good morning," Elle told her as she slumped into the seat next to her.

"Morning," the girl answered as she pushed an empty bowl, the cereal, and the milk toward her. "My dad got a call from our foreman, and he needed him to come back to the farm before he went into the clinic. He said to tell you he'd call you later."

See? It didn't have anything to do with her or the time they'd spent together the night before. It was like she'd thought—he just got called away for something to do with his ranch. So she could stop overthinking everything and blaming herself. "I hope everything's all right."

"He said one of our horses cut up his leg on some barbed wire, and they needed my dad to stitch him up."

"Oh no. That's awful."

"Don't worry, my dad will fix him right up." She pointed to the empty pen in the corner of the kitchen. "He also fed Grace and the puppies and put them in their pen in the backyard. I think he thought you were still asleep, and he was trying to keep them from waking you up." Zane had fashioned a small enclosure in the grass, so the puppies would have a safe place to roam a little and get some sunshine.

"I thought it seemed a little quiet in here." Elle dumped cereal into her bowl, then nodded at Mandy. "Why are you eating that cereal like you're afraid someone's going to take it away?"

"I'm trying to eat fast so I can get back to Roxy."

Elle wrinkled her brow trying to go through the list of names of the menagerie of animals on the farm, but she couldn't come up with a match. "Who is Roxy?"

"The new dog. The one in your bed."

"Oh. I didn't know she had a name."

"I gave it to her. I was thinking about it last night, and it came to me this morning. She's a little dog, but she's scrappy. She didn't give up when those coyotes attacked her, so I wanted to give her a name that showed she was a fighter."

"That makes sense."

"Yeah, but the only fighter I know is the one from that movie Dad likes, *Rocky*. And that's a boy's name. So I changed it to Roxy since she's a girl."

Elle nodded. "Good thinking. It's perfect. Roxy is a great name, and it fits her. Good job."

"Thanks," Mandy said. "Now I just need to convince her to keep fighting. She still seems so sad this morning. She didn't even want to get up to go outside."

"We can try to take her out again when we're finished eating," Elle said. "And we just need to give her some time. She's been through a lot."

"Yeah. I was sad for a long time after my mom died. Sometimes I still am." She stared into the milk left in her bowl. "But sometimes I get kind of mad at her. I know it's not her fault she got cancer, but I still get mad that she died and left me behind." She raised her gaze to meet Elle's. "Is that bad of me to be mad?"

Elle didn't care if Mandy was the tallest girl in her class, Elle still wanted to pick her up and cradle her on her lap. "No, it's not bad at all. I do the same thing. Sometimes I get so mad at my husband for dying and leaving me alone that my chest hurts, and I just want to scream and hit something."

Mandy's eyes were wide as she nodded. "That happens to me too."

"One time I was unloading the dishwasher, and I was stacking these beautiful white plates we'd been given as a wedding gift, and something in me just snapped. I got so mad that I threw every single plate on the tile floor as hard as I could."

"You did?"

"Yep."

"Did they all break?"

"Oh, you bet they did. They broke into hundreds of shards, and the noise was deafening." She would never forget the sound of those plates shattering on the Italian tile or the way they exploded and shot white glass fragments across the floor like a display of fireworks. "It took me hours to clean it all up, and I still find little pieces of those plates on the floor sometimes. But it was worth it."

Mandy nodded. "Yeah. I bet it was. So what do you use for plates now?"

Elle smiled. "I bought new plates. But I didn't get white ones. I found some really pretty blue ones online, and the color reminded me of robins' eggs and the ocean. So now when I see the plates, I try to think of those things and try to let myself be happy instead of sad."

"I like that idea." The girl's gaze returned to her bowl, and her voice dropped to just above a whisper. "One time I got mad and broke my mom's favorite mug. But it didn't make me feel better. I was just ashamed that I broke something my dad might have still wanted. I picked up the pieces and hid them in my closet." She twisted the napkin she held into a tight line. "But now I wish I would have just told my dad and then bought another one to replace it."

"Would you still like to? I can take you to the store if you'd like to pick out another mug that makes you think of your mother, but in a happier way."

Mandy looked up and nodded. "Yeah, I'd like that."

"I'd like that too. Next time we go into town, we'll stop at the Mercantile and see what we can find."

"Thanks, Elle." Mandy smiled, and Elle realized she would take this girl to the ends of the earth and buy her ten thousand mugs if it would take away her pain and bring back that smile.

Elle pointed at the girl's bowl with her spoon. "Why don't I wash up these bowls while you go check on Roxy?"

"Okay." She tilted the bowl up and drank the rest of the milk from the side of the rim. Then she slid from her seat and started down the hall.

Elle stood and picked up the empty dishes. She'd barely taken a step forward when she heard Mandy's quick footsteps running back and felt the girl's arms wrap hard around her waist. She pressed her cheek into the center of Elle's back as she gave her a fierce hug.

Elle tried to turn around to return the hug, but the girl let go and ran down the hallway toward the bedroom. She swallowed back a lump of emotion as she carried the dishes to the sink. But before she had time to wash them, Mandy was back with a concerned look on her face.

"Roxy won't get up. I tried to coax her to come outside, but she won't even stand up. She's just lying there, and she looks so sad, it's hurting my heart."

Elle let out a long sigh. "She is sad, honey. Dogs have feelings too. And she is missing her puppies." Elle followed Mandy back to the bedroom, and she peered down at the desolate little dog curled in the folds of the blanket. She crouched next to her and carefully lifted her into her arms. "It's okay, girl. I've got you. Let's go outside for a little bit and see if a little sunshine helps."

Elle was glad that Grace and her puppies were in the backyard as they carried Roxy through the house and out the front door. The morning was already warm, and Elle gently set the dog in a sunny spot, then sat down in the grass next to her. The dog looked around for a few seconds, then let her head drop into the grass, as if the weight of holding it up was too much for her. Elle tenderly stroked her cheek as she cooed encouragement to the grief-stricken dog. She remembered that exact feeling after she'd lost Ryan and Ava, that weightiness of her body that felt like she couldn't lift even her pinky.

Mandy came out with two small dishes, one holding water and the other a scoop of canned dog food. "Maybe we can get her to eat a little something."

"Good thinking." It was obvious Mandy was a veterinarian's daughter. They put the dishes by the dog, and Roxy lifted her head and took a few laps of water. She sniffed the food but lay back down without even licking it. Poor, sweet dog. "Let's leave her alone for a few minutes while we feed the other animals. Maybe she'll eat if we aren't watching her."

Brody had already fed the horses and the dogs, so Elle and Mandy each sang a song to Glory while Elle petted her neck, then took care of putting out food for the pig and the tortoise.

"What about Otis?" Mandy asked. "What does the goat eat?"

"Everything he can find to put in his mouth," Elle replied. "Bryn told me I could put out some oats for him, but he'll mainly eat grass and sneak bites of all the other animals' food. I swear that goat has a bottomless stomach."

"I think my dad has a bottomless stomach too," Mandy told her. They had made their way back to the barn and the girl climbed onto the seat of the four-wheeler quad Zane had bought for the ranch. "Wanna go for a ride on the quad? We could take it up to the lake and go for a swim."

Just the suggestion of taking a ride on the ATV had anxiety swelling in Elle. "No way. Do you know how many accidents happen on four-wheelers? Hundreds of people die on them every year. They're crazy dangerous." Elle's blood pressure rose just thinking about the fatality rate.

"Dangerous? How can they be dangerous? We could wear helmets and go really slow."

Elle shook her head. "No. Absolutely not." Her hands started to tremble, and she wrapped her arms around her middle.

Mandy's brows drew together, and she slid off the seat of the ATV and hurried to Elle. She threw her arms around Elle's waist and hugged her middle. "It's okay, Elle. I didn't mean to upset you. We don't have to ride it."

Elle hugged the girl to her, embarrassment heating her cheeks. For only being ten years old, Mandy was very in tune to other people's feelings. She rubbed a hand over the girl's back. "I'm okay. Really. I just kind of get freaked out sometimes when I think about the dangers of certain things. Which is weird because I used to do dangerous stuff all the time. My husband and I rode motorcycles and skied, and once, we did a zip line across the top of a rain forest. I used to love it. Did you know that I even jumped out of a plane once?"

Mandy pulled back and cocked an eyebrow. "When it was in the air?"

Elle laughed as she nudged the girl's shoulder. "You're hilarious. Yes, when it was in the air. When it was thirteen thousand feet in the air to be exact."

"Whoa. Were you scared?"

"Yes, but it was a good scared, like it was exciting."

"Would you ever want to jump out of a plane again?"

Elle had to swallow at the panic rising in her. "No. I don't really even like to fly much anymore. I used to like that thrill of excitement, but now I just get terrified and practically have a panic attack just thinking about doing anything dangerous where someone could get hurt. I know that probably sounds weird, but it's just how I am now."

"It's okay." Mandy offered her a shrug. "I'm weird about some stuff now too. My dad says death has a way of changing things. And I guess it changes people too."

Elle nodded. She'd changed in so many ways. And none of them seemed good. She used to be fun and have a thirst for adventure and threw herself into life.

She needed to stop focusing on the past. "Let's go check on Roxy."

Brody's truck pulled into the driveway as Elle and Mandy exited the barn. He got out and stood by the door. His forehead was pinched as he watched them approach.

"You okay?" Elle asked as they got closer. She'd planned to ask him about the night before when she saw him next, but it was obvious from the slump of his shoulders and the set of his mouth that something was wrong. Also by the fact he was back so soon.

"Rough morning," he said with a hard sigh.

"Mandy told me one of your horses had been injured."

"Yeah, he got himself tangled up in some barbed wire. His leg was a mess. I think I put in fifteen stitches, but he's gonna be okay. Then I got to work and some guy stopped in because he'd found a couple of puppies in a ditch by his house. Looked like somebody didn't want 'em so they abandoned them on the side of the road."

Elle gasped and covered her hand with her mouth. Her knees threatened to give way and she put a hand on the hood of the truck to steady herself. What was happening with these poor, sweet dogs?

He scrubbed a hand over his neck. "I just don't get how some-one could do that. They're real cute little things—look like some kind of Golden Retriever mix." He reached into the truck and pulled a small cardboard box from the cab. "I brought 'em out here, and I'm hoping our mama dog will foster them. I don't know how old the puppies she lost were, but she should be able to nurse these if they are the same age or younger than hers were. She's clearly lactating though, and if they'll latch on, she should be able to feed them, at least until they're old enough to be bottle-fed."

Elle leaned forward to peer into the box at the two sweet, sleep-ing bundles. One was a lighter yellow and the other was a dark red-dish color, more typical of a golden retriever. "They're adorable," she whispered, her throat raw.

"The yellow one is a female and the rust is a male," Brody explained.

"Aww. They're so cute," Mandy said, leaning in next to Elle. She peered up at her dad and gave a resolute nod. "Don't worry. Roxy can do it. She's over here. We brought her out into the front yard." The girl hurried toward the little dog.

But Elle couldn't move. Brody glanced her way, then took a step toward her, wrapping an arm around her waist to support her. "Whoa there. You all right, darlin'?"

She nodded. "Yeah, I'm fine. I just feel bad for these dogs. Poor, little Roxy. We couldn't even get her to eat this morning. She's just despondent with grief. And now these sweet puppies that someone threw away like they were trash. And who knows what happened to their mom?" She swallowed as she gripped Brody's sleeve in her fingers. "It's all just so tragic and so senseless. And I guess all this is just bringing up so much of my own stuff."

He stroked his hand across her back. "I get it. And no, it doesn't make sense. But life rarely does. All we can do is keep putting one foot in front of the other, and try to find a little joy wherever we can."

Elle peered up at him. "You are very wise, Dr. Tate."

"Nah, I stole all that from my grandpa. He's the wise one. He told me that stuff when I lost Mary, and I just try to remind myself of his words when I start getting down on life and all the irrational parts of it." He hugged her to him. "You want to go in the house? Mandy and I can do this part."

She shook her head. "No. I'd like to be there for Roxy. And for me too, I guess. I've witnessed the death part of it. I'd like to be there for the life part."

He hugged her again. "Thatta girl." They walked toward where Mandy sat in the grass with Roxy. "I think maybe we should take the dog back into your room," he told them. "If we can make a little nest in there, she might settle in with the pups easier."

"Good idea," Mandy said, pushing to her feet. "There's a box in the laundry room that should work. I'll grab it."

"Smart. I'll bring Roxy in, and we can put that blanket she likes in the box and set it up in the corner of the closet in my room," Elle told her.

"And toss one of those old towels in the dryer for a few minutes," Brody instructed. "The puppies need to stay warm. I've got them resting on a hot water bottle now, but there will be less of a shock to their systems if we have a warm place for them to nest in."

"Got it," Mandy said as she ran up the porch steps and into the house.

Elle carefully lifted the dog and cradled her to her. She noted that she hadn't touched the dog food and the water looked untouched as well. She was going to have to eat if she was going to care for the new puppies, but they'd cross that bridge when they came to it. For now, they just needed to see if she'd accept them.

Brody picked up the water dish and followed them in. Mandy already had the box and the blanket in place, but they gave the towel a couple of minutes to warm up before they wound it into the folds of the blanket. Elle gingerly set the dog on the soft, cozy nest of warm cloth. She looked up at Elle with the saddest eyes, and Elle had to look away for fear she would break down sobbing. "Be strong, Mama. We've got some babies that need you. And only you can help them."

Brody glanced over at Elle and Mandy as he reached into the box. "You ready?"

Elle picked up Mandy's hand and clutched it in hers. They sat down on the floor outside the closet, trying to give the dogs some space but still be able to see them.

Brody lifted the first pup, the female, and set it on the blanket next to the dog's swollen belly. Roxy's tail lifted in a slow wag as she raised her head to sniff the puppy. Her tail hit the blankets with a harder thump as he set the second puppy down next to the first. Roxy let out a soft whimper as she licked the closest puppy's head.

Even with their eyes closed, the puppies' innate sense of survival had their tiny mouths moving as they searched out a place to suckle. They blindly squirmed over and around each other, eventually rolling against Roxy's stomach as she licked one head, then the other. Roxy lay on her side, opening her belly to the new orphans. The female pup finally found a teat and, after a couple of tries, latched on. Her mouth moved in rhythmic motion as she greedily suckled. Roxy nudged the other puppy's head closer to her belly, and he soon joined his sister.

"She's doing it," Mandy whispered. "Look, Dad, Roxy is feeding them."

"I see that," he said, reaching his hand out to scratch the mother dog's head. "You're doing great, Roxy. You're a good girl."

The dog looked up at him, her expression one of affection and devotion. Whether that was due to the fact Brody had bathed her and stitched up her wounds or the fact that he had brought her babies to care for was undetermined. But she seemed to gain a little light back in her eyes.

Elle couldn't speak as she watched this sweet dog who had

lost her babies so graciously take on the care of another mother's orphaned children. Roxy seemed to have already accepted the new puppies as her own as she licked their heads and nuzzled their ears.

"Why don't we give them a little time?" Brody said, nudging his daughter's arm before pushing carefully to his feet.

They tiptoed out of the room and down the hall. As they walked into the living room, Elle spied a blue car heading down the driveway and pulling up in front of the house. She went to the door as Sassy climbed out of her car and pulled a cardboard box from her back seat.

Brody hurried outside and down the porch steps to give her a hand with the box.

"Hey, Sassy," Elle said, stepping out onto the porch. In the time they'd been inside, Tiny had found her way out of her sty and the giant pig was lying in a patch of sun on the front porch, two barn cats curled along her sides. She lifted her head as she must have gotten a whiff of the heavenly scents coming from the box, but the cats didn't budge.

"Now that's a sight you don't see every day," Sassy said as she peered down at the feline and swine pile.

"Tiny thinks she's a dog," Mandy explained.

"Whatever floats her boat," Sassy said, pushing through the front door, then holding it open as Brody carried the box inside. "I made a mess of fried chicken this morning and thought I'd bring some over for you to eat for lunch. I was worried I made too much, but now that I see Doc and Mandy are here, it seems I made just enough. There's some homemade mashed potatoes and gravy in there as well. And a couple of my famous Sassy cakes."

"Oh my gosh, that was so nice of you," Elle told her. "You didn't have to do that. You already fed us lasagna." She held up her hands. "Not that I'm complaining or turning down the chicken. It smells so good, my mouth is already watering. I just hate for you to go to all this trouble."

"It's no trouble. I enjoy cooking," Sassy said. "And I enjoy the company." She'd already bustled into the kitchen after Brody and was wrapping an apron around her light blue tracksuit. She pointed to Mandy. "Why don't you grab some plates, honey, and start setting the table? Brody, if you'll fill the glasses, Elle and I can get this food set out." She pulled the covered dishes from the box Brody set on the counter and carried them to the table.

Within a few minutes, they were ready to eat and took their places at the table. Sassy had also brought a fruit salad and a small tray of veggies.

Elle sat down next to Brody, and he took her hand for the blessing. It was such a simple thing, holding his hand as they bowed their heads, but the plain fact of touching his skin, of having her palm resting in his, had her stomach doing funny little flips that had nothing to do with being hungry for the chicken and way more to do with being hungry for the hunky cowboy.

Sassy said a quick grace, then lifted her head and said, "Pass the rabbit food," as she pointed to the small platter holding a variety of carrot sticks, celery, radishes, and onions. "Don't these veggies look like what you would feed a rabbit?"

Mandy nodded in agreement, taking a carrot stick before passing the tray. "They also look like pig food and goat food 'cause I know Tiny and Otis would both eat all this stuff."

"Judging by the size of that pig, I think it would eat that tray and this kitchen table too."

They laughed and settled into easy conversation as they filled their plates and dug into the food Sassy had prepared.

"I checked in on your house before I drove out this morning since I hadn't seen you there yet," Sassy told Elle. "I know you stop over every day, but I like to keep my eye on things when you're not around. I'm glad the progress seems to be going so well. The contractors like to fill me in on what they're getting done. Since I have a key to the place, they assume I belong there."

"I don't recall giving you a key to the house," Elle said, furrowing her brow as she tried to remember.

"Oh, you didn't. But I always breeze right in, so they don't know that. I told them I'm your aunt, and I've been over there so many times they probably think I live there too."

Elle chuckled, amazed at how this woman had so easily slipped into her life and how much she enjoyed her being there. She reached out and put her hand over Sassy's. "I'm so thankful for all you've done to help me. You've been a really good friend. And I'm so sorry it took me so long to walk across the lawn and get to know you. It was a terrible error on my part. I think I could have used a friend like you the last few years."

Sassy's eyes widened and she smiled warmly at Elle as she rested her other hand over hers. "What a lovely thing to say. And don't worry, honey. Now that we are friends, you're not going to be able to get rid of me."

"Why would I want to get rid of you? Especially now that I know you're such a great cook. Anyone who goes to the trouble of making me fried chicken, mashed potatoes and gravy, *and* a cake will stay in my heart forever."

"I actually made two cakes," Sassy told them. "One is leaded for the adults, it's alcohol-infused, and the other is unleaded for Mandy and anyone who might be driving."

"Unfortunately, the unleaded one is going to have to be for me," Brody said. "I've got to get back to the clinic. So far, every cake I've ever had of yours was delicious, but I'll take a piece just to confirm my suspicions." He gave Sassy a wink.

"I'd better take a big piece too," Mandy said. "Just to be sure."

"Sounds smart." Sassy laughed as she stood to serve the cake.

Elle cleared the plates and carried them to the kitchen. "I'm going to save my piece for later."

"I'll wait too," Sassy said. "We can have ours after we get everything cleaned up."

"You'd better take yours now, squirt," Brody told his daughter. "I'm taking you back to town with me and dropping you off at your grandma's this afternoon."

"Why can't I stay with Elle?"

"You've been with her every day," her father explained. "Let's give her an afternoon to herself."

"Fine," Mandy said, crossing her arms. "But can we come back after supper? You're gonna need to check on the puppies anyway."

He peered up at Elle.

She nodded. "That's fine with me. I'd like to have you check in on Roxy too." *And on me.*

CHAPTER 16

AN HOUR LATER, THE TATES HAD GONE BACK TO TOWN, AND Elle and Sassy had finished cleaning up the dishes. Elle had made coffee, while Sassy prepared plates holding giant slices of cake and carried them into the living room. Elle brought in their coffee as Sassy hurried into the backyard and came back in with the gray-and-white puppy cuddled in her arms.

"I'll admit, part of my motivation in coming out here was to see this precious girl again. I just adore her," Sassy said as she picked up her cake, then settled on the sofa with the cute little animal on her lap. She took a big bite, then let out a sigh of bliss. "I call this recipe 'Better than Sex Cake.' It's that good." She offered Elle a wink and an impish grin. "Although I don't know what kind of sex you're having, so I can't say for sure."

"I just never know what's gonna come out of your mouth," Elle said with a chuckle.

"Speaking of 'cake,' things seem to be going pretty well with the good doctor," Sassy said with a provocative lift of her eyebrows. "I noticed the way he couldn't keep his eyes off you."

Elle almost choked as she picked up her plate and a fork. "Oh, I don't know about that," she said, avoiding Sassy's all-too-knowing gaze.

She needed to steer this conversation train in a different direction. She took a bite of cake, then let out a groan. "Oh man, this is delicious." So much for getting her mind off sex; this dessert was practically orgasmic. The moist chocolate mingled with the slightest coffee flavor, but it also had a bit of a kick. "What's in this? My lips feel numb."

"Oh yeah, that's the Kahlua," Sassy told her. "I told you this cake has a kick. After it's baked, I poke holes in the cake and drizzle extra Kahlua into it, and I also pour a healthy dose into the whipped cream frosting. I make this one every once in a while for my bridge group, and it always makes for a lively afternoon of cards."

"I'll bet," Elle said, taking another bite. Chocolate chips added to the rich chocolate taste, but the light whipped cream frosting balanced perfectly with it. Her tongue was now starting to go numb as well, and she wondered if she should have had such a big piece. Or maybe she should have two. She could use a little liveliness in her life. Although the night before had been pretty lively, she thought as she cut her eyes to the kitchen counter.

Why was she suddenly feeling warm? She needed to stop thinking about Brody—and what happened in the kitchen—and get the focus back on her houseguest. "I noticed Doc Hunter seemed mighty interested in you the other night."

Gah. How was asking about Doc's interest getting the conversation away from the topic of men and passion? At least it wasn't talking about her and Brody's passion.

"Oh yeah, that man's been after me for years," Sassy said with a wave of her hand. "It's the pink hair." She gave a light lift to her pink-streaked curls. "It drives men wild."

Elle chuckled. *Note to self: Check with Carley at the Cut and Curl to see about adding pink to my hair.* "Well, I think he's sweet."

"Doc's a good man. He asked me to dinner this weekend. We go out every once in a while. He was quite a looker in his time. Plus he's a gentleman, a fine conversationalist—and by that, I mean he enjoys talking about other things than his aches and pains and what meds he's currently been prescribed, *and* he's still got all his teeth. It's rare to find all three in a man these days."

"I can imagine."

Sassy peered down at the gray-and-white puppy sleeping soundly on her lap. "I can't stop thinking about this little darling.

I haven't had a pet in the house for years, but I might talk to Bryn about taking this one home when she's ready."

"Aww. I think you should. She seems to already adore you, and I think the companionship would be good. She might even grow up to be a guard dog."

Sassy laughed. "In a town the size of Creedence, there's not much I need to be guarded from, but I do like the idea of having someone to talk to who won't talk back. And I love her coloring. I know she's just a baby, but I think her gray-and-white kind of matches mine."

"Absolutely. All she needs is a pink collar, and you two could be a matched set."

Sassy's eyes lit up. "You're right. Oh, a pink collar would be so cute on her."

"Sounds like we may have found a home for our first rescued pup. I'll put your name on her."

"It's settled then. It will be good to have a little company in the house." She narrowed her eyes at Elle. "How about you? You've been rambling around in that big house for the last several years now. Are you about ready to have some more company in your life?"

"Is this your roundabout way of asking about Brody again, or are you trying to wrangle an invite over for dinner?"

"Both, now that you mention it." Sassy laughed. "But I was really asking about Brody and Mandy. It seems like you've been spending a lot of time with them."

"I have. And I really love hanging out with them. *Both* of them." She twisted the napkin she was holding. "But the idea of starting something with him—I mean, really starting something—scares the heck out of me."

"Why?"

Elle shrugged, fighting tears. "Because I've already had my happily ever after. Well, I didn't get the *after* part, but I got the *happy* part. I had my shot at falling in love with the perfect guy and creating a family, and it just about broke me when I lost it. I can't let myself go through that again. I'm sure Brody feels the same. We've both been in love and thought we had it all, then had it ripped away instead." She focused on the tattered napkin clutched in her fingers. "That changes a person. I can't imagine either one of us would be willing to go all in to commit to that kind of love again."

Sassy nodded. "Well, it's good that you've already decided that for him."

Her sarcasm wasn't lost on Elle. "He's got way more at stake than I do. He's got Mandy to think of. She deserves someone who can go all in—who can be a mother to her and who can love her dad the way he deserves to be loved. And that isn't me. My days of going all in are over. Now I'm more of a stand on the sidelines, holding on to the railing, watch from afar where it's safe kind of person."

"That sounds awful. And *boring*. And desperately lonely."

Elle's voice dropped to a whisper. "I think I'd rather be lonely than take a chance on getting hurt like that again."

"I think the fact that you're even talking about the possibility of a new relationship and that you're having feelings for someone else means you're starting to heal. That sounds like a huge step forward to me." Sassy waved her fork around the farmhouse. "Look at how far you've come in the past month. You've made new friends, you're volunteering at a horse rescue, and you're going *out* into the community. Six months ago, you barely left your house. Now look at you. You're going to the pool and connecting to people, and if I'm not mistaken, you might even be having a little hanky-panky with a hot cowboy." She studied Elle as if she could see into her soul. "Or maybe by the way your cheeks are turning red, you're already doing the dipsy doodle with the dashing animal doctor."

Elle shook her head. "There is no dipsy doodling happening."

Well, what happened on the counter the night before could be deemed as doodling. But they hadn't gone all the way dipsy yet.

Eek—did she just think *yet*?

The fact that she was even considering going dipsy told her she was already in this thing too far.

Sassy put a hand on her leg. "Honey, you're still young, and you have a lot of life ahead of you. I know you're afraid, but that's what life is about, getting up every day and facing your fears and finding joy. I'll tell you love doesn't exist without fear. If the thought of losing somebody doesn't scare the hell out of you, then you're not really in love."

Elle nodded but couldn't speak around the ache in her throat. The things Sassy said made sense.

"I'd be a lot more afraid of *never* falling in love again than I would be of getting hurt again. Something's always going to hurt you. But we don't heal the past by staying in it. We heal the past by moving on and living in the present."

Elle offered her a brave smile. "You're one smart lady, Sassy James."

Sassy shrugged. "My daddy was a preacher. He could spout inspirational wisdom from sunup to sundown. Occasionally some of it stuck." She patted Elle's leg. "You'll find your way. I do believe that. Whether it's with Brody Tate or someone you haven't even met yet, you'll figure it out. When love comes for you, there's no stopping it. And for the record, my money's on Brody."

———————

Elle had just stood to take her and Sassy's plates to the kitchen when she heard a loud clopping noise on the porch. She looked up to see Glory standing at the front door.

"What in heaven's name?" Sassy said, taking a step back as the horse stamped her foot next to the door. "Do the horses around here think they're dogs too?"

"Not usually," Elle said, hurrying to the front door. "How did you get out of the stable?" she asked Glory as she pushed open the screen.

The horse stamped her foot again in response. Then instead of taking a step back, the horse took a step forward, ducking her head as she crossed the threshold.

"Holy crap," Elle cried, leaning her shoulder into the front of the horse's haunches to keep her from coming further into the house. "Oh no, you don't. No horses in the house."

"Is that a rule around here?" Sassy asked, wringing her hands as she backed away.

"I don't know. But it should be." Elle groaned as she pushed against the horse, who stood her ground now halfway into the house. Glory raised her head and let out a whinny, then stamped her foot again.

"Good heavens," Sassy said, grabbing a large bound book off the coffee table and holding it out as if to use it as a weapon against the horse. Thankfully, she'd already returned the puppy to her mother in the pen outside. "What can I do to help?"

Elle glanced back. "I don't think reading her a book is the answer. How's your singing voice?"

"I haven't been kicked out of the church choir yet, but what does that have to do with—" Her words were cut off as Glory advanced another few feet into the house.

Elle's arms were wrapped around the horse's neck and shook with the exertion of trying to hold the horse back. "Sing!"

Sassy dropped the book and planted her feet as she stuck her palm out to the horse and lifted her voice in a clear tenor. "Stop... in the name of love before you break my heart..."

Glory paused in her forward motion and huffed, sending slobber flying as she shook her head.

"Gah." Elle held up her hand to ward off the slobber, then put it back on the horse's neck, twisting her fingers in her mane as she joined in with the chorus, singing loudly. "Think it o-o-ver. Haven't I been good to you?"

"I don't know the rest," Sassy cried.

"It doesn't matter. It's working. Any song will do. This horse loves to be sung to."

"I might have put too much Kahlua in that cake," she muttered.

"Keep singing."

"You ain't nothin' but a hound dog," Sassy sang, giving her hips a little shake. "Cryin' all the time."

The horse took a step back. Elle laughed as she joined in again. "You ain't never caught a rabbit, and you ain't no friend of mine."

They sang through most of the Elvis song and crooned the choruses of a few Beatles' tunes, then Sassy surprised her by going rogue and belting out the lyrics to one of Pink's newest hits. But the tension in the horse eased, and she stepped back out of the house and let Elle lead her toward the barn.

Sassy followed at a reasonable distance but kept up a steady stream of songs.

"I blame you for this." Elle pointed at Shamus who stood in the middle of the yard nibbling on a patch of grass. "How do you keep getting out?"

Shamus chewed a mouthful of grass in response.

"I'll be back for you in a minute," she told him. Thankfully, the other horses were still in the corral. They stood by the fence watching her and Sassy's singing parade as if it were their afternoon entertainment.

She was also thankful that Glory remained docile and obediently walked into the stable.

Elle wiped her arm across her damp brow as she leaned her back against the gate. She grinned at Sassy and held up her hand for a high five. "You did great."

Sassy smacked her hand. "I must say, in all my years of singing, that's the first time I've ever serenaded a horse." She followed Elle out of the barn. "And I'm okay if it's the last."

"Now to get that silly mini-horse back into the corral." Elle peered around the yard, but Shamus was nowhere to be seen. "I don't know how he keeps getting out, but he eventually finds his way back in." Giving up, she walked up the porch steps and almost choked as she spotted the missing horse.

She grabbed the screen door and charged into the house. Neither the mini-horse standing *next* to the coffee table nor the goat standing on *top* of it paid her any mind as they casually licked the remaining cake crumbs from her and Sassy's plates.

"Hold the door, Sassy," she instructed as she shooed the two trespassers out of the living room. "You two rascals get back outside."

Otis bleated his discontent at being evicted from the house, but Elle ignored his annoyance as she herded them out of the house and off the porch. Tiny stood in the yard, peering up at her as if she'd come over to see what all the fuss was about. Either that, or she smelled the cake.

Sassy popped into the house, grabbed her purse, and headed for her car. "I think I've had enough animal excitement for the day. I'm going home to take a nap."

"Thanks for the cake," Elle called with a wave as she steered Shamus toward the barn. Otis had run off and, by the sounds of the yipping puppies coming from the backyard, was probably already trying to sneak back into the house.

Later that night, Elle stared into the refrigerator as she searched for something simple to make for supper. She should have been hungry after her busy afternoon, but her brain was too fried to come up with a meal idea. After she'd finally returned all the animals to their rightful places, she'd cleaned up the dishes and run into town to check on her house. Then she'd spent what was left of the afternoon checking in on Roxy and working on insurance forms and some new marketing ideas she had for the horse rescue.

She put together a simple sandwich and a glass of iced tea, then took them out to the front porch and eased into one of the rocking chairs. She wasn't used to solitude around the place—usually there was so much activity with various people and animals bustling around. But tonight it was peaceful as the horses stood in the corral—*all* of them, and the goat too—and the cows grazed in a far-off pasture. A gray barn cat brushed against her leg, then turned the other direction, stroking her body against Elle's shin in a figure eight before settling down on the porch next to her.

Elle leaned back in the rocker and took a bite of her sandwich as she imagined living a life on the farm. Not this farm, but on a farm with a certain handsome cowboy and his spunky daughter.

She shook her head. No—she couldn't go there, even if it was just in her imagination. Sassy's words churned through her brain, but she couldn't get past the idea that she'd already had her chance. She'd vowed never again to open her heart and let herself love so fully and completely that when that love was ripped from her arms, it left her wrecked and helpless, sobbing in the middle of a cold bathroom floor.

No, she was better off staying safe, sticking to herself and not letting herself ever feel that close to anyone again.

So why did her pulse take off like a jackrabbit as she spotted Brody's truck turning from the highway and heading toward her?

She jumped as a loud bleat sounded from the porch steps and she turned to see Otis clopping up the porch steps. He stopped in front of her to stare at the remaining few bites of sandwich left on her plate. He bleated again, then looked away as if to say, *I don't really need the sandwich, but I'll take it off your hands if you think it will be of some help to you.*

She chuckled as she pushed the plate toward the goat. "Take it. It's yours." She wasn't that hungry anyway.

Mandy waved and climbed from the truck, then barreled toward Elle. "Hey. How is Roxy doing? How are the puppies? Have they been eating? Are they still latching on?"

Elle held up her hands. "Whoa there. One question at a time." She pushed up from the rocking chair. "Or better yet, why don't we go check on them and you can answer those questions for yourself?"

"Good idea," Mandy said, already pushing through the screen door and racing toward Elle's bedroom.

"Sorry," Brody said. "We don't mean to keep bugging you, but she's been dying to get back out here. We won't stay long."

"It's fine. I'm glad to have the company. I was just sitting out here thinking about how I wasn't used to the farm being so quiet." She nodded to the goat. "Then Otis came up and asked to share my sandwich with me."

"I don't know that I would call that goat good company."

He held the door, then followed her inside. His hand brushed over her back as she walked past him, and she wondered if they'd ever have another chance to dipsy doodle. She banished all thoughts of that nature as she walked into her bedroom and saw the mama dog curled protectively around the two new puppies. They weren't hers, but she had already accepted them and lovingly licked their heads as they nursed.

Her tail wagged, and her eyes were bright. She had her head up, and she gave a whine and a butt wiggle as Elle approached the closet. "Hi, sweetie, how you doin'?" Elle cooed as she sat down on the floor next to the dog.

Mandy was already sitting on the other side. She beamed up at Brody and Elle. "She's doing so great. She looks like a different dog—like she's happy now. Last night, she seemed so sad it made my heart hurt. But she's doing so much better today."

"She is," Brody replied, squatting down to take a look at the dog. He lifted each pup and gave it a cursory exam, and Roxy licked each puppy's face as he set it back down next to her. "The pups look good. The mama dog looks good." He lifted the bandages and surveyed her bites and cuts. "She seems in pretty great shape."

"She ate all the food I put out for her and drank some of the water." Elle gestured to the half-empty water dish and licked-clean food bowl that she'd set near the dog's head earlier in the day.

The sound of a horn honking drew their attention, and Elle pushed up from the floor. "Who could that be?"

"Maybe Bryn and Zane are back," Mandy said, racing out the bedroom door.

The honking got more insistent as Brody and Elle followed the girl. Elle didn't recognize the older model Honda that was heading down the driveway, but as they got closer, she recognized the passenger who was waving wildly and leaning toward the driver to hit the horn.

Elle frowned. "What the heck is he doing here?"

CHAPTER 17

"It's Milo," Mandy cried, already at the front door. "And that must be his mom. What's Milo doing here?"

"The better question is why the heck is he honking the horn like that?" Brody asked. He held the door that his daughter had just slammed for Elle, and they walked out onto the porch together.

The kid had the door open before the car even came to a full stop, and Brody heard the boy's mother calling for him to wait for her.

Milo stumbled from the car, a bundled towel wrapped in his arms. "I found them," he yelled, a huge smile cracking his face. "I went back, and I found them."

The woman jumped out the other side of the car and slammed the door. "We're sorry to stop by unannounced, but we were just so excited, and we knew you'd want to know right away."

The boy raced up the porch steps, stumbling on the top one but catching himself before he pitched forward.

Brody grabbed his arm to steady him. "Careful there, son. Slow down and tell us what's going on." Milo's body was shaking, and he couldn't seem to catch his breath. Brody hoped the kid wasn't having an asthma attack.

The boy stopped on the front porch and took a deep breath, then carefully pulled back the top of the towel to reveal two wiggling, cream-colored puppies. "I found them," he whispered, his eyes filling with tears as he passed the puppies to Mandy.

"I can't believe it. I can't believe it," Mandy repeated as she took the puppies in her arms. Tears were falling down her cheeks as she laughed and cried. "You did it, Milo. But how? How did you find them?"

"My mom wanted to go for a walk, and I wanted to try to find your lost shoe. I told my mom what happened, and we decided to look around some more, just in case we saw anything. And we did. We found them between two big rocks back behind where you found the dog. They were really down in there, but we heard them crying. Best I can figure is one of those coyotes must have dropped them and not been able to get to them again."

Brody clapped a hand on Milo's shoulder. "You did good, son. I'd given up on finding either of them. And they wouldn't have lasted another day on their own."

The woman with him held out her hand. "I'm Jillian, Milo's mom." She was tall and curvy and had her long, dark brown hair pulled into a braid that hung over her shoulder. She wore khaki shorts, scuffed hiking boots, and a lavender T-shirt with an open book on the front that read *My patronus is a bookworm*. Her smile was warm and friendly, and she seemed just as excited about the find as her son. "We couldn't believe it when we found them. We were so happy, we just grabbed them and drove out here as fast as we could."

"How did you know where to find us?" Elle asked, not taking her eyes off the puppies. She wasn't crying like his daughter was, but her eyes were brimming with tears as she reached out to tenderly stroke the head of one of the puppies.

She shrugged. "Milo told me about you yesterday and how you'd been so nice to him at the pool and then everything that happened with the dog. I mentioned the story to someone at the library today and they told me about the fire at your house and that you were staying out here. It's a small town, you know."

Did they ever.

"Let's take them back to their mom," Mandy cried. "She's going to be so happy."

They entered the house as a group and followed Mandy down the hall to Elle's bedroom. Jillian hung back by the door. "You all go ahead. I don't want to spook her."

Mandy and Milo slowly approached and crouched on the floor outside the closet door. Roxy lifted her head, her tail already wagging. She let out a whine as Mandy held the puppies in the towel out to her.

The new puppies were asleep, curled against the dog's swollen belly. But Roxy whined and pushed to her feet, trying to get closer to the towel. The puppies looked to be about three weeks old, their eyes were barely open, and they made frantic, whimpering yips as their mother licked their heads and nuzzled their faces. Roxy's tail was going crazy, wagging and whirling at a wild pace. She let out a low moan and flopped down on the floor, nudging the pups toward her tummy.

The puppies seemed to be just as excited about eating as they were to be reunited with their mother. They wiggled their bodies and heads, one of the pup's mouth missing its target in his frantic attempt to latch on. He finally got it and sucked greedily, his body squirming closer to his mother's as he let out a whine.

"Oh, Dad," Mandy said, her eyes filled with tears as she threw her arms around him. "They're so excited to see each other. I'm so happy for them."

He smiled as he hugged his daughter and dropped a kiss on her head. "I know, honey," he said, swallowing back the lump in his throat. He snuck a glance at Elle. She had tears running down her cheeks and wasn't even trying to wipe them away as she watched the puppies cuddle in closer to their mother, both of them nursing now. He wrapped an arm around her shoulder and pulled her into his and Mandy's hug.

Her shoulders trembled as she gripped his back. She offered him a brave smile as she looked up at him. She didn't have to say anything. He knew. He nodded his head and pulled her close, trying not to think about how well the three of them already fit together and the fact that he and Elle were already silently communicating with each other.

Jillian eased into the room and sat on the floor behind her son, who Brody had seen discreetly wipe what could have been a stray tear from his cheek. It seemed no one wanted to leave, and they spent the next fifteen minutes just watching as the other puppies woke up and all of them squirmed and wiggled into a pile together as they all snuggled against Roxy's belly. For her part, the mother dog licked and nosed the heads of all of them, her tail still wagging and her eyes bright as she tended to her new blended family.

"My leg is asleep," Mandy finally said, carefully standing up and shaking her leg.

"My butt is asleep," Milo said, earning a giggle from Mandy as he got up with her and rubbed his rear end.

"Nice, Son," Jillian said, pushing up from the floor. "You sure know how to make me proud." But she smiled as she rubbed her own fanny. She put a hand on Elle's arm. "Thanks so much for letting us stay and watch the puppies."

"Oh my gosh, thank *you*," Elle said, throwing her arms around the other woman. "Thank you for finding the puppies and for bringing them right out here. I think it's safe to say you made all of our nights."

They left the family of dogs and all trooped into the living room to tell Milo and Jillian goodbye. The women hugged again and exchanged numbers, with Elle promising to keep in touch and send pics of the new puppies.

"I've got some hamburger in the fridge," Elle said after the mother and son drove away. "I could make some tacos or spaghetti if you all want to stay for supper."

"Sounds good to me," Mandy said.

"Actually, we can't stay," Brody told her, trying to ignore the slump of her shoulders. "Not tonight."

"Oh. Okay," Elle said.

"It's just that we've got other plans."

Mandy drew her brows together in a skeptical expression but didn't say anything.

"It's no problem. Really. Another night." Elle twisted her hands in front of her and avoided looking in his eye.

Damn. He felt like a schmuck. But he couldn't help it. He needed time to think. And he couldn't do that sitting across the table from her, eating tacos as she laughed and joked with his daughter. They already felt too much like a family.

And what had happened the night before had shook him to his core. He was getting too close, wanting too much. Heck, he'd been here less than an hour and he'd already had Elle wrapped in his arms. He couldn't keep his hands off her.

No, it was best they went home tonight. He needed to figure out what the hell he was doing. And what he was going to do about this woman.

"Let's go, kiddo," he told Mandy.

She frowned as she looked from him to Elle. "Okay. But we *are* still meeting you for the Hay Day Celebration tomorrow, right?"

Elle had been standing at the door, her eyes wide like a rabbit frozen on the highway. Hell, he couldn't blame her for being confused—he was giving off wildly mixed signals. One minute he was kissing her and handling her hoo-haw, the next he was turning down supper and practically racing out the door.

"Um," she said, sucking her bottom lip under her top teeth—a move that drove him crazy. "I'm not sure."

Mandy glared at her father.

"Yes," he relented. "Of course. We're *all* going to the Hay Day Celebration tomorrow."

"And we're going *together*, right?"

"Yes, we're going together."

"Good." Mandy gave Elle a hug, then turned to her dad and tilted her head toward Elle.

Dang. His daughter was so bossy. But he got her meaning, and he would only make things worse if he didn't give Elle a hug now. He stepped toward her and held out his arms. She'd seen

Mandy's gesture, and the hug she gave him in return was stiff and awkward.

But she smelled amazing, and at the last second, he pulled her close and pressed a kiss to the side of her temple. As if the kiss were magic, she relaxed into him and hugged him back. "See you tomorrow," he said into her hair before letting her go.

Mandy had gone into the kitchen to say goodbye to Grace and the puppies, but she followed him outside after he let go of Elle. "What the heck was that all about?" she asked when they were in the truck and heading away from the house.

"What?"

"Don't *what* me. Elle offered to make us supper and you said no and then you *fibbed*."

"Fibbed?"

"Yeah. Fibbed. Or do you want to tell me what are these great *other plans* we supposedly have?"

"I, um, well, I was just thinking we could go out for hamburgers tonight. Just you and me."

His daughter rolled her eyes with the expertise of a teenager. "Oh brother. You're not even good at this. You totally just made that up right now."

Crud. Why did his kid have to be so smart?

He dragged his hand through his hair. "Look, we've been spending a lot of time with Elle, and I just thought maybe she could use a break from us."

"But *she's* the one who invited *us* to stay."

"I know."

Mandy narrowed her eyes. "So really, *you* are the one who wants a break from her."

He shrugged. "I don't know. I guess. Maybe."

"But why? I thought you liked her."

"I do like her." *I like her a lot.* He shook his head. "Which is why I didn't want to stay for supper."

Mandy wrinkled her nose. "That doesn't even make sense."

It didn't to him either. But it had at the time. *Hadn't it?* "It's complicated, kiddo."

"It doesn't seem like it. Either you like her or you don't."

"It's not always that easy."

"You're weird, Dad."

"I know," he said, ruffling her hair and offering her a grin. "But that's what makes me awesome."

The next morning, Elle putzed around the house as she tried not to think about a certain handsome cowboy. She'd already fed and brushed the horses and set up a radio inside the barn so Glory could hear singing whenever she wanted.

She'd dusted, ran the vacuum, threw in a load of laundry, and mopped the kitchen floor. When none of that did the trick, she pulled out her laptop and did some work on the horse rescue website, answered some emails, and scrolled through Facebook. She took turns cuddling Grace's and Roxy's puppies, filling her lap with adorable, fuzzy distractions. She swore Peanut Butter had already gained another pound. But nothing kept her mind from continually coming back to Brody.

What was going on with him? He'd been so weird the night before when she'd invited him and Mandy to supper.

Come to think of it, he'd been acting sort of strange ever since their "close encounter" in the kitchen.

Her phone rang, and she tried not to be disappointed that the call was from Bryn instead of Brody.

Bryn's enthusiastic greeting quickly put a smile on her face. She'd forgotten how great it was to have a woman friend. She found herself pouring out everything that had happened in the days since Bryn had been gone.

She pulled a fresh load of towels from the dryer and stood in the laundry room to fold it as they talked. "Now tell me what's happening with you. How's the trip? How is Montana? How's your cousin?"

"Trip's going great. Montana is gorgeous. And Cade's good. Turns out the reason he was getting evicted was because his building is getting torn down to bring in some fancy strip mall and a chain restaurant. So he's a little salty about that. It took a little convincing on my part, but overall he seems excited about coming to Colorado."

"I can imagine. I've been on the receiving end of your *little convincing*," Elle said, teasing her friend. "So when are you heading back?"

"Probably not for a couple days still."

"Uh-oh. Does that mean you're going to miss the Hay Day Celebration?"

"Yeah. It looks that way. I know Mandy's going to be bummed. And so am I. I haven't missed one in years, but it can't be helped. Family comes first, and I need to take care of mine."

Elle hugged a warm towel as loneliness for her family settled over her like a damp blanket on a cloudy day.

"You're still going though, right?" Bryn asked.

She shook off the gloom and forced a smile. "You sound like Mandy. Everyone's sure concerned about me going to the fairgrounds to walk around and look at some goats. If I really want to see a goat, I can go outside and stare at Otis."

"He'll stare right back until you give him a snack."

"True. And yes, I'm going. I told Mandy I'd be there, and I'm excited to see her and Shamus's costumes. She hasn't let me see them yet. She wants it to be a surprise."

"Take pictures for me. They're going to be adorable."

A knock sounded at the door, and Elle's stomach dropped. It hadn't been Brody on the phone; maybe he'd come by in person to talk. That made more sense anyway. She looked down at the shorts and tank top she was wearing and brushed at the dust that had settled across the front of her shirt from her cleaning frenzy. "I gotta go, Bryn. Someone's at the door. Drive safe, and I'll call you later."

"Sounds good. Have fun today. And text me pictures later."

Another thump sounded at the front door, and Elle pushed her phone in her pocket and hurried from the laundry room.

She came to a full stop in the middle of the living room as she caught sight of who was standing on the other side of the screen door. And it sure wasn't Brody.

CHAPTER 18

ELLE OPENED THE FRONT DOOR AND PEERED DOWN AT HER visitors. "Since when do you knock?"

"Bleat," Otis answered, which could have meant *It's a recent skill I acquired* or *Knocking on doors is only one of my many talents*.

Tiny stood next to him and looked up at Elle with what could only be regarded as a smile on her face. She gave a snuffling snort and pushed past Elle's leg, trotting into the house and lying down on the floor next to the sofa.

"Make yourself at home," Elle said to the pig, then turned back to the goat and pushed out her leg to block his entry. "Not you."

"Bleat."

"Sorry, but last time you were in the house, you ate a throw pillow. Which was quite rude because Bryn left me in charge of her house, and I *had* planned to have it completely intact when she returned."

The goat hung his head, which could have been a show of remorse or, in the case of this goat, could have been a clever ploy to gain sympathy and another chance at a throw pillow. "Bleat."

Elle shook her head and stood her ground. "I'm not going to argue with you. But I will bring you a carrot." She closed the screen door and hooked the latch, learning her lesson from the last time the goat let himself in.

She hurried to the refrigerator and grabbed a carrot, her lips curving in a sly grin as she heard the metallic clink of the latch. "I knew you'd try to sneak in," she told the goat as she caught him with his head pushing against the door.

Releasing the latch, she opened the door and held out the carrot. The dang goat faked like it was going for the carrot, but instead slipped past her and ran into the house.

"Oh no you don't." She tossed the carrot on the kitchen table as she gave chase.

"Bleatttt." The goat jumped onto the sofa, grabbed one of the smaller throw pillows, and took off again.

Elle ran around one side of the sofa, but the goat switched direction and jumped onto the love seat. Squaring his legs, the pillow hanging from his teeth, he stared at her as if daring her to make a reach for it.

"Give me that pillow, you stinker." She carefully approached from one side and made a grab for it. But the goat was too fast. He jumped off the love seat, hopped over the coffee table, and vaulted over the pig as he leaped back onto the other side.

The sound of sharp toenails on the hardwood came from down the hall, and Roxy raced into the living room and shot up onto the love seat next to Elle. Her ears were up as she let out a growl and a warning bark at the goat.

"Aww, did you come to save me?" Elle said, reaching down to cuddle the dog's chin. "I'm okay. He's not hurting me." She turned and narrowed her eyes at the goat. "But I might hurt *him* if he doesn't give me back that pillow."

She made another grab for the pillow, this time snatching a corner. She held on for a second, and Roxy jumped onto the coffee table between them and sank her teeth into the side of the pillow Elle was holding. She shook her head and let out another fierce growl.

Elle tried to keep her stare stern, facing down the goat with a serious glare. But Otis pulled back on the pillow, and Roxy's legs lifted off the coffee table. Elle shrieked, then belted out a burst of laughter as she let go of the pillow and grabbed the dog.

Roxy wasn't letting go of the pillow, so now Elle was playing tug of war with the goat, the pillow, *and* the growling dog in the middle. She was pulling, but she was laughing so hard, she had no chance of winning this battle. She bent forward, crossing her legs to keep from peeing herself. "Let go, Roxy," Elle told the dog.

She let go for just a second, but it was long enough for Otis to yank back the pillow, jump over the arm of the sofa, and sprint around the kitchen table. Roxy let out a yip and chased after the goat. She got another bite of the pillow corner and pulled back, baring her teeth as she widened her stance and held her ground. But the goat was too strong and the hardwood floor was too slick from Elle's earlier polishing.

The goat took a step back and the dog, still in her fighter stance, just slid forward on the polished floor. Continuing back, Otis dragged Roxy another five feet before the fabric of the pillow ripped and the dog's forward progress halted, a corner of fabric and pillow fluff dangling from her mouth. Which seemed to prove to her that she'd won because she dropped her part of the pillow, then flopped down on the floor and rested her head on it.

"Good dog" was all Elle could think to say.

Her phone dinged, and she blew up her bangs and threw her hands at the goat. "Fine. Keep the stupid pillow. It's ruined anyway. But you're not getting the carrot now."

Otis answered her by dropping the pillow, leaping onto the closest chair, and snatching the carrot from the table. He munched at the carrot while raising a bushy eyebrow and fixing her with a wry stare, as if to say, *Oh, yeah? What are you going to do about it, sister?*

She gave up, still laughing as she dug out her phone. Peering down at it, her smile fell, and she slumped on the sofa as she read the text that had just come in from Brody. Apparently they weren't going to the Hay Day Celebration together after all.

———

"I don't know why we couldn't have still picked Elle up and brought her with us," Mandy whined to her father as they pulled into the parking lot of the fairgrounds.

Brody grumbled a response, annoyed at the number of cars already there as he searched for a parking space. He was thankful they'd brought Shamus down in the horse trailer earlier that day. "She's still going to meet us here. But there was no reason for her to come an hour early just so she could sit around and watch you register."

"She could have helped with Shamus."

Dang. What was he? Chopped liver? "*I'll* help with Shamus. You know we got along just fine before we met Elle."

"I know. But I like Elle. And I thought you did too."

"I do."

"Well, most people like hanging out together when they like each other." She narrowed her eyes. "You know, Dad, I'm not a kid anymore. I'm almost eleven, and I know about things."

"What things?" he asked, his voice coming out a little strangled.

"Things like what happens when a guy and a girl like each other."

He smacked his palm against his forehead. "Who have you been talking to?"

"No one. But I watch TV, ya know?"

"That's it—I'm canceling cable."

She rolled her eyes. "Oh brother. Overreact much?" she asked, stealing a quote he often used on her. "All I'm saying is that it seems like you and Elle really like each other. I see how you get all googly-eyed when you look at each other. And since she's been around, you laugh a lot more."

His daughter didn't seem to notice when her dirty clothes were overflowing the hamper or when there was a sink full of dishes to go into the dishwasher, but let him make googly eyes *one* time and *that* she notices. Wait. His lips pulled down in a frown. "I don't make googly eyes."

Mandy shrugged. "Okay. Okay. I'm just saying that if you *did* want to make googly eyes with Elle, or if you wanted to hold her hand or kiss her or whatever, I just want you to know, I'm okay with that."

"I'd be okay with you staying in your lane and keeping *out* of my love life, or lack thereof."

Love life?

Undeterred by his tone, she cocked an eyebrow at him in an expression that far belied her ten, almost eleven, years. "Geez. Why are you so grumpy?"

"I'm *not* grumpy," he practically growled in response.

She kept her eyebrow cocked. "Oh yeah, and I'm the Queen of England."

"You're hilarious."

She raised her voice to a high pitch and feigned a British accent. "What did you say, peasant? I can't hear you from up here on my bloody throne."

This time it was his turn to raise an eyebrow. "*Bloody* throne? What kind of queen are you?"

She dissolved into giggles. "That's what English people always say on television—bloody this and bloody that. And they also say *wanker* a lot."

He almost choked and pressed his lips together to keep from laughing. "I'd rather you not use either *bloody* or *wanker* in conversation."

"What *is* a wanker? Like a jerk, right?"

"Uhh, yes, it is used that way. And I'm not completely certain on the exact definition, but I'm pretty sure it also refers to something about a part of the anatomy that boys have but girls don't."

Her eyes widened, then she wrinkled her nose as if she'd smelled something bad. "Oh."

He laughed and made an effort to change the subject. "Let's quit talking about me and focus on you. I'm excited for your event tonight."

"Me too. I don't have to win, but it would be fun to get a ribbon at least." She gave her dad a side-eyed look, then grinned. "Who am I kidding? I totally want to win."

Brody chuckled. "I totally want you to win too." He reached over to ruffle her hair. "And I'm sorry if I'm a little crabby. It's getting close to five, and I didn't have much lunch. I must be getting hungry."

"Hmm. You mean 'hangry'?"

He gave her a look of wide-eyed innocence. "Who me? I'm not angry." He slammed on the brakes as a guy in a truck pulled out in front of him and gunned it to the empty parking spot he was heading toward. "Hey, watch it, you idiot!"

"Yeah," Mandy yelled, leaning forward in her seat. "Watch it, you bloody wanker!"

This time, it was his turn to give her the side-eye, but the wide-eyed innocent look she tried didn't work any better on him than his had on her.

She offered him a sheepish grin and another shrug. "Sorry, Dad. But at least we proved you aren't angry."

———

The annual Hay Day Celebration turned out to be quite the event. It seemed like the whole town had turned out to wander through the craft booths and look at the livestock on display. Dusk was just settling in and the sugary scent of cotton candy filled the air. String lights crisscrossed over the alleyways, giving the dusty fairgrounds an almost magical feel. Like anything could happen.

Elle casually scanned the crowd of people milling around the craft booths and tried not to be anxious as she waited for Brody. What was she all worked up about anyway? There was no reason to be nervous. It's not like this was a *date* or anything. It was just two friends wandering around a craft show and looking at some animals.

So why did her stomach do a flip when she recognized the

tall man who'd just stepped out of the crowd? The flip had been enough, but now a battalion of butterflies had just taken off in her belly as he saw her and a grin broke across his face. A grin meant just for her.

They walked toward each other, then did that weird thing when one went in for a high five and the other went in for a hug and the whole thing turned into an awkward one-armed chest bump.

Unfortunately, she'd been the one going in for the hug. She pressed her arms against her sides to keep them from embarrassing her again. "So, did you get Mandy and Shamus all registered?"

"Yeah, it took forever. You should be glad we didn't drag you along and make you wait through that."

"I would have been okay. But I was happy to meet you too."

They both looked around as if trying to think of something to say. Which was also weird. They didn't usually do awkward silences.

"You look nice," he finally said.

"Thanks." She hadn't been sure what to wear, especially since her wardrobe choices were so sparse thanks to the fire. But she'd found a cute pink-and-white floral summer dress in her laundry basket that she'd recently worn to go to lunch with Bryn. It was light and flowy in a kind of bohemian style and came to just above her knees. She'd worn sandals with it to lunch, but tonight she'd paired it with her favorite cowboy boots. "So do you."

He did look nice. He had on jeans and square-toed cowboy boots and a light-blue button-up shirt that brought out the gorgeous blue of his eyes.

"Thanks." He looked down the fairway behind her as if grasping for something else to say. Geez, this was getting painful. "So, uh, how was your afternoon?"

"Good. I talked to Bryn, then got into a tug-of-war with Otis."

He chuckled as she filled him in on the fight for the throw pillow, but the laugh didn't go all the way to his eyes.

She nudged his arm as they turned to head toward the first row of stalls. "I can't tell if you're happy to see me. Or not."

"I am." He sighed as he peered over at her. "More than I want to admit."

"That's a pretty heavy sigh for someone who claims to be happy."

"I *am* glad to be here. And with you. I'm just a little freaked out by how happy it does make me."

"Ahh," she said. "I get that. And I can see the happiness practically spewing from your bunched eyebrows and that frown you're sporting."

He let out a chuckle and converted his frown into an exaggerated smile. "Better?"

Elle laughed. "Oh my gosh, *so* much better. Now instead of looking like you ate a sour hedge apple, you just look like you're constipated."

A loud laugh burst from him. "You surprise me, Elle. I love that I just never know what's gonna come out of your mouth."

You could shut me up by planting a kiss on my mouth. And she really wished he would shut her up. Had she really just told him he looked *constipated*? Ugh. No wonder he was confused about if he wanted to be around her or not.

She pointed to a food vendor ahead of them. "How about we put something *in* our mouths and grab some food?"

He grinned, and this time his smile was genuine. "Good idea."

Forty minutes later, after gorging themselves on corn dogs, ribbon fries, and sodas, they had made their way through the majority of the craft booths and still had almost an hour before Mandy's event started.

"What should we do now?" Elle asked, as they stopped at the end of the row. She didn't really care what they did. She was having fun just wandering around with him. He had loosened up a bit as they ate and seemed back to his normal fun self.

And she wasn't the only one who thought so. It seemed like the guy knew everyone there, and they all wanted to stop and visit with him—about the clinic, about their animals, about Mandy. And from all the side-eyes she got, it was obvious they wanted to chat about her too.

Brody took it all in stride, patiently listening to pet stories and answering questions about Mandy. But he was also great at introducing her and bringing her into the conversation. Although she noticed a few snooty stares, especially from single women who didn't seem too thrilled that one of Creedence's most eligible bachelors was wandering around the fairgrounds and laughing with a woman, most people were warm and friendly, a few offering kind words about Ryan or sharing how they knew him.

The reminders of her husband had her cringing. Was she being disloyal to his memory by being here with Brody? Sassy's words of wisdom came back to her. Ryan wouldn't want her to hole up in their house and grieve him forever. He loved life, and he loved this town, and she had to believe that he would want her getting out in it and meeting the people and experiencing all the great things Creedence had to offer. Although she wasn't sure he'd be as excited about her "experiencing" the handsome cowboy.

But Brody had said that he and Ryan had known each other in high school, and that they'd been friends even. And seriously, how could anyone *not* like Brody? He was charming and funny, and it felt like the whole town loved him.

"Hey, Doc," a loud voice yelled toward them as they turned toward the livestock barns. "Why don't you come over here and kiss my ass?"

Hmmm...apparently not *everyone* loved him.

CHAPTER 19

BRODY'S ARMS TENSED AT HIS SIDES, HIS BODY INSTINCTIVELY trying to protect Elle. Who the hell was yelling at him? And wanting to pick a fight?

Although the way his emotions had been running the gamut the last few days, maybe a little brawl was just what he needed to get out some of his frustration. It always used to work when he was playing hockey and would check one of the other players into the boards.

He inhaled, ready to turn and drop his gloves—figuratively, at least.

But Elle's surprise turned to amusement as she peered over his shoulder. She laughed as she turned him around and pointed to the sign of the booth above the heckler's head.

The sign read *Kiss My Ass* in bold letters, then smaller letters in the line below offered a chance to kiss Clyde the donkey for ten dollars a smooch. A donkey wearing a straw hat and a bow tie stood in the pen below the sign. A name placard hanging around the donkey's neck read *Clyde*.

"Come on, Doc. It's for a good cause," the farmer standing next to Clyde hollered as she and Brody laughed and approached the booth.

"Good to see you, Ed," Brody said, shaking the older man's hand. "This is Elle Brooks. She lives in town, but she helps out with the new horse rescue at the Callahan ranch. Elle, this is Ed. His farm is about ten miles on up the highway from Bryn's."

"Nice to meet you, Miss Brooks," Ed said, shaking her hand and offering her a sly wink. "Could I interest *you* in kissing my ass?"

Elle laughed and nudged Brody. "Thanks for the offer, but I think I'm going to let Dr. Tate do the honors this time."

"Suit yourself. Clyde isn't particular. He'll let just about anyone give him a smooch. Although he did get a little riled when old Fred Johnson's widow tried to give him a smack." The farmer lowered his voice conspiratorially. "That woman's got a mustache bigger than mine."

"Oh no," Elle said, covering her mouth. "I hope not." Ed sported quite a thick, silver mustache and a full beard.

Chuckling and shaking his head, Brody dug out his wallet and passed Ed a ten-dollar bill. "What part of Clyde do I have to kiss?"

"Whatever part suits your fancy," the older farmer told him with a grin. "Like I said, Clyde isn't particular."

"I just wish you were a girl donkey," Brody said, then patted the donkey's neck. "No offense, Clyde. I'm sure you're a very skilled kisser."

The donkey lifted his head and let out a loud bray as if to say, *You bet your Clyde I am.*

Elle pressed her lips together, trying not to laugh. "Pucker up there, Dr. Tate."

Brody made an exaggerated puckering motion with his mouth as if warming up for the kiss.

"Wait," Elle said, pulling her phone from her pocket. "I've got to get a picture. We need to capture this moment for posterity."

"More like for *posterior*-erity," he said, with a wry smirk. "Make sure you get my good side." He patted the donkey's neck, then leaned in and gave it a loud smack next to its ear.

"Wait, I didn't get a great shot," Elle said, giggling as she held up her phone. "I think you'll have to do it again."

"That'll be another ten bucks," Ed told them, holding out his hand.

Brody shrugged. "I think I'm tapped out."

"Oh, don't worry. I've got cash," Elle told the farmer, pulling a twenty from her pocket and handing it to the man. "Make it a double." She waved to Brody. "Get in there, sir."

"You should be paying me," he told Ed. "Clyde seems to be enjoying this a little too much. I think he just tried to slip me the tongue."

"You wish," Ed said.

Brody held the donkey's head as he peered at his mouth. "Do you think there's any chance this donkey is going to turn into a princess if I kiss it again?"

"I think it's worth the effort to try," Elle said, smothering a giggle with her hand. "Pucker up."

Brody gave the donkey another exaggerated kiss on the side of his head and held his lips there long enough for Elle to snap a picture. "You're enjoying this way too much," he told her. She was getting such a kick out of the thing, and he loved to hear her laugh. Besides, it wasn't the first time he'd had his face pressed against the side of a donkey.

"Wow, all that smoochin' made me hungry," he said as they waved goodbye to Ed and walked away from Clyde's booth. "And I need to get the taste of Clyde out of my mouth. Let's grab a snack."

"How can you be hungry? You just had a corn dog and ribbon fries."

"That was like half an hour ago. And that was supper. Now I'm hungry for dessert." And he needed something to do with his mouth so he wasn't tempted to pull her behind one of the buildings and eat her for dessert. All he could think about was getting her alone and kissing her senseless. And not like he'd kissed Clyde. Although that donkey really had tried to slip him the tongue.

She shrugged and pointed to a booth ahead of them. "I could go for a caramel apple."

He bought Elle an apple and got a cone of cotton candy for himself. He liked how she automatically held out the apple for him to take a bite. He bit off a section, then offered his cotton candy to her.

She tore off a tiny portion of the sugary floss and stuck it in her mouth. "I don't know how you can eat that whole thing. It's so good, but if I eat more than a little bit, it hurts my teeth."

"Mine too, but I still love the stuff." He chuckled and nodded to her apple. "The caramel on that thing will pull your teeth right out of your head."

They laughed as they walked down the fairway. Brody was conscious of every time her shoulder bumped his or the back of her hand brushed against his. He wanted to take her hand, to hold it as they walked, but he knew doing so would start the gossip chain of Creedence flowing faster than Otis could devour a dandelion. Introducing her around and being seen together was one thing; walking around hand in hand was another thing entirely. That made a statement. And he wasn't sure he, or Elle, was ready for that.

But it was still okay. He felt good, happy, just being with her. She made him laugh, and he just flat-out enjoyed her company. For now, that was enough.

Yeah, keep telling yourself that, buddy.

———

"Now we just need to find Mandy," Brody told Elle fifteen minutes later as they made it to the end of the fairway and tossed the trash from their snacks. "I can't wait for you to see her. Both Bryn and my mom helped her with the costumes for her and the horse." They strolled through the livestock barn looking for the girl. Most of the stalls contained goats and sheep, but a few had the occasional calf and one held a black-and-pink potbellied pig.

"There doesn't seem to be a lot of other miniature horses," Elle noted.

"No, I only saw one other one. Hopefully that means Mandy has a chance at taking a ribbon." He pointed to an empty stall ahead. "That's where Shamus should be. Maybe Mandy took him out to walk him in the corral."

They rounded the last stall, and Elle caught sight of Mandy standing outside with Milo and a couple of other kids. "There she is," she said, pointing toward the girl.

She had Shamus on a lead rope, and the horse looked adorably ridiculous in his costume. He wore a tan horse blanket and had a fluffy lion's mane with two round ears around his face. Four bands of matching tufted fur surrounded each of his legs above his hooves. Mandy wore a blue-gingham dress with a white pinafore, and her hair had been braided into two pigtails and tied with blue ribbons. She wore red cowboy boots that sparkled with ruby glitter.

Elle raised her hand to cover her mouth. "Oh my gosh, they're so cute. She's Dorothy from *The Wizard of Oz*, and he's the Cowardly Lion. That is so great."

But Brody didn't seem interested in their costumes. His arm tensed, and Elle glanced up to see his mouth set in a tight line. "That Jasmine girl is with her. And I think it's high time I gave that kid a piece of my mind."

Elle reached for his arm. "Wait. Remember you told Mandy you'd give her a chance to solve this on her own."

He stopped and glared down at her. "Yeah, well, I lied."

Elle chuckled, hoping he was actually making a joke. "No, you didn't." She pulled him to the edge of the door. From there, they could see and hear the kids, but the kids couldn't see them. "Let's just watch a few minutes before we decide to step in."

Jasmine had one hand planted on her hip. Her two cohorts flanked her either side, like she was Rizzo and they were the Pink Ladies. "What's he supposed to be?" she asked, pointing at Shamus and wrinkling her nose.

Mandy wasn't fazed. "Duh. He's the Cowardly Lion from *The Wizard of Oz*. Anyone could tell that."

Score one for Mandy. She wasn't backing down.

"It figures you have a horse that's a coward. And now we know why you smell like horses. You have one as a pet."

A low growl emitted from Brody's throat, but Elle gripped his bicep, holding him back.

Milo took a step forward to stand next to Mandy. "I think horses are cool. I wish I had one."

Shamus leaned his head forward and sniffed one of the Pink Ladies. The girl giggled and reached to pet the adorable horse's head, then froze, her hand midair as Jasmine glared in her direction. She winced and dropped her hand back to her side.

Mandy looked from Milo to Jasmine, then must have taken courage from the support of the cute boy standing at her side. She pushed back her shoulders and stood a little taller. "Yeah, what have you got against horses anyway? Shamus is awesome." She passed a carrot to the girl standing on Jasmine's other side. "You can feed him. He loves carrots."

The girl hesitated as she cut her eyes to Jasmine but must have decided the act of getting to feed the miniature horse a carrot was worth earning the other girl's wrath, because she took the carrot from Mandy and held it out to the little horse. She giggled as he delicately took it from her hand.

"That's Molly. Mandy said she used to be her friend," Elle whispered to Brody.

"Yeah, I remember her. She's been out to the house a couple of times. But that was before Jasmine moved to town."

Molly hazarded a shy smile at Mandy.

"See how neat that was?" Milo said, rubbing a hand over Shamus's neck. "And he's really soft. You can pet him. This dude is awesome."

The girl raised her chin as she turned to Jasmine. "I agree with Milo. I think horses are cool."

Jasmine glared daggers at Molly. "Don't you dare pet that horse," she threatened through gritted teeth.

"Come on, Jasmine," Molly said. "He's cute. Just pet him once."

The horse raised his head and took a step toward Jasmine, as if he understood what Molly was saying.

"Gah! Get away!" Jasmine raised her hands in genuine fear and stumbled back a few steps. Her back foot landed in a pile of fresh horse droppings and slid out from under her, and she went down hard on her bottom.

For a second, no one moved, then one of the girls pointed at Jasmine and started to laugh. The other girl joined in, but neither Mandy nor Milo did.

"It's not funny," Mandy said as she passed Milo the lead rope and hurried to Jasmine, holding out her hand to help her up. "Are you okay? Did you get hurt?"

Jasmine shook her head but winced as she looked down at her scraped hand. She glared at Mandy's outstretched hand. "I don't need your help," she scoffed.

"Dammit, that girl doesn't quit," Brody whispered.

"Give her a minute," Elle said.

"I know," Mandy told the other girl, offering her a reassuring smile. "But I'm offering it anyway." Mandy lowered her voice. "I know horses can sometimes seem scary. I feel bad Shamus scared you."

Jasmine jerked back. "I didn't say I was scared."

Mandy held her hand out farther, offering again to help the girl up.

Jasmine narrowed her eyes. "Is this is a trick? Why would you want to help me?"

"No trick. I just know what it's like to have other kids laughing at you. And I know that it hurts."

The other girl lowered her eyes and hung her head, shame coloring her cheeks.

"There's a sink in the livestock barn," Mandy told her. "Come on, I'll help you clean off your shoe, then you can pet Shamus. He's real sweet. He's kind of like a cute, little old man."

"You're weird," Jasmine said, but she took the girl's offered hand and let Mandy pull her up.

"I know," Mandy said, holding her chin up and grinning at the girl. "But that's what makes me awesome."

Brody snorted and peered down at Elle. "I love that girl."

Elle's lips curved up in a grin. They were in the shadows of the barn, but she swore she saw proud-dad tears shining in Brody's eyes. "She *is* something. And I adore Milo for standing up for her and for helping to give her the confidence to stand up for herself."

"Yeah, I don't know how to thank that kid. I owe him big-time. Maybe I should offer to pay for his college tuition or something."

Elle chuckled. "He'd probably be happy if you just bought him a corn dog."

"True." He nudged her arm. "We'd better get out of here. They're heading this way."

They backed out of their hiding place and scooted down the alleyway and out one of the side doors that opened to a path between it and the next livestock barn.

They were alone on the path, and Brody grabbed Elle and drew her to him, planting a hard kiss on her mouth, then pulled her against him in a tight hug. "Thank you."

"For what?" she said against his chest. Not that she cared for what; she was reeling from the kiss. His shirt smelled like sheets dried on the line, and he tasted like cotton candy. She wanted to stay tucked in the circle of his arms all day. *And* all night.

"For believing in my girl and for spending time with her and giving her the tools to stand up to that bully." He offered her a sheepish grin. "And for holding me back from charging in there like a giant bull in a china shop."

"You're welcome."

He peered down at her, and his expression changed from amused to serious. "I'm sorry I've been such an idiot the past couple days. I really like you, Elle Brooks."

"I like you too."

"And I really liked what happened with us the other night."

Heat rose to her cheeks. "I wasn't sure. You haven't really talked to me much since then. And you kind of acted like it hadn't happened. So I figured you were just trying to forget it."

He shook his head. "I won't *ever* forget it. It was incredible."

A grin tugged at the corners of her mouth. "I thought so too. But then I couldn't figure out why you didn't come back to bed that night and why you didn't want to stick around last night. I thought I scared you away."

"You did scare me. You scared the hell out of me." Her chin fell, but he tenderly lifted it back up to look in her eyes. "But not because of what we did. Because of how it made me feel. I couldn't even think straight, I was so caught up. All I wanted to do was carry you to the sofa and rip your clothes off. If my phone hadn't rung, I'm not sure I would have been able to stop myself from doing it."

She nodded, a small, solemn bob of her head. "I'm not sure I would have wanted to stop you."

He frowned, pain evident in his eyes. "I'm falling for you, darlin', and that's what scares me the most. I haven't felt like this in a long time, so I'm in uncharted territory." He blew out a sigh. "Forgive me for running away?"

"Of course. I'm scared too. The other night totally freaked me out. I pride myself on staying in control and controlling everything around me, and with you, I didn't just lose control. I threw it completely out the window in a haze of wild lust."

He offered her a naughty grin. "That was some pretty great lust." His expression turned serious. "You know, I just watched my daughter stand up to her biggest fear and not back down to a bully—she was so damn brave. And it makes me think that I need to stop being afraid too. I like you, and the idea of us being just friends is a terrible one. I mean, I want us to be friends too, but I don't think friends spend as much time as I do thinking about what their other friend tastes like."

Her mouth went dry, and she swallowed hard.

He dipped his head, and she met him halfway, anticipating the kiss, but their noses bumped instead, and she let out a nervous laugh. "You taste like cotton candy."

He grinned and nodded as if he were proud of himself. "Nice." He lowered his head and tried again, this time connecting to her lips and giving her a thorough kiss. "You taste like caramel. And mint. And summer."

Her stomach did a somersault, and she couldn't keep the smile from spreading across her face.

"Listen, if my daughter can stand up to her fears, so can I. So I was thinking of doing something selfish, something just for us. If you want to."

"I'm listening."

"What would you think if I asked my mom to take Mandy tonight? And we spent some time together—just the two of us. I'm not on call, so there wouldn't be any interruptions. It would just be you and me. And we'd have the whole night to spend together. What do you think?"

The somersaults in her belly turned into backflips. She and Brody alone together, with no interruptions, for the whole night? The idea terrified and excited her. And by the way the heat was shooting up her spine, the idea aroused her too. "Just to be clear, when you say spend the night together, do you mean like as *friends*? Are you talking cards and playing board games and eating junk food?"

His grin turned mischievous, like he was the Big Bad Wolf who'd just been offered Red Riding Hood on a sleepover platter. "I might want to play some games, but they don't involve cards or dice. Although we *could* play Oregon Trail if I get to explore all the terrains of your body."

Elle's breath caught. Yep, definitely arousal. "Yes," she whispered. "I'd like that. Especially the exploring parts." She offered him a coy grin. "But only if I get to take a turn as well."

"Oh, you can take as many turns as you want. I think it's going to take me several turns just to survey your mountains."

A laugh burst from her, and she held on to his arms as she cracked up.

"Was that too far?" he asked, busting out in his own laughter.

"Maybe," she said between laughs. She held up her fingers to signify an inch. "Just a little."

"I like making you laugh," he said. "Even if it is at my nerdy expense."

It felt good to laugh. Especially the genuine kind of laughter that made her cheeks sore from smiling. She put her hand on his muscular bicep. "Oh, Dr. Tate, when I'm thinking about you, 'nerdy' is not what comes to mind."

"But you *do* think about me?"

She chuckled again. "All the time."

"So you okay with tonight?"

She nodded. She was more than okay. She couldn't wait.

CHAPTER 20

BRODY THOUGHT HE MIGHT EXPLODE WITH PRIDE THIRTY minutes later as he and Elle sat in the bleachers and cheered their heads off for Mandy and Shamus. He clapped so hard his hands hurt. But it was worth the pain to see that grin of pride on his daughter's face.

Milo and his mom sat in the bleachers with them and cheered almost as loud. Brody was surprised to see the three girls from earlier sitting a few rows in front of them, and even more shocked when they yelled and clapped, and Jasmine even waved, as Mandy paraded Shamus around the corral.

For his part, Shamus played his role perfectly, walking next to Mandy and nodding his head as if he agreed with her when she asked him a question. Mandy ended her routine by clicking the heels of her sparkling, ruby cowboy boots together three times and calling out, "There's no place like Creedence," three times in a row. The crowd erupted in applause as she took a bow.

They all cheered and yelled some more when she was presented with the first place prize. Brody loved her beaming smile as she held up the blue ribbon. He probably took fifty pictures. And he had a feeling Elle took almost as many. They grinned at each other like hyenas as Mandy and Shamus marched out of the arena.

"She did it. She won," Elle cried as she threw her arms around Brody and hugged him.

He hugged her back, then looked over Elle's shoulder to see his mother watching him, a slight arch to her eyebrow as she stood at the base of the bleachers. *Uh-oh.* He might have some explaining to do.

His folks had slipped in at the end of the row right before

Mandy came into the arena, and he'd waved but hadn't had a chance to talk to them yet. He and Elle high-fived Milo and his mom as they made their way down from the bleachers.

"That was so cute," Jillian said. "Mandy did great."

"We're heading over to find a funnel cake," Milo told them. "But tell Mandy we'll find her later to tell her congratulations."

"Sounds good," Elle said with a wave.

"Hey, Mom," Brody said, giving his mom a hug when they finally reached her. "Thanks so much for helping Mandy with those costumes. Wasn't she awesome?"

"She was adorable," his mother said, pressing her hand to her chest. "I thought I would burst with pride when she accepted that ribbon."

"Me too." He nodded to Elle, who was standing next to him, a matching smile of pride on her face. "Mom, this is my friend, Elle Brooks. You've probably heard Mandy talking about her. She's the one who's been helping Bryn with the horse rescue and taking Mandy to the pool the last few days."

"Nice to meet you," his mom told Elle, reaching out a hand to shake hers. "I'm Susan Tate. It feels like I know you already. Mandy talks about you all the time." She cut her eyes to him. "My son has mentioned you as well. You seem to have made quite an impression on the two of them."

Elle shook her head. "They've made an impression on me. Both of them have really helped me get through this crazy thing with the fire at my house."

"I heard about that. I'm so sorry. I hope you weren't hurt."

Elle glanced his way, a ghost of a smile on her lips at their inside joke about being sorry, then turned her attention back to his mom. "Thank you. I appreciate that, but I'm fine. I've been so busy since it happened—what with helping Bryn out with the animals and taking Mandy to the pool and finding an abandoned dog and dealing with her puppies, I've barely had time to even think about my house."

"Where's Dad?" Brody asked before his mom started asking Elle more questions he wasn't sure either of them were ready to answer.

He'd texted his mom earlier to make sure they were okay with Mandy staying the night at their house. He'd claimed he had some work he needed to catch up on, but Susan Tate didn't miss much. And the way she kept glancing from him to Elle told him she might have a suspicion about the kind of work he was going to do.

"He went back to help get the horse loaded into the trailer," she told him.

"Dad!" Brody turned just in time to catch his daughter as she launched herself into his arms. "Did you see, Dad? I won first place!"

"I saw," he said, leaning down to drop a quick kiss on her head. She smelled like hay and her orange blossom shampoo and the hard butterscotch candies his dad was known for handing out. "I was so proud of you. You did amazing."

"Shamus did amazing. He is just the best horse." She beamed with happiness as she turned to hug Elle.

"You and Shamus looked adorable," Elle told her as she hugged the girl. "You did so great out there. I was so impressed. And you didn't seem nervous at all."

"I was totally nervous at first. But then Shamus shook his head when I asked him a question and everyone laughed, then I knew everyone loved him, and I didn't feel nervous anymore."

"Good thinking. And they did love Shamus, but they loved you too. You both just did so great."

"Thanks." She let go of Elle and hugged Susan next. Her grandmother showered her with more praise as she hugged her back.

"Well, I should probably go help Dad with the horse," Brody told them. "Then I think I'm gonna head on out."

"Aren't you gonna stay for the talent show and the concert?" Mandy asked.

Brody's mom put her hand on her granddaughter's shoulder. "Your dad's gotta catch up on some work, so you're going to stay with us tonight."

"I am?" She wrinkled her brow at him. "I didn't know you had to work tonight."

His mom cut in before he had to lie to his daughter. "I'm excited to watch the talent show with you. And I think I heard Gramps say something about buying us some corn dogs and getting ice cream before the concert."

Yeah, his mom definitely knew something was up. Since when had his mom become his wingman?

And now he couldn't quite meet her eye.

And he didn't dare look at Elle for fear his mom would see his plans written all over his face. "Well, so I'm gonna go help with that horse now. I'll drop him off at Bryn's in a little bit, if that's okay with you, Elle?"

She suddenly couldn't seem to meet his eye either. "Yep, that sounds good. I was thinking I was about ready to head home too. Sooo, I may see you later, then. If I'm home. But I might not be. Or I might be busy. Or I might see you."

He pressed his lips together to keep from smiling. She would make a terrible spy. But she was kind of adorable in her lack of sub-terfuge skills. If she had some shoelaces, she'd probably trip over them right now.

"It was nice to meet you, Mrs. Tate," she said, not quite looking his mother in the eye either. Then she gave Mandy another quick hug and offered him a wave. "See you later, Brody. Or maybe not. See ya." She turned and hurried away, and even though he couldn't see her face, he was sure her cheeks were pink from a blush.

He didn't realize a huge smile had broken on his face until he turned back to his mom, who was gazing at him with an amused and knowing grin.

"Don't worry about Mandy," she told him. "You can pick her

up whenever you get around in the morning." Her eyes practically twinkled as she tried to hold back a smile. "Hope you get caught up on all that *work* tonight."

"Yeah, me too," he mumbled over Mandy's head as he gave his daughter a hug. "You did great tonight, squirt. Milo said he'd come find you later to tell you congratulations. Have fun with Gramps and Grandma. I'll see you in the morning."

"See ya, Dad."

He gave his mother a quick hug. "Thanks, Mom," he said quietly into her ear.

"See ya later, Son," she told him as she squeezed him back. "Have fun."

━━━━━

Elle paced the kitchen nervously as she ate way too big a slice of leftover cake—the leaded one—and listened for Brody's truck. The cake was delicious, the Kahlua flavor even stronger the second day, and she could feel the tingle of the alcohol on her lips. She wasn't much of a drinker, and she'd considered taking a shot of courage from the bottle of peppermint schnapps Bryn kept in the fridge. *But that wouldn't have been as decadent and delicious as this cake*, she thought as she nervously dug into a second piece.

Her pulse quickened as she heard the rumble of a truck engine, and she reached up to smooth her hair. She'd gotten home fifteen minutes earlier and had fixed her hair, swiped on another coat of mascara, and dabbed a little perfume on her neck before she'd come into the kitchen and devoured the first piece of cake.

She looked down at herself to check her outfit. She'd bought this dress on a whim one day earlier this summer from the dress shop in town. It was feminine and cute, and when she put it on, she'd loved it more than she thought she would. The skirt was flowy, but the bodice was fitted and had an open neckline with small cap sleeves. She had on one of her good push-up bras and had undone the top button of her dress, exposing just the slightest hint of cleavage. She sucked in a breath and, in a moment of recklessness, impulsively undid another button. The extra flash of skin made her feel sexy and a little seductive, and was way racier than her normal buttoned-up business attire. But was it too obvious?

She reached back to button it. *Leave it,* her inner vixen ordered.

Blame it on the cake. A grin tugged at the corners of her mouth as she went out the door to meet Brody.

He'd already unloaded Shamus and was putting him in the corral. The other horses trotted over to the gate, either to greet their little buddy or to check if Brody had any sugar cubes for them. More than likely both.

The little colt wasn't much bigger than Shamus, but he pranced around the mini-horse like he was excited to have him home.

"Hey, cowboy." Elle tried to appear relaxed as she sauntered up to Brody, but her hands were shaking, and she was having trouble remembering how to breathe.

He turned from the horses and grinned at her, and it didn't matter what she remembered because her breath left her completely. Something about that grin held both desire and a hint of promise. And dang if it didn't have a bit of a wicked gleam to it as well, as if he were already imagining her undressed. Or maybe it was her imagining that. Either way, it had heat rising up her back, and she suddenly didn't know where to put her hands.

She crossed her arms but realized too late, as she saw his gaze dip and his grin widen, that the motion only drew more attention to her breasts and the hint of lacy bra on display.

"Hey yourself," he said. His eyes held her gaze, and the rest of the farm, the horses crowded at the fence, all fell away. She was standing less than a foot from him—the air between them felt charged with energy—and her skin tingled, her fingers aching to touch him.

She was nervous like she hadn't been in years, and she couldn't seem to find her voice. Not that she knew what to say anyway. *Good to see you. Thanks for coming over to make out and possibly have some sex tonight.* Yeah, that sounded perfect.

Turned out she didn't have to talk anyway. He reached for her hand and pulled her to him, wrapping his other arm around her waist. He pressed their joined hands against his chest. "Can you feel my heart? It's beating so hard, I'm surprised it hasn't left a bruise."

She smiled up at him, swallowing at the mix of desire and nerves. It was hard to think being this close to him, surrounded by his arms and the masculine scent of his aftershave.

He peered down at her. "I'm glad I'm here, but damned if I'm not suddenly as nervous as a long-tailed cat in a room full of rocking chairs."

She laughed, and the spell broke. This was Brody, the guy who had shown up for her again and again the past week, whenever she needed him. Yes, he made her hands shake and the secret parts of her ache with need, but he was also the guy who made her feel comfortable and who made her laugh. And the guy who she was planning to spend the night with—an idea that she couldn't even have imagined a few weeks ago and that now she couldn't wait for.

She offered him a coy grin as she wrapped her arms around his neck. "Why don't you just shut up and kiss me?"

He chuckled and leaned down to press a tender kiss to her lips. With a second kiss, he dipped his tongue between her lips, sampling her mouth as he pulled her against him.

"Mmm. You taste like chocolate," he told her, licking his lips.

"I was eating cake while I waited for you."

"Sassy's cake?"

"Yep."

"The leaded version or the unleaded?"

A grin curved her lips. "The leaded."

He grinned back. "Is there any left?"

She nodded, and he slid his hand down to cup her butt before giving it a playful tap. "Let's go inside and get a piece."

"Of cake? Or...?" She lifted a shoulder in a flirty shrug.

His response was between a growl and an agreement. "Yes. But we can start with the cake."

He stopped at his truck to grab a couple of grocery bags, then followed her inside. She may have given a bit of an extra sashay of her hips as she walked up the porch steps in front of him. Something about the warm summer night and the hint of promise in the air had her feeling like anything was possible. Like this might be the start of something really great.

She felt flirty and fun as she led him to the kitchen table and directed him to sit. Grabbing plates and forks, she felt his gaze on her as she moved. "You want something to drink?"

"Sure," he said, reaching into one of the bags he'd brought in and set on the table. "I made a couple of stops on the way over and grabbed a few things. I bought some beer, then got a bottle of wine too, for you, since it's classier, I guess."

"I appreciate what I think was a compliment, but I'm good with a beer."

He found a bottle opener and cracked two beers while she served the cake, making her slice much smaller than his. She didn't need to tell him she'd already had two pieces. But there was a hunger inside of her, an insatiable desire that was crying out to be quenched.

They had all night—maybe a little more cake wouldn't hurt.

He handed her a beer and held his bottle up. "To new beginnings."

"To new beginnings," she repeated, then clinked her bottle to his before taking a healthy swig. "Speaking of new things, I don't think I've ever had cake with beer before. With milk and coffee, yes. With beer, no."

"Maybe tonight's about stepping out and trying something new." He settled in the chair and patted his legs, inviting her onto his lap.

She took another swig of beer, then instead of sitting down on his lap, she swung her leg over his and straddled him in the chair. *Holy hot cowboy.* She felt the soft denim of his jeans against her thighs as her skirt rode up.

Let the games begin.

She picked up the fork and stabbed a bite of cake, then held it up to him. His eyes widened, but he obediently opened his mouth. He closed his lips around the fork, then groaned in pleasure. "Damn that cake is good."

He swiped his finger through a dollop of frosting and held it up to her, narrowing his eyes in a provocative dare. She opened her mouth, but he pulled his fingers back just the slightest, just enough to make her lean forward, to come to him. She tilted toward him, taking his finger into her mouth and sucking the frosting from its tip.

He groaned again, but this time it wasn't from the cake.

She wriggled in his lap, feeling his pleasure against her. "Is that your beer bottle, mister, or are you just happy to see me?" she teased.

He chuckled. "Oh, I'm *real* happy to see you, darlin'. And getting happier every time you squirm like that. I don't want you to stop."

I'm not planning to stop. For now, it was scary enough to think the words. She wasn't sure she could voice them out loud.

He swiped another dab of frosting from the plate, but this time paused before he got to her mouth and tipped his fingers, letting the frosting drop onto her cleavage. He gazed up at her, an impish grin on his face, as he lifted one shoulder in a shrug. "Dang. Now I'm gonna have to get that." The frosting had landed just shy of the open center buttons of her dress. He peeled back the fabric, revealing smooth, creamy skin. He dipped his head and pressed his lips to the top of her breast, his mouth skimming the lace edge of her bra as he licked the frosting from her skin.

She moaned as he freed the next few buttons, then drew back the bodice from either side, exposing the swell of her breasts as they spilled over the top of her bra. His hand skimmed up her collarbone and against her skin as he slid her bra strap and the cap sleeve off her shoulder and down her arm, just far enough to tug the cup down and free her breast.

His breath was warm on her skin as he kissed the tender flesh of her breast before circling the tightened nub of her nipple with his tongue. She let out a soft moan as he sucked the nub between his lips, grazing his teeth over the edge as he drew her into his mouth.

She flattened her hands on his pecs, feeling the warmth of him through his shirt. She had a need to touch him, to prove that this thing happening between them was real. That he was real, solid. His chest was hard, muscled, yet she could feel the slightest tremble to his hand as he skimmed his fingers over the top of her other breast, then scooped it into his palm.

Her breasts filled his hands, and his mouth, but she wanted more. She arched her back, aching for more of his touch. She squirmed in his lap, rubbing herself against his hardness.

He pulled back and stared up at her as he blew out a shaky breath. "I think you'd better tell me if you want to slow down, because the more I touch you, the more I want you."

"I want you too," she whispered.

"I haven't done this in a long time. In the last five years, there's been no one who's made me even *consider* getting to this step. And—I can't believe I'm saying this—but now I'm having a hard time considering *not* getting to it. And soon."

She let out a small laugh. "It's the same for me. It hasn't been five years, but there's been no one since..." She couldn't quite bring herself to say his name.

"Are you sure you're ready? Because I can stop if you're not."

She was straddling his lap, the hem of her dress hitching up her thighs, the top of it spread open with one breast bare as it spilled over the cup of her disheveled bra, and practically panting as she squirmed against the bulge of his crotch. She'd say she was pretty dang ready. "Honestly, I'm terrified. But I don't want to stop."

He raised his hand to run his fingers over the top edge of her dress, then eyed her with a wicked grin. "Have I told you how much I love this dress?"

She shook her head, caught in the intensity of his gaze.

"Well, it's gorgeous, but I'd love it even better if it were on the floor."

CHAPTER 21

BRODY HELD HIS BREATH, WAITING FOR HER RESPONSE TO HIS flirty, and somewhat cheesy, invitation to get naked with him.

She let out a hearty laugh. Maybe not the response he was hoping for, but he couldn't help smiling in return.

"It may have been five years, but apparently you've still got the moves," she teased, pushing up from his lap and readjusting her dress and bra to cover her breasts.

Dang. Too bad. Although now he got the pleasure of rediscovering them again. His palms itched just thinking about it. "I don't feel like it. I feel like a terrified teenager showing up for that one date when he thinks he might finally score."

"You don't seem that nervous."

"Yeah? You should have seen me in the convenience store on the way over here. I'm a grown man, and you would have thought I was sixteen the way I was sweating over my purchase."

She tilted her head. "Why? What did you buy at the convenience store?"

He nodded toward the bags on the other end of the table. One held the stuff he'd quickly grabbed from his house—a clean shirt, a stick of deodorant, his toothbrush and his cell phone charger. The other held the things he had stopped to buy. His pulse quickened as Elle pulled the bag toward her.

She peered inside, and a grin creased her face. He knew what was in there. Along with a box of condoms, he'd bought a bottle of Gatorade, two protein bars, a Snickers, and a bag of Cool Ranch Doritos.

"Gatorade? Protein bars? I would ask if you're training for a marathon, but the candy bar and chips might blow that idea."

"Look, it's been five years since I've been with a woman. And longer than that since I've had to go into a store and buy condoms. I didn't want to just toss them on the counter, so I bought some other stuff to mix them in. Although the teenager at the counter smirked at me while he was ringing them up like he totally guessed my condom-camouflaging scheme."

"You could have gone to the grocery store and used the self-checkout."

He smacked his palm to his forehead. "Okay, that would have been a good idea. I told you I've been out of the game for a while now." He offered her a questioning look. "Was it okay that I bought that stuff?"

"Sure. I love Snickers, and Cool Ranch is my favorite flavor of Doritos."

He raised an eyebrow. "You know what I mean. I don't want to presume anything, and I'm okay with whatever happens tonight. But I also wanted to be prepared. And I don't want to embarrass you."

"The only thing I'm embarrassed about is that I didn't think of it first." She smiled as she stepped forward and circled his waist with her arms. "I think it's great that you bought that stuff. I'm planning on you needing everything in that bag."

"Everything?"

"Yeah, *especially* the Gatorade and protein bars...you're gonna need to stay hydrated and keep your strength up."

He laughed as he bent his knees and lifted her into his arms. Cradling her against him, he leaned in and gave her a quick kiss. "Don't worry, darlin'. I've got plenty of strength. *And* stamina." He nodded to the table. "Grab that bag. And get ready for a marathon."

She giggled as she snatched the bag from the table. "I feel like I've been training for this my entire life."

He carried her down the hallway and into her bedroom. The window was open, letting in a cool summer breeze and the room was bathed in the silvery light of the moon. Roxy raised her head from her nest in the closet, the pile of puppies asleep against her. She yawned, then cuddled her head back against her babies and closed her eyes.

Setting Elle down, he took a step back to pull off his boots and tug his shirt over his head. Her gaze raked over his body, and the smile that played over her lips had him wanting to flex and beat his bare chest.

Then his mouth went dry as she slowly unbuttoned her dress, pushed it over her hips, and let it fall to the floor, leaving her in only a lacy bra, a teeny pair of panties, and her cowboy boots.

She nodded to the pool of fabric on the floor. "How do you like my dress now?"

"What dress?" He swallowed and tried to control the racing of his heart. "You are so damn beautiful," he whispered. "I can't believe you want me."

She took his hand and pulled him down onto the bed with her. "I want you with everything in me."

He lay down next to her, sighing at the feel of her skin finally against his. The scent of her perfume floated in the air around him, something floral and feminine and enticing as hell. Pushing up on one elbow, he let his gaze linger over her as he brushed the backs of his knuckles across her chest, over the silky fabric of her bra, then down her ribs. She sucked in a breath and pulled her bottom lip under her top teeth, a move that make him crazy.

He loved the sounds she made when he touched her, the soft sighs, the quick inhales. Hunger rose in him as he peered down at her mouth, her lips full, lush, and so damn tempting.

She had no idea how sexy she was.

He dragged his hand through his hair as he shook his head. "I gotta tell ya, Elle. I'm in trouble here."

"Trouble?"

He skimmed his fingers along the side of her face, cupping her cheek in his palm. Her eyes were wide and trusting, even though her last question was said with trepidation. He knew once he said the words, he wouldn't be able to take them back. "I'm falling hard for you, Elle. Like out of the sky, in a tailspin kind of falling. And I didn't even see it coming. The last time I felt like this, it was a slow burn that kind of crept up on me. With you, it's a flash of heat that gets hotter every day. And I'm not trying to say what I feel is just lust." His gaze drifted over her body, then back to her eyes. "Although I do feel a powerful lust for you, woman. But it's more than that. It's my heart—"

He had to stop, surprised by the burn of emotion in his throat and the prick of tears in his eyes. *Damn, pull it together, Tate.* First time he's had sex in five years—he couldn't go into it by practically crying on the woman.

He shook his head and cleared his throat. "Sorry."

"Don't be sorry. Remember?" Her eyes reflected back the emotions he was feeling, and as terrified as he was, he somehow knew she was feeling the same way.

He shook his head again. "Dang. I don't know why I'm even talking. I've got the woman I've been fantasizing about half-naked in front of me, and I'm running my jaw. I just wanted you to know that you mean something to me. That I'm falling for you. I don't know how to stop it. And I don't know if I want to."

She touched his face with so much tenderness, he almost lost it again. "Then don't. Don't stop. Because I'm falling for you too. I—"

He leaned in and caught her next words in a kiss. That was all she had to say, all he had to hear, that she felt the same. She melted under him, her hands circling his neck as he deepened the kiss. Her lips were soft, pliant, and he lost himself in the warm pull of her mouth.

Her skin was smooth and supple under his hands, and he wanted to explore all of it, to touch and caress, to kiss and taste.

He unsnapped her bra and tossed it to the floor, wanting, needing to see and touch more of her.

She let out a soft whimper against his mouth. He loved the little noises she made and the way her body fit so right under his.

He couldn't get enough of her. Breaking their kiss on the moan, he used his tongue to trace the curve of her neck, then laid a trail of warm kisses over her breasts, stopping to give each one attention, sampling the tight buds of her nipples as he sucked them between his lips.

He pulled back to pause and look at her. He wanted to give her time, to not rush this—hell, they had all night—but he also felt like he couldn't wait another minute. A building sense of restlessness drove him forward, and all he could think was how desperately he longed to have her.

He pushed off from the bed, grabbed the box from the bag and tossed it on the bed next to her.

She pushed up on her elbows and bent one knee, digging the heel of her boot into the comforter, as she looked from the box back to him. Her lips curved into a flirty grin. "I feel at a slight disadvantage here. I'm practically naked, and I think you're wearing entirely too many clothes."

"I can remedy that in three seconds flat." He grinned as he shucked off his jeans and boxer briefs. There was no mistaking the effect her sexy-as-sin pose was having on him. His pulse raced and heat surged through him as he peered down at the combination of her boots and the teeny tiny slip of lace that disappeared between her legs. His gaze drifted over her body, down her legs, and back up as he offered her a wolfish grin. "Boots on? Or off?"

She offered him a playful shrug. "Dealer's choice."

"Okay, then I'm choosing off," he said as he lifted her leg and tugged each boot free. "I want *everything* off." He hooked his fingers under the sides and peeled the panties down her legs. They hit the floor next to the boots. "You can keep your earrings on, but other than that, I want you naked and under me. Then make it over me. Then we can discuss next to me. And under me again."

She laughed, but it had a seductively sexy tone to it. "You really are preparing for a marathon."

He nodded. "Oh yeah. Make no mistake. We're both gonna need that Gatorade." He leaned down and kissed her. Not just kissed her but inhaled her, stealing her breath with his desire.

Her hands ran over his shoulders, and she made another soft kitten sigh. A jolt of carnal need rushed through him, that one sound causing everything else to melt away. And he had to have her.

He snatched the box of condoms, tearing the cardboard as he ripped the top off and sending a shower of packets spilling onto the bed. He grabbed one, tore it open with his teeth, covered himself, and then settled back between her legs.

Her body was warm and languid, molding perfectly to his, her breasts soft against him. Everything about this felt so right as he moved with her in a slow, methodical tempo that increased as they found their rhythm.

She matched his pace, her hands gripping his back, her breath coming in quick pants as low moans escaped her lips. He wanted to be gentle, to take it slow, but his desire overwhelmed him. Demand throbbed between his legs, hot and unyielding.

He loved watching her, loved the way her fingers tightened on his shoulders or gripped handfuls of the sheets, loved the way her body flushed and how her hair spread around her on the pillow. He especially loved feeling the crush of her thighs around his waist as her desire built and overtook her.

The pulse in her neck quickened, and her breath hitched as he increased the cadence of his strokes. His nerves grew taut, and he gritted his teeth to keep a groan from escaping. He wanted all his focus to be on her pleasure, loving the thrill of seeing her arousal and excitement.

The swirl of heat rose, built inside him, but he held it back—until she shuddered and moaned his name. Then his resistance shattered as her thighs trembled, and she gave way to the sensations that seized her muscles. Then everything was too much and not enough, and he couldn't hold back. His chest expanded, and the growl he'd been holding in roared from his throat as he gave in to his release, letting go and drowning in the feeling that was better than anything he'd imagined.

Spent, he collapsed onto the bed next to her and drew her to him, holding her tightly against him as he pressed a hard kiss to her hair. He could feel her trembling, or maybe that was him. Either way, he pulled her closer and knew it was right as she pressed into him and clutched his back. They stayed that way for he didn't know how long.

When they finally relaxed, he rolled to his back and pulled her into the crook of his arm. She laid her head on his shoulder and pressed her hand to his chest. "Thank you for trusting me with this."

Could she feel how hard his heart was beating? He blew out a sigh. He *was* trusting her, even though he wasn't sure he could trust himself. All he wanted to do was give in, to let himself fall.

"I do trust you," he said, brushing a lock of hair from her forehead. "Thanks for trusting me too."

She pushed up on her elbow, and her lips curved in a seductive grin. "Thanks for getting the snacks and the, you know, supplies." She pressed a kiss to his right pec, her breath warm as her lips grazed over his nipple. "Do you need a protein bar, or are you ready to keep racing?"

He grinned as he pulled her on top of him. "That was just the warm-up laps. This race is just getting started."

———

The sun shining through the window woke Brody the next morning. His arm was asleep, but he didn't care because it was under a naked woman whose back was spooned against his front and whose gorgeous ass was curved against his hips. It didn't matter that his arm was asleep, because the rest of him had just woken up and was rising to the occasion.

Elle must have felt his wake-up call because she stretched and squirmed against him, the feel of her body revving his engines more than any cup of caffeine could. She rolled over and pressed a kiss to his cheek. "Good morning, cowboy."

"Damn straight it is." He stretched out his arm, his muscles sore, but in the best possible way, then wrapped it around her waist, running the tips of his fingers softly over her hips. "You want coffee?"

She sat up, and her long hair cascaded over her bare shoulders. Her eyes were sleepy but seductive as she turned and climbed on top of him, straddling his waist and giving him a view that rivaled any artistic masterpiece. "Yes, but first I was thinking we could have breakfast in bed."

"I like the way you think." Hell, he liked everything about her. But he took the next hour to reacquaint himself, just to be sure.

They did finally get coffee but skipped breakfast and instead took a shower together, then tumbled back into bed. Elle was wrapped in a towel and had just reached to release it when Brody's phone rang.

He leaned out of bed toward where his phone sat on the nightstand. His heart gave a quick thud and panic rose in him when he saw the caller's name on the screen. "It's my mom."

Shit. Reality hit him like a punch in the kidney. He was rolling around in bed while he'd left his child with his parents, and now something must have happened. He could feel it before he'd even answered the phone. Guilt churned in his gut. He knew he shouldn't have done this. Whenever he put his needs first, it always ended badly. He'd dumped his daughter on his folks so he could be with Elle, and now he would pay.

He prayed nothing had happened to his daughter as he grabbed his phone. "Hey, Mom. Is Mandy okay?"

"Good morning, Son. Yes, she's fine. But your dad isn't, I'm afraid."

"Oh no," he said, already reaching for his pants. "Did he have a heart attack? A stroke? What hospital is he in? I knew he shouldn't have eaten those corn dogs last night." His words came out in a frenzied rush.

"No. He did *not* have a heart attack. Or a stroke. Geez, what is the *matter* with you?"

"Sorry. I don't know why I am so nervous today."

"Hmm. I thought you would be in a *much* better mood." His mom's insinuation wasn't lost on him. "But you are right about one thing—Dad *shouldn't* have eaten those corn dogs last night. He's in some gastric distress today. I'm sure it was all the greasy food last night. He just *had* to have a funnel cake. I told him not to get it, but I swear that man never listens to me. Anyway, on the off chance that it's actually the flu or some kind of bug, I'd rather not expose Mandy to it.

"So I figured I'd take her out to your house, but thought I'd better call first, just in case, you know, you were still 'working.' And then when no one answered your home phone, I figured you must be *at* 'work' getting caught up on all that 'working' you had to do."

"Okay, I get it, Mom. Stop saying *working*. And I appreciate the heads-up. Give me fifteen minutes, and I'll be there to pick her up."

"I don't mind running her to the house. I just don't want to interrupt anything. I know you haven't had any 'work' like this in a long time."

"For crying out loud, Mom." He raked his hand through his hair. "And for the record, maybe I didn't answer the home phone because I was in the shower." That wasn't too far from the truth. He *had* just gotten out of the shower.

"Yes, I'm sure that's it, dear."

He rolled his eyes. "Just hang tight. I'll be there in fifteen." He clicked off and sat up on the side of the bed. "Sorry, I've got to go."

"Everything okay with Mandy?"

"Yeah, she's fine. But my dad's not feeling well, so I need to go pick her up. I'm sure my dad would rather have my mom at the house, so I'll just take Mandy to the clinic with me."

"Do you want me to go get her? So you can get ready for work."

"Hell no." He rubbed his hand over her leg as she jerked back. "I didn't mean that in a bad way. It's not you. You're a sweetheart for offering, but my mom already thinks she's the lead detective in charge of the Brody romance file or, in my case, the missing files. She's like a dog with a bone with her allegations. She hasn't come right out and said it, but she knows something was up last night." And unfortunately, she also knew the state of his romance file had, until last week, been pretty much a cold case.

Elle chuckled. "I like your mom. And I have the day free, so why don't you bring Mandy out here?"

"You sure?"

"Of course. I could use the company."

"Thanks. I'm sure she would rather be here with you. Especially since my day is slammed. I've still got to go by the house and feed my livestock, then I've got appointments most of the day and a surgery scheduled for later this morning."

"Don't give it another thought. We'll have fun."

He peered down at the woman on the other side of the bed. Her hair was wet and mussed, and she wore nothing but a towel wrapped around her, and she was so damn beautiful. His heart swelled with affection. Not only had they had an amazing time the night before, she didn't think twice about offering to help with his daughter.

His heart gave a hard *thunk*. It wasn't just affection he was feeling for her, and he knew it. It was love, and that thought scared the hell out of him. He hadn't woken up next to another woman in years, but this morning, waking up with Elle curled against him felt so natural, so damn good.

"Last night was good, yeah?" he asked, maybe more to reassure himself she was feeling the same kind of things.

A coy smile curved her lips. "Oh yeah."

He laughed. "I didn't mean it like that. Although I'm glad you took it that way, and I appreciate your favorable reaction." He reached out a hand and touched her cheek. "But I guess I meant like are *you* good? Are we okay? After everything?"

She tilted her face, pressing her cheek into his palm. "Yes, I am good. And *this* was very good." She narrowed her eyes as she reached up to grip his hand. "I like you, Brody Tate. I like you very much. This wasn't an experiment or about me trying to get back up on some horse. For me, this was a new beginning."

He nodded. "Yeah, for me too. But my mom's call just reminded me that this isn't going to be easy. I've got a daughter, and we're a package deal."

"I know that. And I care about that girl and wouldn't ever do anything to hurt her. I'm scared to death of all of this, but as terrified as I am, I'm more afraid of *not* getting to be with you."

"Me too." He leaned forward and pressed a tender kiss to her lips. Her arms circled his neck, her fingers tangling in his hair as he fell back into the bed with her. He lost himself in her, in her kiss, her naked skin—for just a few minutes, relishing the feel of her in his arms. Then she pushed him away.

"Go get your daughter," she said.

He groaned as he pushed up from the bed, glad he thought to bring an extra shirt. His mom was already on the case; no use giving her more ammunition by showing up in last night's clothes. "I'll be back."

He forced himself to leave the room, knowing he had to leave, but all he wanted was to stay.

CHAPTER 22

ELLE HAD JUST ENOUGH TIME TO DOWN A CUP OF COFFEE, slap on a little makeup, and get dressed before Brody and Mandy were pulling back into the driveway.

"Hey, Elle," Mandy said, lugging in a bulging tote bag and dropping it on the sofa. "I wasn't sure what we're doing today, so I came prepared for anything. I've got my swimsuit, some coloring books, a deck of UNO cards, and a few of my favorite books, just in case you need a break from listening to me talk to you." She smiled sweetly.

Elle laughed and put an arm around her shoulders. "I never need a break from that. And I'm glad you were free to keep me company today. Have you had breakfast?"

"Yeah, I ate at my grandma's."

Elle smiled coyly at Brody. "Hi, Brody. Nice to see you today. Thanks for bringing Mandy over. Would you like some breakfast or some coffee?"

The corners of his lips curved into an impish grin. "I'm good. And it's nice to see you today too."

Mandy narrowed her eyes as she looked from her dad to Elle. "You guys are acting weird. Your smiles are all kooky. What's going on? Are you planning a surprise or something?" She covered her mouth with her hands and bounced on her toes. "Am I finally getting a puppy?"

Brody laughed. "No, you goofball. You are *not* getting a puppy. And we're not acting weird. You're weird." He reached down to tickle her tummy, sending her into a fit of laughter.

Nice distraction technique, Dr. Tate.

"Well, you all might not be hungry, but I'll bet the horses are.

I was just about to go out and give them their breakfast. Wanna help me?"

"Yes," Mandy said.

"I'll come too," Brody said. "I want to check on Glory. If she's doing okay, we may move her to the corral this morning."

They headed for the barn, Mandy running ahead. Elle and Brody walked next to each other, and a spark of heat ran through her as Brody brushed the back of his hand against hers.

"Otis is in the feed trough again," Mandy called to them as they entered the barn.

"That silly goat. I swear he has some kind of internal clock that tells him when food is on its way," Elle said, shaking her head.

"I have one of those too," Brody teased. "In fact, I'm starting to get hungry right now." Mandy was facing into the corral, and he ran his hand over Elle's waist and gave her hip a squeeze.

"You're bad," she whispered, playfully swatting his arm.

He leaned toward her ear. "Last night you said I was *good, so good.*"

"Why don't you be *so good* and grab that bale of hay?"

She approached Glory's stable. The horse had her head over the gate and let out a whinny. "Good morning, Glory." She fed the horse the slices of apple she'd brought outside with her. "You ready to meet the rest of the crew today?"

Running her hand over the horse's neck, she marveled at the changes in the animal that had happened in just the past few days. She was still skinny, and Brody said her ribs would be visible for weeks, but her eyes were shinier and her coat looked better. And she didn't have that terrified, panicked look in her eyes. Not that she was totally over it, but the fact that she had her head out of the stall this morning and seemed to enjoy having her neck scratched without being sung to seemed huge improvements over the skittish behavior she'd displayed when she'd first arrived.

Giving the horse's velvety nose a scratch, Elle considered how this horse had probably had a good home at one point in her life. Then she'd been abandoned and had to fight to survive. But she hadn't given up, hadn't laid down and yielded to life's cruelties. And now, with a second chance at a life and a new home, this horse was leaning over the gate, restless to meet the next phase of her existence.

"She looks good," Brody said, coming up behind her. "I think she's ready, don't you?"

"She's ready," Elle agreed, giving the horse a final pat. *And so am I.* She turned to watch Brody greet the horse. He had a lead rope in his hand, and a swell of emotion filled her as she watched him soothe and comfort Glory, talking to her in a low voice as he slipped it around her neck. He clicked the clasp around the rope, then made a loop and slid it around Glory's nose, creating a make-shift halter so he could lead her out to the corral. He was so good with animals, and with kids, and with her.

Brody Tate was a kind man who loved his daughter and his mama and who looked dang fine in a pair of Wranglers and cowboy boots. He had touched her heart the night before when he'd told her he was falling for her. She'd told him that she was falling for him too. But that was a lie. She'd already fallen.

Focus on the horse. She hurried ahead to the gate at the end of the barn, anxious to see how the other horses would greet Glory. They were all there: Beauty, Prince, Mack, and Shamus. The two taller horses had their heads over the gate, while Shamus and the colt poked their heads through the spaces between the bars. It would seem that they were intrigued by the new horse heading their way, but their interest probably had more to do with a hope that Brody had sugar cubes or sweet feed for them.

He led Glory toward them, and as they drew closer, she reared back for a moment, her head held high and her stance stiff. Her tail was raised, and her ears were pointed forward.

"It's okay, girl," Elle soothed as she took a cautious step toward the horse. She held out her hand and slowly approached, getting closer as she saw the mare's body start to relax. Running her hand along the horse's neck, she cooed to her, encouraging her as she and Brody led the horse a few steps closer to the other animals.

Glory's ears were back, and she leaned into Elle. "I think this horse kind of likes me," she told Brody, wonder coming through in her voice.

He nodded. "Oh, I know she does. You can tell by her body language and the way she relaxes around you. And she doesn't do that with everyone, certainly not me. It's obvious you're her favorite."

Elle stood a little taller. "I've never been a horse's favorite before."

"You are now," Mandy said from her perch on the fence where her Dad instructed her to stay.

They were close enough now that the horses could sniff each other, and Shamus raised his head and touched his nose to Glory's. Elle was pretty sure these two had already met since she doubted Glory had let herself out of her stall before.

Beauty leaned her head in, brushing against Glory, then rearing back. Glory wasn't a big horse; she was a hand's length shorter than Beauty and probably two hands less than Prince. But Shamus didn't seem intimated by her being taller than him and he stayed at the fence while Prince let out a whinny as he reared back, then ran around the corral.

"Don't worry," Brody told the horse. "That's Prince, and he's just showing off. He'll beat his chest a little, then he'll get used to you." He carefully eased open the gate, keeping one hand cinched up on the lead rope while he forced the other horses to back up on the other side of the gate. "I put some extra hay out in various spots around the corral while you were talking to her, so there shouldn't be too much fighting over food," he told Elle.

"I hope there won't be any fighting at all," she said.

"Oh, there will be. A little. They'll need to establish their hierarchy and show Glory who's in charge. They might buck a little and even kick or bite at each other, but they should settle down before too long."

Elle gave the horse's neck a final pat. "You got this, girl. You're doing great."

Brody slowly released the rope and slipped the makeshift halter from her head. Free from her restraints, the horse swished her tail, then trotted into the corral and over to the closest pile of hay. Otis was currently munching on the pile. He snatched an extra mouthful and hurried away, leaving the rest to the newcomer.

Shamus and Beauty wandered toward her, closing the distance to touch her head with their noses, then back away. The colt stayed close to his mother, but also hesitantly approached Glory, then pranced away.

Brody closed the gate, then gestured to Mandy that she could get down. The girl hopped off the fence and raced over to stand next to them as they watched the horses get to know each other. Shamus plodded closer and nibbled a bite of the hay she was munching on. "That's a really good sign that she's already sharing her meal with another horse. She's doing great," he told Elle.

A lump formed in Elle's throat as she watched Glory take off and gallop once around the wide-open corral, then trot back to the hay. Her stance was relaxed, her tail hanging loose and swinging freely. Elle blew out a happy sigh. "She's free."

———

After Brody left, Elle and Mandy spent the rest of the morning outside, playing with the puppies, feeding Spartacus strawberries, petting Tiny, and watching the horses mill around and chase each other in the corral. They let Grace and her puppies play in the front yard, but Roxy's pups were still too young, so they stayed in Elle's room in the nest in her closet.

The day was sunny and bright. The temperature had already risen into the eighties by late morning, and there wasn't a cloud in the sky. They were just getting back from a walk in the pasture where they had picked some wildflowers to make a bouquet for Bryn's kitchen table. Otis and Shamus had gone along, and the goat had tried to eat several of their pickings.

"I'm having a conundrum," Mandy told her as they walked into the barn. Their hands were full of wildflowers, and they set them all on the workbench.

"That's a pretty big word," Elle said, although she'd stopped being surprised when the girl tossed out great words. Between reading so much and being in the company of adults, Mandy had a pretty sophisticated vocabulary.

"It's a pretty big problem."

Elle filled a couple of Mason jars with water from the spigot and stuck the flowers in them, keeping her hands busy as she listened. The two had already talked about training bras and gone through facing down a bully together. What kind of prepubescent problem could they tackle next? She braced herself for a question about sex but prayed it was hopefully only period related. "I'm listening."

The girl furrowed her small brow. "It's just that I've spent weeks with Grace and her puppies, and I'd pretty much already picked out Buttercup. She's the chubby white one with the black spots. But now we found Roxy and her puppies, and I really realllly love the light yellow one, and the thing is, I think lots of people will want Grace's puppies. Cattle dogs are real popular around here. But we don't know anything about Roxy's new puppies, and I kind of think one of them needs me more."

Elle blinked back tears as she pulled the girl into her arms and gave her a hug. "I sure do love you, Mandy Tate. You have the biggest heart of anyone I know." She pulled back and brushed Mandy's bangs from her forehead. "I can see you've put a lot of thought into this problem, but has your dad said you could even *have* a puppy yet?"

Mandy shrugged. "No, but I think I'm wearing him down."

Elle laughed out loud as she let the girl go and went back to the flowers.

"I think I'm going to talk to him about it again tonight. He was in a *really* good mood when he picked me up this morning."

We both were. Elle pressed her lips together to keep the grin from taking over her face.

"I tried to get him to play hooky today and take me swimming up at the lake. I even had my suit at Grandma's, but he said he had a full day and a surgery this morning and couldn't get out of it."

Elle pulled at the front of her shirt where it was stuck to her damp skin. "It is a hot one today. What if I took you up to the lake? Do you think that would be okay?"

Mandy's eyes lit with excitement. "Yes, totally. Dad lets me go up there with Bryn."

A niggle of doubt crept in. "I don't know. Maybe we shouldn't. It could be dangerous."

"Dangerous?" Mandy planted a hand on her narrow hip. "Come on, Elle. You have got to get over this. It's no more dangerous than going to the swimming pool. And we've done that together."

"Do I need to remind you that neither of the times I took you to the pool worked out really great?"

"What? Yes, they did. That's where I met Milo. And so what if Jasmine poured a slushie on my head? If she hadn't, I wouldn't have run into the woods and found Roxy and then Milo wouldn't have saved her puppies."

"Dang, girl, I *do* admire your optimism. You have an amazing gift of always finding the bright side."

"Yeah, I'm awesome like that." The girl shrugged but couldn't hold in her laughter. "Actually, it's my grandpa who taught me that. He said you have to try to find the good in things, because if you spend all your time focused on the bad stuff in life, you'll just end up sad and miserable. And if all you do is worry about how things could go wrong, you miss out on all the great things that could go right."

"Your grandpa sounds like a pretty smart guy."

"Oh, he is. He's a veterinarian too, and he knows all kinds of stuff. Both my grandparents are real smart. I spent a lot of time with them after my mom died, and my grandpa used to take me on walks all the time. He still does. He says God gave us nature as salve for our souls." She cocked an eyebrow at Elle. "That's his words, not mine. But he told me what it means and said nature is kind of like Neosporin—it's like the medicine you put on your wounds. He says spending time outside can help heal people when they are hurting on the inside."

Elle swallowed. Apparently she should have spent the last year walking outside more and hiding in her house less. "I think that's true. I know I've sure felt better this summer since I've been outside so much more and started hanging out with Bryn and Zane and you and your dad." She grinned at the girl. "And the horses and the puppies helped too."

"And the mountains," Mandy said. "The mountains help too. My grandpa says ice cream is delicious, but it can't beat a walk in the mountains for curing what ails you."

"You know what? You're right. I think a walk in the mountains is a great idea. Why don't we text your dad, and if he says he's okay with us going to the lake, then we can walk up there and go for a swim."

"Are you sure? It's pretty far."

Her eyes lit on the four-wheeler parked in the corner of the barn. In the past few days, she'd seen this ten-year-old girl face down coyotes *and* a bully *and* her two cohorts and come out the other side feeling like she'd made a new friend and gained a large number of dogs. Brody had faced his fears and spent the night with her and that had gone great for both of them, especially Elle, who had found some of her courage and gained at *least* three moments of utter bliss. "Why don't we take the ATV then?"

"Are you sure?"

"No, but I think we should anyway. As long as your dad says it's all right."

Mandy shrugged. "Okay, although the way you drive, it might be faster to walk."

———

Twenty minutes later, they had their suits on, a lunch packed, helmets strapped on, and were slowly making their way across the pasture. Brody had texted for them to have fun at the lake, and Elle had also texted Bryn to make sure it was okay they took the ATV.

Elle insisted Mandy sit in front of her, and she cocooned the girl in her arms, using her body as a shield to protect the girl. "I wish these things had seat belts," she muttered, as they crept along the dirt path.

"Why? If it starts to roll, you couldn't jump off if you were strapped to the thing," Mandy said, raising her voice to be heard over the engine.

"Good point."

"I think you've got a feel for it now," Mandy said. "We can probably go more than five miles an hour." She leaned her head to look behind Elle. "Although going this slow has made it easier for the horses to follow us."

Elle looked back for a second and grinned at the sight of Glory and Shamus trotting along in the pasture behind them. She straightened her shoulders, gaining courage from the sight of the brave horse. The path in front of them was clear for close to a hundred yards before it curved around a ridge and started the ascent up the mountain. Elle increased their speed to ten.

"Wow. We're flying now," Mandy teased. "Feel that wind in our hair."

"Oh stop it," Elle told her. "It's a big step for me even getting on this thing." Although she could feel the old hum of adrenaline forming in her when she'd turned over the engine and the quad had rumbled beneath her.

"Are you sure you don't want me to drive?" Mandy asked her. "I'm pretty good at it."

"I'm fine." She *was* doing fine. They'd made it all the way across two pastures without any incident. The quad seemed sturdy, the big tires not bothered by the rocky path. She gave it a little more gas and felt the exhilaration swell inside her.

I can do this. She goosed it a little more. The speedometer inched higher.

"Woo-hoo!" Mandy yelled. "Faster!"

Elle laughed and gave it a little more, feeling the power of the machine between her thighs. They were on a straightaway with no obstacles in their path, and Elle experienced the thrill of speed while feeling like she still had control of the quad.

They approached the curve around the high ridge—the path was wide but Elle lessened their speed as she prepared for the turn. Before the quad slowed, a mother deer and her two fawns came sprinting around the edge of the ridge and across their path.

Elle swerved to miss the deer but hit a rut in the path and the quad started to tilt. She goosed the lever, trying to get out of the rut, but overcorrected with the handlebars. The sharp turn and the increased speed already had the ATV off-kilter; then it hit the side of the ridge and started to roll.

As the machine rolled, Elle wrapped one arm around Mandy and pushed off the quad with her other. She thrust her legs and turned her body, trying to use herself as a shield between the rocky path and the girl.

They hit the ground with a hard thud, gravel tearing at Elle's back and legs as she slid across the dirt. Then her head hit a rock, and everything went black.

CHAPTER 23

ELLE HEARD HER NAME AS SHE SWAM BACK TO CONSCIOUS-
ness. She blinked, her vision fuzzy, as she tried to focus.

"Elle, wake up! Please wake up!" Mandy cried as she shook
Elle's arm.

"I'm awake," she said, raising her arm to wrap it around Mandy.
"I'm okay," she said, although the words came out a little groggy
still.

"Oh, thank goodness." The girl practically fell on her in a hug.
Her helmet was on the ground next to her, and she squeezed her
eyes shut as she held on to Elle. "You scared the hell out of me.
And I don't even care if you tell my dad I said *hell*."

Elle gingerly pushed up to a sitting position, taking it slow and
testing her head as she pulled her helmet off. She'd worn a jacket
but had pulled the sleeves up, and she winced at the road rash on
the outside of her arm. A dull pain also emanated from around her
right lower leg.

She ignored the pain as she focused on the girl, thankful she'd
made her put on a jacket and pants. The sleeve of her jacket was
torn, and her pants were covered in dust. "Are you okay? Did you
get hurt?"

"I'm okay," Mandy told her as she sat back in the dirt. The ATV
was on its side behind her, one wheel still slowly spinning. The
horses had caught up and were keeping an eye on them from a
safe distance away. Mandy cradled her arm to her. "I might be a
little banged up but nothing like when I got bucked off a horse
last summer." She glanced down at her arm. "And there's a strong
possibility I may have broken my arm."

"Oh my gosh." Elle dropped her head into her hands. "I knew

we shouldn't have gotten on that stupid thing." She raised her head and pressed her hand to Mandy's leg. "I'm so sorry."

Mandy narrowed her eyes and fixed Elle with a steely stare. "Remember, we don't say that to each other. This isn't your fault. If anything, I'm the one who pushed us to go to the lake and to ride the ATV. But this was an accident. There was no way we could have seen that deer. It just happened."

"Oh, honey, but if only—"

The girl held up her good hand, cutting off her next words. "Stop. You didn't do anything wrong. And you don't have to say you're sorry to me."

Elle nodded, her eyes brimming with tears. She loved this girl so much.

"But we do need to figure out how to get back to town. Your leg is bleeding, and since you passed out, you might have a concussion."

"You're right. Why don't I call your dad while you grab us those waters?" She gestured to a couple of loose bottles that sat in the dirt behind Mandy. Judging by the debris scattered around them, their lunch must have exploded when it flew off the ATV.

She eyed the overturned quad as she dug her phone from her pocket. There was no way she wanted to get back on that thing, even if they could push it back over by themselves. She tried Brody, but his receptionist said he was still in surgery. She left a message for him to call her as soon as he got out. She wasn't looking forward to that call.

She looked at her phone, wishing Bryn or Zane were back, as she tried to think who to call for help. Tapping the phone, she called the only other person in this town who she knew she could count on.

Less than ten minutes later, they heard the sound of an engine and looked up to see an ancient, blue pickup barreling through the pasture. It pulled to a stop in front of them, and Sassy jumped out of the passenger side.

Not only had the elderly woman shown up, but she'd brought reinforcements. Elle would be surprised if she didn't have a lasagna tucked somewhere in the cab.

"Oh my Lord," Sassy cried. "Are you two all right?"

"We're okay," Elle said. "Thanks for coming."

"Of course," she said. "And I brought Doc with me, just in case."

Doc Hunter hurried toward her, a large black medical bag in his hand.

"Hi, Doc," Elle said, gesturing toward the girl. "Check Mandy first. She might have broken her arm."

"No," Mandy said. "Check Elle first. She's bleeding."

"I'm fine, really." She pleaded with Doc with her eyes.

"I'll check both of you," he said, but knelt down next to Mandy first. "Sassy, why don't you grab some of that gauze from my bag and press it to that gash on Elle's leg?"

"Got it." Sassy tore open the package of gauze and gently pressed it to Elle's wound. "I always wanted to be a nurse."

"Why didn't you do it, then?" Elle winced at the pressure. She'd already poured water over the gash, dislodging most of the dirt and pebbles.

"Oh, I don't really like blood." Sassy wrinkled her nose. "Or vomit. Or any bodily fluids really."

"Then it's probably wise you skipped that profession."

Sassy shrugged. "I did like their uniforms. Those crisp, white dresses and cute, little hats. Although nowadays, they all wear those funny scrubs, so I guess it doesn't matter anyway."

After a cursory exam, Doc declared they would both live. "It does look like Mandy's got a buckle-break-type fracture of her wrist. And there's a chance you have a mild concussion. Other than that nice laceration on your leg there and some pretty good road rash, it doesn't appear you've got anything more than some minor bumps and bruises." He peered down at Elle. "It seems you took the brunt of the damage. You must have protected the girl when you fell."

Elle heaved a sigh of relief. "I tried."

"You did good, honey." Sassy patted her shoulder.

"You both need to go to the hospital to get checked out, and Mandy's going to need an X-ray. Let's get you two in the truck, and we'll take you over there." He nodded toward the quad. "Just leave that thing there. We're far enough off the road, no one's going to see it. And Brody can come out and get it later."

Elle groaned. Brody had entrusted her with his daughter, and she'd let him down. She'd let herself down. "We can leave it out here forever as far as I'm concerned. I don't care if I ever see that thing again."

Brody skidded into the parking lot and barely got the door of his truck closed before he sprinted toward the doors of the hospital. A sick feeling churned in his gut. *This is my fault. I never should have stayed at Elle's last night.*

He swore at himself. When would he learn? Every single time he'd tried to put his needs above his daughter's, it had ended in catastrophe. *Please God, don't let this be catastrophic.*

Elle had called and left a second message with the receptionist, telling her that they had been in an accident but were all right except Mandy may have broken her arm, and they were headed to the hospital to get it X-rayed. He didn't know Elle well enough to know if she tended to over- or underexaggerate things in a crisis situation. All he did know was that his daughter was hurt, and his pulse wouldn't be able to stop racing until he saw for himself that she was okay.

The whoosh of the doors sliding open almost stopped him in his tracks—the memories of visiting Mary coming at him with the force of a tsunami. The smells were next—the strong scent of disinfectant, bleach, the cloying smell of get-well flowers, and the underlying hint of cafeteria food.

The waiting room was sparse, an older man leaning forward in his chair to hack a harsh, phlegmy cough into his handkerchief, a miserable-looking teenage boy wearing pajama pants and leaning onto his mother's shoulder, another mother bouncing a fussy infant.

He hated this place, every sound, every smell reminding him of the hours he spent here wishing and praying for his wife to get better as he waited for her to either live or die. Bile rose in his throat as he forced his feet to move forward.

"Hey, Brody," Pam, the receptionist, said as she looked up from the registration desk.

"Where's Mandy?" he asked, not bothering with the niceties. Pam was a friend of his mom's. She went to their church, played bridge with Susan on Tuesdays, and had occasionally filled in as a babysitter for Mandy after Mary had died.

She got up from her desk and waved him toward the emergency room doors. "Come on, honey. I'll take you back. But don't look so scared. Your girl is doing okay. In fact, I think I just heard one of the doctors saying she was trying to tell him a knock-knock joke while he did the X-ray."

"Thanks, Pam. I appreciate your trying to make me feel better, but I need to see her for myself."

"I understand, hon." She pulled back a green curtain. "She's in here."

He rounded the curtain, and his heart nearly stopped.

Mandy was sitting up in the bed, looking smaller than usual, the starched, white blanket across her lap. Her arm was in a sling, but she smiled at him around the lollipop lodged in her mouth.

"Hi, Dad. Guess what? I broke my arm. But they said I could have a pink-and-purple cast. Isn't that cool?"

A nurse stood on the other side of the bed, marking things on a clipboard.

"I'm Dr. Brody Tate. I'm her dad. How is she?" he asked as he gingerly wrapped his daughter in a hug. He kissed the top of her head, then blew out his breath into her hair. "You really okay, squirt?"

"Yes, I'm fine, except I can't breathe because you're squishing me," she said into his chest.

He let her go and took a step back, but kept his hand on her shoulder as he peered at the nurse.

"She's doing great. Other than the buckle fracture of her wrist, she's just got a couple of scrapes." She hooked her pen to the top of the clipboard. "The doctor can tell you more. I'll let him know you're here."

She went out one end of the curtain just as a voice could be heard speaking loudly from the other end. "I'm looking for Mandy Tate. I heard what you said, but I'm tired of waiting. And I'll get back in the bed after I see that she's okay."

He recognized Elle's voice, and the sound of it had guilt rising in him like a tide of floodwater. The rings jangled as she pulled back the curtain and peered inside, her jaw set, her eyes narrowed and determined. Her expression changed from dogged to desperation when she caught sight of him. "Oh, Brody, is she okay? I'm so sorry. I never should have taken her on the four-wheeler."

"No, you shouldn't have." His voice was hard and steely. He couldn't believe Elle had taken that kind of risk with his daughter.

Her shoulders curved inward as she wrinkled her brow. "I know." She was barefoot and wore only a hospital gown. An angry-red scrape covered her lower arm, and a deep purple bruise traveled across her ankle and up her leg, ending somewhere under a large white bandage. Her face was smudged with dirt, and her hair was tangled, the majority pulled loose from the ponytail holder at the back of her neck. Even during the fire, he'd never seen her look so disheveled or this distraught. One part of him wanted to cross the room, haul her into his arms, and kiss away her pain. But the other part, the part that was terrified and mad and nauseated from the swirl of memories churning through him, kept his feet planted and his muscles tense.

"I'm okay, Elle," Mandy told her after giving her dad an odd look. "My arm is barely even broken. And they said I could have a pink-and-purple cast. Isn't that awesome?"

Elle shook her head, her voice barely over a whisper. "No. That's not awesome that you broke your arm."

"Are you okay? Did they check your head?"

"I'm fine. Don't worry about me. What can I do to help you?" She took a step forward, but Brody held up his hand.

"Look, I'm glad you're okay, but I think we need to do this on our own. She's my daughter. I can take care of her."

Elle winced and shrunk back. "Oh, sure, yeah, okay. I understand."

"Dad, it's fine. I want Elle in here."

"It's not up to you," he snapped. "You're the child. And I'm the dad. End of discussion." He cut his eyes away from the hurt burning in both Elle's and Mandy's eyes. *Tough shit.* If he had to be the bad guy to keep his daughter safe, he'd be the bad guy all day long.

He held his ground as Elle slipped quietly out of the room.

"Dad," Mandy said. "What is wrong with you?"

"Nothing." Nothing that he couldn't fix. "I'll be back in a minute, honey. But I'm right out here if you need me," he told his daughter as he followed Elle. He saw her disappear behind another curtain a few rooms away.

She turned as he pushed through the curtain. "Oh, Brody, I know you're angry, and you have every right to be. I can't begin to tell you how sorry I am. Can you ever forgive me?"

She stepped toward him, but Brody took a step back and had to look away from the desperate hurt in her eyes. Head down, he stared at the floor, his gaze trained on a dark smudge on the linoleum. "It doesn't matter if I can forgive you or not. This isn't about that. I just came in here to tell you that I can't do this. This thing with you and me. I thought I could, but I can't. Getting that call and walking into this hospital this afternoon just reminded me of everything I lost. And I can't go through that again. Ever." His voice broke, and he fought for control.

She didn't say anything, and he finally looked up at her. She was staring at her hands, clasped together at her waist and gripping them so tightly her knuckles had turned white. "I understand," she finally said, her voice soft. "It's probably for the best."

"It's just the way it has to be. We need to stop before anyone else gets hurt. It's not just us. It's my daughter too. And I need to put her first."

She raised her gaze to meet his, and the hurt he saw in her eyes ripped through him like a chainsaw tearing through a tree. "Yes. Mandy should always come first." She tore her gaze from his. "You should get back to her."

"Yeah, I should." He pulled the curtain to the side, then turned back, feeling like he should say something else. He really cared about her, and even though he knew it had to be done, this still felt like a shit way to do it. "This isn't how I wanted it to be."

"No. Neither did I." She sighed as she slumped down in the chair.

He swallowed at the emotion swelling in his throat as he pushed through the curtain and headed back to his daughter.

———————

This sucks. Elle's body felt as if it were weighed down by a half ton of cement as she watched the curtain settle after Brody left. What did she expect would happen? That Brody would race in and sweep her into his arms, desperate to make sure she was okay?

Yeah, that didn't happen. Not even close. But what did she think he would do after she so recklessly risked the health of his daughter? What was she thinking anyway?

She had to get out of here.

She stumbled out of the chair and yanked on her clothes, wincing as her sleeve rubbed against the scrape on her arm. That pain was nothing compared to the ache in her heart. She tossed the hospital gown to the floor. She didn't care what the doctor said. She wasn't spending the night here. It was too much. There were too many memories, too many ghosts of the night of the accident. She would have stayed—for Mandy. And Brody. But he didn't want her here.

She wasn't sure how everything had gone so terribly wrong, but the determined look on his face told her there was no fixing it. And she wasn't sure she wanted to fix it. Loving someone only ended in pain.

Loving someone? She stopped and leaned forward, planting her hands on her knees as she tried to ride through the wave of nausea. She wasn't sure if it was the concussion or that thought that had bile rising in her throat, but she tried to focus on drawing in a steady breath, then slowly releasing it.

She *did* love someone. *Two* someones. Whether she was ready to admit it or not, the fact of the matter was that she had fallen in love with Brody Tate and his precocious daughter.

Not that it mattered. Because it was clear from Brody's reaction and the finality of his words to her that he did *not* love her. And he wasn't ever going to.

Which was another reason she needed to leave. Mandy was okay. Well, not okay, but not in any danger. It was Elle's fault that a bone was broken in that precious girl's body. And Mandy could smile and sound as excited as she wanted about getting a pink-and-purple cast, but that didn't assuage Elle's guilt.

She stuffed her feet into her sneakers. She couldn't stay here another minute. The smell of bleach and the sounds of insistent beeps and dings made her head hurt—even the soft *whoosh* of the rubber wheels on the linoleum and the low murmur of voices was too much.

She had no idea where she was going or how she was going to get home, but she'd walk if she had to. She limped down the hallway and out the front door of the hospital. The bright sun blinded her, and she raised her arm to protect her eyes and ran smack dab into another person.

"Sorry," she murmured as she lowered her arm, then relief flooded through her as she recognized the woman she'd crashed into. "Bryn. Thank God you're here." She wanted to sob as she collapsed into her friend's arms. "What are you doing here? How did you know?"

"Aunt Sassy called as we were driving into town. We came straight to the hospital," Bryn said as she hugged her. "Zane's parking the truck."

"Don't bother. I'm leaving."

"Leaving?"

"Where is he?" She ignored the question as she pushed away from her friend and scanned the parking lot. "Let's go."

"Wait. Aren't you supposed to stay here? I thought Sassy said the doctor wanted you to stay overnight for observation."

"I don't care what the doctor said," she snapped. Narrowing her eyes, she stared at Bryn, who, for her part, stood her ground, staring back as she held firmly on to Elle's arms. "Fine." Elle's shoulders slumped forward. "He told me I should *probably* stay overnight, but that's when he thought I'd be home alone. Now that you're back, you can observe me. And really he just said I needed some rest. But if I pass out or start speaking in gibberish, you have my permission to bring me back here."

Bryn's brow furrowed as she looked from Elle to the hospital door. "Maybe I should just take a minute and talk to the doctor myself."

"He's not going to talk to you anyway because you're not immediate family. I don't *have* any immediate family. Remember, mine died in a car accident." She stopped, realizing she was practically yelling at her friend, who was doing nothing except trying to help her. Elle stared at the other woman, beseeching her to understand. "Bryn, please. I hate hospitals. They're full of ghosts for me and too many bad memories."

Bryn's staunch expression crumpled, and she tightened her grip on Elle's arms. "Oh, honey. I am so sorry."

"You don't have to…" she started to say, then had to stop, the recollection of the *so sorry* game she played with Brody and Mandy too fresh, too raw. "Look, I've had a shit day, and every part of my body hurts. Plus, I did something stupid and hurt two people I really care about. And now Brody doesn't want anything to do with me—so now my heart hurts too. I just want to go home and curl up under the covers and sleep. But I don't currently have a home to go to, so I just want to go to your home and curl up there. And I *am* going, whether you like it or not. So you can either take me to the farm or get out of my way and let me start walking."

"All right," Bryn relented. "We'll take you."

As Elle was speaking, a silver king-cab pickup had pulled up to the curb, the back end loaded with stuff tied down under a tarp and pulling a small horse trailer. A yellow palomino stared out through the slats in the trailer, and Zane leaned his head out the window of the truck. "Are you all okay? I saw you standing here looking like you were about to drop your gloves and go at it." Lucky stood on his lap, his tongue lolling from his mouth as he leaned his head out next to Zane's. Hope stood on the backseat, staring at Elle through the window. The collie lifted a paw and scratched at the glass.

"I'm trying to convince her to stay in the hospital," Bryn told him. "But she's determined to leave. She said if we don't give her a ride, she's going to walk."

"Yeah, I heard." He pushed the dog out of the way and got out of the truck. "We'd better give her a ride, then." He opened the back door of the cab.

A cowboy about their age sat in the back. He wore jeans, boots, and a faded blue T-shirt. Elle took a step forward, and her knees almost buckled.

Zane caught her as she pitched forward. He wrapped an arm around her waist. "All right, darlin'. I got you."

Bryn let out an exasperated sigh. "Zane, look at her. She can barely stand up. I think we should take her back in."

"You heard what she said—either we're taking her or she's walking, and this one is just stubborn enough to do it." He grinned down at Elle. "And she doesn't look in very good shape to be walking." He nodded toward the truck. "Between the three of us, we've seen enough concussions to know the danger signs. We can keep an eye on her."

"I'm fine," she told them. "They gave me some pain meds for the road rash, and they're just making me a little woozy. I'll be okay after I get home and get some sleep." Elle pulled her arm from Zane's grasp and climbed into the back of the truck. The man on the other side of the seat held the border collie in a firm grip as she strained to greet Elle.

"Hi. I'm Elle," she said, reaching over to give the dog's ears a scratch. "Hi, Hope. You're a good girl."

The man nodded. "Cade Callahan. Bryn's cousin."

"Nice to meet you. Welcome to Colorado." She might be bruised, heartbroken, and wobbly from pain meds, but she still had her manners about her.

"Good to meet you too." He nodded at her front. "Not that you'd care, but your shirt's on backwards."

"Is it?" She looked down to see the tag sticking up off her collar.

"Well, shit. Apparently it's inside out too. That just freaking figures. But it's about par for the kind of day I've had."

He nodded. His face was serious. But it was a good face, and she saw a little of Bryn in it. He looked like a young Robert Redford, with his sun-streaked light-brown hair, a scruff of beard covering a chiseled jaw, and blue eyes that conveyed amusement but also kindness. "Been there."

She buckled her seat belt and slumped back, so exhausted she felt like she could melt into the warm seat. The truck smelled like a mixture of dog, men's aftershave, hay, and coffee—an almost pleasant scent—one that offered comfort and familiarity. Elle's eyes fluttered closed as the sun beat warm on her face, and within seconds, she was out.

———————

Elle woke sometime later—it could have been ten minutes or ten hours. As she swam to consciousness, she noticed her legs and one arm were asleep and her cheek was pressed firmly against a muscular, jean-clad thigh.

CHAPTER 24

FLUTTERING HER EYES, ELLE LET OUT A GROAN AS SHE TRIED to raise her head. She winced as a sharp pain split through her skull.

"Easy now. Don't try to sit up too fast," the man attached to the muscular thigh instructed.

She laid her head back down, the splitting pain overriding the awkward embarrassment of waking to find herself sprawled across the backseat of a pickup with her head in the lap of a strange cowboy. Strange, but also incredibly handsome, which only added to the awkwardness.

Yeah, right. If he were only a moderately attractive man, waking up in his lap would definitely be less awkward.

He calmly tucked a ticket stub into the center of the paperback novel he'd been reading and set it on the seat. Her opinion of him raised several notches, both for his choice of reading material—a spy thriller—and the fact that he didn't desecrate the book like a monster by dog-earing one of its pages.

The windows of the truck were down, and Elle could hear the rustle of leaves as a cool breeze blew through the cab. "Where are we?"

"At the farm. You fell asleep on the way home, and you sort of slumped over on me. You were sleeping so soundly, you seemed like you needed it. And I didn't have the heart to wake you, so I told Zane to park under the tree by the barn, and I've been catching up on my reading while you slept. You snore by the way."

This guy was a pro at pointing out her flaws—first her backwards shirt, now her propensity to snore. "So you've just been sitting in this truck reading a book while you let a perfect stranger sprawl across your lap and take a nap?"

He lifted a shoulder in a lazy shrug. "That about sums it up, yeah. Although to be fair, I've spent the better part of the last three days listening to my cousin yammer on about you, and everyone else in this town, so it feels like I already practically know you."

That makes one of us because I sure don't know you. "How long was I out?"

"Not long. About an hour, maybe."

Her eyes widened. "You've been sitting in this truck listening to me snore, er, I mean, sleep, for an hour?"

"Give or take. Although, to be precise, I'd been sitting in this truck for at least six hours before we got here. And the last hour was much quieter and with fewer dogs."

"Oh my gosh. How embarrassing." She covered her face with her hands.

"Nah. Nothing to be embarrassed about. I've had my share of conks to the noggin, and I've spent many hours passed out in a much more unpleasant fashion."

"But still…"

He shrugged. "I didn't mind. I was at a real good place in my book. Plus, Bryn brought me out this nice cup of iced tea." He picked up a plastic tumbler and the ice clinked against the sides as he held it out to her. "Want a sip?"

She nodded. Her mouth was dry from sleep and the medication, and it watered at the droplets of condensation on the sides of the glass. "Yes. Actually, I do."

He helped her to sit up. "Easy now."

She leaned back against the seat and wiped the side of her mouth, hoping she hadn't drooled. Taking the cup from him, she took a small sip. The iced tea was heaven on her parched throat. She raised an eyebrow at her seatmate. "I normally wouldn't share a drink with someone I just met, but now that I've slept with you, it seems okay."

His lips curved into a grin. "Bryn was right. You are funny. I wouldn't have thought it at first, but that was a good one. Snuck it right in there and almost made me laugh."

Almost. Story of her life. She took another sip. "Now I'm curious what you *did* think at first."

He cocked an eyebrow as he studied her. "Smart, a little proper, a lot classy."

"Even with my shirt on inside out?"

"Even then. And a little bit fragile. When you came out of those hospital doors, you looked like you might shatter into a million pieces and fracture all over the sidewalk."

"I kind of felt like that."

"Feel better now?"

"No, not really. But at least I'm awake. Although I've got a bastard of a headache."

"I'm sure Bryn's got some ibuprofen. You ready to go in?"

"Yeah, I think so."

"We'll take it slow. Stay right there. I'll come around and give you a hand." He got out on his side and slammed the door.

The sound of the slam was still ringing in her ears as he came around the front of the truck and opened her door. He held out his hand, and she grabbed on to it as she eased out of the seat. The ground felt a little unsteady under her feet, and she let him wrap his arm around her waist as they walked toward the house.

"What the hell?" He squinted at the house. "Is that a hog sleeping on the front porch?"

"Shh. We don't call her that. Her name is Tiny, and she thinks she's a dog."

"Apparently."

A loud whinny sounded from the corral, and Elle turned to see Glory running up and down the fence line, rearing her head up and down as she ran. "Hold on," she told Cade as she stared at the horse. "I need to go over there for a minute. This might sound weird, but that horse was there right after the accident, and I think she needs to see that I'm okay."

Cade shrugged. "I don't think that's weird. I've been around horses my whole life. There isn't much that surprises me about them anymore."

She approached the fence and the horse huffed and reared back her head, then settled as Elle held out her hand. Glory took a cautious step forward, swished her tail once, then moved closer to let Elle rub her neck. Elle leaned her head forward, and the horse tipped her nose down to nuzzle Elle's head.

"Hmm. You don't see that a lot," Cade noted. "You must be pretty close to this horse."

"What do you mean?"

He shrugged. "A lot of horses are affectionate and they'll lean into you, but their nose is one of the most vulnerable parts of their body, so when they open up like that and nuzzle you with their nose, it shows how comfortable they are with you and how much they trust you."

A lump formed in Elle's throat, and she leaned her forehead against the horse's. "Thanks, girl. I needed that. And I like you too, Glory." The horse had visibly settled and stood calmly at the fence.

"All right, she's seen you. Now, I think we'd better get you inside." They crossed the driveway, and Cade rubbed the back of his neck as they walked up to the house. "I might need to get my eyes checked because that looks like a giant turtle standing in the front yard."

"He's actually a tortoise. His name is Spartacus."

"Of course it is. Does he think he's a dog too?"

"No, but he does love strawberries. And cherries. And anything red, so if your toenails are painted red, he might go after them."

"Duly noted. And I think I'm safe on that count. I haven't painted my toenails in weeks."

Elle's lips tugged in a grin as she peered up at him. "Evidently you're funny too."

"Occasionally. But don't get used to it."

The front door opened, and Bryn came hurrying down the steps and wrapped her arm around the other side of Elle's waist. "Oh good, you're awake. How do you feel?"

"Hot, achy, and a little embarrassed. Apparently I've been asleep on your cousin's lap for the better part of an hour. And he said I snore."

Bryn grinned over her head at her cousin. "You do. A little. But it's a cute snore." They walked up the steps, and Cade held the door for them. "I've made some hot tea, and I've got baked macaroni and cheese in the oven. I can run you a bath. Or would you rather take a shower?"

Bryn's actions reminded her of the night of the fire. Except this was different. Because Brody wasn't here, sharing inside jokes with her and turning her insides wonky with his cute smile. "I just want to lie down."

"Okay. I can bring you a tray."

"She could probably use some ibuprofen," Cade said, leaning his hip against the counter and peering around the inside of the house. "I like what you've done with the place. It looks real nice, Bryn. Although from what I've seen so far, it seems you might go by Dr. Doolittle now."

Bryn laughed. "I wish I were Dr. Doolittle. Then I could actually talk to these animals. I think several of them would have some pretty interesting stories to tell."

Just the mention of a doctor had Elle's throat burning again. She nodded at Bryn's cousin. "I can't remember your name right now, but thanks. For everything." She gave Bryn a hug, then shuffled down the hall toward her bedroom.

Roxy looked up as she came into the room, and her heart filled at the sight of the mother dog curled protectively around the sleeping pile of multicolored dogs. Elle trudged toward the closet and sank to the floor, resting her head on her arm as she laid down next to the dogs. Roxy stood and stepped carefully around the snoozing puppies to get to Elle. Her tail wagged furiously, and she licked Elle's cheek, then circled around and laid down in the crook of Elle's outstretched arms. The dog scootched closer, then raised her head and licked the underside of Elle's chin.

Elle let out a laugh that turned into a sob as she cuddled the dog closer and buried her face in Roxy's small neck. The dog gave a soft whine and tried to lick Elle's tears as she wept out the stress and heartache of the day.

"Oh, honey," Bryn said from the doorway of her room. She was holding a glass of iced tea and a bottle of Advil, and she set them on the nightstand and crossed to where Elle lay on the floor. She sank to her knees and rubbed her friend's arm. "I'm not sure what you need right now, but I'm here for you. I can either sit here quietly, or lie down next to you and be the big spoon, or I can help you into bed. What do you need, friend?"

Elle smiled through her tears. "As much as I appreciate your offer to spoon me, I think I should probably get into bed. I just couldn't resist a little cuddle time with Roxy. I really love this dog."

"She really loves you too. She's such a sweet dog. And those puppies are adorable." Bryn stood and held out her hand to help Elle.

Everything hurt as she pulled herself off the floor and eased into bed. Bryn dumped a couple of ibuprofen into her hand, and she took the pills, then sank back onto the pillow, praying the medicine would work quickly.

―――――――――――

Elle spent most of the next few days in bed, reading or sleeping, but Bryn woke her on the third day after the accident with a soft knock on the door.

"Good morning, sunshine," she said, a little too cheerily for Elle's opinion. "I'm coming in, and I've got coffee and a puppy." She set the cup on Elle's nightstand and plopped the wiggling gray-and-white puppy onto the bed. The pup immediately ran to Elle's head to lick and nibble at her chin.

"It's Saturday," Elle said, wincing as Bryn flung open the curtains and let the sun stream into the room. "This is the day you're supposed to sleep in."

"We already did. It's almost eight o'clock. That's like eleven in Country Time."

Lucky's and Hope's dog/human sensors must have gone off because she heard the rapid skitter of toenails on the hardwood seconds before both dogs ran into her room and vaulted onto her bed to join the slobber bath the puppy was already giving her.

"Okay. I'm up. I'm up," she said, pushing herself up against the headboard while trying to give all three dogs a quick pet.

"I talked to the doctor, not about *your case* specifically, but just in general terms of what kind of care to give someone who had wrecked an ATV and had cuts, bruises, and a mild concussion."

Elle raised an eyebrow. "Just in general terms? Right." *Small towns.* "And?"

"And he said rest is good, but it's also good to get up and walk around and stretch your achy muscles. So I'm giving you one hour to drink your coffee, eat breakfast, take a hot shower, and get dressed. Then, we're going for a walk."

Elle blew out a sigh as she shook her head. "I think I need another day in bed before I rejoin the ranks of society." Or another week.

"Tough. You don't get one. Today's the day. Zane already made bacon."

"I can't," she whispered, peering up at her friend. "Everything still hurts too much." She had finally started to feel complete, with Brody and Mandy, finally found a family, and now it was gone. In an instant, in a stupid move on a four-wheeler. Another accident. The irony of it was just too much.

"Oh, honey, I know it does," Bryn said, sitting on the edge of the bed and gathering her friend into a hug. Elle had filled her in on everything that happened with her and Brody while she and Zane had been gone.

"I really like him," Elle whispered.

"I know you do." Bryn stroked her hair, and the dogs cuddled against her legs. "And he really likes you. Which is what I'm sure scared the hell out of him. You have both been through a lot. Cut yourself a break and give it some time."

"He didn't say he wanted time. He did at first, but not this time. This time he said he couldn't do it at all. And he meant it. We're through."

"I know it hurts, but hiding in bed isn't going to make it hurt any less. You'll be surprised at what a hot shower and a long walk in nature will do for you."

"That's what Mandy said too." A vise squeezed her heart. Losing Brody was hard enough, but the thought of not being with the ten-year-old anymore almost paralyzed her.

"She's a smart girl. Now come on." Bryn gave her shoulder a rub before pushing off the side of the bed. "Get up and out of that bed. It's been hot and dry the last few days, and we need to get our walk in before the day gets too warm."

Elle nodded and cuddled the puppy closer to her. "Did you know Sassy has decided she wants a dog, and she's fallen in love with this one? I told her we'd save him for her. Hope that's okay."

"Yeah, she already called me and told me to hold him." Bryn smacked the blanket next to her. "Nice attempt at a stall tactic, though. Now get up."

"Fine. But has anyone told you that you can be kind of bossy?"

Bryn laughed as Elle swung her legs over the side of the bed. She might not have Brody and Mandy, but she still had a good friend, a *best* friend, one who cared enough to bring her coffee, to force her out of bed, and to boss her around. She needed to focus on the positives in her life—even if they were small positives, like the one Bryn had mentioned earlier. Elle followed her from the room, inhaling the heavenly scent that wafted down the hall. At least there was going to be bacon.

———————

Forty minutes later, Elle tried to catch her breath as she and Bryn climbed the trail leading up the mountain behind the farm. "When you said a walk, I thought you meant a leisurely stroll through the pasture," Elle told her. "Not a death hike up the side of a mountain."

"Oh, this is barely a hill. And it's good to stretch your legs. Plus, I like coming up here because you can see all of our land and most of the town," Bryn told her as they crested the top of the treelined ridge. "Just fill your lungs with that clean mountain air." She inhaled deeply, then alarm widened her eyes. "Do you smell smoke?"

She searched the sky and pointed to a plume of dark smoke rising in the air. "There." She ran over the last stretch of the trail that led through the trees and out onto the open ridge, Elle racing at her heels.

"Oh no! It's a grass fire!" Bryn had her phone out, already calling 911 as she pointed her finger toward the pasture below, where a line of flames was licking across the dry grass of the open field.

CHAPTER 25

FORGETTING ABOUT THE PAIN IN HER BODY, ELLE RAN AFTER Bryn as they fled down the mountain and back toward the farm. Bryn had called in the fire, then called Zane and told him what was going on as they hurriedly made their way down the rocky path.

Once they got down and out of the trees, they sprinted across the field and toward the farmhouse. Zane was already tossing shovels and gear into the back of the truck. "Cade's in the barn saddling up. He's gonna go after the cattle and the horses and get them closer to the house. I'm heading to the fire."

"I'm going with you," Bryn said, pulling open the door to the truck.

"How can I help?" Elle asked.

"Find Cade," Zane told her. "You can help with the animals." He gunned the engine and gravel flew as they tore out of the driveway.

Elle sprinted toward the barn, racing inside to find Cade cinching the saddle of his horse. "Zane sent me in to help you. What can I do?"

"Can you ride?"

"Not with any proficiency."

"Well, I'm heading to the west pasture and need to get fifty head of cattle and several horses back to the house. So if you can't ride, then I'm gonna need you to get on that quad and follow me out there, so you can flank my other side and help me get those animals back here."

She glanced at the quad, then back at him, her heart pounding as she shook her head. "I can't."

"Can't or won't? 'Cause *won't* doesn't help me."

"You don't understand. The last time I got on one of those I hurt two people I care about and I lost the guy I'm in love with."

"Well, I'm the last person to tell you anything about love, but I do know a little something about fear. And the only way to get past it is to face it. Grab it by the horns, look it in the eyes, and stare it down."

Do it. She grabbed a helmet and strapped it on but hesitated again as she grasped the handlebar and prepared to mount the machine. "That's easy for you to say. You ride bulls and stare down fear all the time."

"Look, I don't know you. We met like a minute ago, so I don't have time for pleasantries and chitchat." He put his foot in the stirrup and hauled himself into his saddle. Picking up the reins, he stared down at her, his gaze hard and resolute. "But we've got work to do, so if you really want to help, get your ass on that quad and follow me."

His directive spurred her into action.

She climbed on. *I can do this.* Her hands shook as she turned the key in the ignition, then pressed the start button. She fought the panic rising in her as the machine roared to life. *I have to do this.*

"Let's go," Cade shouted as he galloped from the barn.

With a silent prayer, she put the quad into gear, then pressed the throttle and followed him.

Brody rubbed his temples as he pushed back from his desk chair. He'd been trying to catch up on some work at home, but he'd just read the same paragraph three times and still had no idea what it said. He needed a break.

He rolled his shoulders as he picked up his empty coffee cup and headed for the kitchen. What he really needed was to stop thinking about Elle. *Good luck with that.* He stopped as he stepped into the kitchen, and his mouth gaped at the mess his darling daughter was in the process of creating. "What is going on in here?"

Mandy stood on a stool in front of the sink, an apron wrapped around her, and a bag of russet potatoes spilling onto the counter. A YouTube video was paused on the screen of her iPad on the other counter. She turned to him, holding a potato in one hand and wielding a potato peeler in the other, one of his surgical gloves stretched over her cast. "Hi, Dad."

"What are you doing?"

She crinkled her nose, an expression she'd taken to using when she thought he was being an idiot. "I'm peeling potatoes."

"I see that. But why?"

"I'm trying to learn how to make mashed potatoes and gravy."

He approached the sink and peered down into the pan holding close to a dozen already-peeled potatoes. "For how many? That's enough potatoes to feed a small army."

"I just need enough to feed *one* person."

A sinking feeling settled in his gut. "And who would that one person be?"

"Well, one person, plus you and me, so actually three. I'm learning how to make these so I can invite Elle to have supper with us." She planted the hand holding the potato on her hip. "When we were at Bryn's and Aunt Sassy brought over that meal, Elle said that if someone went to the trouble of making her fried chicken, mashed potatoes and gravy, *and* a cake, that they would stay in her heart forever. So I'm gonna need you to help me with fixin' some fried chicken because I want her to love us again."

Oh.

Brody tried to breathe around the sharp knife that his daughter had just stabbed into his heart. A heart that was already struggling to beat from missing Elle too.

He shook his head. "That isn't going to happen."

Her small forehead wrinkled, and her eyes narrowed. "Why not? I know you miss her. You've been as grouchy and grumpy as an old bear the last few days. You're either mopey and sad or angry and mad. I heard you throwing stuff around the basement last night."

"I wasn't mad. I was just trying to find something."

She cocked an eyebrow at him. "Whatever, Dad. I'm not embarrassed to say I miss her, and I'm tired of waiting for you to fix this, so I'm doing it myself. Except for the chicken. But we already have the stuff to make grandma's chocolate dump cake, and I *know* Elle loves cake."

Elle *did* love cake. And *he* loved cake—especially when he was licking it off her perfect breasts. He scrubbed a hand through his hair, trying to force the image from his mind. "Look, kiddo, I appreciate what you're trying to do, and I know Elle would love it too. But things are over with us."

"But why? I thought you liked her." She set the potato and the peeler in the sink and dried her hands on a towel.

"I did like her." *I do like her. Still.* "But after everything that happened with the accident, it was just all too much. And I just don't think I can trust her. Especially with you."

"What? Why? She takes great care of me. She's even more worried about germs and safety than Grandma is. And she never drives over the speed limit. She barely even *goes* the speed limit."

"That may be, but she took you out on the four-wheeler without my permission. What were you even doing on that thing? For all her safety measures, I can't believe she risked putting you in that kind of jeopardy."

"Dad, that wasn't her fault." Mandy cut her eyes to the floor. Her voice was softer as she said, "I sort of told her you said it was okay."

"You what?"

She shrugged and wrung the towel she was still holding between her hands. "I'm sorry. I didn't think you would care. But she was so worried about it, and I really wanted to go swimming, so I told her I checked with you and you said it was okay. I didn't know we would crash."

He shook his head. "I don't even know what to think right now. I'm disappointed in you, I can tell you that. But I'm also glad you told me the truth. I'll figure out how to deal with the lie later."

"I know. I'm sorry. I know what I did was wrong."

"And you both ended up getting hurt."

"Not that bad. My arm will heal, and you heard what the doctor said. He told you it could have been a lot worse. That he's seen some awful damage from four-wheeler wrecks. And he said Elle was in a lot worse shape because she protected me during the crash. That sure sounds like someone you can trust."

He sighed. Did this new information change anything? So Elle hadn't taken Mandy out on the quad without his permission; it didn't change the way he'd felt as he walked into the hospital with fear gripping his body that something had happened to his daughter. Or to Elle.

But Mandy had a point. The doctor *had* said that Elle had risked her own safety to protect his girl.

"I'm glad to know Elle protected you. And yeah, maybe it does change how I feel about the accident. But it's not enough for Elle and me to patch things up. Even if I wanted to. There are two people in a relationship, and I don't think Elle even cares that it's over. She didn't even fight. I told her I didn't want to see her anymore, and she just accepted it and nodded in agreement."

"What did you expect her to do?"

He raked his hand through his hair. "I don't know. *Something. Anything.*"

"Dad, don't you get it? Elle is the one who's afraid. She's afraid of everything. That's why she does all that crazy safety stuff. So *we* have to be brave for her until she can find the brave in herself."

He felt a small frisson of hope. But it wasn't enough. "I love that you see the good in people, and you have a giant heart, but there's more going on than just being brave."

"I don't think so. I think this is all about being brave and going after what you want. I'm not a little kid anymore, Dad. I mean I *am* a kid, but I'm not a *little* kid, and I understand some stuff. Like I understand that in the time that Elle has been with us, it's the happiest I've seen you in…like, ever. Well, ever since Mom died."

He shook his head. "My happiness doesn't matter."

"That's stupid. Why not?"

"Because *you* are what's important. I need to put you first. I put myself, and my career, first when your mom was alive, and I regret it every day. I missed out on so much time with her, and with you. And I promised myself I wouldn't do that again."

"You know that's a lot of pressure to put on a little kid."

"You just assured me that you weren't a little kid anymore."

"Okay, that's a lot of pressure to put on *any* kid. You're saying you can't be happy if I'm not happy. But what if sometimes I want to be mad or sad or upset…which by the way, I've heard happens a lot once I start my period."

He groaned. "Seriously, kid? Can we face one life crisis at a time?"

She shrugged. "Fine, but come on, Dad. For such a smart guy, you sure are dumb sometimes. I'm not going to be happy if you're unhappy. That doesn't even make sense. And having Elle in our lives *does* make me happy—partly because I love her and she's nice and fun and awesome. And partly because she makes you so happy. And I think you love her too."

He blew out a sigh. "Yeah, I think I do."

"So, don't tell me. Go tell her."

"I hear you. But it's not that easy. I already broke things off with her, so what am I supposed to do?"

Mandy rolled her eyes and did the nose-crinkling *you're an idiot* face again. "Go fix it."

Go fix it. It sounded so easy when Mandy said it. But Brody had no idea how to just fix it. *Start by talking to her.* The idea of seeing her again had his pulse racing. It had only been a few days, but damn, he had missed her.

"Okay, I'll go talk to her." His cell phone buzzed, and he pulled it from his pocket to see a text from Bryn. "Aw hell. There's a grass fire out at Bryn's place. We gotta go, kid."

Mandy threw down the dish towel and clamored off the stool. They sprinted to the truck, Brody stopping for only a second to throw a shovel into the back end. He tossed his phone on the seat as they got in. "Call Grandma and get her to come pick you up. Tell her the fire's on Bryn's property out on Highway 9 across from Rivers Gulch."

He pressed the gas pedal, swerving around a compact car that was putzing down the road. He had no idea how far or fast the fire had spread, but if it was on Bryn's land, her house could lay in its path.

"She's on her way," Mandy said, hanging up the phone and passing it back to her dad.

He flew down the highway, racing toward Bryn's—and Elle. Leaning forward, he strained against his seat belt as he looked through the windshield, trying to see signs of the fire.

They spotted the dark smoke rising in the sky and then saw the flames. Pickups and cars lined the sides of the road, several that Brody recognized, and most with the red-and-white Volunteer Firefighter sticker affixed to the vehicles. But in this community, every available rancher showed up to help dig firebreaks and do whatever they could to help the fire department.

Brody pulled up as close to the main area as he could, then jumped out.

"There's Grandma!" Mandy leaned out the window and pointed to the road where Susan's blue Subaru was speeding toward them. She pulled up behind them.

"Go!" Susan yelled as she opened the car door. They all knew how quickly a grass fire could destroy crops and farmhouses.

He raced toward the fire chief, assessing the situation as he ran. Highways on the east and south sides of the property formed firebreaks, but that meant the fire was heading toward Bryn's farm. A tractor hauling a plow element behind it was digging a fire line trench through a pasture on the west side, and he recognized the driver as Logan Rivers, the rancher from across the road.

Two guys were shooting water at a round bale of hay that had caught fire and was a massive ball of flames in the center of the field. Thick, black smoke rose from the hay bale, smudging the blue sky with a gray-and-black trail.

The chief saw Brody coming and waved him toward the tractor. "Help with the firebreak," he shouted.

Brody switched direction and headed toward the tractor. He saw Zane and Bryn working with shovels behind the line and hurried toward them, giving Bryn a quick hug as he reached them.

"You okay?" he asked her.

"I will be when we get this fire out."

"Where's Elle?"

"She and my cousin Cade were riding out to our east pasture to bring the cattle and the horses in. Then I'm sure she'll head back to the house."

He looked toward the direction of the farm and spotted a horse and rider galloping toward them. The rider pulled up short as he reached them and shouted, "We need the water truck. Elle went after a stray calf, and now the fire has her trapped against the ridge."

CHAPTER 26

BRODY'S EARS RANG AS HE TRIED TO FOCUS ON THE RIDER'S words.

"We need to get a truck up there to beat the fire back so we can get her out."

Elle was trapped? Brody turned to the firefighter directing the trench effort and borrowed his insulated coat. Then he reached a hand up to the man on the saddle. "Take me to her," he commanded.

The man squinted down at him. "You the vet?"

He nodded, then grabbed the man's hand as he extended it and used it to pull himself up on the horse behind him. "You the cousin?" he asked as they took off at a gallop.

"Yep."

They didn't need much more introduction than that. Brody pointed to the line of fire. A horse that looked a lot like Glory was racing up and down this side of the flames, kicking out her legs and shaking her head as she whinnied. "What's that crazy horse doing?"

"She won't leave. That's where Elle is—up against that ridge."

Brody scanned the area looking for a way in. He could see where the fire surrounded the ridge, but there was a spot where the flames hadn't made their way up it. He pointed to that spot. "Get me up that ridge, then I can climb down and get to her on the other side."

Cade nodded his agreement and raced to the ridge. He started up the back side with the horse but only made it about three-fourths of the way up before the trees and flames blocked their path.

"I'll go on foot from here," Brody told him, climbing down from the horse. "I'll find her. You just make sure that water truck gets here and clears a path for us to get out."

"Got it. And tell Elle I'll take care of getting that horse back to the house. Although I doubt she'll leave until she sees Elle is safe and out of there," he yelled.

"Then let's get her out of there."

Cade gave him a quick nod, then turned to head back down the hill.

Brody took off at a run, scaling the ridge, then searching the area below him as he crested the top. *There!* He spotted Elle sitting on the ATV, her back against the ridge.

"Elle!" he shouted as he raced down the hill, sliding and skidding in the loose gravel. It only took a few minutes to reach her, but it felt like hours.

She turned at the sound of her name, but he couldn't see her face inside the helmet. Breaking through the sparse trees, he ran down the last section and sprinted toward the ATV.

She scrambled off the quad and ran to him, practically falling into him as he gathered her into his arms.

She hugged him hard, her shoulders shaking. "Brody. Thank God. I can't believe you're here."

"Where else would I be?" He lifted his hands to hold either side of the helmet as he stared down at her. "I was an idiot. I said it hurt too much to fall in love with you, but it hurts a hell of lot more to think about losing you. So I'm getting us out of here, then I have some apologizing to do."

She shook her head. "Remember, you don't have to say you're sorry to me."

His gaze was solemn as he nodded his head. "I appreciate the sentiment, darlin', but in this case, I do."

She nodded back, and a ghost of grin pulled at the corners of her lips. "Okay, then me too."

His spirit lifted. He still had a chance to save this thing. But first, he had to save them.

"The truck is here." He turned her by the shoulder and pointed through the flames to where the water truck had just parked and two firefighters jumped out and grabbed the hose. They pointed it toward the area with the smallest blaze, and a fan of water cascaded onto the flames. "They're going to beat a section of the fire back, and we're going to ride through it as fast as we can. Then we'll shoot across the burned grass where the fire has already been. That's called the black, and it's the safest place since the fire can't come back to it. If you're in the grass, you're part of the fuel. If you're in the black, you're in the safe zone."

She nodded, her eyes red-rimmed from smoke but still full of trust.

He climbed onto the ATV and held out his arms. "I want you to climb on facing me and wrap your arms and legs around me like a monkey clinging to a tree. Then I can wrap my coat around you, and it should protect you from the flames."

He opened his turnout coat, and she didn't hesitate as she scrambled onto the quad and pressed against him. Clinging to his body, she shouted over the roar of the quad's engine, "One monkey, ready to go."

He grinned as he folded her inside his coat, cocooning her against him. Scanning the flames around them, he gauged their best point of exit in the section of fire the firefighters were working on. He pushed the throttle and moved them closer, tensing for action as soon as he saw a way clear.

"Get ready," he yelled as he saw a break in the flames. "Hold your breath when we go through the smoke. Here we go." He pressed the throttle, pushing the ATV to accelerate while still keeping control. It wouldn't do them any good if he tipped them in the middle of the fire.

Heat from the blaze pushed against them, and he sucked in a

breath before riding through the curtain of thick smoke. They shot out the other side of the flames and raced across the blackened field. A swath of blackened grass cut through the center of the pasture, and they passed another truck that was shooting water over the flames as it drove along the line of fire from inside the burned area.

He spotted Zane and Bryn walking across the field and headed toward them. More people had gathered on the other side of the highway to watch the fire.

Brody pulled to a stop and felt Elle hug him hard before she released him and climbed off the ATV and into Bryn's embrace.

"Oh my gosh, I'm so glad you're okay," Bryn said, hugging Elle to her.

Elle pulled off the helmet and took a deep inhale of air. "I'm fine, thanks to Brody."

"And Cade," he said. "He told us you were trapped and gave me a ride to the ridge."

She shook her head. "I couldn't believe it when I saw you come over the side of the hill. I was so scared, but when I saw you, I just knew everything was going to be okay."

"I guess you can also thank Glory. She was going crazy, racing up and down the field on the other side of the flames. Cade said she wouldn't leave with you stuck in there. But he said as soon as he saw us get out, he'd drive her back toward the house."

Elle grinned. "I love that horse."

Zane wrapped Elle in a quick, tight hug, then told them, "They've got the head of the fire out, and they're just putting out spot fires now. They've got it contained, and it shouldn't take much longer to have it fully out."

"That's great news," Brody said, scanning the crowd for Mandy.

"We told your mom they had the fire contained, and she took Mandy to our house," Bryn told him. "I figured we could all meet up there afterward."

The tightness in his chest eased now that he knew his family was safe. And that included his mom, his daughter, *and* Elle. He picked up Elle's hand. "I've got to go see what else I can do to help make sure this thing is completely out, but if you want to wait for me, I'll take you back to the house. I've got my truck here."

"What about the ATV?"

"I'll take it back," Bryn said. "I want to head back in a few minutes anyway, just to check on the house and the animals."

"Wait for me then?" he asked, his gaze trained only on Elle. Her hair was a tangled mess and her face was smudged with dirt and soot, but she still looked beautiful. All he wanted to do was take her in his arms and kiss away all the hurt they'd been through the past few days. He held his breath as he waited for her reply.

"Yes. I'll be here." She narrowed her eyes as if trying to convey a stronger message. "I'll wait for you. As long as it takes."

"Good. I'll be back as soon as I can." He squeezed her hand, then let go, and he and Zane headed for the chief.

———————————

It took another few hours to get the fire completely out. Elle and Bryn stood outside for a while, then Bryn took the ATV back to the house, and Elle climbed into Brody's truck to wait for him.

Her heart leaped as she looked out the windshield and saw the tall cowboy heading her way. He tossed his shovel in the back of the truck, then opened the door and slid in next to her, bringing in the scent of smoke and ash. His face was covered in soot, and his hair stood up in sweaty spikes from where he'd pushed it off his forehead, but he looked gorgeous to her.

She scooted across the seat and threw her arms around his neck, hugging him tightly, then pulled back and pressed a hard kiss against his lips. She took his soot-covered cheeks in her hands and stared into his beautiful blue eyes. "Just so you know, I'm planning to fight for you."

A grin tugged at the corners of his lips, then it spread wide across his face. "I'm glad to hear it, because I'm planning to fight for you too."

"I've spent the last few days being miserable without you, and I somehow convinced myself that that's what life was going to be for me now. That because I'd already had my shot at a family, I somehow didn't deserve another one. But today, when I was trapped in that fire, I swore to myself that if I made it out alive, I would really live. I would fight for a chance at a life with you and Mandy. And then you came over that ridge, and my heart just about exploded with joy."

"I thought—"

She put a finger to his lips. "Wait. Don't say anything yet. I've been sitting in this truck thinking of everything I wanted to say to you, and I need to get it out."

He nodded. "Okay."

She reached up and lightly touched the corner of his mouth. "We once talked about how the other one tasted. You remember that?"

He nodded again, an impish grin curving his lips.

She shook her head, trying to hold back her own smile. "Anyway...I told you that day that you tasted like cotton candy. And other times I've kissed you, you've also tasted like chocolate and cake and cinnamon gum." Her voice lowered. "But what you mostly taste like to me is *home*."

He blinked, and she wasn't sure but it looked like his eyes shone with tears. She loved that about him. He was this tough cowboy who could wrestle a steer into a corner to give it a shot, yet he also had this sensitive side. She'd seen it when it came to his daughter—and now, apparently, when it came to her.

She swallowed against the dryness in her mouth. "And it's been a long time since I felt like I really had a home. Or a family. Until you and Mandy came into my life. And now I feel like I have a chance at both." She twisted her hands in her lap. Her thoughts were all over the place, and she had no idea if she was making sense to him, but she couldn't stop talking. "I was thinking about something Sassy told me the other day when she was over, and we were getting tipsy on the alcohol-infused cake and talking about love and relationships. And also about sex, but that's another story."

Brody covered his ears with his hands. "Please do not tell me anything about Sassy's sex life."

"I won't." She laughed, then regained her concentration. "Her thoughts on sex aside, she did have some really great insight about life and love. She said we don't heal the past by staying in it. We heal the past by moving on and living in the present. And I'm ready for that now. I'm tired of drowning in the past, and I'm ready to live in the present, with you. Well, I don't mean *actually* live with you. I'm not saying we should move in together, at least not right now," she stammered, trying to keep her focus while she backpedaled.

Brody picked up her hand. "I know what you mean. And what she said makes good sense. I'm ready to stop living in the past too. Even though it still scares me, I'm ready to start living in the present and looking toward the future."

The future? She liked the sound of that. But he'd also just said he was scared. "It's okay to be scared," she told him, gripping his hand. "That's another thing Sassy said—that love doesn't exist without fear. And if the thought of losing somebody doesn't scare the hell out of you, then you're not really in love." She lifted her hands to cup his face in her palms. "I'm still scared too, but I'm not gonna let fear stop me anymore. Because I know one thing as sure as I'm sitting here." Her voice found its strength as she looked him straight in the eyes. "Brody Tate, I *am* in love with you."

He paused and gave her a questioning look. "Is it okay if I say something now?"

She nodded, her heart pounding hard as she waited to hear what his thoughts were on the jumble of things she'd just told him.

"First of all, I want to repeat what I said before, that I had already decided to fight for you too. I was just getting ready to come tell you when Bryn texted me about the fire."

"Really?"

"Really. And I don't know why, but it seems like fire keeps forcing us together. So I think for our overall happiness *and* the safety of everyone involved, we'd better just stay together forever this time."

"Forever?"

"Yeah. Forever." He lifted one shoulder as he held her gaze. "I don't care that it happened fast. I'm just glad it happened. You crossed my path and my life changed direction." He tucked a loose strand of hair behind her ear, then held the back of his fingers to her cheek. "When I look into your eyes, I see everything I need, everything I want. And I don't want to lose that. Or you."

"Me either."

"I don't know what our present or our future looks like, but I know I want you in it. And so does Mandy. I know it's a lot to ask you to step in and be some kind of a mom to another mother's child."

"Actually it's not," she said, thinking of Roxy curled in her closet and how she didn't even hesitate to nurse the orphaned puppies. "It's the easiest thing I've done in a long time. I love you, and I love *her* too. She was already one of my favorite people before I ever even met you, but the last few weeks, spending time with her, she has totally captured my heart. And it would be my honor to be *any* kind of a mom to her."

A grin spread across his face that felt to Elle like the sun coming out on a cloudy day or, in their case, like blue sky when the black smoke clears away. He pulled her to him and kissed her, a tender kiss filled with love and promise.

Brody couldn't stop smiling as he pulled into the driveway of Bryn's farm ten minutes later. He held Elle's hand firmly in his and despite the stink of smoke in the air and the soot and dirt covering their clothes, the broken pieces of his life—and his heart—felt like they had been put back together. Maybe not in the same way, but in a new way, forged together through fire and forgiveness and a second chance at something amazing.

He stopped the truck and turned off the engine, then turned to Elle. "Look at all these cars here. There's Aunt Sassy's sedan and Doc Hunter's truck, and there's Milo's mom's car too. I think we both have a lot more family than we give ourselves credit for."

Elle grinned up at him. "I think you're right." Her eyes cut to the house at the sound of the screen door slamming. "We'd better get out of the truck because the best part of our family just came out the front door, and I, for one, am dying to hug our girl."

Our girl. His smile returned as they climbed from the truck and his daughter launched herself into his arms.

She hugged his neck. "I heard you were a hero, and you saved Elle from the fire."

"Nah," he said, pulling Elle into the hug with them. "I think she saved me."

A huge grin spread across his daughter's face. "Does this mean you fixed things?"

"Yeah," he said, chuckling. "We fixed things."

Mandy looked from him to Elle and back to him again. "So does this mean we get to be a family? All three of us?"

"Well, not exactly." His tone turned serious, and he felt Elle and Mandy stiffen. "I think we're missing something. But it's just a *little* something."

His daughter's eyes went from dismayed to delighted, and her body wiggled with excitement. "Do you mean a *little* something that has a wet nose and a waggy tail?"

This kid knew how to read him. He tried to keep his expression serious, but he couldn't pull it off, and a huge grin spread across his face. "Yeah, I think we should get a puppy."

"Yes!" she shouted, then threw her arms back around her dad's neck. "I love you so much, Dad." She wriggled out of his arms so she could hug Elle too. "And I love you too, Elle. Especially if you helped talk him into this."

Elle hugged her back and pressed a kiss on her head. "I love you too, honey. But I didn't have anything to do with this. I didn't even know about it until this second. It was all your dad's idea."

Mandy looked from her to her dad and back to Elle again. "I think you had more to do with it than you think."

Brody chuckled. *The kid is right.* He nudged her shoulder. "You better go tell Bryn not to give away all of Grace's pups."

She shook her head. "I changed my mind. I don't want one of Grace's puppies. I mean I do, but unless you're going to let me have twoooo puppies…" She paused, tilting her head as she gave him a side-eye.

"Don't push your luck."

"That's what I thought, but I had to try. Anyway, if it's okay with you, Elle, I would really like one of Roxy's foster puppies. The yellow one. And I'm pretty sure Milo's got his mom talked into letting him have the reddish one."

"That's absolutely fine with me. And it works perfectly, because I've decided I'm keeping Roxy and at least one of her original puppies."

Brody raised an eyebrow. "You're going from zero dogs to two? Or maybe three? That's a big leap."

She tilted her chin and offered him an impish grin. "I just went from zero family to two. And really, with us *and* the dogs, *we* just went from a family of three to a family of six." Her smile widened. "Or maybe seven."

"Yes," Mandy said, raising her hand to give Elle a high five.

Brody groaned. "Wait, I think I'm changing my mind."

"No way, Dad."

"No takebacks," Elle told him. "But you should know that after all of Glory's heroics, I might also be taking on a horse. *And* I'm thinking I might get a cat. *And* maybe a goldfish. But I'm absolutely drawing the line at a pig." She laughed and tickled Mandy's side. "And I for sure don't want a goat. That Otis is a kook."

Mandy giggled. "I'm with you on the goat. But I'm all in for a pig."

Brody slapped his forehead as he laughed. "I said yes to *one* puppy, and suddenly we're getting a farmyard full of animals."

"I'm going to go tell Milo we're getting puppies." Mandy hugged them both again, then raced back to the house.

Elle put her arms around his waist and peered up at him. "Maybe I should have mentioned that thing about Roxy earlier."

"It's all good," he told her, hugging him to him. "I agree with you about the goat, but as for the rest of it—three people, three dogs, a horse, a cat, and a fish—I'm all in. In fact, I'm so happy right now, you might even be able to talk me into that pig."

Elle laughed. "I think we'll have enough mouths to feed without adding a pig."

"I think you're right. And speaking of mouths to feed, I have another request. Mandy and I would like to invite you for dinner tonight, and we'll be having fried chicken, mashed potatoes and gravy, and chocolate cake for dessert."

She raised an eyebrow. "That's a pretty specific menu."

"It is. That's because I found my daughter in the kitchen this morning watching a cooking video and peeling a mountain of potatoes because she was trying to learn how to make mashed potatoes for you."

"For me?"

He nodded. "Apparently, she remembers you telling Aunt Sassy that if someone went to the trouble of making you fried chicken, mashed potatoes and gravy, *and* a cake that they would stay in your heart forever."

"Awww." Her eyes widened and brimmed with tears. "I would love to come to dinner, but you don't need fried chicken or gravy to win my heart—it's already yours. *And* hers." She pressed a quick kiss to his lips, then grinned up at him. "Although a little cake is always a good thing."

THE END...
...AND JUST THE BEGINNING...

ACKNOWLEDGMENTS

As always, my love and thanks goes out to my family! Todd, thanks for always believing in me and for being the real-life role model of a romantic hero. You cherish me and make me laugh every day and the words it would take to truly thank you would fill a book on their own. I love you. *Always*.

I can't thank my editor, Deb Werksman, enough for believing in me and this book, for loving Brody, Elle, and Mandy, and for making this story so much better with your amazing editing skills. I appreciate everything you do to help make the town of Creedence and the motley crew of farmyard animals come to life. Thanks to my project editor, Susie Benton, for all your encouragement and support, and a HUGE thanks to Dawn Adams for this amazing cover and every other awesome cover you've given me! I love being part of the Sourcebooks Sisterhood, and I offer buckets of thanks to the whole Sourcebooks Casablanca team for all of your efforts and hard work in making this book happen.

A big thank you to my parents—all of them. I appreciate everything you do and am so thankful for your support of this crazy writing career. Thanks to my mom, Lee Cumba, for so many lunches where we talk writing and plots. And thanks to my step-mom, Gracie Bryant, for your encouragement and support, and to my dad, Dr. Bill Bryant, for spending hours giving me ranching and farming advice, plot ideas, and guiding me through some of the tough aspects of rescuing horses.

Special thanks goes out to Lou Kaylor for your fire department expertise and for all the tips and advice you offered me on Elle's house fire.

Special thanks goes out to Drs. Rebecca and Corbin Hodges, my sister and brother-in-law, who are always willing to listen and offer sound veterinarian counsel on my farmyard crew of animals. Thanks Bec especially for all your help with Spartacus, the tortoise. Thank you to my nephew and nieces, Caleb, Leah, and Eden for all your tips and expertise on being kids and sharing ideas for what would be sprawled all over a family's car, words that kids use, and books you like to read. Special thanks to Corbin for spending an hour patiently helping me work through the hard scenes with Roxy and her puppies getting taken by the coyotes and fostering the new dogs.

Thanks to Melissa Chapman—my hairdresser and friend, who spends my time in her chair talking through story ideas and plot holes. Your encouragement and belief in me means so much.

Thanks always goes out to my plotting partner and dear friend, Kristin Miller. The time and energy you take to run through plot ideas with me is invaluable! Your friendship and writing support means the world to me—I couldn't do this writing thing without you!

Huge shout-out thanks to my agent, Nicole Resciniti at the Seymour Agency, for your advice and your guidance. You are the best, and I'm so thankful you are part of my tribe.

Special acknowledgment goes out to the women who walk this writing journey with me every single day. The ones who make me laugh, who encourage and support, who offer great advice and sometimes just listen. Thank you Michelle Major, Lana Williams, Anne Eliot, and Ginger Scott. XO

Big thanks goes out to my street team, Jennie's Page Turners, and for all of my readers: the people who have been with me from the start, my loyal readers, my dedicated fans, the ones who have read my stories, who have laughed and cried with me, who have fallen in love with my heroes and have clamored for more! Whether you have been with me since the first book or just discovered me with this book, know that I write these stories for you, and I can't thank you enough for reading them. Sending love, laughter, and big Colorado hugs to you all!

ABOUT THE AUTHOR

Jennie Marts is the *USA Today* bestselling author of award-winning books filled with love, laughter, and always a happily-ever-after. Readers call her books "laugh-out-loud" funny and the "perfect mix of romance, humor, and steam." Fic Central claimed one of her books was "the most fun I've had reading in years."

She is living her own happily-ever-after in the mountains of Colorado with her husband, two dogs, and a parakeet who loves to tweet to the oldies. She's addicted to Diet Coke, adores Cheetos, and believes you can't have too many books, shoes, or friends.

Her books include the contemporary western romances of the Cowboys of Creedence and the Hearts of Montana series, the cozy mysteries of the Page Turners series, the hunky hockey-playing men in the Bannister Brothers books, and the small-town romantic comedies in the Cotton Creek Romance series.

Jennie loves to hear from readers. Follow her on Facebook at Jennie Marts Books or Twitter at @JennieMarts. Visit her at jenniemarts.com and sign up for her newsletter to keep up with the latest news and releases.

Also by Jennie Marts

COWBOYS OF CREEDENCE
Caught Up in a Cowboy
You Had Me at Cowboy
It Started with a Cowboy
Wish Upon a Cowboy

CREEDENCE HORSE RESCUE
A Cowboy State of Mind